BY AVA REID

The Wolf and the Woodsman
Juniper & Thorn
A Study in Drowning
A Theory of Dreaming
An Archive of Romance
Lady Macbeth
Fable for the End of the World
Innamorata

INNAMORATA

INNAMORATA

BOOK ONE
OF THE HOUSE OF TEETH
DUOLOGY

AVA REID

DEL REY

UK | USA | Canada | Ireland | Australia
India | New Zealand | South Africa

Del Rey is part of the Penguin Random House group of companies
whose addresses can be found at global.penguinrandomhouse.com

Penguin Random House UK,
One Embassy Gardens, 8 Viaduct Gardens, London SW11 7BW

penguin.co.uk

First published in the US by Del Rey, an imprint of Random House,
a division of Penguin Random House LLC 2026
First published in the UK by Del Rey 2026
001

Copyright © Ava Reid, 2026

Grateful acknowledgement is made to Peters Fraser + Dunlop for permission
to reprint an excerpt from *Gormenghast* by Mervyn Peake. Reprinted by permission
of Peters Fraser + Dunlop on behalf of the Estate of Mervyn Peake.

The moral right of the author has been asserted

Penguin Random House values and supports copyright. Copyright fuels creativity, encourages diverse voices, promotes freedom of expression and supports a vibrant culture. Thank you for purchasing an authorised edition of this book and for respecting intellectual property laws by not reproducing, scanning or distributing any part of it by any means without permission. You are supporting authors and enabling Penguin Random House to continue to publish books for everyone. No part of this book may be used or reproduced in any manner for the purpose of training artificial intelligence technologies or systems. In accordance with Article 4(3) of the DSM Directive 2019/790, Penguin Random House expressly reserves this work from the text and data mining exception.

Book design by Edwin Vazquez
Part-title art: Halyna/Adobe Stock
Endpaper art: Mary Metzger

Printed and bound in Great Britain by Clays Ltd, Elcograf S.p.A.

The authorised representative in the EEA is Penguin Random House Ireland,
Morrison Chambers, 32 Nassau Street, Dublin D02 YH68

A CIP catalogue record for this book is available from the British Library

ISBN: 978–1–529–91066–7 (hardback)
ISBN: 978–1–529–91067–4 (trade paperback)

Penguin Random House is committed to a sustainable future
for our business, our readers and our planet. This book is made
from Forest Stewardship Council® certified paper.

He had emptied the bright goblet of romance; at a single gulp he had emptied it. The glass of it lay scattered on the floor.
—*Gormenghast,* Mervyn Peake

CONTENTS

BOOK I

I:	The body of Adele-Blanche	7
II:	Liuprand	14
III:	The origins of our custom	18
IV:	The library	26
V:	A good set of teeth	32
VI:	The ladies of the House of Teeth	35
VII:	A historic flight	39
VIII:	Castle Crudele	41
IX:	The Sluggard	46
X:	Waltrude	50
XI:	A meeting	55
XII:	Adele-Blanche visits	58
XIII:	As the prophets did	63
XIV:	The library again	65
XV:	Ruinous fruit	74
XVI:	Two gowns	80
XVII:	Half a soul	86
XVIII:	A feast for all but one	91
XIX:	Agnes alone	97

XX: Unstained sheets	100
XXI: The language of rustling wings	104
XXII: The Most Esteemed Surgeon	116
XXIII: Truss and Mordaunt	124
XXIV: Dissolved through death	136
XXV: The martyr's price	143
XXVI: Mother	155
XXVII: Waltrude is stricken	170
XXVIII: The dagger slips	182
XXIX: Mistress of Teeth	186
XXX: A very heavy silence	195
XXXI: The House of Blood	199
XXXII: Pliny	207
XXXIII: Gray for grief	215
XXXIV: With flowers in her hair	222
XXXV: The mute tongue moves	236
XXXVI: The casks of Lord Fredegar	253
XXXVII: Sequelae	265

BOOK II

I: What cannot be reversed	275
II: The Just	282
III: Ninian	289
IV: The mummers	299
V: Life and death	308
VI: Spare	314
VII: Wanting, which lies like sleep	325

VIII: A thousand candles burning	330
IX: What might break apart the world	339
X: Tantalus	348
XI: Asunder	355
XII: A stone turned	359
XIII: Innamorata	365

BOOK III

I: Agnes in love	371
II: Humanity's other inheritance	380
III: Lavender and wax	387
IV: Maleagant	392
V: An encounter in the tower	398
VI: Milk, teeth	406
VII: A reward bestowed	414
VIII: Parts are chosen	420
IX: The procession	426
X: The sanction of the Sluggard	430
XI: Gamelyn	434
XII: The fruits	441
XIII: Happy and dauntless, and sagacious	447
XIV: With barbaric luster	454
XV: The princess and the mistress	464
XVI: Distant embraces	469
XVII: Rimmed in red	476
XVIII: An immodest proposal	484
XIX: One speckled, one white	488

XX: The Master of Eyes	491
XXI: Progeny	498
XXII: The chains of desire	502
XXIII: A wet nurse's sorrows	506
XXIV: Flowers at bloom, cut too soon	515
XXV: Wounded lion and trodden serpent	520
XXVI: Progenitrix	530
Appendix: The great houses of Drepane and their retainers	535
Acknowledgments	539

INNAMORATA

It was the castle of Nicephorus the Sluggard, and before that it had been the castle of Widsith the Precious, and before that Berengar Who-Fights-Alone, and before that the island of Drepane had no king, no duke, no count, and only death lay upon the marshes and peaks and sickly-white beaches, until blood watered the earth and the great monument flowered up, stone upon cruel stone.

BOOK I

I
THE BODY OF ADELE-BLANCHE

No corpse could be left to lie long enough for maggots, but there were leeches. There must be leeches. As befit a woman of her stature, fourteen leeches stood gathered around the body of Adele-Blanche, two furnished by each of the great houses of the Septinsular Covenant. They wore sepia-colored robes, the shade of teacloths stained with tea.

In order to give the leeches room to work, the noble guests stood at a distance, on smooth, elevated pews of marble, which formed an oval around Adele-Blanche's body. Her body lay on the ground as the mud from the previous night's rainstorm cosseted and fondled her bare limbs. The mud pooled in the hollow place between the two halves of her rib cage, each half thrusting upward like a crested white bird. Her breasts sagged like empty waterskins, only loose, wrinkled flesh with no fat to engorge them. Her nipples were shriveled chestnuts.

It bothered Agnes only a little that her grandmother's nakedness was on display. The dead were afforded no dignity in Drepane.

The leeches stood about with arched backs, their spines compressed like a snake before it strikes, as the Most Esteemed Surgeon tottered up to his dais.

He could not ascend without assistance, and it was one of the leeches who offered his hand. The hood of the leech's robe fell back to reveal his bald, age-speckled head. There, just at the crease where the back of his throat connected to his skull, he had a very large, raised, and jagged birthmark in the shape of a leaping fish. At least, that was what it looked like to Agnes, from her vantage point. She supposed that Marozia, who was standing to her left and a bit forward on the pew, might think it looked like a sickle or a sliver of melon or a half-smiling mouth.

At last, the Most Esteemed Surgeon was settled and standing upright. He cleared his throat four times. Agnes didn't blame him. It was an especially moist morning, with mist oozing between the black tree branches.

"This woman is dead," he intoned. "Expired. Extinct. Forever gone."

When his voice reached Agnes's ears, it fizzled like water dissolving on a hot pan into steam and nothingness. Her mind generated its own words to fill the space.

Adele-Blanche, Mistress of Teeth, ruled her noble house for a very long time. Agnes did not know her grandmother's exact year of birth, as it was forbidden to record such figures, so her mind supplied a rather poetic estimation. *Her eyes had seen at least three-quarters of a century. She outlived her two daughters, Manon and Celeste. She is survived only by her grandchildren, including Marozia, heiress to the House of Teeth.*

Agnes did not include herself in this accounting of her grandmother's life. She was unsure of where she belonged. But she held fast to these facts as if they were a piece of parchment that threatened to be snatched from her hand by a vicious gust of wind.

As her own private, silent remembrance ended, the voice of the Most Esteemed Surgeon reasserted itself.

"May you be consumed as a coal upon the hearth. May you dry up as water in a pail. May you become as small as a linseed grain, and much smaller than the hip bone of an itch-mite, and may you become so small that you become nothing."

Then it was time for the desecration. By decree of the Septinsular Covenant, this process required adherence to the strictest of tactics and the most ordered of schemes. Yet it had been performed upon all the dead of Drepane for a hundred years or so, and thus there was no hesitation among the leeches, who sank to their knees before Adele-Blanche's body, immediately sullying their sepia robes.

First came the leeches from the House of Blood. Their task was the most elaborate, their equipment the most baroque. One leech carried under his arm a fluted vessel, girthy at the bottom and then narrowing to a minuscule hole, an aperture too small even to accommodate a traditional wine cork. What it did accommodate, however, was the end of an extraordinarily thin leather tube. This tube at first hung as the limp cord of pig viscera that it was, until the leech blew into it and it inflated at once, as rigid as a man-at-arms. The other end was then fixed to a glinting metal spigot, hardly larger than a sewing needle but much sharper. This pierced the flaccid throat of Adele-Blanche.

Given that the pig-viscera tube was translucent, all the attendants could clearly observe Adele-Blanche's blood sluicing from her veins and into the fluted vessel. It was rather pulpy, and each time the tube clogged, one of the leeches flicked it with a single finger, the way one might repel a horsefly.

A curious thing occurred as the blood dripped into the vessel, though it happened inside Agnes's mind, where no one else could see. All of a sudden the blood became a quotidian liquid, like bathwater or soup broth. The blood was not her grandmother. Her grandmother was gone.

But just as suddenly as the realization occurred to her, with all its lovely weightlessness, it vanished again. Her grandmother's posthumous existence—that awareness, that truth that even in death she was not truly gone—dropped down upon her shoulders like a hissing, heavy house cat. She swallowed and tasted the bitterness of black henbane, the tongue-curling sweetness of mandrake.

Beside her, Marozia watched their grandmother's blood drain. She did not blink; her dark eyes did not even glisten.

Oddly, there was no representative from the noble House of Blood itself in attendance, only an ignoble member of their household guard. The leeches had some difficulty bringing him the now-filled vessel. It swayed between them like a pendulum, and the mud sucked lecherously at their boots. These three servile delegates then departed wordlessly, vanishing into the dense wall of mist.

"An insult," Marozia whispered, her lips barely moving. Her fingers reached out and gripped Agnes around the wrist. "Don't you think?"

Agnes touched her cousin lightly on the shoulder. Then she tipped her head to indicate the retinue of gray-clad guards standing on the other side of the mud pit.

Marozia inhaled sharply. "An insult to the prince, you think?"

Agnes nodded.

"Well." Marozia's mouth thinned. "That's a good sign, isn't it? That already the Master of Blood equates our house with the Crown?"

Agnes stared down at the increasingly lugubrious mud. Perhaps she made too much of the House of Blood's absence. Perhaps it was no more than coincidence that the Master of Blood, their venerable patriarch, could not attend himself. But even if illness or other business prevented him, surely he could marshal up a son or nephew to appear in his place? It was hard to deny the overtness of this breach of etiquette.

Still, she did think it must be directed at the Crown, if it was indeed an insult. It was the royal family who so ardently enforced the articles of the Septinsular Covenant, day in and grueling day out, corpse after corpse after corpse. Her grandmother would not have minded if the other houses declined to partake in this service. In fact, she would have been gleeful to know that her blood would not be drained and carried away in a fat-bellied cistern, would have been pleased at some glimmer of rebellion.

Yet rebellion it would be. The prince's line had won Drepane by blade, and the laws of the Covenant they forged must be executed. Even in the Master of Blood's rude absence, the ritual was fulfilled.

Thrasamund, Master of Eyes, fancied himself a man of exceptional charisma, so as his leeches set to work, he orated.

"How many gentle faces in attendance! The gentlest, of course, is of our dear prince. He has journeyed through reeking swamps and up miserable cliffs, through the gloomy stench of mist, to the peak that upholds the Peake. What a dreadful odyssey. But the House of Teeth has always enjoyed its inscrutable isolation. Let us hope for the sake of the honorable and merciful prince that there will be no more deaths within Castle Peake for a good long time."

"There will not be," Marozia said.

It had started to drizzle. Thrasamund grinned widely under his beard. The beard was itself a momentous thing. It draped over the curve of his stomach in wry, fox-red curls. As if to maintain some sort of filamentary equilibrium, the hair on his head was entirely gone. His baldness shone like the back of the silver spoon his leeches used to scoop out Adele-Blanche's eyes.

Luckily, the task of his leeches was quite simple, and so they were spared more of his speech. The eyes, once removed, were placed inside a leather purse. Staggering out of the mud pit, the leeches handed the purse to their master.

Unluckily, Thrasamund and his leeches did not depart. The Master of Eyes rocked back and forth on his heels and watched in a serene manner as the leeches from the House of Teeth descended upon their mistress's corpse.

They had been her grandmother's leeches, and they were Marozia's leeches now. Agnes had known them both since she was a little girl. One was named Swallow, and the other was Wrestbone. She had seen them polishing their pliers in preparation for the event. Swallow held her grandmother's mouth open with a gentleness none of the other leeches had afforded her body. Then Wrestbone removed each tooth with a brisk, dexterous tug, the tendons on the inside of his wrist tensing and bulging. For thirty-two teeth, this process was completed in under a minute. Then the teeth were deposited inside a velvet pouch, bunched closed with a drawstring.

It was Wrestbone who presented the pouch to Marozia, panting slightly from the exertion of scrabbling out of the mud pit. This was the first time Agnes saw her cousin's eyes well up. But the tears stayed lodged resolutely along her lash line, like beads on a taut chain.

Innamorata ~ 11

"Give them to Agnes," she said. And then Marozia turned to face her. "Hold them, will you?"

Agnes nodded and accepted the pouch. She clasped it between her hands, as a child might clutch a firefly she had captured while frolicking in the purple dusk. Once, Agnes had held her captive too clumsily, mashing its fragile body between her finger and thumb. She had cried then, out of guilt and grief but also slightly out of envy, because Marozia's firefly remained a lustily glowing little prisoner in her more delicate hands. Agnes knelt in the grass and smeared the juices of the insect's demise into the dirt. When she stood up again, all evidence of its death was gone.

The leeches from the House of Hearts and the House of Lungs could do their work in tandem. All four bent down over the body, obscuring the finesses of their labor under reaching limbs and flapping robes. When they rose and stood back, Adele-Blanche's chest was sliced down the middle in one grave stroke. The loose folds of skin, which parted to reveal the dark cavity half empty of organs, were now the purview of the House of Flesh.

"I don't want to watch this," Marozia said. "It's raining again. Can't they hurry up?"

They could not, Agnes knew. Indeed, this was the fastest she had ever seen the desecration performed. Perhaps it was the foul weather, or perhaps the other houses were merely treating their grandmother in death as they had treated her in life: as a disagreeable, vaguely malevolent presence that one feared either offending or overly flattering. To be in Adele-Blanche's favor was just as unpleasant as being her enemy. Agnes understood this better than anyone.

Amycus, Master of Bones, had the most material to recover and the heaviest consignment to carry away; his leeches groaned and shook under the weight of their trunk, loaded with Adele-Blanche's disassembled skeleton. But Amycus was a shrewd and efficient man, putting all things in his power to their best use. It was said that he slept on a bed frame constructed out of femurs and fibulae, and that his torches all burned inside sconces made from the ribs of children.

There was very little left of Adele-Blanche's body now. None of what remained was the inheritance of any great house, yet by Article III of the Covenant, it all must be obliterated immediately. The Covenant also restricted the methods of expunging it: There could not be a pyre; vultures could not be permitted to feast upon it; it could not be sent out to sea; and, of course, it could not be buried. So here at last was the paramount duty of the Most Esteemed Surgeon.

Both Swallow and Wrestbone helped the Surgeon down from his dais and allowed him to grip their arms for balance as he maneuvered toward the very last remains of their departed mistress.

The Most Esteemed Surgeon wore heavy wooden clogs. Holding on to Swallow and Wrestbone, he stomped Adele-Blanche's entrails into the mud. Thudding, squelching, like he was mashing grapes for wine, until the red matter of her grandmother was reduced to invisible bits and mixed with the dirt so as to be completely, utterly irretrievable.

II
LIUPRAND

The rain spent itself, and the clouds broke apart to show strips of hoary light. Marozia nudged Agnes meaningfully, and Agnes stepped down from the pew onto the sodden earth that infected her flesh with goosebumps. She raised a hand to help her cousin descend, and Marozia followed her down primly, nose wrinkling as her feet met the same cold ground.

"Come on, come on," Marozia urged. "He's going to leave."

Marozia never *rushed*. This manner of locomotion did not befit a noble lady. But the impatience in her cousin's voice had Agnes stumbling forward, half tripping over her muddy skirts, desperately trying to blaze a trail for Marozia, newly anointed Mistress of Teeth. It would not do for Marozia to be observed faltering and fumbling. Particularly by Thrasamund, Master of Eyes, who, congruous to his title, had the perception of a carrion bird. He steepled his hands over his stomach and watched Agnes's awkward efforts.

Fortunately, the gray mass of guards did not move. Each stood as straight as an upright sword and, clad as they were in armor and mail, looked more metal than man.

Agnes bent down to brush some of the mud from Marozia's skirt, taking this moment to catch her breath. From inside the mass of soldiers came a stately voice: "Part."

No sooner had the command left the mouth of their master than the guards each took one step to the side, forming a gap through which the prince was at last revealed. Agnes stood quickly, not wanting to be perceived in such a cowed position, but when she turned her eyes toward the prince, she had the sensation of being cowed twice over, in fact almost blinded.

It was more so the contrast between the prince's emanation and the dismal surroundings than anything innate to His Highness, though it could not be denied that he was an inordinately and surpassingly beautiful man. Gold was his hair, but a dark gold, like sunken treasure. His face appeared carved, with the adoring, if not slightly lascivious, ministrations of a master sculptor, one who took great care in shaping its aquiline nose and august brow, who caressed the statue's high, prominent cheekbones as though it were a lover.

He wore a doublet of midnight blue, banded with opulent braids of gold, a cape held to his shoulders with gilded epaulets. The prince trod the path created for him by the Dolorous Guard and stopped before Agnes and Marozia. With this proximity, Agnes could properly appreciate his stature. He was of a greater height even than Thrasamund, but he had none of the latter's adipose indulgence. His broad figure was led by bone and muscle rather than by fat and flesh. And with the grace that Thrasamund had ascribed to him earlier, he smiled down at his subjects.

"My good ladies," he said. "I did not have the occasion to meet your grandmother, but I grieve the loss of such a distinguished woman."

"Thank you, Your Highness," Marozia said. "I will endeavor to fill her slippers."

"It is a great honor to meet the new Mistress of Teeth so early in her incumbency." He turned and looked Agnes directly in the face. "And who else do I have the pleasure of meeting today?"

He was Liuprand, eldest and only son of Nicephorus the Sluggard, heir to the throne of Drepane, already well loved by his subjects, already affixed with half a dozen potential epithets: *the Golden, the Great, the Just, the Illustrious, the Fair, the Ready.* He had no reason to know her.

"My dear cousin," said Marozia, touching the small of her back. "Agnes."

"Agnes," Liuprand repeated. "You must be mourning the great old woman as well. I have heard she was especially attached to her grandchildren. How is your heart?"

"Aggrieved, Your Highness, of course," Marozia said. She gave Agnes's back a soothing pat. "But your attendance honors our house and warms our cold spirits."

The smallest of furrows ran along Liuprand's noble brow. His eyes left Agnes briefly, flickered to Marozia, then returned to her. "And you, Lady Agnes?"

The bile of nervousness rose in her throat. The prince's gaze was not malicious, but it was probing. Quickly, before the silence could stretch on too unpleasantly, Marozia took her hand.

"Aggrieved as well, Your Highness," she said. Her voice was smooth, cloaking any strangeness the prince might have observed. It would not do to have him unnerved or suspicious. They were meant to be mending the bridges Adele-Blanche had broken, treating the old wounds she had inflicted, draining the moats she had dug around the House of Teeth.

When still Liuprand regarded Agnes in that rather puzzled manner, Marozia hastened to say, "But she, too, is cheered by your presence."

"I am glad," he said, finally lifting his eyes from Agnes's face. The furrow, however, did not disappear from his brow. "Perhaps when your grief is not so fresh, we may discuss the future of your house's relationship to the Crown."

A joyful flush filled Marozia's cheeks. "Yes," she said. "I would like that very much."

"I mean no disrespect to your grandmother's memory, of course. But with the House of Teeth under the purview of a new mistress, there may be a path forward yet untrodden."

"It is to be my first act as Mistress of Teeth," Marozia said. She squeezed Agnes's hand in a very significant way that almost hurt. "If it please Your Highness, I will visit Castle Crudele within the month to discuss these arrangements."

"It would please me very much, Lady Marozia." Liuprand nodded at her. And then he looked to Agnes again. His eyes were a water-bright blue but seemingly without depths, such that they reflected her own countenance back at her. These two cerulean mirrors showed a blanched oval face, thin dark eyebrows, and imperturbable lips.

"Lady Agnes."

She dipped her head in acknowledgment and performed a half curtsy. It was a perfect gesture that would have pleased her grandmother enormously. Acquiescent enough to satisfy the superior being, yet still withholding complete submission.

As he turned, the Dolorous Guard were inspired to life again, forming a phalanx around the prince. Now only the crown of his golden head could be seen, rising atop the bobbing gray helmets. He was escorted into the waiting carriage, which was made of a splendorous soldered metal that seemed not to show the mud that must have accumulated on its wheels and its belly as it clambered up the mountain to Castle Peake.

Marozia was standing on her tiptoes to watch his departure, one hand braced on Agnes's shoulder. Agnes stood flat on her feet and felt the mist creep around her with a cold, solicitous grip.

On the top step of the carriage, Liuprand looked back. He had a curiously unimposing gaze for a prince. It was an intense gaze, to be sure, but it did not demand. It seemed merely to ask. And for a reason Agnes could not comprehend, his gaze lay not upon the black tree branches that fingered into the flat gray air, nor upon the mud pit that contained her grandmother's infinitesimal matter, nor upon beautiful Marozia in the deep-red gown that impressed her on the world like a passionate stain of blood, but upon *her*.

Silent, grim Lady Agnes, wearing bruise-colored silk.

His stare could not have rested there for more than a quarter minute, yet it felt the length of hours. Then without warning, Liuprand ducked into the carriage, and a member of the Dolorous Guard stepped forward to close the door behind him.

III

THE ORIGINS OF OUR CUSTOM

Castle Peake, the ancestral dwelling of the House of Teeth, was the object of ridicule and drollery among the people of Drepane. Nobles and peasants alike sneered at its ugliness, its remoteness, the bleak, gloomy color of its crumbling walls, the battlements that staggered unevenly along the edge of the mountainside, as if the structure were a great layered cake gone mealy and rotten with time. The treacherous peaks around it, which had given the castle its name, rose into the gray sky like the scutes of a slumbering dragon. Masons and millers who lived miles away, who could barely glimpse the mountain range from their huts and hovels, grinned toothily over pints of ale and said, *I would sooner climb to Castle Peake than wed my daughter to you, you copper skink. I would rather listen to a screaming owl than the groans of Adele-Blanche. They say the Mistress of Teeth has filed her teeth into points, like a horned viper.*

None of them would guess that Castle Peake was in fact teeming with flowers. Behind those moldering battlements and the rusted barbican, the courtyard bloomed with betony and bitter nightshade, monkshood and catnip, fuchsia and sea thistle. Foxgloves rustled like wind chimes, and heliotropes turned their humble faces toward the rare and precious beams of sun. Spines of sea holly pierced the air like the minutest daggers. Wisteria clambered up the columns with the powerful muscularity of a snake. Altogether, they filled the air with pollen so thick that it clogged the throats of any who passed through, and left behind its yellowish powder on their clothes and hair. If one were unwise enough to take the path near the shrubbery, the crown-ofthorns and blackberries might tear holes in one's skirts. One might become sticky with sap or pricked with barbs. All such small perils awaited any visitor to the House of Teeth.

Agnes was still holding her grandmother's teeth in their velvet pouch as Marozia led them to a small plat of dirt near the drooping fuchsia.

"He was charmed, don't you think?" Marozia asked. "He invited me to come. I should go right away."

Agnes shook her head. With the one hand that was not occupied by the pouch of teeth, she made a scribbling motion in the air, as if there were a quill pinched between her forefinger and thumb.

"You're right," said Marozia. "I should write first. Just to be certain— you will write the letter, won't you?"

Agnes nodded.

"Tomorrow?"

She nodded again.

"Good." Marozia smoothed her skirts in an anxious manner. "I shall practice. I shall have new gowns made . . . and the necklace. Will you bring them to the metalworker?"

She was looking down at the velvet pouch. Agnes met her eyes and once more nodded in agreement. Silence blossomed between them in the moist, sullen air.

"She would be pleased by this, wouldn't she?" Marozia's voice was quiet. Atypically so. If there was one thing Agnes thought her cousin lacked, it was the skill of subtlety, of subterranean machinations. "Grandmother trusted us with this."

Yet Marozia had a certain clear-eyed perception of the world that allowed her to easily ascertain the desires of others. If this skill were not so often trodden under the heels of impatience and frivolity, such that Marozia could make little use of it, perhaps their grandmother would not have needed to rely so heavily upon Agnes.

And yet even then, there were burdens Adele-Blanche's heiress could never be permitted to bear. These duties, too, fell to Agnes.

Marozia took Agnes's hand and waited expectantly, watching her face. Agnes squeezed her cousin's palm.

Innamorata ~ 19

With that, Marozia threw back her shoulders confidently, drew herself to her full height, and let go of Agnes.

"Very well," she said.

Then she turned away and navigated through the cruel garden, though she did not quite manage to avoid its hazards entirely. Before Marozia reached the door to the great hall, the hem of her skirt was torn in several places, and burrs of soft agrimony were caught in the scarlet fabric.

With her cousin departed, Agnes took her own well-beaten path to the innards of the garden, its central cavity, so ruthlessly protected by Adele-Blanche. She bypassed fragile sweet peas and crinkly hellebores. She knelt down at the feet of the black henbane shrub, its sallow flowers curving up out of the ground in a single large stalk, like vertebrae. She plucked out twelve leaves and pressed them into her palm. She then shifted to where the mandrake bloomed in starry clusters, a violet cosmos. She dug around until she freed one of its roots—small, white, and tender, curled in a fetal shape.

Agnes kept these bits of vegetation in her right hand and held her grandmother's teeth in her left. She deposited the teeth with the castle's metalworker, who would very meticulously carve them into flat disks, set them inside rings of gold, and add them to the chain that her cousin would wear from this day until her own death.

Then Agnes went to her own chamber, where the small iron pot and her other supplies waited. She dumped the old water out the window and refilled it from the jug that sat on the floor beside her bed. It was a dark chamber, even on the sunniest of days, and when she lit her firesteel, it became the room's most persuasive light. The shadows scuttled away and held themselves at a distance, occupying only the cold corners of the room.

While the water boiled in the pot, Agnes mashed the mandrake root and henbane leaves with her mortar and pestle. When fat bubbles swelled and burst and the water frothed like a mutt's spittle, she scraped the mashed roots and leaves into the pot. Sweet-smelling steam unfurled in miasmic wisps of purple and green.

Agnes set down the mortar and pestle. She placed her hands flat on the table, steadying her weight against the wood. Then she leaned forward, inhaled, and committed the highest of treasons.

This had all been set upon its course a hundred years ago, long before Agnes was so much as a dream in her mother's mind. Some said it was rats, stealthily boarding one of the many creaking trade vessels that sailed each moon from the mainland republic of Seraph to Drepane. Others said it was the fleas that traveled as parasitic passengers upon the backs of these rats. Still others said that the island itself birthed the scourge, in protest of the humans who brusquely planted flags upon it, soiled its ground with spilled blood, poisoned its waters with their waste, and drove its wolves and wild boars up into the black mountains for refuge. Whichever of these stories was true—if any at all—death came to Drepane like an enormous bird of prey, shadowing the whole island beneath the darkness of its oily wing.

First, it was a fever, though perhaps this is too quotidian a word. It was a fever that drew every drop of moisture from the body and dappled it in hot-cold sweat across the skin. It was a fever that turned eyes a blind, leucitic white, then boiled those eyes inside the skull like pearl onions in a cooking pot. Those few who survived roved sightlessly across the island, driven to a madness that compelled them to fight stray dogs in the gutters for carrion and offal.

Yet if the fever broke, it only gave way to the pustules, strange growths that pushed upward through the flesh, bulging and tumescent. When these pustules burst, they spilled into a lava field of blood and pus, leaving behind open wounds through which maggots could tunnel and lay their eggs. This was a slow death of hours, sometimes of days, being eaten alive with the most infinitesimal insect teeth.

Doctors donned beaked masks and slathered on every poultice they knew, forced tonics and elixirs down their patients' seizing throats.

Priests prayed to God for deliverance, for salvation. Prophets in their caves predicted the end of the world.

Mothers tore their hair and scratched at their eyes as their children were wrenched from them and tossed upon burning piles—until at last there were more corpses than there were corpse-burners, and bodies were stacked, naked and swollen, in the streets, where vultures and weasels began to masticate their flesh. The subjugated wolves crept down from the mountains to feast.

The nobles hid away in their castles and closed the drawbridges to the serfs who pounded desperately at the doors. Only the remotest, most hard-hearted houses survived. The stench of death lay so oppressively upon Drepane that even in their opulent fortresses, these nobles began to grow mad with isolation, and still fever crept in beneath the closed doors, like the scent of ash from a pyre.

And so these noble houses of Drepane, of which seven remained, began to meet in secret, each bringing along all of their doctors and priests and even dragging the prophets from their caves. They scoured medical compendiums and holy texts and asked the prophets what visions they saw in pools of water, in the entrails of crows, in the mists of their dreams.

It was one noble, from a house within the remotest black peaks, who came first to the answer. Yet what they discovered was not a cure for sickness, but instead a cure for death.

The medical compendiums offered the herbs. The holy texts offered the words. And the prophets offered some intangible magic that knitted all this knowledge together into a spell, a ritual that, when performed, cracked through the husk of death and drew from the corpse a living, breathing creature, slathered in fetal oils like a newly hatched bird.

These creatures were nearly human, but not quite. They knew their names and the faces of their mothers and fathers and children. They were pale and gangly, with jutting bones and strange, mincing gaits. Yet they were not diminished. They were imbued with a preternatural power. Strength beyond that of an ox, hunger beyond that of a starving monk, thirst beyond that of a fish. Even the resurrected children could splinter stones in their tiny fists. The men broke the backs of horses when they rode them. The women stuck their hands in open fires and their flesh did not burn.

And so, death ruled Drepane.

Perhaps the island would have been left to writhe beneath the sepulchral might of these monsters if their ravening did not become so great that it bloated past the island's borders. These revenants swam to the mainland, their pale limbs arcing and knifing through the waves like ivory-handled blades. They terrorized the shores like ghoulish pirates. They slaughtered fishermen in their huts and devoured their eels whole, crunching the bones in their teeth.

It was the council of the luminous city-state of Seraph, on the mainland, that responded in kind. With gleaming swords forged from the finest tempered steel, they struck down the revenants and tore apart their twice-dead bodies. And one man among them, a Seraphine knight of uncommon courage, sailed to Drepane itself to stamp out this scourge at its fount.

This man was Berengar, great-grandfather of Liuprand. His soldiers cut down every revenant from the mountainous crest of the island to its marshy pediment. And the seven noble houses, crushed under this mainland muscle, bent the knee rather than taste the conqueror's blade. He took the masters of each great house to the table, yoked them in like oxen, and bound them with a treaty called the Septinsular Covenant.

It was a formidable document, cloaked in jargon that disguised the brutality through which its articles were executed. First, power was to be divided equally among the seven houses, as a body is anatomized upon a table. Every man, woman, or child who died upon the island would be desecrated, their parts distributed to the master of each house. But this still risked a show of odd unity among the houses during which they might put aside various discords to reclaim their grave power.

So Berengar gathered the doctors, the priests, and the prophets, and slit their throats upon the foundation of his new castle. He burned their books and their herb gardens, demolished their churches, and walled up the prophets' caves. From the mainland he brought leeches, lay monks who could perform the crudest of medical tasks, and appointed the eminent among them, the Most Esteemed Surgeon, to oversee each corpse's desecration. It was forbidden even to record dates of birth and death, in case some latent magic lurked in these numbers. It was forbidden to grow herbs or cast stones or even pray to God.

And then, at last, he killed every noble who had ever heard the secret words spoken and the secret ritual performed. Any memories of magic perished with them, dismembered and ground into the earth, quashed like worms after a rainstorm, leaving widowed, weeping women, maddened by their loss, and bewildered children, confused at their sudden elevation.

The house to emerge from this massacre with the greatest vestiges of power, with unequaled stores of ancestral wealth, was the house that had remained most cold-blooded. That had kept out, from the plague's very first hour, the sickness and the pleading serfs at all costs. That had retreated immediately to its remote mountain castle, armoring itself in apathy. That had slaughtered any fever-stricken supplicants with cruel alacrity. That had, during those clandestine meetings, discovered and proposed the ultimate solution. That had cured and thus mastered death.

The House of Teeth perched resplendently on its peak, both hideous and supreme, admired and reviled in equal measure. Like all the other houses, it had lost its patriarch. Yet unlike the rest, it had no male heir crouched and waiting.

And that was how, at the tender age of fifteen and already gravid with twins, Adele-Blanche, Mistress of Teeth, became the most dreadful and illustrious woman in Drepane, second in her power only to the king himself.

Her grandmother's face did not appear to Agnes that night in the throes of her induced dreams, but she did not expect it to. She was too freshly dead. It had taken weeks, a whole month perhaps, for the purple smoke to help conjure images of her mother, Celeste's pale, overly youthful countenance floating like the moon at its fullest. So Agnes lay in bed, her vision clouded with strange hazes, bizarre images that rippled from one to the next without coherence or reason. A mason laying stones. A parchment-colored moth landing on the inside of an anonymous wrist. A parade of masked figures in dark, candlelit chambers. She had the vague sense that they were important, as they were the result of Adele-Blanche's treasonous designs, but she recognized nothing within them, could pry from them no deeper meaning.

Sweat broke out across her skin as it always did, and she began to tear at her clothes, though the herbs turned her fingers numb and clumsy, her movements sluggish.

Marozia's gentle hands chased back the apparitions, clearing the haze until it was wisps of smoke at the edges of her vision. Without speaking, she unlaced Agnes's dress and removed the pins from her hair. She peeled off her stockings and released her from her corset. At last, when she was naked save for her gauzy shift, Marozia arranged her body into a fetal pose upon the bed, then lay down beside her.

Instinctually, Agnes drew her arms around her cousin, pulling Marozia to her chest. The notches of Marozia's spine prodded at her breasts. Agnes slowed her breathing until they were inhaling and exhaling in tandem.

And then, as she did every night, Marozia took Agnes tenderly by the wrist and drew her hand upward toward her mouth. Agnes felt a shiver dance across her skin, first cold, and then warm, settling into a heavy need at the bottom of her belly. Marozia put Agnes's thumb to her lips and sucked until they were lulled into twin slumbers.

IV
THE LIBRARY

Sleep, however, could not keep Adele-Blanche at bay. She was a more virulent illness than her daughter; in fact, it seemed almost as though death had augmented her. She stormed Agnes's dreams. In this misty terrain of unreality, her grandmother stood, clad as she always was in black, and stared with her unblinking, lidless eyes.

"Bring back our house's glory," she said. "Do not fail me, granddaughter."

I will not fail. I swear it. Even in her dreams, Agnes did not vocalize.

"Marozia is the snake's hypnotizing gaze, but you are the snake's deadly fangs. Do you understand?"

Yes.

"Then waste no more time."

And then her grandmother vanished, as if swept away by a sudden, terrible gale, snatching her black dress, the white shock of her hair in its long braid. Yet her posthumous existence woke Agnes like a knife in the dark, and she shot up in bed, panting.

Marozia still slumbered unperturbed. Outside, dawn had not begun to wriggle into the starless sky; there was not even a pale band of light at the horizon. Agnes wiped at her eyes to banish the film of sleep, then stood.

The damp air around Castle Peake often smothered the torches, despite the best efforts of the servants and the sconces, so Agnes lit a candle and dressed by its murky orange glow. Marozia shifted in her sleep, mewled like a cat, but did not wake. Agnes slipped out the door, brandishing her single candle against the vast solidity of the night.

What had aided in keeping the House of Teeth safe from the ravening of the plague was their castle's ungainly stone walls, its windowless towers, its slimy green moat. All of this was a marvelously effective bastion against sickness and supplicants, but it made an ungenial home for its inhabitants. Shadowy corners and empty hallways were gorged with rats. The gargoyles, once grimacing boars or reposing lions, had been eroded by thousands of putrid storms, soiled rainwater eating at the stone like acid. Now they were all moldering, lumpish monsters, curdled into sameness.

The qualities of cold and damp both thrived in the dark. The stairs to the library were slippery with mold, and Agnes took them in slow, ponderous steps, one hand braced against the equally slick wall. Her breath unfurled in wisps of white. The thick, gloomy air clutched at these vapors, holding them in icy suspension, so that they hovered before her like ghosts. Agnes thrust her candle forward, and the light spooked them away.

At the top of the stairs was a door constructed entirely of unpolished obsidian. Her candlelight spasmed off the stone, trying to gather in its grooves but each time repelled by its matteness. The hinges and knob were bereft of rust, as they had spent less than half a century embedded in the door and all that time had been scrubbed regularly and lovingly. Often Agnes climbed the steps to clean the metal herself.

She turned the knob and hurled her body against the colossal mass of stone. The dull pain in her shoulder portended a bruise, but her efforts were rewarded, and the door groaned open.

Of all the many grim chambers in the castle, the darkness of this room was the most complete. A clever, truly evil darkness that seemed to threaten any who entered it, taunting them with the possibility of irrevocable blindness should their candle extinguish and they not manage to stumble their way to the door again. The silence was not tinged by the scabbering of rats, though they should have found much to chew on among the manuscripts. The cold, and the darkness, and the lingering memory of Adele-Blanche repulsed them. The library was a place where only Agnes dared tread.

Innamorata ~ 27

But her single candle labored bravely on, and with its light she reached the first of seven torches mounted upon the wall. She lit it, and then the others.

The brightness seemed almost perverse in the immediate aftermath of such malevolent black. In some ways, it was more terrifying to know both light and darkness. Always it was uneasy shifting from day to night, never allowing one's eyes to adjust. Agnes often wished that, if she could not walk with other humans in the sun, she could be a nocturnal animal, one that thrived and fed itself in the dark. Instead she was a withering intruder in both worlds.

The torches painted every manuscript in gold, even those whose pages Agnes had not yet gilded. They also shone down softly on the table and the two velvet-backed chairs, one of which would be empty forevermore. Adele-Blanche's chair was more plush, more well stuffed, and Agnes briefly considered sitting in it, but her grandmother's memory, her stubbornly posthumous existence, gusted across her in a cold draft, and she quickly scuttled to the other side of the table.

Quill and ink and parchment were still set out neatly on the table, like a lord's uneaten meal, because Adele-Blanche had died as she lived, armoring herself in words. Agnes had been scribbling so furiously that at first she had not noticed that her grandmother had stopped dictating, and indeed, when she finally looked up, she saw that her grandmother's head was tipped back, her mouth open just slightly, her blank eyes reflecting the torchlight.

At first, she thought her grandmother had merely fallen asleep.

And then Adele-Blanche slumped forward onto the table, cracking her skull against the wood. Red liquid dribbled out from around her hair, which meant that the House of Blood had been robbed of some meager portion of its inheritance.

Agnes sat. She stared down at the parchment, at her grandmother's arrested final words, committed to the page in Agnes's elegant script. These words were nothing remarkable. In fact, Agnes had copied them down half a dozen times before, because Adele-Blanche's memory had grown frayed with age and her stories had begun to repeat themselves like thread around a spindle. Yet Agnes did not dare crumple the parchment up.

Instead she set the sullied parchment aside and took a clean sheaf. She opened the jar of ink and dipped her quill, but doing so seemed to chase every thought from her mind. She sat vacant and stupid. *The letter. You must write the letter.* If only Adele-Blanche had lingered long enough in Agnes's dreams to offer further guidance.

Her grandmother had given her little practice in writing anything of her own invention. The manuscripts that occupied the shelves were fat with page after page of baroque script, accompanied by painted illustrations in brazen reds and greens and blues, bound steadfastly between covers of leather and held together with clasps of bronze. Each one was a beautiful object, the covers engraved and set in jewels, the edges stenciled or lacquered in gold. And yet none contained a single word that Adele-Blanche had not dictated herself.

They were the stories of their family, of their house. Of Agnes's great-grandfather, killed by the cruel sword of Berengar. Of Castle Peake's tremendous old library, turned to ash in accordance with the laws of the Covenant. In each story, the House of Teeth was noble and grand, wise and capable, so far exceeding the crass manner of other humans that they were almost another species entirely.

Technically, this was not treason. There was no specific law of the Covenant that prohibited the relation of old tales, though Agnes knew the king would not be pleased to know of Adele-Blanche's actions and might have tried to punish them in some indirect manner—if he held any real power at all over the machinations of Adele-Blanche within the obscure rooms of her castle.

When she was young, before Adele-Blanche had halted such indulgent frivolity, Agnes had scribbled away at some small stories of her own. In them, the mutilated gargoyles came to life and fluttered around the courtyard on their scabrous stone wings. A man and a woman fell in love, but at night he was cursed to turn into a green serpent. During the day they slept, ate, and made merry as husband and wife would, but at night, she kept him locked in a cage and fed him mice through the bars. Another man and another woman fell in love, but they drank from poisoned fountains that filled their hearts with hate, and in the end they murdered each other. Only then, in the throes of death, did the fountain's magic loosen its grip. They came to weeping on a bloody bed of grass, curled together like mollusks, a lover's dagger in each belly.

Of the gargoyles, Marozia said, "They would sooner fall apart than learn to fly."

Of the green serpent: "I would not labor so much over such an ugly creature as a snake."

Of the lovers' sad end: "There is no such thing as magic fountains."

Agnes showed the stories to her grandmother, who read them all very intently. Once, then twice. Her brow crumpled over her tiny black eyes.

"What is the meaning of this first one?" Adele-Blanche asked, lifting her head. "That you can imagine a statue stirring to life? Anything in the world can be imagined, yet not all things are worth putting to paper, unless there is a meaning to them. I can perhaps see the motive of the other two stories. In the first, romance overcomes tragedy; in the second, tragedy overcomes romance." She smiled her close-lipped smile. "They are not so poorly written. But do you see how simply I cut straight to the heart of it? For such silly tales, it is better if they are confined to your mind. You may play with them like a horse-on-a-string. Like your cousin dresses her dolls. If you wish to use ink and paper, I must ask that you craft a tale of steeper heights and greater depths. Do you understand?"

Agnes nodded.

"But they are charming little tales. I shall keep them." Adele-Blanche folded the parchment and tucked it into the sleeve of her gown. Agnes never saw it again.

Agnes could not decide on the opening of the letter. *My dear Liuprand* was overfamiliar, yet *Your Highness* was too formal. And of course it had to appear as if Marozia had written it herself. There must be some supplication, but Adele-Blanche's legacy resisted the act of total surrender. And although Agnes did not know the prince beyond their single brisk meeting, she thought of his gracious eyes and could not be convinced he was the breed of man who was infatuated with his own power, who fell in love with the grand performance of kneeling.

And so he must fall in love. On this, her grandmother had been unwavering, even as her eyes clouded over and her gaze lost its bright edge; she had impressed it upon Agnes the very hour before she had slumped over in her chair. Had Adele-Blanche not perished, she would have penned this letter herself. But she was gone, and so by any means, and against all odds, Agnes was to arrange this.

And while Marozia yawned and stretched beside Liuprand in their marriage bed, Agnes would crawl on her belly through the winding halls of Castle Crudele, overturning every brick, leafing through every book, until she found what Berengar had stolen from them, the ritual that would reassemble the body of Adele-Blanche, who would then take her vengeance upon the royal line and upon Seraph, and would bring the island of Drepane under the rule of death again.

V

A GOOD SET OF TEETH

The metalworker carved and hammered away by candlelight, and when the sun rose, so did he, climbing the rank stairs from his basement forge to the great hall, and then to the apartments of the castle's mistress. He had the necklace strung between his fingers like a cat's cradle, pulling gently to make sure the chain would hold, that the hammered rings of gold would not snap and clatter to the floor. Sixty-four teeth, carved into flat disks, shining like inlays of pearl. The teeth of the first master to live by the rules of the Covenant: Adele-Blanche's grandfather, whose throat was opened under Berengar's blade. Now the teeth of Adele-Blanche. It was precarious work. In the mistress's old age, her teeth had begun to wither and furrow like her skin. One impatient stroke of his hand and the teeth would shatter, and the new mistress would be bereft.

The metalworker was not above having contingency plans, however. He often considered how quick and easy the theft would be: The dungeons were a tomb for all the dead's teeth. Each set was arranged into a mold, and then added to a sumptuous marble frieze. The sculptor was forever chipping away at this frieze, adding new faces for every set of teeth that made its way into his hands. This scene stretched for nearly a mile along the north wall of the dungeon, and the older teeth were indeed forming fissures, sometimes falling from their molds and into the foul puddles below. And of course, the marble was always under siege by the water that dripped from the upper floors, green rot defiling all these carefully sculpted figures. But the newer teeth, the teeth of the freshly dead, were more intact than the teeth of the ancient woman, and thus more fitted to his delicate task. Would her granddaughters know if he made this surreptitious replacement? He did not dare. They were both the blood of Adele-Blanche and would not forgive any such transgression.

The scene of the dungeon's frieze was selected by Adele-Blanche and portrayed the history of their house. A parade of lords, each more eminent than the last, braver in battle and more pious in prayer, and of fairer face, as though the sculptor was each time improving upon his craft. He carved supplicating peasants, always with their mouths gaped open—wide enough to accommodate twice as many teeth. The wise man works only half as hard as the fool, and Adele-Blanche would never employ a dullard.

Then there came the gash in the frieze, representing the violent intrusion of Berengar, which broke the old customs apart to the new. Where the House of Teeth had once had masters, there were now only mistresses, for Berengar, in his deceitful cruelty, had left alive no male heir. While he had allowed the other great houses to elevate their sons or nephews or grandsons, on the condition that they swear him endless fealty, knowing their paramount role in the raising of the dead, Berengar had punished the House of Teeth unduly, perhaps hoping that it would crumble to extinction in the absence of men.

But Adele-Blanche, even pregnant and not long after her first blood, was no cringing creature. She rebuilt the House of Teeth in her own shape, ruled by daughters rather than sons.

The metalworker sometimes shuddered to imagine what became of the boy children born to Adele-Blanche's line. He did not believe the freakish stories, that Adele-Blanche slathered their nude bodies in honey and left them to be feasted upon by flies. But the truth was beyond the metalworker's purview.

Her daughters, the ladies Manon and Celeste, had been pregnant each three times. When their bellies first swelled, they were shut up in their apartments, all food laid outside the door. If they even screamed in labor, the metalworker did not know it; in those months, the halls were silent enough that eggs could be heard cracking in the kitchens.

Then the ladies would emerge, twice empty-handed, and once, at last, with girl children squirming in their arms. Never did the metalworker see any men visit their rooms. By what strange means the ladies had been bred, he did not dare to guess.

The lady Agnes was the elder, but Marozia was firstborn of Adele-Blanche's firstborn, and thus was her grandmother's heiress. Two more different ladies there could not have been. Sometimes it beggared belief that they were born from the same blood. But Adele-Blanche, with the perception of a sentry and the mind of a horse trader, saw these discrepancies and played her granddaughters like draughts tiles, ordering them into their most fitting positions, as she did all things within Castle Peake.

Now the great old woman was dead, and the metalworker held her death in his hands. By the laws of any other kingdom, he would not be an important man. But here, he was as essential as a good set of teeth.

VI

THE LADIES OF THE HOUSE OF TEETH

"He brought it to me."

Agnes found Marozia in the great hall. She was perched on a stool, plucking the strings of her harp in an aimless way, and the untuned notes were like the squeals of a small caged bird protesting its entrapment. They were painful to hear, yet the tic seemed rather unconscious to Marozia, as the scratching of an itch. She did not look down at the twanging strings as she spoke.

"Do you think it befits me? I've not yet seen myself in the mirror."

The hall was dark, and Agnes had to come closer to catch the gleam of the necklace. It had been wrapped twice around Marozia's throat, with another unfixed strand dangling pendulously over her chest. The gold chain complemented her, but the teeth, in truth, did not. Their pale sheen gave her skin a yellowish cast. Sallow, like Adele-Blanche had been in her last years. Thankfully, Marozia's beauty was a cup that threatened to overrun; this small defect would not lower the level of liquid but merely keep it from spilling over the rim. Adele-Blanche would have accepted this transaction: Marozia's loveliness was still lesser in value than the advantage of keeping her yoked to their grandmother's posthumous will.

Agnes said none of this. She merely held out the folded parchment.

Marozia abandoned her aimless plucking and took it. Unfolded the paper and read it twice over with a wrinkled brow.

When she finished, she looked up at Agnes and said, "It is good. Except perhaps the last line? Does it fail to flatter the prince enough? I worry—but you are the one who knows the trick of the quill."

Agnes took back the letter and reread the last line. It was mere instinct that had compelled her not to overly compliment Liuprand. But withholding full flattery would please her grandmother; she was certain of that. There must always be a hatch for escape, a bastion that could be hurriedly constructed, just in case. Berengar Who-Fights-Alone had taught all of Drepane this lesson well. One could never leave oneself entirely to the mercy of Berengar's line. His betrayal echoed through the ages.

And the restrained nature of the letter left room for further acquiescence, should the prince meet their initial terms. If Liuprand carried the blood of his great-grandfather, it surely meant he did not care for anything that submitted too easily.

"I leave it to you, then," Marozia said. "Please send the letter at once."

The imperious words did not yet suit her—they made her voice tremble like the strings of her harp. But they would soon. She was the Mistress of Teeth, and she would come to wear that power like the most exquisite of jewels. It would knit together perfectly with her beauty, with her skill in the gentle arts of a lady, such as the playing of a harp. And Agnes would compensate for any and all things that she lacked.

And Marozia was not given to know the full truth. Adele-Blanche had entrusted it only to Agnes; their plot was now hers and hers alone. Her grandmother had assumed—and correctly so—that Marozia would be pleased, as any girl would, to marry a prince, and would think only of how it augmented her own status, the honor of her own house.

Agnes often felt as if she were observing Marozia from a great distance, even when their bare limbs were tangled in bed. She could not fully fathom a creature with such bald and simple desires. With such straightforward charms.

"I have been practicing," said Marozia. This time, when she plucked the string, the note sang out splendidly into the reposing early-morning air of the great hall. "I shall learn a new song before we leave. Let me play it for you."

Agnes had nowhere to sit so she stood, hands clasped at her waist, while Marozia strummed her harp. But her mind warped and stretched around the moment, the music fading into the backdrop as she thought of all else that had come together to compose it. It was like the scene of a masque, so impeccably arranged, down to the minutest detail.

Marozia had the eyes of Adele-Blanche: dark, small, snapping like the beaks of crows. Even at her palest, there was spring beneath her skin, the warmth of moss-green veins that crept up to her cheeks and gave her a liveliness, the flush of a ripened peach. Agnes had the cast of winter. Her veins were ice-blue tributaries, and when she flushed, it was the shade of a rose before its rot, too pink and sickly. Her eyes were a lacking, unshowy gray. Dense, like stone, such that their color could hardly be discerned from a distance.

Marozia's hair curled by nature, not quite in ringlets, but in waves, thick like wool newly sheared. To hide it would be an impairment to her beauty, so she wore her hair long and loose, held back by a plaited hood with biliments of gold. Agnes's hair was of the variety that slipped through one's hands like water. It was stubborn in this straightness. Even if all day she wore her hair in braids tight enough to make her scalp prickle, when she unplaited them, her hair would fall in its same gauzy, unrumpled sheets. This was no asset to her. So Agnes wore her hair in a braided crown, sometimes threading it through with ribbons of silk or teardrop pearls on a string.

Only the hair's color, dark like peat from a bog, suggested any relation. Marozia's nose was straight and sharp. Agnes's nose turned upward, incongruously pert. They were precisely the same height. The soft curves of Marozia's body showed themselves even through the wrappings of silk. Agnes's skin stretched tautly over her bones, with little flesh to fill the spaces between. She always felt herself a narrow, slippery thing, a diaphanous shadow, a pale-bellied newt.

Marozia was the fairer. This truth was not relayed to Agnes bluntly. Rather, it lurked under the surface of things, the green lagoon water beneath its scummy top. The kitchen boys jostled about when Marozia passed, whispering and smirking and growing red in the face. Those same faces grew cold and thin-lipped when Agnes stood before them, mollified by her discomfiting presence.

Her grandmother said, *The right hand is far more useful than the left, but at least the left is lovely and can be adorned with rings.* Extraordinarily precious rubies bulged from the fingers of her grandmother's left hand, like knots on the branch of a tree. The right, meanwhile, was lithe, assiduous, unconstricted by luxury. It gripped a quill with no hindrance, and a carving knife without restraint.

Agnes was not uncomely, but mundane beauty did not interest Adele-Blanche. Anything that was not exceptional was worthless.

The song finished, and Marozia's hand slipped from the strings. "Did you like it?" she asked.

Silence fell like a velvet drape. The basking air grew still. Even close as they were in the chamber, Agnes felt again that great distance, watching her cousin from above. Pale, and passionate, and so embodied, and believing that all had been arranged for her own pleasure. And to an untrained eye, it would appear to be precisely so.

Agnes dipped her head in acquiescence to her new mistress, and Marozia smiled, preening already, as if the stool she sat upon were a throne.

VII

A HISTORIC FLIGHT

The nightjar that carried Agnes's letter down the mountain had a difficult task. The first difficult task, however, had been finding a bird that was fit and obliging. The barren peaks did not make hospitable homes for many creatures, save for goats, which were likelier to eat the letter than deliver it, and snakes, which were sadly short of any appendage that would make them suitable for letter-carrying. There were vultures, which had been Adele-Blanche's favored of all beasts, but they were too wicked to be tamed, even when tempted with the ripest pieces of carrion. Agnes lacked her grandmother's affinity for vicious things.

So Agnes had chosen a nightjar, luring him with beetles and writhing pillbugs. He was perhaps smaller than she would have liked, but he saw better in darkness than in light, which would be useful for the business of flying through the valleys of the black peaks where the sun barely reached. His camouflage was impeccable. He blended perfectly with the bark on rotted branches, or among the dry, underfed grass.

And perhaps most important, he was a peculiar creature, fit only to serve the House of Teeth. He would remind any who received his missive that Adele-Blanche's strange customs were still followed, that they had not been driven into the mud with her innards. Let the other houses keep their dull and familiar messengers.

The nightjar's journey was a harrowing one. He had never flown farther than perhaps half a mile down the mountains, and so the lushness of the green scrub he encountered at their base was arresting, confusing. The dirt was white—sand, an element he did not know. And the bright air was pricked with salt, a bitter, pungent smell that confounded his senses. He landed on the branch of a tall, narrow tree that resembled a pine if it had been shaved down nearly to its trunk. He scratched the white dirt from his feathers. He blinked salt from his eyes.

But the nightjar did not fail at his task. He landed upon a windowsill, chirped to announce his arrival, and allowed the letter to be unclipped from his leg. He took this time to rest on the sill while the letter was read, while humans moved in and out of the room, murmuring to themselves, poring over the parchment until it crinkled and dampened.

As was his nature, he slept during the day and was woken in the evening, to a man fixing another letter to his leg. The man had hair the color of wet gold, and though his body was large, his ministrations were gentle.

The nightjar fluffed his wings. The darkness was not so dense here, not so complete. The castle walls were ablaze with moonlight—powerful, silvery beams that shot to the ground like arrows. The nightjar flew in a swooping, diving pattern as if to dodge them. The sand captured the light and held it, spread it until the whole beach sparkled like glowworms on the ceiling of a cave.

The nightjar was relieved when the shadows of the mountain overtook him again, slicking him with their oils. He carried the letter to Lady Agnes, who waited in the garden, under the gloom of a willow tree. She rose and took the parchment from him, feeding him a centipede to thank him. He was too much an animal to understand that he had accomplished something momentous: The letter he delivered would summon the lady and her mistress down the mountain, and Castle Peake would stand precarious and empty, not even groaning with the footsteps of ghosts.

VIII

CASTLE CRUDELE

It was a colossal thing, and—christened with the blood of his enemies—Berengar Who-Fights-Alone had seen his castle rise like mushrooms in a rainstorm in the age immediately following his conquest. It was a palace that had no infancy, no floundering juvenile years, only the maturity that bleached its walls with accumulations of salt, scruffy and pale as a septuagenarian's beard.

Not a palace so much as a fortress, Agnes amended as their carriage approached. It was connected to the main island of Drepane only by a narrow stone bridge. The rest of the land had collapsed around it, leaving the castle to float like its own tidal island. The whole ocean was its moat. The walls supporting the parapets were a sheer, steep drop directly into the sea. It would be an easy death, sleek as the cascade of water from a fountain, if one stepped over the edge. Agnes could imagine it within the eye of her mind. A woman falling and vanishing into the waves, no jutting stones to break her body apart during the descent.

The enormity of the castle stretched the limits of her vision. There were outer walls with ramparts, moss growing thickly over the white stone. Flanking towers notched with arrow slits. Between the outer and inner walls were wards so large that they could each accommodate many buildings. Stables and smiths, kennels and servants' dwellings. There was room enough for a whole town enclosed within this fortress, yet as their carriage trundled through, Agnes was struck by its gloaming silence. The windows did not redden with firelight; there were no chuffs of greasy smoke from the chimneys; the air did not ring with hammers beating against their anvils. No horses stomped at the dirt and no chickens squawked in their coops. The foul odors of life did not even drift upward: no steaming chamber pots or moldering hay, no pile of vegetables or meat declared too rancid to risk eating.

Or perhaps it was the ocean that smothered all these mortal scents. The waves crashed mightily and spewed their brine like the breath of God. This was no stagnant green pond, holding frogs and minnows and wilting lily pads in swampy, timeless suspension. This water seemed too furious and primordial to contain such mundane forms of life.

Agnes was cowed by its vastness and shrank back into her seat, turning her head away from the window. Her grandmother had felt so supreme, the House of Teeth so unchecked in its power, but they ruled over a domain that seemed painfully diminished now. A vulture might declare itself lord of carrion, but it did not take long for a corpse to be picked clean. Such seemed the potency of their house as Agnes beheld this great fortress rising from the sea.

"It's so beautiful," Marozia whispered. Her fingers danced across the window glass. "Isn't it? All the colors."

There were indeed more colors than Agnes regularly had the privilege of observing within Castle Peake. These were colors she saw only as threads for embroidery, as paints for her manuscripts. The azure waves lipped the white sand. The navy-and-gold flags of Seraph snapped in the wind. The strange, thin trees, which reminded her of upended chimney brushes, were coniferous gashes through the cloudless sky.

Their carriage reached the inner wall, and the stone gate ground open to allow them passage. As the portcullis rose, slowly, Agnes saw behind the latticework a long row of silver helmets, flanking the path. The Dolorous Guard? But when the grille was fully open and the carriage rattled through, she saw that they were only helmets, empty helmets without bodies beneath them, each one held up upon a wooden stake. The wind beat them around like bells, yet no incorporeal soldier abandoned his post. Sunlight darted off the dents in the polished metal.

Marozia drew a breath and pushed away from the window. These were the helmets that had belonged to Berengar's enemies, nameless soldiers who had died like cut flowers under his superior Seraphine steel. Yet if Agnes recalled, it was not Berengar who had mounted them there. It was his son, Widsith the Precious, in his grandest act as king. There was more function than feeling in this deed. Widsith had inherited none of his father's blustering passions, his fiery loves and hates. Widsith only lazily observed that perhaps the noble houses were growing restless beneath the grinding weight of Seraph's rule, that perhaps they were forgetting the violence visited upon them a generation ago. The emptiness of the act echoed in the unoccupied helmets, each one roughly as fearsome as a crab's abandoned conch.

At last, the innermost gate. Its portcullis rose with a shout from an unknown source, and there was some commotion in the courtyard. Sand was kicked up into the white air. The carriage halted in the shadow of the Castle Crudele's tallest spiraling tower. Here was the site where her great-great-grandfather's throat was slit, where he was betrayed by Berengar, punished for his guileless acquiescence. Here was the structure that rose, watered with his blood. In this sense, Castle Crudele was the most elaborate and largest grave marker on earth.

And it was elaborate, a symphony of stone, all shades of gray and white and the dark age-spots of moss. Agnes stepped from the carriage and had the urge to touch the earth, as if she might feel her ancestors' bones reaching up from underneath the sand and the soil, like a plant tendril searching blindly for the sun. Ordinarily she was not disposed to such imagining. But Castle Crudele was the only place on Drepane where the dead were consecrated. The bodies of the ancestors had not been defiled. They lay beneath the castle, seething, languishing.

Perhaps blooming.

This, she believed, was the power Adele-Blanche sought. Perhaps Agnes would have to tunnel under the palace like a mole and root out these hoary corpses. She bent over. The sun scorched the back of her neck, and her grandmother's posthumous existence slid like a knife through her ribs. With every breath, it shifted, and she felt the pain of it.

"Lady Agnes?"

Her head snapped up and her spine straightened at once. Liuprand was standing over her. The prince. He had approached and she had not even noticed, had not noticed the Dolorous Guard treading the courtyard, had not noticed Marozia climbing down from the carriage, wearing her very coyest smile.

Agnes stepped back at once. Her fingertips were thinly grimy where she had touched the earth. She wiped her hand on her skirts.

"Are you well?" Liuprand asked.

He was wearing a pale-blue doublet this time. Some seamstress had painstakingly dyed its threads to perfectly match his eyes—which, upon seeing the ocean for the first time, Agnes now understood to be precisely the same color. The braids of gold across the breast and the epaulets that fixed his cape to his shoulders seemed, likewise, to have been sewn to match his flaxen hair. Standing in the sunlight, unhampered by the gloom as he had been on Adele-Blanche's desecration day, he was more beautiful than any knight Agnes could have painted in her manuscripts or that the sculptor could have carved into his great frieze.

Liuprand the Golden, they would call him, when he came into his crown. There could be no other epithet. At least now when she blinked furiously and raised a hand to shield her eyes, she could fault the blazing sun and not the emanation of the prince himself.

Before Agnes's silence became a breach of etiquette, Marozia rushed to her side.

"Your Highness," she said, in a breathless way, having taken the steps down from the carriage two at a time. "Thank you for meeting us yourself. I am honored. Castle Crudele is magnificent."

"I am happy to see both of you fine ladies again," Liuprand said with a very sincere tip of his head. "And should it please you, I shall give you a tour about the grounds."

Agnes's ears pricked. It was not often that she wished to lift her veil of silence, and after so many years, the instinct had nearly drained from her utterly. Her tongue lay heavily in her mouth like a dead thing, disused, sometimes despised. She could recall only dimly the sound of her own voice.

Yet in this moment, the beginnings of words curled in her throat. If she were to uncover the secrets of Castle Crudele, she would need to learn its premises, committing the curve of every corridor to memory.

She dug her fingernail into the cuticle of her thumb, pressing until the white band of flesh broke apart and blood spurted free. It gathered in a red ring around her nail bed but did not drip.

"Oh, yes," Marozia said. "A tour would be lovely. If first we could leave our things—"

Liuprand lifted a hand to indicate the Dolorous Guard, who had already opened the carriage and begun removing the trunks. They thudded down heavily onto the white sand. "They will be brought to your chambers. And—my apologies that you cannot first rest after your journey—but my father wishes to see you at once."

IX

THE SLUGGARD

His noises preceded him. Before the doors to the throne room had even been cracked open, Agnes could hear the snuffling, tearing, gulping sounds. Sounds like pigs in a stockyard, jostling for room at the trough.

The Dolorous Guard parted the doors and Liuprand led them through, his footsteps nearly soundless on the long ruby carpet. Liuprand was so tall that Agnes could not see over his head even if she craned her neck, and so her first glimpse of the king was not until they reached the foot of the dais and Liuprand stepped aside, holding out one arm to present Agnes and Marozia to his father.

Yet the king himself had not quite reached the throne. He was flanked by two members of the Dolorous Guard, each gripping one of his arms, and he leaned upon them heavily. Despite there being a low ramp up to the dais, the king's every step was painfully trodden, eliciting groans and pants. His brow beaded with sweat. The guards did not fare much better: By the time the king was finally slumped on the chair, they were breathing hard as well.

There was no denying Nicephorus was in some manner a great man—not quite of a height to Liuprand, though perhaps only shrunken by his age and his great weight. He shared his son's broad shoulders. But he had not been titled *the Sluggard* without cause. The once-vibrant young man he had been was decades gone to greed and sloth.

Agnes lifted her head very slowly to take in the full figure before her, starting with his feet. He wore sandals, not boots, and his flesh bulged from between the straps, his toes swollen and purple like grapes. Her gaze traveled up his calves, which were bare to the knee, as he wore a loose linen tunic with seemingly no trousers underneath. Yet he need not worry about exposing what was between his legs—his thighs were massed with fat, more lumpy and loose than taut, as though small pustules were pressing up from beneath his skin.

The tunic was strained over the paunch of his stomach, like cheesecloth wrapped around a gross wedge of cheese. His neck was not so much a neck as a slack mountain of chins, upon which there was a very light, stubbly beard, the shade of dry scrub grass. His lips were very pink and looked to Agnes like worms. He used his scummy tongue to wet them over and over again, perhaps in preparation for speaking.

Only this far in her gaze's journey did she begin to see any shades of Liuprand in his father. There was the nose, proud and aquiline, though the king's veered sharply to the side, as though it had been broken and not properly set. This would not have surprised Agnes; in the king's youth, he had been known for relishing every form of fight, from bare-knuckled brawling to the controlled violence of the joust. His sweaty brow sloped down heavily over his eyes—weak, watery eyes, the whites shot through with red. Once, she imagined, his hair had been golden, but now it was the color of mucky hay, with bald patches that showed his sweat-shiny skull.

The crown gripped him like a dead insect, its limbs bent and seized in rigor mortis. Agnes felt her own scalp prickle with sympathetic pain.

The king's gaze ghosted across them, eyes welling with effort. When he spoke, it was in a moist, gargling voice, as though he could not manage to contain all the spittle in his mouth.

"Which one is the old cunt's heiress?" he asked.

At her side, Agnes felt Marozia stiffen.

Liuprand gestured toward Marozia. "Allow me to present Marozia, Mistress of Teeth. And the other is her cousin, the lady Agnes."

"Two? Two of Adele-Blanche's striga spawn? Why have you brought me two?"

This time, it was Agnes who flinched. He could banish her back to Castle Peake with a flick of his finger, and then she would never exhume the palace's secrets; worst of all, Marozia would be alone. That last thought must have crossed Marozia's mind as well, because she opened her mouth to speak, but Liuprand's tongue was quicker.

"Surely you would not ask the Mistress of Teeth to leave behind her closest confidante," Liuprand said. "They grieve their grandmother still and would not wish to be parted in such fraught circumstances."

Marozia smiled tremulously and said, "We are each other's only family now."

King Nicephorus gave a wordless grunt and rolled his tiny wet eyes, but at least he did not order Agnes gone.

"We do not ask your hospitality in exchange for nothing," Marozia went on. She took a step closer to the dais. "Among our trunks is an offering of our house's wealth. I hope it is to Your Highness's liking."

This pricked the king's interest. He sat up slightly in his seat, as much as he could manage on his own. "Well, let us see, then," he grumbled.

Two members of the gray-armored Dolorous Guard stepped forward, hoisting the largest of their chests between them. Their knees quivered as they carried the chest to the foot of the dais, and although their faces could not be read from beneath their shuttered helmets, Agnes heard little puffs of exertion from their mouths as they passed. At last, they knelt and laid the trunk before the king.

"*Open it*, you dumb oxen."

Swiftly, they undid the latches and lifted the lid. As soon as the chest was opened, the throne room's meager sunlight piled upon its contents and then was reflected back, as golden as the sun itself, painting the walls and the face of the king in chiaroscuro. King Nicephorus strained even farther forward, chins quivering as his neck jutted out, and the mottling of light and shadow could not obscure the look of pleasure in his eyes.

The king made some huffing noises of approval and then said, "Your grandmother could have fed her cattle and pigs on gold and still not gone wanting for a single ducat, hm?"

No matter how crude the king's affect, Agnes knew this was not selfish, quotidian greed. The news had traveled to the remotest parts of the island, even winding its way up to Castle Peake: The power of Seraph was faltering. The once-luminous city-state could no longer afford to finance the occupation of Drepane. No more Seraphine nobles could be prevailed upon to send their daughters across the sea to marry into the royal family. It was whispered that Liuprand's mother, the long-dead Queen Philomel, would be the last Seraphine lady to set foot upon the white sand of this heathen island. It would be a domestic bride for Liuprand, or no bride at all.

And with its bursting stores of ancestral wealth, the House of Teeth was the most desirable alliance for the royal family. Adele-Blanche had held fast to this power, waiting for the proper moment to deploy it, when she could hope for the greatest return. With each passing year that no blushing maiden from Seraph arrived on Drepane's shores, with each ducat that was spent with no return, the desperation of the House of Berengar became more dire, and the House of Teeth stood to gain even more by answering their need. Adele-Blanche had bided her time, to immense profit.

"It is a gift," Marozia said. "To honor Your Highness and to endear our two families. I believe there is much to be gained for us both in a partnership. Should you wish to proceed."

The king was silent for a long moment, the golden light dancing across his tumescent face.

"Hm," he said at last. "Show the ladies to their chambers."

X
WALTRUDE

It was the chamber of the wife of Widsith the Precious, the sweet and pious Iphigene, who decorously turned her eyes away while her husband impressed himself upon squires and serving boys. Iphigene had the look of the most ancient, most noble houses of Seraph. Golden hair, cerulean eyes, skin as luminous as a pearl. She embroidered tapestries of wolf hunts and played both the flute and the viol.

Waltrude had sat many a time in this chamber, nursing the future king Nicephorus at her breast. In his infancy, he was anything but Sluggard; in his adolescence, he had jousted with such reckless fervor that he broke apart his leg bone on a post in the tiltyard, and the splinters of wood remained buried in his thigh to this day, beneath a pulsing, black-blooded sore. This wound had led him down the path of Sluggardry, and Waltrude's heart still ached when she saw him limp onerously up to the throne, remembering the lively suckling babe he had been.

After dear Iphigene had taken ill and perished placidly in her sleep, as if she did not want to inconvenience anyone with her dying (*as in death as she was in life,* a forbidden phrase, meant to be struck from the collective memory of Drepane), the chamber had lain empty for years, with only Waltrude visiting each day to brush the dust from her beloved mistress's bedspread. And then Nicephorus took Philomel to wife, another quintessential Seraphine beauty, though lacking the polite reticence of her predecessor. She dared to raise her voice to her husband, to keep his son from him when he had displeased her, and the king and queen's scrapping was often so loud that it seemed to tremble the walls of Castle Crudele.

Yet within this vortex of detestable misery, Liuprand was the most placid child Waltrude had ever encountered. He wept only rarely, and even then, it was a series of little gasps, not Nicephorus's profane screams and gurgles to which she was accustomed. Perhaps it was because of the wretched circumstances of his infancy, the war that had waged so ruthlessly between his mother and father, and not despite them, that even as a babe Liuprand had learned to make himself unobtrusive, to maintain peace, at the cost of his own innocence.

Waltrude had not felt near enough loyalty to return to the chamber after Queen Philomel died—shrieking, protesting (*as in death*), if the stories could be believed—so now she climbed the steps in a hurry and began to dust off the covers, fluff up the pillows, and stoke the hearth for the first time in years. Her back ached terribly when she bent over. Her fingers, when gripped around the metal poker, looked like the pale, gnarled tentacles of a squid. There were moles on her face that had not been there when Liuprand was a babe, and many of them were growing long, gossamer white hairs. Her eyebrows had become denser. She could not stop the dried spittle from gathering in the corners of her mouth.

There was some scuffling from the corridor. Waltrude stood up and heard her bones crunch.

The door opened and spit out the spawn of the House of Teeth. The first came like a rush of blood, red skirts spilling over. She had crow's eyes, black and flashing, though they could not be convinced to rest in one place for very long. They darted all around the room, skimming right over Waltrude.

The second came with hardly even the sound of footsteps. She stood back with her hands folded at her waist, hair braided into a very dark crown, only a few strands fluttering free to graze her jaw. Her eyes were the gray of rain-dampened stone, her flesh utterly colorless, her body narrow and dry. She had overall the look of a statue, dour and frozen in time, and she was as silent as one, too.

"Hello," the first said in a pert voice. "Are you Waltrude?"

"Yes, my lady."

"I am Marozia, Mistress of Teeth. And this is my cousin, Agnes."

Mistress of Teeth, indeed. She wore that ancestral necklace, held at her throat like a string of delicate pearls. Her face was ruddy, impassioned. If she had not known, Waltrude would not have guessed she had ridden down from the black, hideous mountains of Castle Peake, where every tower was draped in dismal fog. There was too much life to her—exorbitant, aggravating life.

"It is an honor to meet you, my lady," said Waltrude. *Lady* was the term her status afforded her, but she and her cousin both looked more like girls. They were of age to Liuprand, who was just barely straining out of boyhood. Or perhaps Waltrude was merely too old now to perceive the delicate subtleties of youth.

Marozia nodded, and her gaze spasmed about the chamber again. "Where are the trunks?"

"The trunks?" Waltrude's wrinkled brow wrinkled further. "They are here, my lady. The Dolorous Guard delivered them."

"*My* trunks, yes. But where are Agnes's?"

Waltrude chafed at this impatient tone. "They have been put next door. In the lady's chamber."

"No," Marozia said forcefully. "That won't do. Bring them here."

"Lady," Waltrude said, feigning a placidness she did not feel, "Castle Crudele has ample room to accommodate you both. The prince concerns himself with your comfort. You need not be so familiar with each other—"

The shadow that fell across the face of the Mistress of Teeth bewildered Waltrude into silence. Marozia's chest expanded as she gathered her breath.

Then Waltrude feared she had been too easily stifled. After all, had the king not ordered the peasants within the Outer Wall to go into the huts and their workshops, to darken their windows, to muffle the mouths of their children and the braying of their animals, so that the ladies would not feel overly welcomed? Had he not schooled all his servants to treat the ladies less as guests and more as interlopers? The king may have capitulated to the desires of that hoary mistress of the black peaks, but he would make his revulsion and antipathy known.

And now, already, Waltrude felt the imprudent memory of Philomel engulfing the chamber, rolling off Marozia like smoke. Philomel, too, had come to Castle Crudele with such imperiousness and vigor, though it had not spared her a cruel fate. Perhaps this Mistress of Teeth would be luckier.

And Agnes, the statue-girl, was unfortunately no resurrected Iphigene. The old queen would have smiled, laid a hand tenderly over her cousin's arm, endeavored to soothe her vexation and rid the room of its hostile mists. Waltrude was thus made to consider the difference between quiet and silence. Agnes did not speak, but there was nothing demure or self-effacing in her. And though she had not known her longer than a few moments, Waltrude somehow had the sense of her silence as total. Even her eyes communicated nothing at all.

"That is *not* my will," Marozia said. "And Agnes does not like it, either. Call the Dolorous Guard and tell them to place the trunks in this chamber instead. The other room is of no use to us."

Waltrude glanced at the statue-girl, whose expression had not shifted. Yet her silence could not be mistaken as deafness or muteness; there was nothing dull about it. It was a sharp-edged silence, bristling like barbs, as though she were trying to punish the world by withholding speech. Her lips were so pale as to be almost white—unused, Waltrude thought, for a very long time.

Perhaps she was wrong. She did not much care to find out. It was the other lady, Marozia, who ought to be the subject of her mulling. She would be queen, sooner or later, when Nicephorus could be convinced to put aside his hatred of Adele-Blanche. Would her manner please the prince? Would her looks? Certainly he could not take issue with the latter; for all her impertinence, the Mistress of Teeth had beauty enough to compete with a purebred Seraphine.

But Waltrude did not know the prince's proclivities. Never had she observed Liuprand lingering about the quarters of the serving girls, nor returning to his own room late, hair mussed and clothes rumpled with the evidence of nocturnal trysts. Likewise she had not observed him taking a suspicious number of squires under his wing, as Widsith had. Sometimes he seemed above such corporeal appetites.

One thing she knew with certainty was that he would perform his duty, as he always had. So she ought to endear herself to Marozia, even if her old, embittered soul protested it. Like Liuprand, Waltrude had always performed her duty.

She gave Marozia a nod of deference and turned for the door. On her way out, she stole one last look at the statue-girl. Lady Agnes was not unlovely. But her beauty was that of a corpse, death laid over her with its gentle, lambent stillness.

XI
A MEETING

Agnes cast a horrified glance at Marozia and rushed out of the room after Waltrude. She was not horrified for the same reason as Marozia, whose bed she had shared since they were old enough to no longer need the nearness of their mothers—though in truth the idea of trying to sleep at night with a heavy stone wall between them made her insides shrink and coil, too. Neither she nor Marozia could tolerate the other's absence.

But more immediately, Agnes had to reach her trunks before the servants began unpacking them. She had to hide the treasonous cargo—those herbs and potions inside.

She was in such a hurry that she did not hear footsteps on the floor behind her; in fact, she heard nothing at all until the prince's voice echoed down the hall.

"Lady Agnes."

Instantly she halted. There was an imperiousness to his tone that well befit a prince. Had her treason already been uncovered?

Stiffly, slowly, she turned. Liuprand had already taken his great long strides down the corridor and now stood so that she was in reach of his arms, should he grasp for her. But he did not. He only stood. And Agnes wondered if she would ever become accustomed to his beauty; if ever it would become as mundane to her as a painting or a tapestry on the wall she passed every day.

"Have you settled?" he asked. "Are your accommodations to your liking?"

Coldness crept up her spine. If she nodded, she was a liar, and if she shook her head, she invited more questions that she could not answer without provoking suspicion. So she remained silent and did not move or even blink.

Liuprand stared down at her, and his gaze was searing. "Well?"

A mere two meetings and he had already discerned her. Agnes wished that Marozia had followed her into the hall. She wished for her cousin's voice, always ready, always fluid, always perfectly tuned, to fill the palpable silence.

"Answer me," Liuprand said. His pitch had grown lower, and Agnes flinched.

He barely let another moment pass before he prodded at her again.

"You must speak. I am your prince. You cannot refuse my orders."

Her stomach pooled with ice, but the ice she knew, and it was like armor to her. Agnes stared back up at him.

"Open your mouth," Liuprand said.

She was not afraid of the prince, not really. Even now, his orders had been without malice; his face showed no cruelty, only strength of will. Rather, she became afraid that he might somehow see the things she had, over the years, consumed. As if there would be plainly visible the scummy, variegated stain on her tongue, or the fleshy bits caught like maggots between her teeth.

Her lips were trembling. She opened her mouth.

Gently, with a single finger, Liuprand tipped up her chin.

"You have not been maimed," he said bemusedly as he peered down the dark cavern of her throat. "Everything is intact. So why do you not speak?"

She had not anticipated being confronted like this, and certainly not by Liuprand. This matter was well beneath him. What did he have to gain in coaxing words from the mouth of his bride's cousin? Agnes would serve Marozia as she always had, in dutiful silence. It had been a long time since anyone had spoken to her and expected speech in return.

The silence stretched out and filled the space between them. It felt like a solid mass, something that could be cleaved by a sword. Still

Liuprand held her chin, and his gaze ran itself over her face, as if her eyes might divulge something that her mouth would not.

If she tried, Agnes could thrust her silence out around her until it became less a shield and more a weapon, a spear-point, a dagger. She could make it wound anyone who dared to come close—who dared to stay close for so long, as Liuprand did. Would he feel the prick of her blade? It did not appear so. His eyes were steady, and his finger rested there just below her bottom lip, and with every moment that passed her skin warmed beneath his touch and chased away the ice that ran through her veins.

At last, Liuprand dropped his hand. "Very well," he said.

Agnes felt the loss immediately. Winter rushed back into her blood. "You may go."

She gave the slightest of nods and waited for Liuprand to leave. He did not. He continued to watch her until at last Agnes turned around out of pure mortification, because there was a very uncommon blush rising to her cheeks. Even as she went, she felt his gaze on her. She dared to give the inconspicuous look back, just a quick glance over her shoulder.

Liuprand had dropped his eyes, in an almost mollified, boyish way, and was staring down at his own hand, the one that had tipped up her chin. She wondered if her skin had leached its coldness into him, as his had bled warmth into hers. But she dismissed the thought. She was nothing, a shadow, a white curl of breath in the dark. She could not leave a mark upon Drepane's golden prince.

Yet as she turned and walked briskly down the corridor, her heart pulsed within the iron vise of her sternum, like a caught bird in a clutching fist.

XII
ADELE-BLANCHE VISITS

"He was pleased, don't you think? The king? It was a good amount of gold." Marozia fiddled with her necklace of teeth. "Perhaps we should have brought more jewels. Or had the metalworker forge the gold into goblets. Perhaps the king would have preferred that."

Agnes half listened, but she was much more intently focused on the mortar and pestle and henbane and mandrake arranged before her on the desk. The steady motions of the task were so well known to her now that it was an unconscious act, like the drawing of breath. She carefully placed six berries in the mortar and one mandrake root. This was the least of what the ritual required. She would have to be sparing in her usage of the materials until she found some secret place to safely grow the plants.

Marozia knew of these heady rituals she performed, but she did not inquire about their purpose. Adele-Blanche had never allowed her into the library, into that cold workshop, protecting her heiress by armoring her in ignorance.

Her cousin was perched on the edge of the bed, running her finger along the gilded edge of the coverlet. "I do think the prince was pleased," she said. "He is so courteous in his manner. And so, well, lovely to look at. Surely even *you* can agree."

Agnes nodded and then absorbed herself again in the arrangement of berries. Liuprand's manner was gentle, she now knew; her cousin would not marry a man who would treat her meanly. That should be enough to satisfy her.

"Liuprand has already been charmed." Marozia's smile was softer now, more private, as if this victory were hers alone to enjoy. Perhaps it was. "Do you think I should work on endearing myself to the king? It will be an ugly task, I know."

Agnes was sure to catch her cousin's eye when she nodded. Marozia would certainly not find a willing audience in Nicephorus, but the betrothal could not proceed without his approval. She considered how best to advise Marozia. After a few moments lost in deliberation, she took a parchment and quill and scribbled on it, then handed the paper to her cousin.

Marozia read it with a furrowed brow. *"Dine with him?"*

Agnes nodded.

"I suppose that *is* the king's favorite activity." Marozia put a hand to her mouth to stifle a giggle. "Then I shall. It might be best to become allies with the castle cook. They surely are the king's closest confidante." Laughter spilled from between her fingers. "Better than befriending that old crone Waltrude."

She wished Marozia had not been quite so impertinent with Waltrude. Marozia had no experience in endearing herself to her lessers; at Castle Peake, all of their servants had been in the employ of the House of Teeth for longer than Agnes or Marozia had been alive. Even if their servants did not love them, they had been taught to worship their blood. The servants of Castle Crudele had no such natural loyalty. They might kneel at Marozia's feet and then spit behind her back. When Marozia was less overwrought, Agnes would suggest naming Waltrude Mistress of Robes, if she could not be Lady of the Bedchamber, as was now Agnes's official title. A show of goodwill.

Agnes picked up her pestle. But before she could grind it down, Marozia shot to her feet and snatched it out of her hand.

"Agnes!" she exclaimed. "No, you mustn't. The smoke will smell and bring guards to our chambers. It will alert that nasty Waltrude. You cannot do this now."

Clenching her empty fingers, Agnes looked at the mortar and then up at her cousin.

Marozia bit her lip meditatively. "It will still work if you consume them, will it not?"

So perhaps Marozia had paid more attention than Agnes had imagined. Agnes had caught her, once, lingering outside the library door, but Agnes felt her own embarrassment as well as her cousin's shame, hot in her blood and on her cheeks, and neither had ever spoken of it or acknowledged it.

This new room was made of gray stone, and although it was large, it felt in this moment very small, as small as their bedchamber in Castle Peake, and despite the air that blew in from the window in large cold gusts, Agnes suddenly found that she was aching for breath. The heaviness and pallor of their old home spread out over them and then descended upon her, like a mantle made from the gaspings of ghosts.

"Well?" Marozia prompted, very gently.

Agnes felt herself nod.

"Here," Marozia said, and rose from the bed. She took the mortar with its bellyful of black berries; it looked inordinately heavy in her hand, like a blunt instrument for stoning. She sat back down on the bed, then beckoned Agnes toward her.

Agnes rose and came to sit at her side. The weight of hours was dragging at her body. All of the sand that was clumped into the soles of her slippers, the mud at the hem of her skirt, the filthy vestiges of Castle Peake. She wished to be relieved of it all. She exhaled with a force that was almost sound, but not quite.

She lay her head in Marozia's lap. Marozia stroked back the strands of hair that seemed always to slip from her braided crown and fall against her cheeks. Marozia tucked them behind her ears, once, then again when they fell, and then at last the hair stayed in its proper place.

Marozia dipped her delicate fingers into the mortar and removed one of the berries. Agnes opened her mouth, like a weaning babe. She let herself be fed the berries, one after another after another, until the black juice was running down her chin. Marozia wiped it clean with greatest devotion. Agnes took her cousin's fingers between her lips and sucked until they, too, were rid of that dark nectar.

Agnes closed her eyes, lashes fluttering against the red silk of Marozia's skirt. The bitterness of the berries parched her tongue, but when she swallowed, she tasted the human sweetness of Marozia's skin. It coated the inside of her mouth.

"Shhh," Marozia whispered. She bent over Agnes, lowering herself until their foreheads touched. "Tonight I shall dine with the prince and the king. I shall tell them you were too fatigued from our journey to join us. They will not take offense. Do you agree?"

Icy perspiration had begun to bead along Agnes's brow. It required momentous effort to nod.

Marozia arranged her body in the bed, on her side, close enough to the edge of the mattress that her fingers could brush the floor, should she let her arm hang down. The world was a swampy tangle of light and shadow behind Agnes's eyes. Then Marozia lay the dusty coverlet over her, smothering the last embers of her consciousness.

The mists and vapors of the dream-world hung heavily in the air. Three Adele-Blanches fluttered down and landed before Agnes like crows. One held a spindle, red yarn unfurling from it and into a heavy pile at her feet. A dead serpent, limply coiled.

Another held a brass scepter, though the top had been broken off, whatever idol had adorned it now forsaken. There were small cracks running down the remaining length, as though the entirety of it risked shattering with a single indelicate movement.

The last held a pair of enormous shears, which glinted with great evilness, like the sneer of a striga. These shears were too large for any domestic task. They were meant for snapping weak branches from bothersome trees.

"Well, you have found your way here, though it took rather longer than I expected." It was the one with a scepter who spoke.

I know. I am sorry. There were matters at hand—but now we are at Castle Crudele and Marozia dines with the king.

"That is the least of what you can do," said Adele-Blanche with the shears. "Every wasted moment is a drop of precious death-blood."

"Leave nothing up to your cousin," chimed the spindle-clutcher. "Let her ply the prince in peace. She will draw his attention while you seek, seek, seek."

I shall. I thought I might start—

"With the tomes," the scepter-holding Adele-Blanche cut in dryly. "Indeed. Did I misuse my years teaching you strategy? Of course you will start with the tomes."

You did not misuse them. The words, unvocalized, still somehow caught in Agnes's throat. *The tomes, and then the tomb. There must be a way inside.*

"There will be." This came from the Adele-Blanche with the shears. "The words will be in the tomes, and the bodies will be in the tombs. If you forget, take off your gown and read your own stomach."

XIII
AS THE PROPHETS DID

A violent force wrenched Agnes from the murk of her dream. She felt the bed lurch up at her, as if she had been dropped from a great height. Her throat was ablaze with the taste of bile, and when she opened her eyes, she saw that she had vomited all down her chin and the side of the mattress, and it had dripped down her outstretched arm, puddling onto the floor. It was thin and rheumy and laced with the black dye of the berries. But because Marozia had laid her on her side, she had not choked.

Marozia's arms were around her, pulling Agnes's body against her chest. Her snoring was high and soft, like air passing through the reed of a flute. With greatest care, Agnes sat up and removed herself from her cousin's grip. As soon as she rose, her vision turned milky and obscure and her head started to ache; meanwhile Marozia merely rolled onto her other side, clutching at a pillow instead.

Tiny needles drilled into Agnes's skull, but she stood anyway. The light through the open window held a clarity that she had never witnessed before, unhampered by fog or the general damp grime that hung in the air around Castle Peake. It was already past dawn and the sky was a virtuous blue. There were no clouds to besmirch it.

When her vision sharpened and stabilized, Agnes noticed that there was a plate of food on the desk. Marozia must have brought it up for her. A goblet full of wine, watered down to its weakest pallor. Bread that had already been peeled of its hard crust. A wedge of crumbly white cheese.

Agnes dug into the bread with her fingernail and removed a bit from its center, where it was airy and light. She rolled it into a ball in the palms of her hands and then nibbled it slowly, grateful that she did not have to worry about any hard sharp bits finding their way into her mouth.

The cheese was not for her, but the wine begged to be drunk, so she drained the goblet. The sleeve of her gown was soaked through with bile. All of a sudden this was more sensation than she could stand, so she tore at the stays of her corset, yanking and ripping even when they smarted against her ribs, until it loosened enough that she could slip the dress off her shoulders and step out of it.

With the washbasin in the corner, she wiped her mouth and chin clean. Then she opened her trunk. Inside was a monochrome array of silks and satins, the shades only as distinct as stone at various levels of dampness.

Agnes did not tread near red; that was Marozia's dominion. She kept to unassuming colors: skulking violets, dusky plums, occasionally a lavender wrung out like laundry, if ever Castle Peake was touched by an odd joyous moment. She selected the most taciturn of gowns today. It was a murky, nameless color somewhere between mauve and gray. She examined her fingers, to make sure there were no greasy smears of bile or black juice dried into the lines of her palms. She peered at her shuddery reflection in the bronze mirror. Her teeth were white, her tongue pink. Unless she was examined closely, no one would suspect her treasons.

The cruel glint of Adele-Blanche's shears flashed through her mind. The scepter with its annihilated idol. The spindle and its endless red yarn. The images layered behind her eyelids until the real world was only a blur, something glimpsed vaguely beneath the surface of the water.

Agnes picked at the white ring of flesh around her fingernail until the nail bed brimmed with blood. The images dropped dead. The real world resurrected itself. She wondered if this was what the prophets saw in their caves, if their visions enveloped them like sticky swarms of flies. She wondered if it made them sick to their stomachs.

 # XIV
THE LIBRARY AGAIN

Castle Crudele was not silent as she navigated its halls. Through the wide-open arched windows, sound poured in. Voices and clanging anvils, heavy footfalls, the snorting of horses, the sea hushing against the rock. If the castle had seemed eerily lifeless when she had arrived, it was no such thing now. Smoke from newly stoked fires and the other odors of humanity floated up, all cut through by the brine of ocean air.

But perhaps there had been no great change at all except the change of her own perception, accustomed as she was to the overwhelming silence of Castle Peake. Her ears were as sensitive to the noise as a babe newly born. Yet—these sounds did not perturb her as Agnes had expected them to. She had anticipated being galled, rubbed raw by the sheer force of life around her—so different from her forsaken home—but it was not like that. The sounds filled her, nourished her, yet in a strange way that reminded her starkly of her own emptiness and hunger.

Agnes was not disposed to lingering. So she was surprised to find herself pausing before one of the large windows, placing her palms flat on the sills, listening in earnest as one might drink deeply of a cup of wine. She stood there until she felt very foolish. Then abruptly she pulled away and hurried down the hallway again.

Her grandmother had told her: *They will keep the books deep down, in the remotest corner of the castle. Near the bodies. Like and like. Hoarding their power in one vault.* So Agnes descended through corridors of white stone. If at any point she heard strange footsteps on the ground or strange voices through the threshold, she stopped and waited, holding her breath and pressing her back flush against the wall.

The corridors drained down and down, but she remained undetected. Then abruptly she found herself staring down a long and narrow hallway with a bright mahogany door, and in front of it stood a gray-helmeted soldier of the Dolorous Guard.

She could not see his eyes, but by the way his head inclined, Agnes knew he saw her. She froze, then took one heedful step forward, then froze again. The guard did not shift at all.

If she could be put off by the presence of a single soldier, Adele-Blanche had indeed wasted her years in training her. It was this thought that at last propelled Agnes forward, her gait precise and serious. Her figure, of course, was too slight to intimidate him, but her status afforded her much to compensate for that, even if she did not speak. So she reached the mahogany door and grasped for its golden knob.

"Wait, lady," the guard said. "This is the library."

She merely looked up at him and nodded.

"You are not permitted to enter alone," he said.

Agnes blinked. Surely King Nicephorus was not so petty as to deny her access to such a simple thing as a library. She wondered if Marozia had done something at dinner last night to gravely offend him. But as she worked it over in her mind, she realized that it was with not pettiness but prudence that he had made such a decree. Despite the imminent betrothal and the joining of their blood, she was still a lady of the House of Teeth. Still a granddaughter of Adele-Blanche. Of course she could not be trusted among the relics of Berengar's power. Her grandmother's memory ran cruel and deep.

To find herself stymied so early in her quest was dreadful. Agnes felt her insides twist, her empty stomach grinding against itself. The shears, the scepter, the spindle. Strength, tradition, craft. All of these qualities that had been so carefully inculcated in her since infancy seemed to abandon her now. The only thing she could do was keep her gaze on the guard, trying to peer through the grate of his helmet and glimpse his eyes. She saw only their jelly-like whites.

Her silence was a bluffer's gambit. No matter how great in size or in stature, one eventually folded against its totality. Usually it was from sheer discomfort, but this in and of itself was no tool to be easily dismissed. She had spent a long time honing its effectiveness.

The silence filled the air like filthy smog, as sour and thick as what rose from the hovels of the Outer Wall. The guard shifted on his feet.

The longer her silence persisted, the greater its effectiveness. Agnes had not gotten here through weakness of will. Ordinary humans, she had learned, were so unaccustomed to silence that its endurance sooner or later became intolerable. And this guard's spirit was made of no stern stuff.

"Well," the guard said—at last, and Agnes could, without sight of it through the helmet's grate, perceive the redness rising to his face—"I suppose I may permit you inside. But you must be observed."

Agnes nodded fervently, trying to appear relieved. In fact, she *was* relieved, but this was far from the end of her trial. Would the guard restrict her from particular tomes? Would he keep notes of what books she selected and report back to the king? In truth she thought it unlikely that he could read, though she could not be sure.

He pushed open the door and held it so she could enter.

She did, and found herself in a room far taller than it was wide, which rose in tiers of bookshelves like the spiraled mound of rock jutting up from a cave floor. There was a single window at the very top of this columned chamber, like the aperture of a spyglass, and because the whole room was furnished in that same mahogany, the light that fell through turned amber, and the dust motes drifted slowly through its shafts like flies caught in resin. A single faint breeze, from an unknown source, lifted the smell of parchment and ink into the air.

All around, there were winding staircases to bear one to the upper floors, and rolling ladders to reach the topmost shelves. And indeed every shelf was crammed to its edges, the spines of the books gleaming in shades of emerald and indigo, deep burgundy and richest gold. Although Agnes was on the ground, she had the sensation of standing somewhere very high, the edge of a cliff perhaps, and she felt that height in the soles of her feet, her stomach swooping, gull-like, with astonishment.

The library held no dampness, no evil darkness, no putrid stench of fear. The candles on the walls were not lit because they did not need to keep any shadows at bay. The air was heavy, but it was a serene and pleasant weight, like being wrapped in a soft woolen cloak.

Agnes moved in an almost unconscious state to the nearest bookshelf. She ran her fingers along the spines, and the pad of her thumb did not come away smeared with dust. This library was not abandoned; it was kept lovingly, visited often. By whom, she did not know. It overwhelmed her, filled her in that same strange way that also illuminated her own desolation.

She turned to see the guard—true to his word—watching her intently. She did not fear his scrutiny, not now that she was inside. If anything, the cues of the guard's eyes might help her navigate through the labyrinth of shelves. If she grew too close to a tome that contained unrealized treason, she assumed that he would stop her. But he merely stood there, an impassive sentry, his hidden face revealing nothing.

There was no indication of where to start. Even the voice of Adele-Blanche had been silenced, the images of shears and scepters and spindles evicted from her mind. Her grandmother's posthumous existence seemed to have been shut out of this place, her memory emptied from Agnes's consciousness. So Agnes pulled down from the shelf the first book she had touched and opened it.

At first, she could not even make sense of each word individually. What overtook her instead was a breathtaking realization that these were not *her* words, not the words dictated by Adele-Blanche; they had come from someone else's mind and been transposed onto the page. They were proof of a world that stretched far beyond the dark room in Castle Peake, past the forbidding black cliffs that breathed and swelled like a mighty beast with mountains on its back. The writing was beautiful, not for what it said, but that it existed at all. And Agnes was so overwhelmed that she could do nothing but drop herself into a seat at a nearby table, the book open in front of her, the epiphany bowing her head over the page as if in prayer.

When she did manage to read the story, it was not particularly remarkable. It was a story about the slaying of a hydra. A noble knight in green armor with a breastplate in the shape of a bearded head. It was something she might have written as a child, something without steep heights or great depths, but it captured her mind anyway. The image of the hydra's many necks, stretching outward from its cave like vines, flashed brilliantly across the insides of her eyelids.

Agnes no longer had the sensation of being watched, though the guard had not moved from his post. His gaze, mostly blank, was as light as air compared with the steely sharp eyes of her grandmother. There was parchment and ink on the table—the ink was fresh, with a blackened quill nearby confirming it had been used recently—and Agnes found herself plucking up one sheet, dipping the quill, and putting it to the paper. The guard watched her closely still, but he did not intervene. Clearly she had not chosen a tome whose secrets would threaten the supremacy of King Nicephorus the Sluggard and the House of Berengar.

The library was still and quiet, and gold as the inside of a vault, and warm enough even with the narrow slanting of sunlight that Agnes could feel her muscles relax, her body going soft within the velvet arms of the chair.

And then—a sound. The door creaking open.

At the same time that her head snapped up, the guard's head declined in a dutiful bow. So Agnes should have known, even before she saw him tread down the narrow walkway between two enormous heaps of books, that it was the prince who entered. She would have heard the king much sooner.

Liuprand wore only a sky-blue doublet, no cape, no epaulets, and he looked just as surprised to happen upon Agnes as she was to encounter him. It would have been proper to stand, of course, perhaps curtsy, but Agnes was far too stunned to move.

Incredibly, however, Liuprand merely nodded and said, "Lady Agnes," and then sat down beside her.

He had been carrying a book under his arm and now set it on the table. Agnes tried to glimpse the title on the cover, but she could not. Liuprand's presence was still too perturbing; she could not resettle herself. Although she was obviously the intruder, she could not help but be shocked that the prince was the one frequenting this place, that *he* kept its tomes lovingly free of dust, that he handled them regularly and gently. Liuprand the Scholar?

"You were missed at supper last night," he said.

She nodded slowly and tried to assume a weary, dour expression. It did not take much effort on her part. There were dark circles carved deeply beneath her eyes, and in the mirror, her face had looked particularly waxy and wan.

"Your cousin said you were too worn from your journey. I hope you have recovered your strength."

He said it so sincerely that it seemed almost funny to Agnes. It painted a gloss of absurdity upon the entire scene. If she spoke, she would have been tempted to ask him, quite bluntly, why he concerned himself with her condition at all.

Instead she merely nodded again, blinking in an attempt to brighten her eyes.

Then, to her greatest astonishment, Liuprand looked up at the guard. "You may go," he said.

"Surely Your Highness has greater matters to attend," the guard replied, sounding uneasy.

"And surely you have better sense than to question the directives of your prince."

Agnes could nearly see his face redden behind the grate of his helmet. "Of course, Your Highness." He dipped his head once more, and then he was gone.

Now they were alone, and neither of them spoke. Was he borrowing her tactics? The idea flustered her. Agnes wondered if the prince meant to conquer her, too; if he thought of her silence as a motte and bailey, as a siege wall. If he thought he could starve her silence out.

But Liuprand was not a conqueror. None of these Seraphine nobles were, not since Berengar. Berengar's son, Widsith, was so well known for his complacency that he was named *the Precious*. And of course there was Nicephorus the Sluggard, so idle that he left even his own form unguarded, allowing his body to grow indolent with flesh, swelling beyond the borders of doublets and trousers.

She guessed the prince at only one-and-twenty. He had not yet been given his epithet. Agnes regarded him.

He watched her back intently, gaze measured and steady. Liuprand the Constant?

If indeed he meant to mirror her silence, the strategy was wasted on her. No matter how strong his will, Agnes had years on him, years to craft her silence like the thickest and most ponderous of battlements. He could never triumphantly besiege it.

As she expected, he broke his own silence within minutes.

"It has been many years since I've had company in the library."

This, however, was not at all what she had expected him to say.

"My father is no scholar," he went on. "It was my mother who fed me on books. She had many of these tomes imported from Seraph. My father said, if he had known, he would have offered books as her dowry instead of gold."

Queen Philomel had died in Liuprand's youth, though of course the precise date was not documented. The circumstances of her death were still lusty food for rumormongers and talebearers even so many years later. The most flavorsome morsel of all was the story that one night, during their coupling, and when he had already been titled *the Sluggard,* the king had crushed her into their marriage bed and smothered the life out of her. The longevity of this gossip was remarkable. Agnes had heard the kitchen girls in Castle Peake whispering about it mere days before their departure, although they could not have been more than babes when this unpleasant and lurid tale first emerged.

Even if Agnes did speak, she would never be so crass as to ask whether this accounting was true. But she was intrigued by the notion that the old queen had been a reader. Such a thing was rare in Drepane, given the annihilation of their ancestral texts by Berengar. A century later, the quality of inquisitiveness was not especially prized. If they did title Liuprand *the Scholar*, it would not be an epithet of reverence.

Perhaps this was why Liuprand posted a sentry at the library door. Not to keep others out, but to hold his secret safe inside its walls.

All this time she had been occupied in her own thoughts, Liuprand had not taken his eyes off her. Now his gaze skimmed downward and settled on the piece of parchment on the table.

Luckily she had not written anything damning. In fact, she had not written anything valuable at all. She had scribbled banal little notes, testing whether the story had any heights or depths, and if she could scale or plumb them. *The hydra lures but also terrifies. The knight is brave but also lusts for glory. The pursuit is selfish. The hydra has inflicted no harm upon humanity.*

He stared at the paper for a moment, then lifted his gaze again to meet hers. "You wrote the letter," he said.

There was a gap between the speaking of his words and Agnes's comprehension of them. But once the understanding had lowered its weight upon her, she snatched up the parchment, crumpled it in her fist, and shook her head furiously.

"No, I did not mean to alarm you," Liuprand said quickly. "I merely recognized your penmanship. It was not a recrimination. Marozia is a lady of great power and esteem, and one in her position cannot always be expected to perform such tasks. I take no offense to it. As you proposed in your letter—the betrothal will proceed."

So already it had been decided, likely last night at supper. Agnes should have felt joy; at the very least, relief. But an odd feeling invaded her instead. It was some hazy echo of what she had felt when Marozia had clutched her firefly in gentle, uncallused hands while Agnes was smearing the sticky remains of hers on the grass.

Slowly, Agnes nodded. She tried to mount an enthusiastic expression. Clearly she was not very successful, because Liuprand then frowned and asked her, "Does this please you?"

She nodded again. Still Liuprand did not look particularly convinced, but it did not matter much. Her pleasure or displeasure was nothing that would affect the political maneuvering of princes and kings.

Liuprand left the topic behind, gaze skewing toward the book she had open. "What an interesting tome you've chosen," he said, the corner of his mouth quirking.

Frowning, Agnes looked down at the book. She could not tell what amused him about it. Then she turned the page.

But queer enough, when the knight came to the hydra's cave, she was not a serpent at all but halfway to a woman, her body patterned with green scales and her hair black as tongues, breasts heavy with venom rather than milk. And when he thrust into her, it was not with the point of his sword.

This was accompanied by a wondrously vivid drawing. Heat rushing to her face, Agnes slammed the book shut.

Liuprand seemed to be biting back a smile as she rose immediately and returned the book to its place on the shelf. Still blushing profusely, she took down the next book she could find and, after leafing through it to ensure she had not selected another surreptitious tale of obscenity, returned to the table. She sat and refused to meet the prince's eye. Silence curled through the heady golden air.

"You may read whatever you like, you know," he said at last. "There is a time and place for all tales, even the bawdy and bestial ones."

Amusement made his voice light and musical, but Agnes did not feel that he was mocking her. It was too gentle for that. Liuprand turned to his own book, the title of which she still could not manage to glimpse, and opened it to a marked page. After casting one final, secret glance in his direction, Agnes opened her book as well.

And then, heads bowed, they read in a strange but companiable silence.

XV

RUINOUS FRUIT

The Exarch rose from his cot in total darkness, as had been his custom ever since Widsith the Precious had sealed off the one window into the chapel. He lived now as a dove in a dovecote, and the melted wax on the walls and on the altar were like his droppings. The tattered ends of his ceremonial robes dragged on the floor behind him, clearing a path through the dust that had gathered as thickly as a layer of ash over a decimated city.

He must light one candle on each end of the seven-pointed altar and then work inward, slowly, moving from point to point, until the whole altar glowed like a star. It would have been easier of course to start in the middle, and light every candle on each arm of the star, but this was not the will of God. The Exarch also did not concern himself with his own longevity. If the sleeve of his robe caught fire and he burned to death, that would be the will of God. Because he believed God's will existed only within these walls, and nowhere else on this dreary, death-soaked island, he must do all he could to preserve it.

This ritual was also important because it was the only manner by which he could measure time. It took fourteen seconds to light each candle with his tremulous, age-spotted hand. And then sixteen seconds to shuffle to the next altar point. By the time he was finished, that was the morning, and the brightly flaring altar was his dawn, and his breakfast would be arriving soon.

The Exarch then sat back on his cot. He lifted the hem of his robe to examine the tumescent bulge on his left leg, which had been at first only the size of a grape but now was a throbbing purple mass that more resembled an eggplant growing beneath his skin. It made his gait even more labored. But if the tumor had grown within these walls, it was the will of God. He was God's garden and in him God had planted a ruinous fruit. Who was he to try to chisel away at the architecture of his impending demise? He would be no better than the godless heathens of Drepane, who thought they could pilfer from death like four-fingered thieves.

The thought of fruit made the Exarch's stomach whimper. His breakfast should have come by now, delivered as it always was on a very tottery silver tray. He considered rising, but why? The door to the chapel locked from the outside and could not be breached. And on the highest floor and in the remotest tower, he could bellow and pound on the walls and no one would hear. He could even set fire to the chamber, and it would be hours before anyone glimpsed the smoke.

Before he could ponder whether or not God had decided that today should be the start of his starving to death, with all the many implications of that conceit, the door rasped open.

From the hallway came a shaft of light, uncommonly gold. The Exarch squinted as the light planked his face.

"Good morning, Your All-Holiness," said the prince.

"You?" The Exarch coughed out this syllable. "What need have I of you?"

Lit from the back, with the candle flames dancing in his overly blue eyes, the prince smiled. "You have need of breakfast, I presume."

He was carrying the Exarch's silver tray, piled with all its usual satieties. There was the bread, only the tough ends of the loaf, toasted until their crust was blackened and they tasted equally of flour and ash. There was the dollop of honey, which he would smear on one piece of the bread using his thumb. And then, in the center, in a glazed green dish, there were six gauzy strips of cured ham, crumpled like soggy parchment. The Exarch liked to stretch out each piece until it snapped and went limp in his hand. Sometimes he amused himself by rolling the gummy meat in his palm, forming a red-and-white marble that could roll quite assuredly across the altar. Then he would lick his sticky palm clean, savoring the perspired oils of Seraph.

Of course he could not perform this ritual in front of the prince, so he would have to wait, which made him cross.

"Set it here," the Exarch said, waving his hand toward the altar. There was one square of empty stone upon which the melting wax did not intrude, and the tray fit within it perfectly.

The prince set down the tray so decorously that it hardly made a sound. Then he stood back, hands clasped at his waist and head angled down, an oddly penitent position for a man born in the hurricane-eye of this heathen island, who had never once touched the radiant shorelines of Seraph.

But Seraph had touched him. The prince had hair the color of the sand on the Seraphine coast, eyes the shade of its jeweled lagoon, and the broad, powerful build of the bronze statue that stood over the entrance of the bay, ships passing beneath its spread legs, its reflection painting the water below in ripples of gold.

This softened the Exarch's gnarled and rancorous heart. He pinched a strip of meat between his finger and thumb and lifted it, light shining through the translucently pink and white-veined morsel.

"This animal knew the scent of the Dogaressa's perfume," he said. "Rosewater and morning dew. It counted every feather on the winged lion as it walked through the city gates. It heard the arias from the opera house. It felt the gentle lilt of a canal boat on a hazy summer night."

"Then this was the most illustrious and genteel pig in Seraph."

"Liuprand the Droll. I might prefer your father yet. He never tried to make anybody laugh."

The prince thinned his mouth. "Go on, Your All-Holiness."

"Widsith's men slaughtered the animal on the deck of a ship bound for this barbarian little place," the Exarch said. "Since then, it has been butchered and cured, and kept in its preeminent barrel. You must have heard the cook say as much to you. I will not eat a bite of meat that was born on this island. I will not taint the vessel of God."

"As you wish it." The prince regarded the tray. "And you may have your meal in sacred isolation, but first I must invoke my rights as your sovereign."

"My sovereign?" the Exarch repeated sourly. "My sovereign is the Dogaressa."

"And the Dogaressa has sent you here to serve the royal family of Drepane."

The prince had been standing halfway in the room, his knee holding the door ajar, and at this point he stepped inside fully, letting the door shut behind him. Now again the only light was from the incandescent altar, and from the gleam of one hundred and twenty candles gathered within the prince's marvelously blue eyes.

The Exarch could have been staring directly into the lagoon of Seraph.

"What would you ask of me, then?" he barked. "Say it quickly."

"Tomorrow you will climb down from your tower and bless my marriage."

A marriage. Had a new Seraphine bride been smuggled to the island like the most precious plunder? Would she have hair the color of sun-drenched sand and carry the scents of rosewater and morning dew? The Exarch allowed himself to hope. He imagined breathing into the nape of a Seraphine woman's neck, inhaling against the holy column of her throat.

"Tell me of her," the Exarch said. "Your bride."

"She is a noblewoman."

"And?"

"And it is a profitable match," the prince said.

Sitting so close to the candle flames, the Exarch's meat had begun to sweat. "And? Can you lay no plaudits upon your betrothed? Do her manner and form not move you to poetry?"

"I am not Liuprand the Bard," he replied. "You will be fetched at first light."

The Exarch felt as though something was slipping away from him, something he was not even aware he had held at all until it was gone. Like water, pouring from the cracks in his wizened hands.

"Tell me her name," the Exarch said. "Seraphine names are each themselves a psalm."

The prince was silent for a long moment.

At last, he said, "My bride has no Seraphine name."

"No," the Exarch croaked, like some dull little frog. "It cannot be. No. God will not permit it."

The prince said nothing, allowing the Exarch's world to crumble down around him, allowing the Exarch to lie gasping in its ruins, choking on the ash of desolation, seizing with visions of a million matches, all burning to their ugly blackened ends.

"*I* will not permit it," he said, speaking as a dead man.

But the prince's mouth quivered into the slightest of smiles. "Do you not wish to partake in this civilizing mission? You will be the herald of Drepane's new age."

"She will poison you," he rasped. "That viperess, that striga who will share your bed. She will suck the fine blood of Seraph and leave you a gray corpse. That is the aim of all women, all creatures, on this apostate island. You will allow yourself to be the vile serpent's prey?"

He did not like this prince, this too-beautiful, too-canny prince. But he loved him, as a hungry man loves the last morsels of meat on the bone. He would worship at his feet, kiss him for the faint taste of morning dew on his mouth.

"You do not even know what you do not know," the Exarch whispered. "I would cut out your eye to show you—how it is the precise color of Seraph's waters. Liuprand the Last, they will call you. Worse than a Sluggard, leading your line to its demise. Do you not ponder your own condition? Do you not fear for the fate of your soul?"

"I ponder the condition of the island and the fate of all the souls upon it."

A breath came out of the Exarch's mouth. It was as cold as the murmur of a ghost.

"God cannot help you," he said. "Liuprand the Ill Portent. You are already lost."

"Tomorrow," the prince said. "At dawn."

He turned then, his cape fluttering mightily over his shoulders. He grasped the knob on the door, but rather than stepping through and then shutting it again, he thrust the door wide open and held it to its hinges, letting the light pour in.

"Adjust your eyes, Your All-Holiness," Liuprand said. "You will need them to read the rites."

The Exarch cried out and threw up a hand, but still the light beamed through his skin, through his eyelids, and boiled his eyes right in his skull. The altar candles flickered only dimly, cowed as he was by the totality of this external light. White was this light, not gold, white like the sourest pear, the most unready apple, divested too early of its peel.

The prince propped the door ajar and left the Exarch trembling on the floor, bargaining with God: *Please,* he prayed, *let my tumor burst before dawn.*

XVI

TWO GOWNS

The gown was an elephantine thing, almost a creature itself. The bodice was ivory, stitched through with the most intricate embroidery of gold, flourishes and vines and minute flowers, and whenever Agnes looked closer, she could see some shape that she had previously missed: a bird caching itself among the leaves, an upside-down cat's face camouflaged among volutes and plumes.

The skirt swelled from beneath the bodice like a puff of pastry, planked with alternating stripes of ivory and gold. A narrow, plaited belt was fixed around the waist of the gown, and chains of gold draped down, giving the appearance that Marozia was wearing a second skirt made of delicate and impractical mail. It also created no small amount of commotion when she moved.

The sleeves were fitted and again stitched through with gold, baring tiny diamonds of Marozia's skin between the embroidery. But most exceptional of all were the shoulders. They jutted up tremendously, crafted not out of cloth but out of corset boning, and looked for all the world like a rib cage picked clean. Agnes imagined that the dressmaker had thought of this feature's avian qualities, that he had intended for it to resemble wings, but she could not dispossess her mind of its glorious horridness. Unintentionally, the dressmaker had crafted the most fitting gown for a noble lady of Drepane.

Marozia's throat bore the ancestral necklace of their house. Her hair was held back with the high bridal hood, a braiding of white and gold, the cumulus veil floating out behind her like a spirit escaping its vessel. The golden train was so heavy that Agnes had to practice lifting it, trying to determine the proper way to haul its weight without her knees buckling.

She tested this as Marozia paced about the room, oblivious to Agnes's endeavors.

"It suits me perfectly, does it not?" Anxiously Marozia fingered the necklace of teeth. "Every stitch and seam. It was the old queen's wedding gown. The dress of Liuprand's mother."

Agnes let the train tumble out of her arms in fear that she would split the seams of her own gown if she continued in this enterprise. Her dress had also been provided by Castle Crudele, and it perfectly suited Agnes's stature as well. It was a greatly diminished version of Marozia's, lacking those wondrous bird-sleeves, and where the golden embroidery gleamed radiantly against the ivory of Marozia's gown, Agnes's dress was stitched in silver. The color did not shine against the cloth's overall hue, which was a very diluted lilac, so pale as to almost be white, and even resembling gray in certain ungenerous slants of light. Her hair was caught up in a silver hairnet.

"It needed no alterations, the seamstress said. That is a good portent, surely. That this gown was meant for me."

Agnes nodded. She had not had much occasion to examine her own reflection in the mirror, but she caught a glimpse of it now. Those two fickle strands of hair had come loose to frame her face, and she felt a startlingly powerful surge of anger when she saw them. The strength of this fury surprised and terrified her.

Marozia inhaled suddenly, a quick but lusty gasp. "Agnes," she said.

So rarely did her cousin address her directly by name that this startled Agnes further. She looked up.

"Is it wrong," Marozia said softly, "to be afraid?"

A slow moment passed between them, silence wreathing the air.

And then Marozia came to her in such a brisk manner that it was violent, crashing into Agnes and seizing her about the waist, pressing their bodies flush together. Agnes tucked her face against her cousin's shoulder. Even with layers of silk and corset boning between them, her liveliness was overwhelming, the urging of her breasts against Agnes's, the overly sweet smell of the orange blossom oils in her hair.

Marozia raised a hand to caress the back of her neck. She gently fingered the ribbons of Agnes's corset. Then she whispered, "Swear to me. Swear you will always be my Lady of the Bedchamber, even when I must share my bed with the prince."

Agnes closed her eyes, lashes feathering against Marozia's bare collarbone. In the matter of an hour, she would be princess-consort, the most powerful and esteemed woman in Drepane. Her words were no longer requests; they were orders. And somehow this made it far easier for Agnes to lift her head and meet her cousin's gaze and nod without hesitation.

Marozia smiled at her. She tucked back the strands of hair from Agnes's face. Then she murmured something about ill-fitting slippers and rushed from the room, dragging that heavy golden train behind her as if it weighed nothing at all.

Agnes stood in place, arms fixed at her sides. The strands of hair slipped down again, and this time she made no effort to push them back into place; she simply let them fall, and with her head bowed they obscured her vision, filmy streaks of black like wet lashes, though of course she did not cry. Her eyes did not even burn with the desire to weep.

For weeks, preparations for the wedding had busied and diverted her attention; she'd not had the time to return to the library or search elsewhere in the palace. Agnes would have gone to the library again, eagerly, even if she had found nothing there, in the hope of seeing the prince again—yet now that foul and perfidious desire passed over her, like a stone skimming the water's surface.

What she did feel, rooted there, was far worse. The slippery and foul bile of envy. She felt it in her stomach. She tasted it in her throat. And each time she thought she had crushed this sensation, anatomized it, desecrated it, she could pass weeks, sometimes months without it, but then it would come seeping back. And worse still was the fear that it was a part of her, as essential as a heart or lungs or a set of teeth, without which one could not eat, and if she tried to kill it or starve it out, she would wither and die before the envy did.

But these thoughts broke like a fever as the door to the bedchamber scraped open.

It was Waltrude, dressed for the wedding in a very simple shift of white, tied at her waist with what appeared to be no more than a tasseled rope. Waltrude regarded her up and down, and it was only now that Agnes realized she had very canny eyes. Guarded, icy green, and sharp.

"My lady," she said. "The ceremony is nearly upon us."

Agnes nodded.

Waltrude did not prod further. Instead she crossed the room until she was standing before Agnes and held something out in the open palm of her hand.

"Here," she said. "I was instructed to give this to you. A gift, from the prince."

It was a ring: a thin silver band with very fine engravings, so delicate she could have spent no small amount of time examining them to see every detail. And in the center, two modest white pearls enclosing a larger—black, but iridescent when it was turned to catch the pale shafts of sunlight. She had never seen one with this coloring before.

She looked up at Waltrude in bewilderment.

"I was not given to know the prince's reasoning," Waltrude said. "But perhaps he meant it as something like a dowry. You are the bride's only family, after all."

If that was so, it was overly generous, beyond what propriety demanded. If he had meant it as a gift for her, unconnected to her kinship with Marozia, it was a clever one. Nothing so opulent as to disgrace his wife, yet still solicitous enough to flatter, showing he knew the color of her gown and had perhaps even noticed her preference for silver over gold. It sat just within the boundaries of decorum, pressing at their limits but not infringing them.

That was too absurd for Agnes to entertain. Liuprand must have seen this as some way of fulfilling his bridegroom's duties, nothing more. She had tried to evict the memories of their encounter in the library from her mind, and it would not help, in such efforts, to wear a reminder of the prince on her person.

Still, it would be a garish breach of etiquette to refuse, so Agnes took the ring and slipped it on her finger. The pearls did not glint powerfully in the light as a precious stone would, but their chameleonic sheen showed a soft rainbow of colors, subtle and almost secret.

Then, quick as the bite of a viper, Waltrude reached out and grabbed her wrist.

Numbed by shock, Agnes did not protest as Waltrude took her other wrist as well, yoking them together and pulling them toward her. Waltrude turned Agnes's hands over in hers, eyes narrowing as she inspected them.

"Why do you destroy yourself?" she asked.

One of Agnes's nail beds was bleeding. She must have picked at them just now, unconsciously. She tried to tug her hands away, but Waltrude would not let go. She was then forced to inspect her own hands with just as much scrutiny, greater scrutiny than she had really ever given them before.

She was surprised by how gruesome she found them. Not only had all the nail beds been stripped away, but the skin around them had also been picked and peeled until all was a tender dark pink, pulsing with below-surface blood. In some places, the breakthrough of blood was merely imminent; in others, the barrier had already been breached, and red was scored through the mangle of white, transforming her fingers into something that resembled meat more than living flesh.

Agnes lifted her head and met Waltrude's gaze defiantly.

"You are a lovely girl," Waltrude said. "Not as vibrant as your cousin, but some men prefer a remote beauty. It is a shame to ruin yourself when you are young and might still find a fruitful match."

At last Agnes managed to jerk her hands free. She stalked to the opposite end of the room and glared fiercely at the old woman, until, with a loud, indignant sigh, Waltrude turned and left her.

It was only after she was gone that Agnes considered a third possibility. She had spent those many hours sitting beside Liuprand in the library. He had taken notice of what she had read and written. Had he taken notice of her hands, too? Perhaps—she tried not to think it, yet the notion fought its way to the forefront of her mind—he wanted her to know that he had seen them. Always, she realized, he had seen her. When no one else bothered even to look.

XVII
HALF A SOUL

The great hall had no dais upon which the bride and bridegroom could kneel and be raised above their gathered guests. Rather, on either side of the aisle, there were four square depressions in the stone, like garden plots, and several pews within them. Eight plots in total, for each of the seven houses, and one at the front for the royal family and its attendants. Arranged within their distinct depressions, every house made a showing, except for one.

There was Hartwig of the House of Lungs, a handsome man who dressed in brocade of garish colors, his cloak, showing each shade of the rainbow, fanned out behind and beside him, filling every seat in his plot. The hair on his head was gray, but there was gold in his mouth: a grille that latticed his white-toothed smile. There was a ruby in each ear, and it was said that his most delicate part had also been pierced and studded with gems, but Agnes was not given to know if this was true.

There was Amycus, Master of Bones, who was of such slight stature that his seat had to be padded so that he could watch the ceremony. Evidently his attendants had anticipated this problem and brought with them a number of fatly stuffed silken pillows. Perched upon them, black hair combed flat, his face round and uncannily free of the furrows and blotches of age, he had a doll-like prettiness and looked closer to a child than a man. However, his age showed in the way his voice had withered to no more than a croaking whisper, and so he muttered into the ear of the raven that sat ever-presently upon his shoulder. The raven, a clever creature, then squawked out its master's words.

The House of Hearts made the fairest showing, Lord Rabanus and his wife both wearing vestments of rosy pink. They sat shoulder-to-shoulder, occasionally dipping their heads to whisper to each other. They had been wed for longer than Agnes had been alive and the lady had given her lord four children, but the coy smiles they exchanged were those of a courting couple, fresh and flushing in their love. Love? A marriage for love was rarer than an ivory tusk.

The Master of Flesh, Vauquelin, did not himself appear, but he avoided terribly offending etiquette by sending his most valuable son in his stead. His heir had also arrived bearing the most generous of wedding gifts, two creaky chests bursting with gold. This had pleased King Nicephorus enormously, and Agnes suspected he would indeed have been happier to see the pews filled with piles of gold rather than human guests.

The House of Eyes had the plot behind the king. Thrasamund was leaning forward, his words moistening the skin below the king's ear. To Agnes's surprise, Nicephorus appeared to be listening quite intently, nodding every now and then, even occasionally deigning to grumble back. Agnes could not imagine what Thrasamund could be saying to evoke such enthusiasm, other than oily flattery. Was this a particular defect in Nicephorus, or was there something about the condition of being king that made one vulnerable to the world's toadies?

His power has grown as soft as his flesh, Adele-Blanche had said.

Across the aisle was the empty plot where her grandmother would have sat. The effect of seeing it, utterly devoid of life, was more poignant than Agnes had expected. As she hefted the enormous train down the aisle, trying to match Marozia's measured steps, she was looking toward that empty plot rather than the bridegroom and the Exarch ahead. It made her realize, truly, the fruitfulness of the laws imposed by Seraph to conquer death. The desecration left not even a shallow grave behind, an absence that could still impose itself upon the world.

In the otherworldly theater behind Agnes's eyelids, a ghost flowered up. She wore all black, with a netted veil that hid her face, but the end of the white braid, like a boar-bristle brush, peeked out from beneath the macabre attire. Adele-Blanche's pale impression turned, raised one crooked hand, and beckoned Agnes to her side.

Marozia settled herself before the Exarch, throwing back her shoulders beneath the avian adornments. Agnes let the train drop, golden cloth spilling from her hands like honey wine. The eyes of aristocrats were upon her. She had to remove herself from their line of sight, but where? On one side, her grandmother's ghost floated fractions of an inch above the stone bench. On the other, Nicephorus the Sluggard regarded her with his limpid, unreadable eyes.

Their power crushed her in, like an insect between clumsy hands. The force of life and the force of death. In the end, it was Marozia who made the choice for her, turning around and hissing between clenched teeth, "*Go on.* Sit beside the king."

So Agnes did. Adele-Blanche's ghost withered into empty air. Agnes wondered if she was the only one of the wedding's attendees who understood the significance of this: Finally, the better part of a century after Berengar's conquest, the House of Teeth had been anatomized.

But this epiphany did not rest upon Agnes for long; the gravity of the impending ceremony stole away its force. Instead, her gaze was drawn upward, toward Marozia, the Exarch—and Liuprand.

Liuprand wore a doublet of white, braided through with gold, and gilded epaulets that fixed a white cape to his shoulders. Next to Marozia's marvelous dress, it was not an especially grand outfit, but his very presence was so luminous that standing beside each other they looked like two winking stars, part of their own private constellation.

It flooded her again, that noxious, treasonous feeling. When Agnes swallowed, she tasted its bile. And when she could no longer bear to look, she lowered her gaze to her own hands, fisted in her skirts, and the pearl ring that gleamed softly among the folds of pale fabric. Still she could not figure out its significance. It was not gaudy enough for anyone else to notice; the mystery was hers alone to contend with. He had not managed to wrest speech from her, but if Liuprand had intended to invade her mind, he had succeeded.

Agnes lifted her head again when the Exarch began to speak. He was a small, hunched man with eyes that resembled two spills of sour milk, and his voice was, shockingly, full of hate.

"In Seraph, it is believed that God divides every soul in two, and upon birth, each of his vessels is gifted with half a soul. With only half a soul, one lives half a life, and spends all one's days seeking one's matched half. One searches in sleeping, in waking, and especially in dreaming. Once one's search has ended and the two souls have been joined, nothing may keep them apart. It is more binding than any treaty, more supreme than any law; it exceeds any power that might be exercised in the mortal world. If ever this bond is threatened, there is no limit to the violence one may enact to restore it, and if ever it is severed, there is no end to the brutality one might wreak as vengeance. This is God's holiest promise: In death, these souls will be united forever and ever as one."

The royal plot was situated behind Marozia, and Agnes could not see her face. But she watched Liuprand closely. All through this oration, his expression did not shift. He did not look at Marozia; rather, he kept his eyes on the Exarch, his jaw set in a nervy way, some private rancor filling the air between him and the priest.

"They keep up this farce, you know. In Seraph."

Agnes whipped her head around. King Nicephorus had leaned over, his lips mere inches from her ear.

"This soul nonsense," he went on in a gruff whisper. "Here on Drepane, they are just words . . . but in Seraph, they are as real as the food that fills your mouth. There is a rite—one man may duel another to the death if he feels this bond threatened. It is the law above the law. A law of God, superseding the law of man."

Agnes tried to shift away from him as he spoke; he was so close to her ear that she felt the muggy warmth of his breath. But already she was near the end of the pew.

"What a relief it is to live on this godless island," Nicephorus said, "where marriage is only ink and paper, and all the rest is fucking."

And then his hand was on her thigh, crumpling the fabric of her dress. His fingers were enormous, swollen between the rings that had been jammed on painfully, the tips so pink they were like boils ready to burst.

Agnes could not move; she dared not even draw breath. Encouraged by her lack of protest, Nicephorus moved his hand higher, fingers scrabbling in the silk to keep his grip tight. In this, he hardly seemed sluggardly at all—as Liuprand and Marozia spoke their vows and knelt for the Exarch's blessing, the king worked himself over in the pews, one hand fondling Agnes's thigh.

"Bleeding traitors," Nicephorus panted as he rubbed himself fiercely. "He should be named Master of Stabbed Backs."

With his chin, the king gestured over Agnes's shoulder. She turned, the nape of her neck still damp with the king's breath. It was only then that she realized the plot of the House of Blood was empty. All that occupied it was a wedding gift: a single bottle of wine, set upright on the pew, like an accusatory finger jabbed at the obstructed sky.

XVIII
A FEAST FOR ALL BUT ONE

Though the king had satisfied one craving, he had not divested himself entirely of his appetites. As they processed into the great hall for the feast, Agnes heard his stomach growl deafeningly, lecherously, his footsteps growing swifter, lumbering and eager. But he overestimated himself. Two more lurching steps and he had to stop, catching his breath and grasping Agnes's arm for balance. She felt the slick, nauseating heat of a fever crawl up her skin from where the Sluggard's fingers touched her.

Marozia's train had been snipped by this point, rolled up like a long and ponderous parchment, and carried away, so she could walk without assistance. She and Liuprand led this procession, though they did not touch each other—the moment that the ceremony had concluded, Liuprand had let go of her hand. Such fondness may have been expected in Seraph, where marriage was a union between two souls, but in Drepane marriage was a quotidian, corporeal contract, which expired when the mortal bodies of its signatories did. Yet both traditions dictated that Liuprand and Marozia must share a bed. A child, whether a product of love or convention, was a necessity.

Agnes did see Marozia's wedding band flashing on her unencumbered finger. Gold was the ring, with a ruby gemstone large enough to pluck like a grape from a vine. Agnes looked down at her own ring, this thing of secret, unshowy beauty, and wondered again what thoughts had crossed Liuprand's mind when he had it made for her.

At her first step into the great hall, Agnes was suddenly overcome.

A memory invaded her, a memory that was not her own, perhaps something her grandmother's posthumous existence had pressed into her mind; perhaps something her own brain had conjured, born of so many treasonous inhalations. She saw, for a moment, all the furniture cleared, the carpets pulled up from the floor, the candles gone cold—a dark, grim room, absent of all ornamentation. In its center, a man stood. He emanated the puissant golden aura of Seraph. He held a sword so thin, it looked carved by a lathe, as though a sewing needle had been magicked to an appalling length.

Before him knelt seven men. Their faces were covered in hoods, yet their clothes were rich; this was no common execution. The doomed men likewise did not beg, did not weep, did not shiver or exude the wispy vapors of fear. In fact, they were so still they seemed already dead, corpses arranged in stiff positions only to simulate life, like taxidermic animals. And the scene was all the more grisly for its lack of motion, as Berengar drew his sword, the cruel sword for which the cruel castle was named, and slit each of their illustrious throats.

Agnes was jerked forward, and the vision dissipated with an eyeblink.

"Come," Nicephorus grunted. "Mulish little thing, eh?"

Agnes was led through the room where the throats of the patriarchs had been cut, watering the castle's foundation. Had they been buried here? she wondered. Beneath the neatly laid stone and the deep-red carpets with their damask pattern that looked like the false eyes of moths? She could not focus her mind on the living; Nicephorus had to haul her up onto the dais and to the banquet table, as she was haunted and more haunted by the dead.

Still blinking through these visions, she was bewildered to find herself seated not at Marozia's side, but at the king's. Nicephorus had arranged her between himself and Liuprand.

"Oh," Marozia sputtered. "My dear cousin—won't you sit next to me?"

"She is plenty comfortable here," Nicephorus said. He was still clinging fast to her.

Liuprand looked over. In one sweeping glance, he took in his father's hand, Agnes's fingers clenched hard enough to turn her knuckles white, and said quietly, "Perhaps she would be more comfortable if you released her arm."

The stare that passed between father and son was not as pointed as it could have been, since their guests were getting settled in their chairs, clinking their glasses and dinnerware, murmuring among themselves, and all these sounds pricked through the silence, sapping its power—yet the look in Nicephorus's eyes was petulant and defiant, near to being hateful, as though he were the errant child and Liuprand the severe patriarch.

At last, his face ruddy with anger, the king relaxed his grip. He did it in slow increments, fingers uncurling one at a time, as moments passed staggeringly, like droplets from a tincture. Agnes's arm throbbed, her skin mottled with red marks that swore to be bruises.

Liuprand watched intently, and of course this meant he saw Agnes wearing the ring. She wondered if he had intended all of this as some elaborate tactic to get her to speak; as if he could draw out the words *thank you* from her throat by activating some deep-seated instinct of politeness. But his gaze was steady and without expectation.

As she slid her aching arm from the table, Liuprand merely gave her a single nod. And though she did not open her mouth, she looked into his eyes—she had much practiced this method of communicating—and, with her stare alone, impressed upon him her gratitude.

"Be well, Lady Agnes," was all he said, and then he rose, in a powerful surge of white and gold, to address his guests.

"I am grateful for your attendance, that you have left your homes to bear witness to this binding between my house and a noble house of Drepane. You are also bearing witness to what I hope will be a new day for the island. For too long my house has ruled on high, remote from its subjects. Now, with the mingling of my blood with that of the island's most ancient line, we will become more familiar to each other. One kingdom, allied in custom and in virtue, in language and in arms.

Just as I promised my loyalty to the lady Marozia, princess-consort, I make this vow to all of you."

When he spoke, the very air seemed to ripple and bend, as if it were nothing more than a conduit for his words, carrying them to the ears of each noble in the hall. So resounding was his voice, so eloquent his locution, that not a single eye averted, not a single lip pulled back into a contemptuous sneer, not a single scoff formed in a skeptical throat. Even Thrasamund, ever garrulous, was silent.

Liuprand the Silver-Tongued? Agnes could see this epithet scrawled there beside his name, ink drying on the legacy of what was sure to be Drepane's most illustrious king since Berengar. Only one house had still truly chafed beneath the Seraphine rule, and now that house was expired, extinct, forever gone, mixed with the royal blood so as to be utterly irretrievable. Marozia was now princess first, and Agnes alone wore the House of Teeth's both drab and glorious gray.

And was the other missing house merely absent, not extinguished? The table that should have been occupied by the House of Blood was empty, the plates and dinnerware set out for no one. She wondered if the bottle of wine had been retrieved, to be sent back to the brazen Master of Blood, or whether the king would make a show of having it shattered and stamped upon; either way, such an insult could not be left to lie.

The spell that Liuprand's voice had cast appeared to be broken, as Thrasamund now raised his cup.

"Let us drink," he crowed, "to this gracious golden prince and his exquisite wife, the beautiful blooming Marozia."

Hartwig, rubies glinting in his ears, raised a cup as well. "To the fair prince and his fairer wife."

Amycus's raven squawked out his praise: "To the sweet-voiced prince, his lovely bride, and the halcyon days to come."

Rabanus, stately and sharp-eyed, lifted his cup and said, "To the joining of hearts and the prince of great promises."

Vauquelin's son said, "To the bridge of flesh between great house and great house."

No words, of course, came from the Master of Blood. And the Mistress of Teeth smiled, preening like a flower indeed, petals opening under their exultant praise.

Agnes looked down at her goblet. The wine inside had not been watered; it gleamed with the hue of a ruby. When etiquette demanded that she raise her cup, she did, and put it to her lips, but she only mimed drinking, and did not let even a drop of the rich liquid touch her tongue.

At last came the feasting. Good cheer returned to Nicephorus's face, his petulance drained away. A swan was carried to the table on an enormous platter; intact even in death, its neck curling like a white-gloved hand. Crumbling cheese drowned in honey. Bread loaves in the shape of winged lions, flour dusting their false feathers; olives in the place of their eyes. Pale-green melon cut into crescent-moon slivers. Agnes watched these plates arrive in the arms of servants, like grains of sugar carried by ants, and with each one that was placed on the table she felt her stomach knot with dread.

And then came a tray of silver fish, coiled so that their tails were in their mouths. Relief struck within her, and then it was quickly snuffed out. This was not the flaky white meat of the freshwater fish that seemed to hang suspended in their stagnant ponds, the fish whose needle-thin bones Adele-Blanche crunched in her teeth. Its flesh was bright pink, like a pair of painted lips.

Agnes leaned forward, trying to catch Marozia's gaze. Her cousin was absorbed in the candied pear that was being placed upon her dish and cut for her by a servant, who leaned decorously over her shoulder. But she sensed Agnes's need of her.

Marozia looked up, cast her gaze across the table, and then prodded the servant.

"Water the lady Agnes's wine," she said. "It is too rich for her. And bring her plain bread with butter from the kitchens."

"Yes, Princess," the servant murmured. The request was not exceptional, though Agnes worried that the king might perceive it as rudeness. Her arm still throbbed from the memory of his grasping hand.

But it was only Liuprand who reacted to this. He turned to her and asked, "Are you feeling ill, lady?"

"Not especially," Marozia said. "But my cousin has a deficient stomach. The misfortune of a too-early birth. As an infant, she could not even suckle. She had to be weaned upon the milk of goats."

Liuprand's gaze was heavy upon her. "That is an unhappy burden. How fortunate, then, that your elder cousin is so vigilant of you." Something false tinged his tone.

Agnes gave a small shake of her head.

"No?" Liuprand frowned.

"She means she is the elder," Marozia said, with undisguised exasperation. "By five days, nothing more. My mother was meant to have given birth first, but Agnes insisted on rushing out a month too soon. It was thought she would not survive. And it has maimed her for life, you see. She is a fragile creature now, and always quite poorly."

Liuprand looked at Agnes for a long moment, though the emotion in his gaze could not be read. At last, he said, "She does not seem such a fragile creature to me."

The conversation was interrupted by the arrival of the water and the bread. All around her, there was feasting, laughing, fair faces going red with drink, promises made of hunts and future banquets, and Agnes sat, sipping her pale wine, picking at her bread, and feeling grateful that her hunger had been excised from her long ago, like the sawing of a gangrenous limb.

XIX
AGNES ALONE

Marozia was gone, to the prince's chamber with her new husband. The sun had sunken into the ocean, yet no moon rose in its place; the clouds were too dense to be penetrated by its silvery emanation. And thus, only the torches on the walls and the fires in the hearths gave light to Castle Crudele.

The hearth in her chamber was cold. Her chamber, Marozia's chamber, their chamber, for since the moment of Marozia's birth they had never slept apart; their bodies had grown in tandem under the same sheets, as weeds sprout from the same plot of dirt. Yet more life had gone into Marozia somehow. She had leached more water from the earth, soaked more sun from the sky. And perhaps she had left Agnes bereft of these things, or perhaps she had drained them directly from Agnes herself, like a snake's teeth are milked for venom, which is then brushed onto the arrow-tips of men.

Agnes sat upon the empty bed. Visions of the living assaulted her now, scenes that played out mere rooms away. She imagined how Marozia would bloom even more brilliantly once within the privacy of Liuprand's chamber, how his large but gentle hands would unlace her corset, then run over her waist and her naked hips. But her imagining stopped dead here. She could not picture a wanton stare on Liuprand's face. It seemed beneath him somehow; at the feast he had not even eaten much more than Agnes. As though he could subsist on nothing more than air. Agnes wondered if his father's appetites disgusted him, whether the king's revolting indulgences had turned Liuprand into a remote creature who could not bear to want or need.

She could easily summon to mind visions of the king, however. When she rolled up the sleeve of her gown, she saw the nascent bruises, in their pulsing, sickish violet. It was then that fear rippled through her, a roiling sensation in her belly that almost approximated hunger.

You must refuse all mortal desires. You must summon visions in smoke. You must consume the knowledge of every plant. The secret covenant of Adele-Blanche, sworn between her and her anointed granddaughter. Agnes touched her stomach through her dress. She felt each jutting bone of her ribs. She felt the slight rising of her small breasts. She felt the letters that ran across her skin.

The ritual to raise the dead from the earth required priest, prophet, and surgeon. And so Adele-Blanche had cultivated in Agnes the asceticism of a monk, the future-sight of a sibyl, and the medical wisdom of a doctor; all of this in preparation for the day she would find the secret words that had been buried in the boneyard of time, in some clever place within the walls of Castle Crudele, guarded more jealously than gold.

Agnes dug into the nail bed of her left thumb. Blood loosened and ran a path down her palm. When she was hungry, she feasted upon pain. When her body throbbed with need, she indulged in this passionate torture. Rich foods and rich wine may have been forbidden to her, but she had learned, like a dog, how to gnaw the marrow from a naked bone.

Her fear then was that somehow she had violated her grandmother's hidden covenant. The king had found his pleasure while kneading the flesh of her thigh. Was this enough to ruin her; had she failed to live as an ascetic, thus preventing her from ever performing the ritual Adele-Blanche required? Exhaustion lay across her heavily, but now Agnes feared sleep, lest her grandmother rise like a specter in her dreams.

She raised her hand to her face and examined it, this gruesome instrument, which itself had suffered so many ignominies yet also inflicted them; it was both the weapon and the wound, her nails working with the steady rhythm of embroidery to peel back her own flesh. Her hand, the instrument that had guided her to Castle Crudele, that had led Marozia to the prince's bed.

The pain had become familiar to her: the endurance of it and the execution. It was this pain that she curled up beside in the bed, holding it as if it were a warm body. Blood traveled along the creases of her hand, dyeing the sheets a fresh and vivid red.

Sleep did not visit Agnes alone. It came only to brush her eyelids shut and then vanish before she could be pulled under. In her mind, she shouted out for it: *Please, wait, come back.* But the words, like all others, would not fall from her lips.

XX

UNSTAINED SHEETS

A visitor did come to her, in the most arcane hours of the night, and it was not sleep. It was a living creature, flesh and bone, and it came to her racked with heaving sobs. Marozia.

Agnes shot up in bed, blinking away the film in her eyes. The shadows were glimmery and deep, like the realm beneath the surface of the water, when rippled through with overworld light. Marozia thrust the door shut behind her with a thud loud enough that it would surely wake Waltrude in the next room over. Hurriedly Agnes got to her feet.

"He would not touch me," Marozia bawled. Her hands were curled up into fists and pressed to her eyes, obscuring most of her face. "He invited me to his bed, yet he left such a berth between us that I could not even reach out and brush his fingers. When he slept, he faced away from me. He averted his gaze as I undressed. As though I disgusted him."

So bewildered herself, Agnes could not very heartily comfort Marozia. She drew her cousin into her arms and patted her back, but her movements were made stiff with shock.

Marozia's tears ran into her skin, slippery and hot. They soaked her exposed collarbone and the hollow of her throat. Marozia's forehead was pressed so powerfully against Agnes's shoulder that she felt like a mule under its burden, and she tried to shift subtly without disturbing her cousin. Then at last, at last, Marozia raised her head and spoke.

"He hates me," she whispered hoarsely. Her face was as red as a fever, and her eyes had the gloss of tears. "Am I not lovely enough for him? Not as beautiful as a bride of Seraph?"

In her gauzy nightgown, which clung to the curves of her body as if it were soaking wet, and even with her countenance so flushed by her impassioned weeping, there could be no disputing Marozia's beauty. Vibrant, ripe, and soft, like a flower-field nymph in a painting of old. She was not the blood of Seraph, true, but was that not the purpose of their union? Why would Liuprand have pursued this match, only to rebuff Marozia so coldly in their marriage bed?

A union was not fruitful until it bore fruit. Until there was a child born who would yoke the royal line to this ancient house of Drepane, a child who might serve as a bridge between two feuding families, a child who might be held up as shining proof that there could be a peaceful joining of old blood and new, that the Seraphine planned no longer to coldly rule from their fortress but rather to mingle among their subjects, coming down from on high like a god from his mount.

Agnes doubted that Marozia was considering all this as her body trembled with now-muted weeping. The insult had been to her person, not to the House of Teeth. Agnes felt her belly go soft with pity, and it was a strange feeling, unfamiliar to her. There was a sharp and acrid morsel of perversity in it. The wine inside the watered-down drink, bitterness just barely coating her tongue.

She was surprised by how quickly that little poison began to spread. Because she was then able to step away from her cousin, and lean over her desk, and scrawl something on a bit of parchment, all while feeling the strength that this small venom pulsed through her blood.

She showed the paper to Marozia, who was still swallowing thickly to contain her sobs.

Try again, it read.

The words of Adele-Blanche, as dictated by her ghost.

Marozia blinked her tear-daggered lashes. "Try? But he . . . he did not want me."

Agnes was not certain this time whether it was her grandmother's posthumous existence that moved her quill.

Try harder.

Silence. Finally came the haughty breath, the hackling of Marozia's shoulders. "You are not the Mistress of Teeth."

Agnes grew still, her breath gathering like dust in her throat.

"You are here to give me *counsel*," Marozia went on, sniffing. "Not orders. Not as our grandmother would have done . . ."

Agnes remained frozen, hands clasped at her waist. The shadows rippled and deepened, as a great fish leaves its wake in the water. For several more moments, Marozia simply gulped air, chest rising and falling, but there had never been a silence that her cousin did not know how to fill.

"Tell me, then," she said at last. "Not *your* will. Tell me what Grandmother would wish for me."

Agnes had never been sure how much Marozia had known. The profit of her elixirs and potions, her grandmother's ministrations, or the constitution of her dreams. Marozia knew that Adele-Blanche plotted for their house's advancement through this marriage, yet what more? Her grandmother had always wished for Marozia to be ignorant of the truth. Of that much, at least, Agnes was certain.

Agnes tore the pieces of parchment into the gasping hearth as Marozia let out a small whimper. Then she went to her trunk and took out the mandrake and henbane, the ingloriously crumpled leaves, edges tinged with rot. They were her last and she could not use them now; she had to save them, so that she could plant more.

Marozia approached her and took Agnes's mangled hands in her own. Never once had she remarked upon the carnage wrought by and wrought upon her cousin's fingers, just as she had never asked what secrets lay within the library, what thoughts preyed upon Agnes's mind. She merely turned Agnes's hands over, and then over again as she pleased, as one would an embroidery hoop.

"Tomorrow," she said softly. "I am so . . . I must sleep."

And so she, the Mistress of Teeth, guided her Lady of the Bedchamber into their bed. She covered them both with the blankets. She curled around Agnes, as a mollusk folds its own legs under itself, and brushed Agnes's lips with her thumb. She did not seem to notice the blood on the sheets, the blood spilled by her cousin's impassioned torment, yet Agnes was gripped in the rictus of this knowledge: that here, in their bed, the sheets had been bloodied, but in the marriage bed where Liuprand slept alone, the sheets were white and clean. No lust had sullied them.

Sleep did not deign to visit Agnes alone, but even it bowed to the whims of Drepane's newly anointed princess. When Marozia yawned and sniffled, burying her face into Agnes's shoulder, sleep drew its mighty arms over them both.

XXI
THE LANGUAGE OF RUSTLING WINGS

Adele-Blanche could not manage to twist her way into Agnes's dreams, yet her sleep was not unperturbed. She was assaulted instead by a bizarre array of visions, which did not particularly disturb her but were vexing nonetheless for the little sense they made and the lack of continuity between them. She saw again a stonemason laying bricks. She saw an ancient man in stained white robes, lying face down on a cot, his hoary face painted in candlelight. She saw a set of enormous stone doors, impenetrably gray, with frayed ropes fed through small notches in the rock so they could be forced open; so heavy they were that a simple knob would not do. The bolt across them was pure steel, and it gleamed with its great mass. It would take two men, perhaps three, to lift it. A vault? What could be so precious that it required such elaborate means to hold it within?

These were dreams she had never had before, not since coming to Castle Crudele. And she had dreamed them without the aid of herbs and smoke. The same question as always pricked at her: Fantasy or prophecy?

But Agnes was thrust into the waking world before she could glean any more knowledge from her dreams. She had not closed the drapes last night, and now sunlight drenched the chamber as if poured from a golden urn. Removing Marozia's hand from her waist, she rose.

The matter of Liuprand's rejection fell heavily onto her shoulders the moment she stood. In the clarity of day, no longer warped by night's freakish shadows, it seemed less strange, yet even more dire. This was Marozia's one task, to make the prince fall in love. And though she had not failed precisely, Agnes did not know a man alive who could be persuaded into love without the coercion of corporeal pleasure. No affection could blossom in a bed of cold bodies.

She did not truly want the directives of her grandmother in this matter. Agnes knew she would not see it as Marozia's failure alone. To Adele-Blanche, Marozia was half a child still, and it was Agnes's duty to arrange her into her place, no matter how ignominious or ugly the task became. She picked at the pale band of flesh around her nail. An old scab, tiny and black like an itch-mite, came loose and fell to the ground.

It was then that she saw the ring. She had not removed it last night. Unaccustomed to wearing jewelry, Agnes had forgotten she had it on at all. This revived her wondering: What was the purpose of the gift? Had he always intended to rebuff Marozia and, if so, did he hope the ring would help smooth over the pain and tensions wrought by this great slight? This thought made her want to remove the ring and retire it to some secret corner of her trunk, but she could not afford to be seen snubbing Liuprand so openly. And in the most obstructed and forbidden part of her mind—her heart?—it would have pained her to be rid of it.

She remembered how concernedly Liuprand had looked upon her at the banquet, with the king's grip forming bruises on her arm. She remembered Nicephorus's hateful, slinking glare as he released her. Liuprand had maligned his father for her sake, why? It made no sense to try to endear himself to the one cousin, and the lesser lady by far, while planning to offend the other, greater cousin, his lady wife.

All this rumination without agenda was useless. Agnes dressed in her accustomed violet-gray and tucked the seedlings into the pocket of her gown. While she pondered the wiles of the prince, she could at least play her role to perfection.

She sought a garden. This was no simple task. Castle Peake was known for its maze-like halls, its dark and vexing stairwells, and its confounding, precarious parapets, but Castle Crudele was a beast of another order. She guessed it as three, four times larger, if not in height then in area, for the moment that she turned one corner, she would be confronted with no less than three distinct paths down different corridors, which, at least, were flooded with light from the many windows near the high ceilings.

However, this gave her the disadvantage of being unable to peer through them to gauge her proximity to the courtyard. Agnes went down one hallway that was decorated on both walls with garish, heavy tapestries, depicting a massacre of revenants. She stopped to examine the embroidered renditions of these pale creatures and was surprised to find they had a certain unearthly beauty about them.

Their limbs were overlong, their skin blanched to terrible whiteness, but death and its undoing chiseled their features to loveliness, as a sculptor carves a statue. Old men lost their wrinkles and regained their rotted teeth. Children replaced their tottery steps with a graceful, loping gait. Sharp cheekbones emerged from previously flabby cheeks; broken noses were slanted back into place. And their eyes, while black from end to end, glittered richly, like water under a midnight sky.

Agnes traced her finger across one of these beautified faces. Did the clandestine cure for death lie here, in the threads of this tapestry? She would return to study it later. Perhaps she would ask her grandmother what she thought when they spoke again in the misty terrain of her dreams.

For now she needed to hurry on. Should she be caught wandering the halls alone, much less regarding this particular tapestry with so much scrutiny, she would be made to explain herself. Granddaughter of Adele-Blanche, overly engrossed in death. The king would be leery, even furious.

So she turned the corner, leaving the tapestry behind.

Yet another corridor was lined on both sides with spears, their tips reddened with ancient blood. Another was glutted with cats, fat-bellied tabbies with mauled ears who raised their hackles at her and hissed until Agnes retreated. Another was lined with birdcages, though these cages held no birds, only feathers and crusted droppings. Did death lurk here, in their absence? Agnes felt increasingly fearful that she would be discovered, and she quickened her pace yet more.

The most curious corridor of all was one that was empty save for a glazed clay statue at the end, in the shape of a handsome youth with a collar around his throat. There was a crown askew on his head, and he was missing his hands. Agnes could not tell if they had been broken off, or if they had never been sculpted in the first place. The statue bore the cracks of age but had no coating of dust, suggesting it was visited and polished regularly.

The youth's stare was so baleful that it made Agnes shudder. She turned away and hurried down another corridor, then immediately thought she should have examined this statue more closely, for perhaps it held a secret clue. It was surely the most enigmatic thing she had encountered on this treasonous journey. But when she tried to retrace her steps, she could not find it again.

At last, as a current carries a fish, a narrow corridor bore Agnes into the daylight. She blinked and raised a hand against the sudden brightness of the sun. The courtyard was rather compact, dusty, more scruff and yellow earth than growing leaves and reaching vines. It was not wild enough to look untamed; rather it appeared merely abandoned, the plants left to their own apathetic devices. Agnes fingered the stem of a dandelion, which curled upward from a spindly nest of goosegrass. So light a touch, and still the plant resisted her, releasing its seeds instantly. The white down scattered and then was carried away on a thin breeze.

Here, in this courtyard, she would commit treachery. Even in the sunlight, she felt cold; she glanced again and again over her shoulders, scanning the windows that looked down into the area from above, searching for watchful faces. And though she found none, she could not exorcise her fear. If she were caught, not even Marozia's new status as princess would protect her.

But this was her task, as ever, and so Agnes knelt. With a cupped hand, she began to dig a small hole in the yellow, cracked earth. The soil did not come away easily. It burrowed up beneath her fingernails. She reached and reached, searching for the deeper place where she might find moisture, yet it was dry all the way down. Nothing would grow here. A dejected feeling started in the center of her chest and unfurled outward. It made her limbs feel leaden, and her head too heavy for her neck to hold aloft.

Once more she had failed. Agnes pressed the petals into her palm, feeling the bite of pain as her tender fingers flexed. She was mired in this gloomy mood when she heard someone call out her name.

"Lady Agnes?"

By now she recognized the sound of these syllables on the prince's lips.

Yet when she did turn, Liuprand still found a way of surprising her. It was not his presence alone, which was unexpected, for why would the prince find himself in this neglected corner of Castle Crudele where even the plants only halfheartedly sought out the sun? Rather it was his aura, which ordinarily seemed so preeminently golden but was now somehow paler, reduced. His doublet was perhaps a shade closer to gray than to blue. His stride, always deliberate, was hesitant, as if he approached a creature he thought might startle and run at the very sight of him.

Agnes was no such creature. She rose, dusting off her skirts and brushing her palms clean. She was long past being afraid of him. In fact, when she lifted her gaze to meet his, she felt a bristle of defiance.

Liuprand held her gaze, but she did not miss the swallow ticking in his throat. "You always appear to me in the strangest places."

Marozia had left their bed and he had risen alone. He must know that Marozia had told her of their failed consummation, of his cold refusal. Perhaps this was why he appeared slightly diminished. It was not only Marozia's duty to please her husband, but his duty to furnish the realm with an heir. The fault and blame for this was always assumed to lie with the woman, if no one was any the wiser. But Agnes knew the truth of what had occurred in his bedchamber—or rather, what had not.

"Your cousin tells me you do not speak at all," Liuprand said. "Not since you were a child. I had thought that maybe you spoke to her alone, where none else could hear. But she tells me this is not true."

It was bold of him, Agnes thought, to mention Marozia. She also thought it was odd that she had been a point of conversation at all, in such close proximity to their marriage bed. Still, she did not understand the prince's interest in her speech, or lack of it. Many others found it a mild curiosity, at first. But with time its novelty wore, and they abandoned their interest in her muteness, and usually in Lady Agnes altogether. If their interest did persist, it was only because they found the totality of her silence maddening. Yet never had Liuprand seemed angry.

"Is it fear?" he asked, quite baldly. "Do you think you will be punished if you speak?"

Agnes pressed her lips together. She shook her head.

"Are you afraid of what you will say, if you cajole your tongue to move?"

If Agnes did speak, she would have told Liuprand that he would tire of this guessing game long before he could defeat her silence.

"I would not think you weak, if you were afraid. We all armor ourselves against our fear the best we can."

Agnes examined the prince's beautiful face. She had not precisely grown accustomed to its beauty; it was more that she could now appreciate its subtleties and finesses, having had the opportunity to look upon him so closely all these times. She saw the faint cleft of his chin. She saw that his hair was not that pure dark gold, but in fact woven with strands of lighter flaxen, which caught the glare of the sun and held it. And she saw, with some alarm, the bruised circles under his eyes. They were not dreadfully deep, but she had never seen such a human-looking imperfection upon his face. If Marozia had slept uneasily, it seemed as though he had not slept at all.

There was a shifty, slippery feeling in her belly. It occurred to her that perhaps Marozia had not told her the whole truth of what had occurred in that bedchamber. But her cousin had never lied to her before. Why would she begin now?

Innamorata ~ 109

Liuprand then said, "Will you come with me?"

Agnes stiffened. She still had the roots and buds in her gown pocket and did not want to risk losing them, and with every moment they wilted and grew less liable to bloom when they were put into the earth. And what if—by some measure of misfortune—Liuprand discovered them? He was perceptive, and in their every meeting he watched her intently, almost overly so. Still she could not guess why the prince found her such an intriguing creature.

She also found herself unable to shake the indignation she felt on Marozia's behalf—no matter the details, he had not deigned to lie with her; that much she knew Marozia would not fabricate.

But for all Liuprand's lack of forcefulness now, he was still her prince. She could not outright refuse.

So Agnes merely nodded and allowed Liuprand to lead her through a white stone archway on the east side of the courtyard. There was a narrow dirt path shaded by vaulting olive trees, and the sun came warm and dappled through the branches.

A low rustling sound reached her ears, which she thought at first was the wind among the leaves, but the olive trees remained unruffled. It was only when the path ended and bore them both into the courtyard that Agnes could see the sound's source: a great flurrying of a hundred pairs of wings.

It was a proper garden blooming with a riot of colors, almost too garish to be real, as though it were a scene embroidered in a tapestry. Roses turned their bright-pink faces to the sun. Hydrangeas clambered up their lattices, their flowers blooming between the plaits of wood in great, round bunches the size of beehives. The tendrils of willow branches waved in the breeze, and pear trees scattered their white petals through the air like flurries of snow.

And among them, perched on every stem and branch and leaf and petal, were moths. Moths of all colors, all patterns, and all sizes, from some that were small enough to fit on the pad of her finger to others that could sit upon her shoulder like Hartwig's companionable raven. Sunlight filtered through their membranous wings, showing the spread of veins beneath. The greater moths had thoraxes as large as honeycombs, and legs that flexed and bent like copper wire.

One large moth swiveled its head and pinned Agnes with bulbous black eyes. She could see her own bewildered reflection in those shiny eyes, but more, she saw a keenness beyond that of an ordinary animal. This was no base creature, operating only on instinct. It took to the air, flicking off pollen, and fluttered toward Agnes. It hovered before her, wings pulsing. There was a true intellect within, she realized, couched inside its deceitfully common insect body.

The moth seemed to perceive this realization from her and be pleased by it. Slowly, it lowered itself onto her shoulder and nuzzled her cheek fondly.

Alarmed, Agnes looked over at Liuprand.

"Gray is for grief," he said. There was a slight, enigmatic smile on his face.

She merely stared back, mouth ajar.

"Gray is for grief," he repeated. "False eyes for a false surrender. Sapphire for fires; gold for relief. A clear wing calls for a defender. This is the language of moths, conceived by my ancestor Berengar. He sought to pass furtive messages to his generals stationed on other parts of the island and across the sea in Seraph. But he feared a letter could be intercepted. He needed a secret code known only to himself and to his allies, so he devised this system, one built upon the qualities of Drepane's great variety of moths."

Agnes warily regarded the moth perched on her shoulder. There was no insect of such an astounding size anywhere near Castle Peake. The only moths that fluttered around the ancestral home of the House of Teeth were tiny, dull, wax-colored creatures, which could be swatted dead with the errant swipe of a hand. Agnes imagined slaying an animal like the one nuzzling her cheek would require an arrow or a spear meant for a beast.

"At first this code was quite rudimentary," Liuprand went on. "Red for retreat, violet for victory, cobalt for a sound defeat. The like. But as his conquest wore on he realized he needed to pass more complex messages. So he began the task of breeding these moths for particular traits—size and pattern, in addition to basic color. If white was the shade of displeasure, and silver the shade of regret, and a larger moth meant a stronger sentiment, then what could Berengar's general be given to know when a great white moth with stripes of silver landed upon his arm?"

He looked to Agnes expectantly, as though he thought she might answer. She wondered if he would ever give up this task of drawing out her speech.

When she did not reply, Liuprand deflated very subtly, his golden aura growing paler.

"Well," he said, "since Drepane has been at peace, the moths have not been formally bred for many years. But they propagate among themselves, as you can see, so nearly every sentiment known to the human heart can be expressed, if you can find a moth with all the particular qualities. They are intelligent creatures, too, at least as clever as ravens and crows, and their breeding has engendered in them a desire to make bonds with humans."

The moth perched on Agnes's shoulder was gray all over, a wholly patternless gray, dense and matte, such that the sun could scarcely manage to leak through its parchment-thin wings. The membranes did not show clearly; they were disguised by this solid color. There was a steadiness to its dark gaze—if an insect could be said to have a gaze at all—and its weight upon her was warm and solid.

"Fuchsia for a forward march." Liuprand was watching her as intently as ever, and his voice grew low. The breeze pulled down petals from the pear tree, scattering them through his golden hair. "Emerald for a true surrender. One dark wing and one white means resolve. This type of speckling, here, which is like the bark on a birch—that is for an apology. This iridescence—it is subtle; you must wait for the wing to catch the light—means love. And this precise shade of green is for sacrifice."

The moth Liuprand indicated was the color of a ripe lime, and its wings were banded with gold—or was it yellow? There seemed to

Agnes an awful lot of room for error in this system; what if someone mistook sapphire for cerulean? And she could not imagine there was any need to transmit a message of love during wartime.

The lime-green moth fluttered off its perch on the neck of a rose and landed on Liuprand's outstretched hand. It was a tiny insect, small enough to fit within his palm. Little, lime green—a minor sacrifice? Agnes frowned as her own moth shifted somewhat discontentedly on her shoulder.

"You see," Liuprand said, drawing himself up to his full height and now exuding the full force of that potent golden aura she had come to know him by, "this is why we with tongues and mouths and human minds use our words to communicate. Without speech, things so easily become muddled."

A flush rose to Agnes's face. She turned on her heel and marched past the hedge lattice, through the willow fronds. Her sudden movement dislodged the gray moth on her shoulder, and it fluttered away to ornament the stem of a hydrangea.

Agnes's gaze searched among the flowers and plants. She carefully inspected the arrangements of petals, the pattern of bark on the trunks, and of course the moths fixed to them or fluttering through the air. She glimpsed one through the hedge lattice and slowly worked her way toward it. She was surprised by how easy it was to coax the moth onto her finger.

Then she returned to Liuprand, marching back through the softly undulating willow branches. The moth on her finger tittered. It was the size of a sparrow and had one black wing, one white.

Gently, Agnes raised her arm and urged the moth into the air. It flitted across the space between them and landed on Liuprand's outstretched hand.

A wry, pleased smile turned up Liuprand's mouth. He allowed the moth to crawl along his fingers and settle in his cupped palm.

"Black and white for resolve," he said. "Very well."

He retreated then, vanishing among a tall cluster of foxgloves. When he returned, he had another moth held aloft on his arm. Larger, sturdier, like an adolescent falcon. He urged it into the air, and Agnes raised her own arm to receive it.

It landed nimbly upon the inside of her wrist. She turned her hand over to examine it, yet the color could not be mistaken. It was a deep and vivid fuchsia, and when the sun shot through its papery wings, Agnes swore she saw a glimmer of iridescence. But then the light changed, and she could not find that shimmery effect again.

Fuchsia, for a forward march. She looked up at Liuprand, who was still smiling in that clever way.

"You will not drive me back so easily, Lady Agnes," he said.

Liuprand the Dauntless. Liuprand the Resolute. There were many epithets for brave kings, for gallant, unfaltering kings. As if the annals of history would be writ with his success in coaxing one inconsequential lady to speak. He should be seeking other ways to dress his legacy in gilt and armor. Of course—his legacy would not be guaranteed until he gave the realm an heir.

He was such an inscrutable character, this prince. So preeminent when he faced his subjects, so gracious with his nobles, courting them with civility, never seeking to instill fear. Forceful but not malicious in his dealings, even when it was past the point of propriety. Remote in affect, cold and unyielding, but never cruel. And yet—

He hid away in libraries, sought his pleasure among the pages of arcane books. He forsook his lawful wife in their bedchamber only to waste his hours endearing himself to her cousin, the lesser lady in all respects, hardly worth noticing, much less befriending.

Agnes looked down at the ring. Nothing passed beneath Liuprand's attention; he would have seen her wearing it. All of this for what? She began to think the prince was as secretive a creature as she was, his true nature unknown to all others, perhaps obscure even to himself.

The fuchsia-colored moth fluttered off her wrist and disappeared among some large stalks of lavender. Agnes left Liuprand again and returned with a moth whose wings had large, optical-looking spots. When it fluttered from her hand to Liuprand's, he laughed—openly, as she had never heard him do before. False eyes for a false surrender.

Agnes found that she quite liked the sound of his laugh. She found that she wanted to draw it out of him, again and again. And she found that she *could*, through this droll casting of moths back and forth. That was how she came to know the language of rustling wings.

The sun rose to its highest point in the sky as they spoke without speaking. And by the time duty called them both away, her back to Marozia's bedchamber, Liuprand back to whatever princely business, Agnes realized she had entirely forgotten to plant her grandmother's treasonous seeds.

XXII

THE MOST ESTEEMED SURGEON

"No," the Most Esteemed Surgeon said. "Not you."

He was standing at the center of one of the villages within the Outer Wall, upon an improvised podium that was no more than an overturned crate. Flies swarmed heavily. The leeches he had brought along—Truss and Mordaunt, his favorites—attentively swatted at them with horsetail staffs. Yet this had the additional effect of blowing the scents of the village directly into his nasal cavities. Boiling offal, teeming latrines, and the brine of seldom-washed bodies.

The Most Esteemed Surgeon sighed and tried to breathe only through his mouth. All these gross odors of humanity made him despair. Was this a hopeless endeavor?

The girl he dismissed slunk away, head hanging low. Behind her, the line had swelled to two dozen, maybe three, all jostling over one another's shoulders to catch a glimpse of the Most Esteemed Surgeon and his retinue. So many smudged, leery faces. Not a single one stood out to him or even dared to meet his gaze.

Mordaunt waved the next girl forward. The Most Esteemed Surgeon regarded her.

She had her dun-colored hair tucked beneath a kerchief, and her brow was tacky with sweat. Under that brow, however, were the most curious eyes. One was a kaleidoscopic gray, the color of pebbles on the beach. The other was a clear, sharp blue.

The Most Esteemed Surgeon studied those eyes. "Name?"

"Ninian," she answered softly. Her pert chin quivered.

The Most Esteemed Surgeon squinted at her until his own eyes watered. Sensing the need of his master, Truss reached up and dabbed at his unshed tears. The Most Esteemed Surgeon blinked to clear his vision. And then he looked at the girl again.

Fair she was, for an islander. There was a naturalness to her features that would not be found in Seraph, where every cheekbone and nose bridge and brow was sculpted as if by the deft hand of God himself. But her lips were pink, her lashes full, her face mostly symmetrical—except for those astonishing eyes.

And yet, when he looked upon her, the Most Esteemed Surgeon felt nothing at all.

Nothing, not even a quick skipping of his heart, not even a quiver in his stomach, not even a faint warming of his veins or a catch in his throat. There was no great, encompassing emotion that eradicated all else, that made the foul odors and the voices of his leeches recede into the background, so that it seemed as though the only two people on earth were him and the girl with mismatched eyes. In fact, the nothingness he felt made the scents and noises assert themselves even more dramatically, and he found himself wrinkling his nose and resisting the urge to clap his hands over his ears. Somewhere a horse snorted and pawed the dirt. A woman tossed the contents of a chamber pot into the street.

Truss and Mordaunt both watched him expectantly. With a weary exhale, the Most Esteemed Surgeon shook his head.

He had been at this increasingly fruitless toil for weeks now. It had all begun when he heard that the prince was to be wed to a noble lady of Drepane. *Impossible,* he had thought, at first, until her carriage clattered down from the morose mountains surrounding Castle Peake. And he had been taken by her loveliness, the lady Marozia, Mistress of Teeth (now princess-consort). He had not imagined such beauty could exist on this grim, forbidding, godless island. If the prince could not import a Seraphine bride, this was the next best thing.

And so the Most Esteemed Surgeon began to wonder if he, too, could find a mate among the women of the island. Surely there was at least one woman here who was to his liking. He would accept half, even a quarter of the beauty of a purebred Seraphine, if she was gentle in her manner and eager to please him. He thought he would have his best luck searching among the inhabitants of Castle Crudele, as if, through their proximity to the royal family, they might have leached a bit of Seraph's graces. Yet he had already moved through nearly every dwelling within the Outer Wall and found nothing. And with each day the search wore on, he became more and more despondent.

Perhaps he should not have had such high hopes. For, in truth, beauty and gentle manner were not enough to soothe the soul-deep yearning that he felt. This was both the blessing and the burden of having Seraphine blood: Every Seraphine has one great love, the other half of his soul, and no other can compare. Even the kisses of the most beautiful woman would taste like ashes in his mouth if she were not his true mate. Her words of adoration would be hollow and cold. Their marriage bed could only ever be as barren as a salt flat.

There was, in fact, a pamphlet commissioned by the Dogaressa of Seraph that offered guidelines for any man in search of his great love. These rules were adhered to as strictly as the laws of the city that prohibited theft and ravishment and murder.

Marriage is no excuse for not loving.
He who is not jealous cannot love.
No one can be bound by two loves.
No one should be deprived of love without good cause.
A true lover never desires the embraces of anyone save his lover.
Love rarely lasts when it is revealed.
An easy attainment makes love contemptible;
a difficult one makes it more dear.
Every lover turns pale in the presence of his beloved.
When a lover suddenly has sight of his beloved, his heart beats wildly.
He who is vexed by thoughts of his love eats little and seldom sleeps.
The true lover believes only that which he thinks will please his beloved.
Love can deny nothing to love.

In desperation, the Most Esteemed Surgeon had begun to forgo sleep, to refuse eating, as though he could trick his soul into believing it had found its matched half. But this only left him tired and hungry and no closer to sating his soul with love.

Yet . . . perhaps. *Perhaps* there was still some hope. His gaze *did* keep wandering back to the girl. Ninian. He had thought at first it was merely the unexpected strangeness of her eyes. But could it not, he wondered, be love? He had not felt his heart flutter. He would have to ask Truss and Mordaunt if they noticed his face growing pale. Perhaps the *seed* of love was here, and he would have to tend it, coax it out of the earth, protect it from harsh winds and bitter frosts and trampling feet until it flowered to its fullest. Could that, he wondered, be love? The steady and patient hand?

Before the Most Esteemed Surgeon could wrestle further with these questions, the crowd of girls and women parted. There was some disquieted murmuring, gazes turning to the ground. And then two members of the Dolorous Guard marched through the cleared path and right to the base of the Most Esteemed Surgeon's crate.

Their faces, mostly disguised behind the grates of their helmets, revealed nothing. One of them said, "We have been looking everywhere for you."

"Why?" the Most Esteemed Surgeon asked.

"There is a grave matter of state," he said. "The Exarch has been found dead."

Dead. The word floated up like a cold plume of smoke. It chilled the Most Esteemed Surgeon's blood. For a moment, he could not speak.

At last, he managed, "How? Was it . . . a natural expiration?"

The guards glanced between themselves.

"It appears to be so," one said. "But the prince calls for your judgment. There are many questions to be answered and many decisions to be made."

Slowly, the Most Esteemed Surgeon nodded. He reached up and, with the sleeve of his robe, patted his brow. Then he looked across the crowd of women again, feeling so terribly alone.

"Let us go, then," he said. Truss and Mordaunt helped him down from the crate. "And you, girl. Ninian. Come with us."

The Exarch's body lay face down upon the floor of the chapel. His limbs were splayed; even his fingers extended as far as they could reach, as though he had been dropped from a great height and landed flat on his belly, killed the moment of impact. His gray robes were pulled up around his hips, baring his thighs and his buttocks. The life had only recently gone out of him. His veins still bulged with bluish blood, vast, spidery networks of them, like the mold in a crumbly wedge of cheese.

But it was clear immediately what had arrested his life. The Most Esteemed Surgeon's gaze traveled down to the Exarch's right calf—or at least what remained of it. An enormous, currant-colored pustule had erupted through his skin. Where the tumor was exposed to the air, it had turned an ashy, putrid black, like the crushed wick of a candle. The innards of the tumor so strongly resembled jam that the Most Esteemed Surgeon caught himself envisioning a knife slicing through the jellied red, then scooping and smearing it onto a crust of bread.

Truss and Mordaunt were enlivened by this, so different from the dull, quotidian deaths they ordinarily oversaw. They whispered to each other, eyes growing bright with glee. At their side, Ninian clapped a hand over her mouth to muffle a squeak of horror. Her face drained of color, and the Most Esteemed Surgeon felt a twinge of chagrin. Not because he had frightened her, but because he feared that no true love of his could be so stricken at the sight of a corpse. His mate would have to be hardier than this.

"Well, obviously he is dead," said the Most Esteemed Surgeon. "Pity. On Seraph he could have lived fifty more years, at least."

The Seraphine were not immortal and certainly not immune to disease, though the close pulse of Seraph's power extended the length of their lives. The Dogaressa herself was two hundred. She had seen the erection of the winged lion statue and watched it turn mossy and green with time.

"Perhaps so," said Liuprand.

The prince stood in the doorway of the chapel. From behind his large body, light streamed in, the only light that could repress the darkness of the chamber, chasing the shadows to the farthest corners and the highest vaults of the ceiling. Not a single candle flickered against this immense blackness. They all had been extinguished and burned down to their ends, leaving only a waxy film behind, which dripped off the altar in frozen suspension like icicles on eaves.

"I have no further wisdom to give," said the Most Esteemed Surgeon. "He is dead. A tragedy, I suppose, if I did not believe he had long been vainly awaiting his ascent to heaven."

The prince's eyes narrowed. He was truly a beautiful man; the most virile and refined blood of Seraph. Along with his new bride, they made quite an appealing pair, if one could suppress prejudice against the native people of the island.

"I do not need your wisdom in this matter," Liuprand said. "I merely wish to know whether you advise performing the desecration."

Surprise jerked his head upward. The Most Esteemed Surgeon glanced askew at Truss and Mordaunt. Though they knew better than to speak, a single look shared between them communicated their shock. And Ninian's brow furrowed, her hand still pressed over her mouth.

"He is Seraphine," the Most Esteemed Surgeon said at last. "The last holy man who remained on this heathen island. You would subject him to such ignominy, as no such Seraphine has been subjected before? The bones of your mother and grandmothers and grandfathers were returned to Seraph and buried there beneath the earth."

"Death is an inherent state of ignominy. He perished on Drepane. His corpse should be dealt with according to the articles of the Covenant."

The Most Esteemed Surgeon scoffed. "Surely you cannot mean that. He is not some idolatrous serf. His teeth are holy instruments.

His eyes stared deep into the blue lagoon. His lungs inhaled the Dogaressa's perfume. His heart beat with love for his true home across the sea. His bones are the apparatus of God. And his blood sings the divine song."

"Sang," the prince said flatly. "And all that may be true, but it does not exempt him from Drepane's customs. For nearly a century, he lived on this island. That is cause to wonder what, truly, is the nature of home."

"You tread close to heresy." The Most Esteemed Surgeon puffed out his chest. "Nicephorus will not live to be an old man. That much we all know. Is this the sort of king you wish to be?"

"I will be no king at all if I do not abide by the laws of my own ancestor's invention."

"Careful," the Most Esteemed Surgeon warned. "Berengar was a conqueror. He was not a god."

"Yet he created the laws of this land. He built a castle where there was nothing but dirt and stone. Perhaps this is cause to wonder what, truly, is the nature of a god."

The lightness of the prince's tone belied the ferocious blasphemy of his words.

"Stop," the Most Esteemed Surgeon said. He shook himself all over, as though he were a damp dog. "I shall hear no more of this."

"Very well. But you will perform the desecration nonetheless. It is my decree as prince."

The Most Esteemed Surgeon drew a breath. At his back, the darkness shuddered and bloomed, threatening to engulf him. The light filtering in from the corridor now seemed dubious, unfaithful. It would only take Liuprand stepping away and letting the door close behind him to plunge them all into irrepressible blackness. This prince who looked in all respects an ethereal child of Seraph yet, with every word, strove to make himself an apostate.

Was it the princess, that Mistress of Teeth? Had she seduced him into this heathen conduct? *The true lover believes only that which he thinks will please his beloved.* The Most Esteemed Surgeon shuddered. Perhaps he, too, had been too ensorcelled by her beauty; perhaps her comely face hid her poisonous heart. Perhaps their marriage was no more than the union between a dead tree and the rot that consumes it. Perhaps there could not ever be true love between a Seraphine and a native of Drepane.

"Your earthly decree." The Most Esteemed Surgeon spoke slowly, so that every syllable fell from his mouth like a hard fat raindrop. "It spits in the face of God."

"Then let God try to prevent me," Liuprand said.

And then he was gone. He did not leave them all in darkness; the Most Esteemed Surgeon almost wished that he had, for it would have made it easier to loathe the prince—this arrogant, impious prince, who might yet be the ruin of his line. Rather, he propped the door open so that light still drained into the seething black chapel, but it seemed diminished now, a watery light, closer to gray than to gold, as if the prince had taken some of the luminance with him.

The Most Esteemed Surgeon stood with great stillness for a moment, half bathed in the prince's discarded light. A thin bile pervaded his stomach and then rose up to his throat, so that when he spoke, each word was touched with poison—renewed as he was in his revulsion for these islanders. And yet—he sounded more weary than hateful in the end.

"Take the body to the pit," he said, nodding toward Truss. Then, tipping his chin at Mordaunt, he said, "And let me not lay eyes on this girl again."

XXIII

TRUSS AND MORDAUNT

The Most Esteemed Surgeon turned on his heel and marched out of the chapel, mumbling irately, white robes flapping like the wings of a flustered seagull. Truss stood and watched for a moment, grieving his master's turned back. He also grieved for himself the ugly task that awaited. Because he had been in his master's favor for so long, he had been exempt from performing desecrations; his own hands had remained unsullied, his fingernails clean, his palms uncallused, his back unbent. He did not trust his own dexterity or his own strength. Perhaps with a clumsy stroke of a scalpel, he would let the inheritance of the House of Blood spill out into the dirt. Perhaps his knees would buckle beneath the weight of a trunk full of bones, and they would all clatter to the ground.

He was not, however, concerned about the blasphemy of these actions. Truss had been born on the deck of a ship bound for Drepane, a liminal space that had formed a creature who was neither believer nor apostate. His relationship with God was akin to his relationship with his neighbor's cat: He would pet it, if it came asking, but he did not care whether it lived or died.

"Trade with me," Truss said. "I'll take the girl, and you take the body."

Mordaunt was his elder. He styled his hair with oils imported from Seraph even though no one ever saw it from under his leech's hood. Truss had never observed him praying, but occasionally, in moments of great emotion, he heard him murmur, *"Dear God."*

"No." Mordaunt, yet another exiled son of Seraph, shook his head. "Master will know if we swap. He won't like it."

"He won't know. He has gone to stew. Come, you are more charismatic with the dead than I am."

Throughout all of this, Ninian had not ceased looking thoroughly horrified. Now she dropped her gaze to the floor, white-knuckled hands fisting her skirts, and whispered, "I do not mean to be any trouble to you."

Truss ignored her. To Mordaunt, he said, "I will play you for it."

"Play? Play what?"

From the pocket of his robe, Truss removed a trachy. One side had gone green and soft with rust; the other still showed the Dogaressa in profile, though it was an old relief, or perhaps merely an idealistic one, as she was bereft of her second and third chins. He traced the coin's jagged edges with the pad of his thumb.

"You are a worm," Mordaunt said, sniffing.

"Here. I will let you have the Dogaressa's face. That is the lucky side."

"I do not think you understand your own game."

"Even better odds for you, then," said Truss. He worked the trachy onto his thumbnail and then flicked it up into the air. In the murky darkness, it winked like a falling star.

He caught it in his palm, closed his fingers into a fist, then slapped it on the back of his other hand. The Dogaressa smiled blithely up at him. Truss groaned.

"There," said Mordaunt. He rolled back his shoulders and jutted his chin. "You have failed your gambit. And you have lost your touch a bit, yes. You must reacquaint yourself with the dead. You may have forgotten, but they are quite good company, once you get to know them."

The chapel was in the very tallest tower of Castle Crudele, and the pit, as its name suggested, was in the ground. Truss steeled himself for his journey the way he imagined a soldier girded himself for battle. In this case, his only weapon was the clothespin he used to pinch his nose shut. The erupted tumor reeked like burnt hair and rotted fruit.

Truss hooked the Exarch's ankles with his elbows and pinned his legs on either side of his chest. Then he dragged the corpse behind him as if it were a wheelbarrow. A wheelbarrow, he thought, would have been useful. But there were so many stairs to heft it up and down. Truss merely hoped that all this jostling would not knock out any of the Exarch's teeth. Curious, he peeled back one of the Exarch's wormy lips and saw that there were only six teeth to be knocked out. A pitiful inheritance for the princess.

As he walked, pain wriggled like maggots through his back, and he loathed Mordaunt. They could have at least taken the body together. The Most Esteemed Surgeon would not be any the wiser. He was robed in his rage and would not make himself seen again until the day of the desecration.

The corridors of Castle Crudele were empty, and despite the light that drained in from the overhead windows, they were rather cold. There was only so much that could be done to heat such inhumane stone. A structure built upon the blood of the dead would never be hospitable to the living. A hundred years had passed, and Berengar's cruelty still echoed in these halls like the groaning of ghosts.

Truss heard voices ahead. He stopped abruptly and let the Exarch's ankles drop, his heels thudding to the ground like stones. At first he thought he had stumbled upon a true specter, a grim apparition, but no. These were the voices of men with pumping blood. And indeed they were lusty, incensed voices that, even disembodied, filled Truss with dread.

"I will not abide this, boy! Yes—you heard me, *boy,* for so you are. You may whisper into your folded hands each night, *Oh, I wish my father would leave this earth,* but I am not dead yet. So you are no king. You are merely an unruly son, and a father may punish his unruly son however he sees fit. Your head will be too deformed to wear a crown when I am done with you."

"You shame yourself making such toothless threats. And you shame the House of Berengar by refusing to listen to reason."

Truss would know the prince's voice anywhere. So fluid, so resolute, even when the words themselves were incendiary. Anyone would balk at such eloquence. Momentarily, it seemed to mollify the king himself.

But then Nicephorus rejoined with, "Ah, well, it is a pity your mother is no longer here to stand between us."

Abruptly, there was a great scuffling, some heavy thudding—footsteps on the ground, an elbow jammed? The slightly sticky sound of flesh and fat meeting flesh and bone. It was the king who grunted—this noise, at least, could be mistaken for nothing else—and the prince who let out a huff of exertion. Leather squeaked and fabric chafed upon stone.

Truss remained still, as quiet as the bleak walls around him. If he had not known it was the royal line struggling against itself, he would have thought it no more than a tiltyard tussle. Rowdy squires blackening each other's eyes before they could be pulled apart. There was quite a limpid slapping sound and then, from the prince, a cold and hollow laugh.

"You might have prevailed if I were still a child," Liuprand said, "but I am a man grown."

Nicephorus wheezed, "A man grown, indeed. Let me see the proof."

The air hissed. There was more scuffling, what sounded like hands scrabbling among fabric. And then a tremendous, solid thud, grim and final. The king panted heavily, hatefully. Truss could hear the mucus rattling in his throat.

"Enough, Father," said Liuprand.

"You are no son of mine," rasped the king. His voice was so scratchy and feeble that Truss had no choice but to imagine this: Liuprand's hand jammed against his father's windpipe, pinning him to the wall. No mean feat. They were of a height, but the king was half as heavy as an ox. "You are your whore mother's progeny and the seed of whatever common wretch she cuckolded me with."

"I almost wish it were so. It disgraces me to share your blood. Now listen. Seraph has cut the rope bridge between our island and its glimmering shores. The Dogaressa is too addled with age to remember the name *Drepane*. We must not let this relinquishment become known, and we must do all we can to forge stronger bonds with the noble houses. This means, yes, merging our lines, and indeed, following their customs."

"You are as paranoid as a prophet. Always predicting doom."

"Am I? The Master of Blood has washed his hands of us. It will not be difficult for him to encourage other houses to do the same. We *must* have this desecration. We must let them see that we, too, will follow Berengar's law to the letter. And we must let them see we do not cling too fiercely to the ancient mores of Seraph. That the Exarch's bones are no more sacred to us than the bones of any other dead man."

A pause. The king panted wetly. "What epithet are you angling for, boy?" he asked at last. "Liuprand the Prostrate?"

"It speaks to your dull nature that you think diplomacy is submission. These are the means by which any king would seek to strengthen his position. I have heard enough from you. The desecration will be performed. I will send missives soliciting leeches from each noble house. This matter is settled."

The king garbled out a curse, but the prince's footsteps were already brisk upon the floor, fading into the distance. Truss exhaled. His knees felt as weak as jellied broth.

He would not resent again the menial tasks of draining blood or pulling teeth. Being only a leech, he was not obliged to look skyward while the prince and the king tussled overhead like angry gods. Truss bent down, picked up the Exarch's ankles again, and continued his slow, descending sojourn. Mordaunt had been right, he admitted to himself, somewhat sourly: He would no longer underestimate the charms of the inexorably silent dead.

Mordaunt, meanwhile, was wishing he had taken up Truss on his offer. That nine-times-out-of-ten fool had been right on this occasion: He did prefer the company of the dead.

Not that the girl was such lively company. She did not speak as he led her through the chilly corridors; she kept her gaze on the ground, only rarely daring to steal glances up at him with her strange eyes. In Seraph, such eyes would be considered portentous. Here on Drepane, Mordaunt kept his superstitions to himself. But he would be glad to deposit her back in her village and not think of her again. Horror-touched eyes, they were. Each time he was caught in their path, Mordaunt shivered.

"You will not speak of what you have seen here today, girl," he said.

"Of course, Your Scrupulousness," she murmured.

They were not even halfway to the main courtyard gate when footsteps approached from the opposite direction. Mordaunt stopped and thrust out an arm to prevent Ninian from taking further paces. A maid, he figured, or perhaps an errant member of the Dolorous Guard. In truth, the last figure he expected to see turn the corner was the prince himself.

It had not even been an hour since the prince had left them at the chapel, yet now his affect was entirely changed. Gone was the imperiousness, the slight defiant tilt of his chin. Now there was a hollow quality to the prince's gaze. His eyes were as bright and sea blue as ever, but without the oceanic depths behind them.

"Your Highness," Mordaunt said, in shock. He bowed, and after a moment of floundering, Ninian found her way to a passable curtsy.

"Where are you taking the girl?" the prince demanded.

Further disconcerted by the lack of preamble, Mordaunt replied hesitantly, "Back to her village, Your Highness."

"Then for what cause was she brought here in the first place?"

Mordaunt swallowed. He did not want to reveal his master's activities. It was not strictly forbidden for a man of his position and stature to seek a bride, but he suspected that the prince would not like the means by which he was conducting his search. Liuprand was oddly beneficent toward his subjects, far beyond what propriety demanded. To even the dullest, most inconsequential serf, the prince extended his protections.

"Her eyes, Your Highness," Mordaunt said—and he was surprised by his own quick inventiveness. "The Most Esteemed Surgeon thought perhaps she was suffering in some manner. But he swiftly determined she was not in poor health. Just a caprice of breeding."

Liuprand regarded the girl thoughtfully. "It is not the result of an illness?"

"No, Your Highness."

"I was asking her," said the prince, "not you."

Mordaunt's mouth snapped shut.

"I am not ill, Your Highness," Ninian whispered. "I was born with these eyes. As was my mother, and her mother."

The prince nodded. "And what is your name?"

"Ninian," she answered softly. Then added, "Your Highness."

The prince stepped forward, out of the falsifying shadows into the beam of light from the window, which made plain a startling truth: His hair was slightly disheveled, as if someone had run through it with an errant hand, and his clothes were rumpled. All of this was not distressing on its face, but because it was Liuprand, the soon-to-be Golden, Mordaunt had to swallow down an appalled gasp. The prince had never appeared any less than flawless in every sense, a marble façade without a single crack, without even a chip in the paint—so these subtle imperfections were as garish and ghastly as an open wound. He might as well have staggered toward them, bleeding shamelessly.

Liuprand was of course perceptive enough to register Mordaunt's shock, and in response, he let his gaze rest heavily upon him, like a sword on a would-be knight's shoulder. The weight of it galled him. He schooled his expression to one of neutrality, and it felt entirely unconscious, as if God himself had reached down and rearranged his features.

Then as quickly as it had been fixed, Liuprand's gaze flickered away and to the girl's face instead. "The princess has need of a new handmaiden," he said. "If you are hale enough, I offer the position to you."

Mordaunt could not keep back the appalled gasp this time. No, this diabolically marked girl could not be allowed to remain in the castle, much less in such close proximity to the royal line itself! The Most Esteemed Surgeon had been seized by a momentary lapse in judgment, moved by his desire for love, but he had corrected this slip of faith within himself quickly and ordered the girl gone. Yet now—the world would never forget the error his master had made. And this ill-omened creature would serve at the feet of Drepane's future queen.

Say no, Mordaunt prayed silently, vainly. *Dear God, girl, refuse.*

But though it had been framed as a proposal, the prince's word was always an order. The girl was wise enough to know it.

"Oh," she said, a flush rising to her face, "yes, Your Highness. That is terribly generous. Yes."

"Good," said Liuprand. His tone was clipped. "His Scrupulousness will see that your family is informed and compensated. And he will show you to the princess's chamber."

Madly, mutinously, Mordaunt did. He walked like a prisoner to his own execution, chains rattling inside his mind. The girl did not even have shame enough to hide her pleasure. A small, quivering smile kept returning to her face, and her eyes were gleaming like two marbles, polished with the spit of the devil himself. A full-bodied, lustful hatred rose in him.

"You will have to learn all the habits of a good lady," he said. "Bend low when you curtsy. Your deference should make your knees crack."

"Yes, Your Scrupulousness."

"And keep your head down unless you are addressed. Your neck should carry the weight of your servility."

"Yes, Your Scrupulousness."

"And do not, ever, speak without being called to. Ignoble voices grate upon noble ears."

"Yes, Your Scrupulousness."

They arrived at the door of the princess's chamber. Mordaunt drew in a breath through his mouth and then let it out through his nostrils. He inhaled deeply of his own animus. Then he raised a resentful hand and rapped once, lightly, upon the wood.

Silence. Perhaps the lady was out of her rooms. Yet Mordaunt doubted he would be so fortunate.

No voice called out from inside, but within moments, he heard footsteps on the floor. The door opened, and the lady Agnes stood in the threshold. He had been expecting the princess, and to see her cousin instead made him flinch. The shock was like drawing out a babe from between a mother's legs, only to have it slip, purple and stillborn and silent, into your arms.

"Lady," he said, once he had grieved and then made peace with her presence. "Is the princess within?"

The lady glanced over her shoulder, eyes flickering beneath dense lashes. Though she moved, her expression never changed; the light did not even seem to refract differently within her shifting gaze. What an odd creature she was, closer to the dead than to the living. But Mordaunt quickly amended this thought. It was not as if she had lived and then perished; it was more as though she had not lived at all. A preexistent being. A cold flower that had never bloomed.

She must have caught the eye of someone within, for Lady Agnes nodded, then stepped aside to let them through.

The princess was indeed within, wearing a gown of rich, choleric red. Her cheeks had a matching color, and she seemed to radiate warmth, though it was not at all a genial warmth. It was a burning heat, better observed than touched. Her lips were full but unsmiling.

"Princess," Mordaunt said, bowing until his back ached. Beside him, Ninian gave a much-improved curtsy. "I come to you with a gift from your lord husband."

Immediately, her dark eyes flared. "A gift?"

Her voice was so hostile that Mordaunt felt physically pricked. "Yes," he said, rising again. "He said you have need of a new handmaiden. This is the girl Ninian."

"I am honored to serve you, my princess," said Ninian, and looked up earnestly, breaking both the third and second rules he had impressed upon her only moments ago.

But the princess did not react to this brazen interjection. Her knife-point eyes never left Mordaunt's face. "Why did he say I have need of a new handmaiden?"

"I suppose because he believes you do."

The princess was a curious creature as well, though perhaps more so when taken in symphony with her cousin. He could not fathom two more different strains of lady. They were alike only in the shade of their hair, an ashen black, and otherwise so dissonant it was perturbing. Yet—they moved in an unerring sort of consonance. If the princess's gaze moved to another part of the room, Agnes seemed to know immediately which object she desired from that area and fetched it for her. If a question was ever posed to Agnes, the princess immediately offered up the answer in her cousin's stead.

It struck him then, and Mordaunt felt foolish for not realizing it before. This strange symbiosis between the ladies had to be the result of unfortunate circumstance—how many handmaidens could there be in that ghoulish, remote castle the House of Teeth called home? They had learned to attend each other's needs in such an unconscious way out of necessity, and seeing this, Liuprand had sought to relieve Agnes and the princess of this shared burden. A perceptive man he was, and a good husband. Mordaunt was quite impressed.

But the princess did not appear remotely grateful for her husband's gift. Her mouth—which was a very pretty mouth—twisted and made itself rather ugly. Light bounced sharply off the beads of that gruesome chain around her throat.

"I have no need of a new handmaiden," she said venomously. "You may tell my husband that."

Ninian looked so crestfallen that Mordaunt almost pitied her, and he might have been moved even to kiss her with how relieved he was that the princess was rebuffing the diabolical creature. Joy began to rise in him at the thought of returning the girl to her village, watching her vanish among the crowd of stinking peasants, never to be seen again. This dalliance with devilry would be dashed from the castle's memory.

But before he could reply, the lady Agnes began to shake her head furiously.

Brow furrowing, the princess took her cousin's hand and guided her to the far corner of the room. There Mordaunt could hear snatches of her whispering, though he could not pick out any words. He craned his neck, desperately curious to know if Agnes would speak to the princess in return. It was said that she remained completely silent by will alone, not for any physical muteness. Of course, rumors spread nonetheless—rumors that the lady Agnes *did* speak, yet only for her cousin's ears.

But Mordaunt could not glimpse her mouth moving; her lips stayed pressed into a nearly colorless line. She nodded and gestured but formed no words. He again had the impression of her as a preexistent being, or perhaps as a babe born too soon, without all the faculties and functions that made one fit for the human world. Mordaunt had delivered such babes: cold, tearless creatures with their hearts on the outside of their bodies, too small or ill formed to pump blood.

In thinking of this, Mordaunt suddenly found the lady Agnes mightily interesting. Her cousin was the beautiful one, but her bright liveliness was easily processed. She required no further inquiry. But Agnes—he could have pinned her down under glass and studied her as he would a peculiar insect.

So lost was he in these thoughts, he did not notice the princess stomping back over until she spoke again.

"Fine," she said. "I will take the girl. And tell my husband thank you."

The words sounded like half-chewed food, spat out because she did not like the taste.

"Very well, Princess," said Mordaunt.

He turned to go, and he should have been happy at his dismissal, happy that he would no longer have to bear witness to this folly, that he would no longer be compelled to look into those unholy eyes. But he felt inexplicably bereft. And so partway across the threshold, he glanced back over his shoulder.

The scene had changed within moments, the players rearranged, as if the room were the set of a masque: Agnes and Marozia stood slightly apart, facing each other, yet neither meeting the other's eyes. And Ninian stood between them, several inches shorter, though perhaps only as a consequence of the poverty that left every peasant with a burdened and stooped back. A few weeks in the castle, sleeping on feather mattresses instead of straw, and she might be of a height to the ladies.

She looked especially grubby now, the dirty and sun-chapped cast to her skin thrown into harsh relief against the marble-white faces of the cousins and their fine aristocratic features. But the shock of seeing Ninian between them was not this physical reality; rather it was something intangible and felt only in the air, an atmospheric augury. He had the sense of a great lute string being plucked, reverberating out a lonesome final note, and then snapping. And he felt a removed sort of grief for the bard whose broken instrument would never be played again.

 # XXIV

DISSOLVED THROUGH DEATH

A gnes had the pins in her mouth and Marozia had the curse on her tongue, but only Marozia spit hers out.

"By the hands of the Surgeon, I hate this dreadful match," she said. "I cannot bear it, being scorned and now insulted . . . the prince does not know me and does not care to. But he is my husband, and nothing can remedy that."

With a gentle hand, Agnes burrowed one of the pins into her hair. She hoped the steady motion, like a needle through cloth, would comfort Marozia, but it did not. Rather she turned around with such abruptness that several of the pins came loose. This undid an hour of Agnes's work—yet Agnes was so alarmed by the suddenly heightened distress of her cousin that she couldn't be bothered to grieve the time lost.

"Let us go," she whimpered. Unfallen tears made glossy her dark eyes. "Let us return to Castle Peake. I want to go home."

Agnes let her hands fall from Marozia's hair. The room was drowned in silence. And like a lamprey, the posthumous existence of Adele-Blanche lithely parted the dark water.

"Grandmother is dead and gone." Marozia's voice trembled as she spoke the words. "Truly, she is. Nothing can remedy that."

What she spoke was akin to treason. Agnes removed the pins from her mouth, set them down upon the table, and felt a tremor go through her entire body. It was a tremor of fear—Adele-Blanche's abyssal mouth and its needle-thin teeth edged ever closer—but there was a thread of anger within it that shocked her.

This anger pulsed in her palms, almost unrealized violence. Of course Marozia spoke so facilely of this; she had never been permitted inside the library; she did not dream of the dead. She did not know that the profit of her grandmother's work was already unfolding before them, Marozia's marriage, Agnes circling and circling her quarry, with each day spent searching Castle Crudele. Her own rage frightened Agnes so terribly that she stepped away from her cousin, letting the unsanctimonious emotion be expelled like a long-held breath.

"You still believe her stories. About the once-greatness of our house and how it must be restored." It was an accusation. Marozia got to her feet. "They are only that, Agnes—*stories.*"

Agnes looked back at her cousin, whose stare crackled like lightning in the limpid summer air. The revelation she had then was so simple, she was almost embarrassed to tell it to herself. Yet there it was. As she stood, cloaked as always in her silence, Agnes realized that she was by herself in these dark waters. Marozia's dress did not lift and ripple in the current; her skin did not grow cold beneath the watchful eel-eyes of Adele-Blanche. For all Agnes floundered, she floundered alone.

When had this lonesomeness begun? All their lives, she and Marozia had shared the same bed. They had both fed of her mother, Manon, until they were old enough that they began to grow breasts of their own. *Marozia is the snake's hypnotizing gaze, but you are the snake's deadly fangs.* And indeed Agnes had believed this, but now she knew they were not different aspects of the same animal. They were separate creatures entirely. One knew the sky and the sunlight, and the other knew only murk and depths.

In this realization, Agnes began to feel obscure not only to her cousin but also to herself. Her spirit was escaping its vessel. She pressed her hands hard against her abdomen as if to keep it in. When she felt the words on her skin, the familiar stroke of pain was like a key turning in a lock, and it trapped her insolent soul inside.

If there was any force to rival her silence, it was Marozia's anger. The lightning still cracked behind her eyes. So Agnes plucked up a piece of parchment and a quill, bent over the desk, and scrawled a message. She held the paper out to Marozia, who snatched it from her hand.

A marriage pact can only be dissolved through death.

Marozia read it once and then crumpled the parchment in her fist. The ink had not even dried, and now it bled its black color into the lines of her palm. It pleased Agnes for some strange reason to see it.

Before Marozia could make a reply, there was a knock upon the door. A cheery voice called out, "Princess?"

Agnes flinched. And Marozia—for all her impatience and lack of wiles—noticed. An unpleasant smile turned up her lips.

"Come in," she said.

It was not only the fact of being interrupted that galled Agnes; rather, it was who interrupted them. Ninian opened the door and minced her way into the room, her gait something akin to a puppet with tangled strings. It was the shoes she wore, with their wooden soles. Unaccustomed to this small luxury, which kept her feet dry and relatively clean, unlike the leather slippers of peasants, she walked as a young child would, clumsy on its new feet.

There could hardly have been a more inferior interloper, and Agnes had to wonder what, precisely, Liuprand had been thinking. Marozia was accustomed to Agnes's agile, aristocratic hands. She would never have imagined that her cousin would accept such a coarse creature to attend her. And yet . . .

Ninian's gaze passed briefly over Agnes, like a bird's wing skimming the water, before her eyes landed on Marozia's face and brightened. She seemed not to register Marozia's barely checked anger at all, oblivious to the hard set of her jaw and her quivering lips.

"My princess," Ninian said with a deep curtsy. "I came to see if you perhaps needed help with your dressing."

There was nothing *wrong* with the girl, Agnes had to reluctantly admit, aside from her curious eyes and her rough peasant manners, not yet smoothed by noble graces, but the circumstances through which she had come to them confounded her. Again, Liuprand had proved himself obscure. His behavior turned her inside herself for answers; it was as though his very soul protested being understood.

Sending the girl was all he had done to even acknowledge Marozia since their disastrous wedding night. And what a strange gift she was, if Liuprand was indeed trying to smooth tensions with his spurned wife. Agnes herself had not seen him in the two days after their meeting in the garden of moths. And Marozia, out of both petulance and shame, had refused to leave her chamber, ordering all her meals to be left outside her door and, other than Agnes, accepting Ninian as her only visitor.

Yesterday Agnes had made her way back to the moth garden and successfully planted the seeds of her grandmother's treasons. Her intention in returning was surreptitiously twofold—as much as she could barely admit it, even to herself, she had hoped she might see Liuprand there. She had hoped to speak to him again in the language of rustling wings. Yet the garden had been empty, and more and more their meeting had felt like something out of a dream, a hallucination that left no physical evidence behind. Agnes did not think she was mad enough to conjure up such an elaborate fantasy. But around the prince, she had begun not to trust the things about herself she had always known.

"Yes," Marozia said pertly, jolting Agnes from her thoughts. "Come here and finish my hair."

Eagerly and without reserve, Ninian minced across the room toward her. Marozia sat back down in the chair, facing away from Agnes. Ninian bent over, still-callused fingers running gently through Marozia's hair, with eyes so soft they were almost lambent. For a moment, Agnes watched them. Marozia preeminent and attended to; Ninian in her worshipful pose.

Bile rose in Agnes's throat, but it was not a thin bile; it was rich, richer than any wine she had ever been allowed to drink. It was steeped in malice, yet the aftertaste was pure pleasure. She could not comprehend this exquisite poison. She fled the room, afraid of what was at work inside her soul.

The Exarch's body reeked. Death had been at work on his corpse for two days now, which was not such a long time, but the manner of his passing seemed particularly solicitous, seducing forth the dark tendrils of decay. Maggots writhed inside his burst tumor with such vigor that it almost reanimated him, his limbs twitching with the rapacious feasting of parasites. And the flies swarmed so thickly that it looked as if his corpse were laid over by a blanket knitted of iridescent wings and glittering black bodies. The drone of their ecstatic repast was almost deafening.

"May you be consumed as a coal upon the hearth. May you dry up as water in a pail. May you become as small as a linseed grain, and much smaller than the hip bone of an itch-mite, and may you become so small that you become nothing."

The Most Esteemed Surgeon nearly had to shout. Fortunately for him, there were not many gathered around to hear. There was Agnes, her hands tucked into the folds of her dress. There was Marozia, staring ahead with a fierce wetness in her eyes. There was Ninian, devotedly swatting the flies away from her mistress's face. And across the pit stood the king and the prince, two paces apart from each other, both of their expressions cloaked in some unreadable sentiment.

Agnes should not have been doing what she was doing, which was trying to catch the prince's gaze. She felt embarrassed to find herself making such an effort. His face was inscrutable to her at a distance. Yet his posture was poor, his back hunched, his shoulders drawn up around his ears. This alarmed her. She remembered the bitter stares that had passed between him and the Exarch at the wedding; surely he could not be grieving the man now. Something else troubled the prince's soul.

The other noble houses had not been invited to the desecration—the Exarch was not and had never been the conduit of God to them—but their leeches were in attendance. And when the Most Esteemed

Surgeon finished his service, he raised a hand, beckoning the first of them forward.

Yet none within the gathered flock shifted. Every sepia robe lay still against its wearer's body.

The brow of the Most Esteemed Surgeon wrinkled. "Come, then," he said. "The blood is ready to be harvested."

Still there was no movement. The sky was as taut and blue as a cauterized wound, and not even the faintest breeze rustled the heavy parchment-colored cloth.

There was some movement at last, though not among the leeches. King Nicephorus took a mighty step forward, the dirt flattening under his foot, as if the very earth shrank from him.

"Well, then?" he called out. "Where are the representatives of the House of Blood?"

The air itself was stiff, hard as it would have been in winter. The only movement was the tapestry of flies, which rippled like it was being shaken out. Agnes did not realize she was pulling apart the skin of her thumb until a blood drop fell into the dirt.

"Answer me!" the king snarled. "I am your sovereign!"

At last came a creaking voice from one of the leeches: "They are not here, Your Highness. We are twelve only."

Several flies came loose from their mass and seized upon the drop of blood from Agnes. They feasted until the red was gone.

"Not here?" Nicephorus echoed. "They were summoned by royal missive. Does the Master of Blood think I was merely inviting them to tea?"

No response came from the throng of leeches. They all stared penitently at the ground, as though the shame of this belonged to their whole order. Perhaps it did. Agnes did not think the king would be particularly discerning when it came to punishing this offense. He would not seek to carry out justice; he would merely seek to sate his rage.

And the rage was clear on the king's face. It devastated his features.

His lumpy brow sagged down further over his eyes, and it broke out in beads of sweat that made his skin look even more slack and greasy. His cheeks were flushed, the broken blood vessels as pink as boils. His jowls quivered, and spittle formed in the corners of his grimacing mouth.

"This is an unacceptable slight," he thundered. "And it will not go without remark. The Master of Blood will feel the full might of Berengar's line—"

"*Father,*" Liuprand said at last. He laid a hand over Nicephorus's outstretched arm. "This is a petty slight. A tiltyard taunt. It does not require a rejoinder of clanging blades. I will travel to the House of Blood myself, if I must, to make things right."

"And what do you plan to do?" The king sneered. "Share a cask of wine with the traitor? Make peace over roast pig and fish?"

No one else among the crowd dared to speak, and even Marozia angled her gaze away. Discomfort spasmed across the Most Esteemed Surgeon's face, while the leeches still stared determinedly at the dirt. Their thoughts were all the same: that the king and the prince shamed themselves in this public scuffle. These matters ought to have been discussed behind closed doors and in even tones, the conclusions then communicated through pronouncements and orders. It was as awkward to witness as any spat between father and son, only swelled to truly galling proportions by the preeminence of the quarrelers. Two such powerful beings in so ignominious a struggle.

Liuprand seemed to realize this, for his voice grew low. "Let us discuss the subject later," he said. "For now, the desecration must be performed. Truss and Mordaunt can fill the role of the House of Blood. Then we will give the leeches their sustenance and send them on their way."

XXV
THE MARTYR'S PRICE

There was no pretense of esteem or reverence as the leeches were led into the castle. This was the basest courtesy, one any man proffered to his guests, even if all he could marshal up was some bread and wine. A meal was laid out. And so it had been, across every table in the great hall.

Agnes was last into the chamber, so she did not have the chance to see the expressions of the leeches when they first looked upon the food presented to them. Yet she could easily imagine their appalled shock. As she followed Marozia to the high table on the dais, she cast her gaze about the room, and her heart stuttered. She saw bread. And she saw wine, diluted to little more than red-tinted water, as if someone had pricked their finger and allowed only the smallest drop of blood to fall into each goblet.

It was a meal for an ascetic, a meal fit for the lady Agnes, such a one as she had eaten half her life. And as she watched the leeches curl their lips in distaste, she felt, for the first time in so long, her own deprivation. Their lack shone silver like a pool under the moonlight, and the warped, shuddery reflection of a starving girl stared back. Agnes had to look away from them.

She glanced instead at Marozia, who had already taken her seat and allowed Ninian to push her chair in. Marozia met her gaze yet did not say a word. The spark of anger remained behind her eyes. Yet Agnes knew that there was turbulence within her mind. Marozia was no fool: She, too, saw the churning waters of chaos below, and how close this discord between the king and the House of Blood had pushed all of Drepane to its precipice.

Before Agnes could sit beside her cousin, Nicephorus snapped, "No. Here."

With a tilt of his head, he indicated the chair to his right. Agnes's stomach pooled with dread. Of course she could not refuse. With heavy footsteps, she made her way around the table to the king's side and sat. The hunger in her stomach had turned quickly to nausea.

This new position meant that Liuprand was at her right. He stood for a long moment, holding to the back of his chair and facing away from her. Agnes tried to catch his eye and felt bereft when she could not. Had *she* done something to offend him? Yet when at last he dropped into his seat, she understood. On his left cheek, stretching from ear to chin, was a large and throbbing bruise. He had been careful with how he angled his head in order to hide it, but now they were so close that he could not.

The bruise was a garish mottling of red and violet. Agnes, familiar with the ripening process of wounds, guessed it at two days old. When finally, *finally*, she caught the prince's eye, she raised a hand and, very hesitantly, touched her own cheek. She knew the gesture made her question clear.

Instantly, almost unconsciously, Liuprand mirrored her and touched his bruise. He gave the tiniest wince as his fingertips grazed the tender skin.

"It's nothing," he murmured.

She merely frowned at him.

And then in response, Liuprand looked down at her hands. She had picked at them so recently that there was fresh blood welling in the beds of her nails, and the mangled skin appeared particularly gruesome, as if parasites had come to feast upon her fingers.

"Speak the truth of your wounds, Lady Agnes," he said, "and I will speak the truth of mine."

She wore the ring still, as she had since the day Waltrude had dropped it into her palm. The prince saw that, too, yet offered nothing to sate her wondering. There were so many truths Agnes wished she could release from him. Liuprand laid his own hand on the table, so close to hers that their fingers nearly brushed. Nearly.

It was not as if there were a wall between them, but rather that they were each creatures trapped in ice, and their own husks of cold kept them always at the slenderest distance from each other. She did not know what it would take to crack through. She did not know if she was even brave enough to try.

The back of her neck prickled with heat. She turned and then was dreadfully aware that Nicephorus was watching her. Had he been this whole time? The king's eyes were like the ends of two blades, freshly lifted from the forge and still ablaze.

Then abruptly he clapped his hands together with enough force to make her flinch.

"Come then," the king said. "Let us all feast according to our virtue. I have laid out a meal that agrees with your principles and complements your fine qualities! Stale bread for your stale honor. Watered wine for your weak faith. Eat now. Eat of your own deficiencies. Glut yourself on your lapses and offenses."

The great hall was silent. Not a single knife was lifted, nor a single goblet touched.

Nicephorus's face glowed as if lit from within by an incandescent candle of pleasure. "And I," he said, raising his cup, "will feast according to mine."

The doors to the great hall broke open and two servants entered. They carried between them an enormous silver platter, upon it the carcass of a boar. Steam still rose from its crackling brown skin. Around it were not the ordinary garnishes of green vegetables but rather a ring of those gaudy silver fish. Where heat had split apart their scaly bellies, the flesh underneath showed through—that lecherous red-pink flesh that tempted Agnes as much as it revolted her.

Fear scalded her throat. She knew what would happen, and yet when it did, the foreknowledge did nothing to lessen her horror. The platter was placed ceremoniously before the king. The vapors of steam mixed with the natural oils of his face and gave his countenance a grisly, iridescent sheen, like rot on a slab of meat. Still illuminated from within by that self-made pleasure, Nicephorus picked up his knife and speared one of the fish through its belly. He lifted it whole, as flaky chunks plummeted from it like rocks in an avalanche, and in one gluttonous bite, he tore off its head and swallowed it.

The silence of the room was now ripped through with the sound of retching. One of the leeches had doubled over, hand across his belly. Agnes could not deny that she felt the strong urge to do the same.

It was not the king's ravenous appetite that sickened her, nor even the scent of his perspiring flesh, so close she could almost feel its aura infecting her, too—it was this unrestrainedly grotesque show of power. If ever he did care for his own legacy, his own honor, how his name would be recorded in the annals of history, these could not be salvaged now. He had given himself over entirely to his Sluggardry. It was eternal, as intrinsic to him as his hand or his mouth. And all for the sake of—what? Instilling terror in those who would never have the strength to challenge him anyway? They were insects. He was a ruler of men. Their existences were incomprehensible to each other.

As the king indulged hatefully, masticating with his mouth open to let the spittle leak down his chin, crunching the bones of the fish in his teeth, there was a sound. A voice, somber and singular. It reverberated like a harp's plucked string.

The retching leech had raised his head again. His eyes were misty, and his skin had a gruesome shimmer of green. But when he spoke, it was without reserve or contrition.

"No true king gluts himself while his people starve," he said.

It was as if he had shattered the window glass and let in a blast of cold. Every muscle and limb in the room froze. Some hearts even momentarily stopped—Agnes's among them. Faces seized mid-scowl, mid-frown, mid-whisper, suspended in grimaces of shock.

The king lowered his knife. "What did you say?"

His tone was hideously mild. The leech swallowed, his throat bobbing.

"No true king gluts himself while his people are left hungry," he repeated. His voice trembled faintly now. "And we have done nothing to deserve this indignity. Your quarrel is with the Master of Blood. We are all obedient men here; we have fulfilled our duty. Do not punish us in his stead."

With eerie decorum, King Nicephorus set his knife down upon the table. He dabbed at the corners of his mouth with his sleeve. The cast of ice across the room did not thaw or recede. Each drag of Agnes's heart was painful, a twitching rabbit within a snake's tightening vise.

Nicephorus laid a hand over his chest. "This entreaty has moved me, Your Scrupulousness. Indeed, it was not your actions that provoked my ire. It was the Master of Blood who vexed me. You were correct in that accounting." His pause was gravid with sincerity. "Yet that was before you spoke."

"Your Majesty—" the leech started. His face, now naked in its fear, was as bald as a boiled egg.

"You say I am no true king," Nicephorus cut in, "for no true king feasts while his subjects are bereft. You must be a philosopher, then, as well as a sucking insect. But let me ask your fellow leeches if they are in accordance with your beliefs. Are they philosophers, too? Do their minds toil at night on the true nature of a king?"

With one swift motion, he brandished his knife again. Agnes flinched, ducking her head. But the king merely used it as an instrument to point and gesture. Indicating the nearest table of leeches, he said, "You. Tell me, do you believe I am a true king?"

There was a rattle of mucus as the first leech cleared his throat. Stiffly, he regarded the king. "Yes, Your Majesty," he whispered. "You are a true king."

"How very generous of you to say." Nicephorus's smile was both remote and resplendent. "And you, Your Scrupulousness? What do you say of my kingly virtue?"

Around the room he went, pointing to every leech in turn. When he reached the end of the twelve, Agnes thought he might be through, but this hope was as false as any she had ever had. Next the king pointed toward the Most Esteemed Surgeon himself, who sat at the foot of the high table, flanked by his two favored leeches.

There was a brief spasm of surprise across his face as he stared down the end of the king's knife. But submission came easily to this Surgeon, who was really only a leech with finer robes and a more tuneful voice.

"Yes, Your Majesty," he said earnestly. "You are a true king. Truer than any who preceded you."

But even this abject slavering did not fill him. Nicephorus pointed to the leech at his left, a short and rather dumpy man with strawlike hair that peeked out from under his hood. "And you, Truss?" He then angled his knife to the other, a taller man with a narrow triangular face, like a marten. "Mordaunt? Do you believe me a true king?"

The two leeches answered in unison, mouths opening and closing like trout on twin hooks: "Yes, Your Majesty."

"I am mightily blessed to have such faithful subjects." Nicephorus's gaze shifted. "And you, Prince Liuprand? A father always holds in high regard the opinion of his son."

From beneath lidded eyes, Liuprand looked at his father. The loathing in his stare was hard to fathom. Not for its intensity, but for its dimension. It shone like a diamond, the light refracting through so many angles and sides, each showing another facet. It was captivating and kaleidoscopic. A refined and almost beautiful hate; precious, rare.

Yet running beneath was the gleam of Liuprand's innate and unperturbable wisdom. No good could arise from challenging his father now, before this audience of men. He knew it, and still the words came wrenched out of his throat, steeped so deeply in that exquisite vintage of disgust.

"Yes, Father," he said softly. "You are a true king."

It was then that Agnes understood, though a part of her had known it since she had first seen the wound. The bruise on Liuprand's face was in the shape of the king's hand. And with this knowledge, a frightening emotion rose up in her. It heated the blood in her veins, like molten steel poured through a mold. She was afraid of the hideous, powerful blade it might fashion. A cruel sword, like Berengar's, soldered of insolent rage.

But she remained still and without words. The metamorphosis occurred inside her, invisible to the eye. If anyone were prevailed upon to look, they would only see what they always had: the silent Lady Agnes, more akin to the dead than to the living.

The king's lips formed a tremulous smile, like two wriggling worms. "I see at last you have learned some deference, Liuprand. Prince you may be, but it is the duty of all sons to obey their fathers. Even if we were two stinking peasants, still you would bow to me."

Hate gleamed from Liuprand like the winking white light from a shower of stars, but he did not speak. Cold silence ruled the great hall again with as much preeminence as the king himself.

Nicephorus's voice deposed it. "And you, Princess—what is your judgment of my kingly virtue?"

Marozia inhaled. Her breath shuddered and her chin quivered, but she was perfectly decorous in her reply. "You are a true king, Your Majesty," she said. "I would not ever think to question such a thing."

The capitulation in her tone was unimpeachable. Marozia, whose voice was as impeccably tuned as her harp. Still, the king had not eaten his fill. He turned to Agnes, and their faces were so close that she could feel the gust of his sour breath as he spoke.

"You, Lady Agnes, last of all," he said. "I would be happy to receive your judgment. Am I a true king?"

Her heart beat in that strangled-rabbit way. With as much vigor as she could manage, she nodded.

"What was that, lady? Speak."

This silence was the most callous ruler yet. More bitter, even, than the king. As cruel as the stones of the castle itself.

"I speak for all the House of Teeth in this matter," Marozia said, hurriedly, before this horrible regime could grow more entrenched. "You are a true king, Your Majesty; my cousin would not ever think to question your virtue, either."

"Enough from you," Nicephorus said. He waved his knife vaguely in her direction, and Marozia closed her mouth at once. "I am asking the lady Agnes. I would like to hear her speak it, in her own voice."

His gaze rested upon her. It was not a hateful gaze; it was not even angry, particularly. Where the blazing emotion had been, there was now only icy assurance. He was certain that he could make her speak. He did not even need to shout or snarl. He already felt half victorious.

Agnes stared back at him, her tongue lying limp in her mouth.

Seconds passed, as droplets from a tincture. The king blinked, and a bit of impatience leaked into his voice. "Well? Speak, Lady Agnes. Speak."

She did not.

"What is wrong with you, girl?" he spat at last. "I am your *king*."

His spittle sprayed onto her face. She did not even try to wipe it away.

"Father," Liuprand said tersely, "leave her be. She has proven her obeisance, as have we all."

The king's gaze cut the air like a whip as he shifted to look at his son. "She has proven nothing until I say so. Nothing will satisfy me but her voice. So *speak,* Lady Agnes. Or if you cannot, I will have to wrest the words from you myself."

And then he drove his knife down, right through the center of her hand.

There were screams enough to butcher the silence for good, though none came from Agnes's mouth. She did not even whimper as she looked down. The blade had driven straight through the meat and muscle of her, pinning her hand to the table. There was no blood at all. And the shock had, in fact, smothered most of the pain.

She regarded the bloodless wound with a removed sort of curiosity. She felt almost buoyant. Though her hand was held fast to the wood, her mind floated freely, watching herself from above.

The king regarded her with his mouth ajar, stupid like a gutted fish. He had meant to surprise her voice out of her, as if her silence was an animal that could be spooked. Yet the act was so brusque and quotidian that Agnes felt almost embarrassed on his behalf. He had no wiles, not even imagination. And true torture required a bit of both.

And then at last came the anger, gathering on his brow like black storm clouds. He released the knife, leaving it to stand perfectly upright, held in place by her constricting flesh. Over her head, he gestured to the leeches at the end of the table.

"Truss," he said. "Mordaunt. Come."

They shuffled across the dais toward him. The remove Agnes felt made her sluggish, her reflexes slow. By the time Truss and Mordaunt reached her, she could not manage to wrest her hand free. And then, at the king's gruff instruction, they each took her by one shoulder and thrust her down onto the table.

"Father!" Liuprand's voice rang out in horror. "Stop this—let her go!"

With her cheek pressed roughly against the wood, Agnes could not see what scene played out above. She heard scraping as Liuprand pushed back his chair and stood. The king stood, too. Marozia was letting out little wordless squeals of panic, muffled, as though she had one hand clapped over her mouth.

Metal clattered against metal. She could glimpse only the legs and feet of the Dolorous Guard as they cracked the doors and poured into the room, storming the dais. They crowded the table like weevils upon a crop. Agnes struggled to turn her face up until at the blurry edge of her vision she managed to see four of them holding Liuprand back. Their steel-clad arms gripped him about the waist and the chest, and then two others came and grasped each of his wrists.

She had not given Nicephorus enough credit, she realized hazily. He had some wiles after all. This was no impulsive turn; it had been planned and calculated, arranged like an act of a grand masque. And this masque had a theme to impart upon its audience: *Do not ever mistake Sluggardry for idleness. The slumbering bear is not complacent in its den. It is merely working up its appetite again.*

Adele-Blanche had made this error. And now Agnes would pay a martyr's price for it.

The knife was removed, and blood spurted from the wound like a spray of seawater. Agnes barely had the chance to draw breath before the blade was driven down again, this time into the tender webbing of skin between her finger and her thumb.

Pain broke through at last. It spiraled outward from her hand, bright and sharp and burning. Tears gathered along her lashes, and her eyes burned like sun-scorched stones.

Above, she heard Truss and Mordaunt—who, if they knew nothing else, at least were experts in the anatomizing of a human body—directing the king. When he raised his knife again, one of them whispered, "There, drive it right there; you will not be slowed by her knuckles."

It came down again, yet this time the blade twisted and wrenched, burrowing into her flesh. Bands of sinew snapped like cut ribbons. Blood pooled on the table around her hand, ruby-hued and thick. There were maggoty bits of flesh floating within the blood, like ice floes in a slowly melting river, which then branched into many tributaries and dribbled down onto the floor. It seeped toward Agnes's face, still pressed hard against the wood, and she had to close her mouth to keep from tasting it.

The air was heavy and, as with the stench of a wildfire, it reeked of both warmth and death. Marozia was sobbing. The leeches were retching. The king was panting, in equal parts exertion and pleasure, and Agnes wondered if he was working himself over on top of her, if she might soon feel his splatter on her back. And Liuprand raged, beating himself upon the chests of the Dolorous Guard, his unprotected flesh pounding against their metal breastplates. He was seeding a field of purple bruises, she thought, to match with the one on his cheek.

"Fucking scream, won't you?" rasped the king. "What kind of sick creature are you?"

Agnes watched through her lashes as the knife was raised and brought down again. This time it ran along the length of her fourth finger, stopping only when the point of the blade hit upon her ring. Liuprand's ring. There was the faint, tinny sound of metal meeting metal, and the even fainter reverberation that Agnes felt shiver through her skin. Her finger had been split open, like a furrow carved in the earth, deep enough that the bone showed itself under loose flaps of flesh and burbling blood.

Agnes was left-handed. It occurred to her, quite suddenly and almost trivially: *I will never hold a quill again.*

It was certainly not the punishment Nicephorus had in mind, but the pain of this epiphany entered her, and it did make her lips tremble. That was all. Her tongue was still limp and dull in her mouth, a dead thing. And her throat was an empty chasm that even agony could not fill with words.

Her cheek was sticky and hot, drenched in blood. Her hand seized now of its own accord; she could not make it move through power of will. Her eyes, too, seemed to close of their own volition, the lids too heavy for her to hold open. Blackness was eating away at the corners of her vision. Yet just when she thought unconsciousness might take her—or rather remove the world from her knowledge, and with it all wretched earthly sensations—there was a furious, almost animal snarl, and the pressure of the leeches' hands on her shoulders lifted.

With great effort, she looked up, though she could not raise her face from the wood. Liuprand had at last managed to free himself. He grasped Mordaunt and hurled him away from her so that he stumbled into the metal-plated chests of the Dolorous Guard. Then he took Truss by the collar of his robe and thrust him hard against the wall, his head knocking back on the stone with an audible but quite hollow thud.

At last Liuprand had his hand on his father's throat.

"You are the most loathsome man to ever walk this earth," he breathed, and through each syllable was laced that gleaming, splendid hate. "You have never been, and will never be, a true king. You are lowlier than a worm and viler than a maggot. Nothing but depravity runs through your veins."

But Nicephorus did not protest as his son's grip tightened around his neck. He merely spluttered out a laugh and dropped the knife. It clattered to the cruel stone floor.

"Such vicious chatter, and yet so empty," he said hoarsely, with a twitching smile. "The damage to the lady's hand has been done, and you could not stop it. But perhaps it was no damage at all. I do not think she feels pain; she is too inhuman. It is like visiting violence upon a corpse."

"Do not," growled Liuprand, "speak another word."

"Please," said Marozia, her voice barely more than a whisper. And then it seemed she could manage nothing else, for her head dropped down, her gaze on the ground.

Liuprand's eyes flickered to her, hand still on his father's throat. "Take the lady Agnes to her chamber. *Now.*"

But the lady Agnes was gone.

XXVI
MOTHER

Liuprand followed her into the corridor. Agnes quickened her footsteps. His legs were longer, and he could have easily caught up and even outpaced her, yet he kept himself at a slight distance—perhaps a yard or two behind. He was still near enough that he did not have to shout to be heard.

"Agnes," he said, slightly breathless from the effort of chasing her, "please. Wait."

She did not stop or turn to face him.

"*Agnes*," he said again. His tone was more pliant this time—nearly desperate. "Listen to me, please. Just for a moment."

She only quickened her pace again.

Liuprand was not deterred. He, too, hastened his steps, and he did not relent until he was at her side. Agnes stared straight ahead; she could not even force herself to blink, and it made her eyes burn. Liuprand reached out, nearly touching her, but he let his arm drop before he could grasp her hand.

Her hand. She had it clutched to her chest, wrapped in the fabric of her dress, yet it dripped persistently through, soaking the fabric and splattering to the floor. Agnes had left a trail of blood in her wake, a path of red from the great hall through the corridor, like the tracks of a fleeing animal.

She reached her chamber, though exhaustion was beginning to drag at her. The wounds would not kill her—Truss and Mordaunt, with their anatomical cunning, had made sure of it—but the loss of blood was great, and it made her dizzy. Despite this she managed, one-handed, to turn the knob and fling the door open. Yet before she could step through, Liuprand wedged his body into the threshold, one arm jammed against the doorframe, preventing her entrance.

In this position, she had no choice but to face him at last.

Liuprand's eyes were dark, with more depths than she could fathom. She had not realized how changeable they were—like the ocean, one shade of blue at a moment, and then another with a shifting of the sun's beams or the rippling of sand below the surface. Now they drew in no light at all.

And Agnes saw herself reflected in these inky cobalt pools. Her hair was bedraggled, the crown of braids coming loose. Blood was smeared and drying scarlet across her cheek, but her skin held no innate color. She was as white as a naked bone.

"Agnes," he whispered one final time. There was a desolate look on his face, soft yet almost crazed. "I'm sorry."

Apologies did not come easily to a prince, even one such as him. But Agnes merely pushed past him into the chamber. He stood there for one moment more and then slipped from the threshold, shoulders sagging, as if all the vitality had been siphoned from his noble form.

She shut the door firmly behind him, then turned with her back against it and slid down to the floor.

Agnes sat upon the hard stone until the sky outside the window turned glossy and deep blue. If there were stars about, none of them winked at her through the darkness. Time was her enemy. It perched like a hideous gargoyle on her shoulder, hissing reminders of what had been done. Memories did not fade with the passing of moments; they only strengthened, as an oak grows thicker and sturdier in its years. She pulled her legs to her chest and rested her chin in the crevasse between her knees.

And they pressed upon her, the memories: Of the king's frenzied panting as he worked over her. Of the sight of the knife driven through her palm. Of Marozia's quiet, wordless weeping. It was this memory that played itself over most relentlessly of all. It was not what she had done, but rather what she had not. She had not spoken up in Agnes's defense. She had only cried at witnessing the horror, mourned for her own stomach, which certainly churned, and her own mind, which would now be mutilated with these memories, too. But the ruination would be inside, where no one else could see, while Agnes would wear her wounds openly, always. No one who saw it would forget what occurred. Nicephorus had left his mark on every soul in the great hall; he knew it, and the knowledge filled him, glutted him even, as an endless banquet of pig and fish.

And Liuprand. She had lost something there, though she could not precisely discern what. Perhaps she had diminished herself in his eyes—perhaps he, like his father, thought her inhuman, little more than a walking corpse. Perhaps now he would look at her and think about nothing but the mangle of her hand and the violent debauchery of the scene. Or worst of all, perhaps he would look upon her and see only what he could not do. He would look into her eyes but see his own shame and failure reflected back: how too late he had wrested himself free; how he could not protect her, nor the kingdom of Drepane, from his father's horrible appetites.

One thing Agnes did not do, as she sat, was look at her hand. It remained cloaked within the folds of her gown. The blood would not cease spilling, and the red stain flowered outward, like a burst of poppies, opening suddenly and violently in the summer heat.

When nearly all the force of life had drained from her, Agnes rose, unsteadily, and walked toward the bed. Marozia had not come; no one had come. She was as alone as she had ever been. She collapsed onto the mattress and dove into the dark water of dreams.

She had expected Adele-Blanche to rise out of the eerie mist like a wolf raising its head mid-feast, bloodied muzzle pointed to the moon. But it was Celeste who came, shedding the mantle of clouds as if they were a white-furred cloak. She was as pale as any lady from the House of Teeth, and her black hair was wet, plastered to her forehead and cheeks. She stepped out of the water, and the cattails rustled as they were parted by her naked knees.

Mother.

Celeste was clutching a bundle to her chest. She rocked it gently and hummed a tuneless song. She kept her gaze to the ground as she walked, stopping before Agnes, though not close enough that she could have reached out a hand and touched her. She kept the same watchful distance that a vulture keeps from an animal that is dying but not yet dead.

"Agnes," she said, at last raising her head. "What has happened to you, my daughter?"

Agnes looked down and realized that her hand was still dripping blood. But in her dream-world, the blood was a silvery color, not red, like the slime on a rotten fruit. She looked away again, momentarily squeezing her eyes shut, as if she could make this dream vanish.

She could not. Even her dreams had never been her own. Celeste stared back, water in her dull dark eyes.

"I didn't mean it," she whispered. "I didn't mean it, darling, I didn't know."

If she had not already known she was dreaming, Agnes would have known it then. Her mother had never called her *darling*.

Liar. The word was not vocalized, but Celeste stiffened at once, a sharp inhale making her lips quiver.

"Why are you so cruel?" she asked, and tears gathered on her lashes but did not fall. "Is it not enough; have I not paid the highest price?"

The bundle in her arms began to shift. A fold of the blanket fell away and revealed the squirming child beneath. It had no eyes, and no mouth, and only two slits in the place of its nose. Yet still a noise came from it, a muffled, impossible keening.

Agnes's heart jumped into her throat. *Get that thing away from me.*

Celeste's eyes widened, and she clutched the bundle closer to her chest. "No! You cannot take him!"

Agnes wondered if her dead mother was somehow dreaming her own dream. She wondered if, in her dream, she could not distinguish between her own daughter and Adele-Blanche. Perhaps they had always been the same to her: one twisted creature, though her grandmother had been the hands and Agnes had been the mouth.

The not-child's fleshy arms were riddled with bite marks. Bile pooled in Agnes's belly.

It never would have lived. These were Adele-Blanche's words, but they were Agnes's words, too. *You chased a corpse over a cliff. You left your living child behind.*

"I didn't *know*," Celeste insisted, jutting out her chin. A shiny trail of mucus ran down from her nose. "How could I have known?"

Easily.

And then one dream shimmered away into another.

All seven torches were aglow, painting the stone walls of the library in daubs of orange and gold. Light gathered along the spines of the books and set them gleaming as well, bright as goblets of yellow nectar. Adele-Blanche stood, which was strange on its own. In the library, her grandmother always sat. If a tome needed to be fetched, Agnes did it. If a torch needed to be relit, that was Agnes's duty, as well.

Stranger still was the presence of Wrestbone. As a rule, Adele-Blanche allowed none within the library but Agnes and herself. It was Agnes who dusted the shelves, who scraped wax from the wooden table, who wiped up spills if her grandmother toppled a cup of wine. Even Marozia was forbidden to enter, not that she would have wanted to.

"You are especially silent today, Agnes," Adele-Blanche said. "Is it your mother's fate that troubles you still?"

Agnes bit her lip. "I keep thinking how I might have stopped it. How I might . . ."

"Come now. It could not have been prevented. She has always been a tricky one. In some ways I am surprised it did not happen sooner."

Agnes dropped her gaze. She did not want to speak of this in front of Wrestbone. The leech did not appear comfortable with it, either. His beetle-black eyes kept shifting, from her grandmother's face to Agnes's and, oddly, to the unoccupied table behind them. His eyes lingered longest on the table, as if he were seeing something there that Agnes could not.

"Perhaps it was an accident," Agnes tried. "Perhaps she merely fell."

Wrestbone shook his head grimly. "I recovered her body myself. There were wounds open on both her wrists. The House of Blood is bereft, and the House of Bones will have to make do with little more than scraps and dust. The House of Flesh—"

"Enough," Adele-Blanche cut in. "We do not need an accounting. There will be time enough for that during the desecration."

Wrestbone nodded and fell silent.

"But she was driven mad by grief." Agnes felt her hands trembling and tucked them into the folds of her gown; she did not want her grandmother to see this weakness in her. "Because of what we did."

A slant of light came into Adele-Blanche's eyes. She advanced upon Agnes and grasped her by the collar of her dress. It was not a gesture fierce enough to be painful, but the shock of it made Agnes flinch. Yet she did not try to get away.

(Often, she wondered what would have happened: if, in that moment, she had wrenched herself free of her grandmother's grasp, pushed past her and Wrestbone, and fled into the corridor. Would she have been chased? Would she have been caught anyway? These were wonderings that could drive a person mad.)

"Listen to me, Agnes," Adele-Blanche said. "Your mother forsook the customs of our house, and she paid the price for it. Do you understand why a lady of the House of Teeth cannot be permitted to have unsanctioned dalliances with some common serf?"

When she did not answer, her grandmother gave her a rough shake. Adele-Blanche was a small woman—at fourteen, Agnes was taller—but sometimes it seemed as though her body were no more than a frail mortal shell for some arcane and deathless power.

"Yes," Agnes whispered back.

"And do you understand why a boy child born of a forbidden affair could not be allowed to live?"

A hard stone formed in Agnes's throat. "Yes."

"Why? Speak it aloud to me."

"Because." Agnes swallowed. "The line of the House of Teeth is carried through the firstborn daughter. Any son would challenge his sister's or his cousin's birthright, and he would easily find allies among the other noble houses of Drepane who chafe at the notion of a woman inheriting titles."

"Good." Her grandmother's grip loosened slightly, but still she did not let go. One of her cold knuckles rested in the hollow of Agnes's throat. "The child had to die. And perhaps Celeste would have chosen another manner of death, but her indiscretion cost her any sway she might have had over the affairs of our house. She was the second daughter anyway; a spare. At least her folly served some greater purpose."

Agnes could still taste the blood of her infant brother on her tongue.

"But it did not work," she said.

"Who are you to say it did not? No effort in this great endeavor is wasted. You will taste the flesh of a thousand children, if I command it. If I believe it might restore our house's power. You are the spare, but you are much cleverer and more useful to me than your ingrate of a mother."

Her grandmother's voice did not blow across her, like a wave of heat from that inner flame; rather it was a gust of chilling air, as if from a flung-open window. There was no passion within Adele-Blanche, even when her words were so full of lust. Her power came from her icy cruelty, the remoteness that had shielded and sustained the House of Teeth through the darkest days of the plague. Her cold

Innamorata ~ 161

preeminence was legendary. Castle Peake and its teeming stores of gold were a great monument to Adele-Blanche's frozen heart.

"Do you wish to be my successor?" her grandmother asked. "Not in title, of course—that belongs to Marozia—but do you wish to someday hold the true power of death in your hands?"

Agnes uncurled her fingers and looked down at her open palms. If she stared and stared until her eyes watered, she could see the blood still staining each crease. The blood of the infant that had screamed as Adele-Blanche had broken apart its fragile bones and pulled its organs through the gashes in its newly born flesh.

The word seemed to lift from her throat as if elevated by some external force. It came out in a wisp of white air.

"Yes."

Adele-Blanche looked over at Wrestbone and beckoned him with a jerk of her chin. "Then let me mark you," she said to Agnes, "so you will carry with you always the edicts of your duty, and so you will never forget the oath you have sworn to me."

Had that answer, that one word, been an oath? Before Agnes could make any sense of her grandmother's declaration, Wrestbone was upon her. Truly upon her, his heavy body forcing her down and onto the table. She squealed, more out of confusion than fear, and this bewilderment made her go as stiff as a doll. Her clouded mind could not even conceive of fighting him off.

Once she was laid out there, her back flat against the wood, Wrestbone let go. Agnes tried to sit up, her movements still sluggish and flustered—but then her grandmother was upon her, pinning her arms down.

"Be still, Agnes," Adele-Blanche said. "Wrestbone has a steady hand, but you do not want to chance a mis-struck cut."

Out of the folds of his robe came a knife, shining. It was the same type of blade the leeches used to pare flesh away from bone and carve lungs from cracked-open chests.

"Wait," Agnes choked. "Please—"

But the knife was not for her flesh, not yet. It was to slice open the front of her dress. The fabric fell away in two even sheets, baring her belly, the mound between her legs, and her still-budding breasts. The cold air swarmed to her skin and made it prick like a thousand beestings.

Agnes yelped and tried to move an arm to cover herself, but her grandmother's grip was unrelenting. She could not break free. She tried to cross her legs over her exposed center. Yet Wrestbone parted her knees easily and came to stand between her legs, his hipbones hard against her soft inner thighs.

He was hard, too, between his own legs. But it was an unconscious hardness, born not from true lust but from the base mechanics of his anatomy. Though her nakedness aroused his body, his mind was surgically focused on his task. He pushed her small breast aside and then drove the knife down on the taut skin that cloaked her rib cage. Her flesh was so thin there that she could feel the blade scraping her bone.

Agnes screamed.

The blade traced a path along her rib cage, from the underside of one breast to the other. It was not an unbroken path; at intervals, Wrestbone lifted the knife and then brought it down again, in straight, short lines and long curved strokes, as if he were penning a note.

The fog in her mind had cleared, and now there was nothing between her and the world's bitter truth. Everything was clear and sharp. The pain was bright and burning. It whetted her senses; she was aware of her grandmother's brutish knuckles grinding into her wrists, the cold air that turned her nipples stiff, and the strange slickness at her center—her own arousal, base, anatomical, though it served a different purpose. Should something be thrust inside her, this slickness would ease its path, protect her from the worst of the dragging, scraping agony. She would not be violated in that manner, but neither her mind nor her body knew it yet. She would only be grateful, afterward, that it was her grandmother's intention to always leave this part of her untouched.

Yet now the blade cut and cut and cut.

"*Please*," Agnes sobbed. "Please, please, please stop—"

The knife trailed gashes down her belly, deliberate and neat. She could see very little through the film of her tears, yet she saw the sweat gleaming on Wrestbone's bald head. His hood had fallen back with the exertion of his movements, and it bared the jagged birthmark on the side of his skull: a leaping fish, a slice of melon, a quarter of a moon. She would remember this small detail very keenly, even when the rest of the scene's ephemera faded from her mind.

She tried thrashing, yet her grandmother's fingernails dug into her wrists when she did, deep enough to draw forth blood. Her blood was hot and slippery and everywhere, pooling in the hollow of her belly, dripping off her and onto the table, and then farther onto the floor. The stench was pure copper and brine, and it made the air thick.

With each new slash of the blade, Agnes screamed. Her tongue was a heavy, lolling thing, swollen with bite marks, and it made her voice slur as she tried to speak. The froth of spittle, the mucus running down and into her mouth—through these vile human moistures, she managed to cry out, "Please, Grandmother, make him stop! *Please!*"

Adele-Blanche's only response was to rub the inside of Agnes's wrist with her thumb. A calming gesture, though without any words to accompany it. Her grandmother's face hovered above her, utterly expressionless. It was like staring up at a cold and constant moon.

Agnes pleaded anyway. She begged, and when she could not make her spent, gushing mouth form any coherent sounds, she merely screamed. The pain obliterated all sense of time; the torture wore on for what felt like hours, until her throat was itself like an open gash, scraped and raw, until she began to wonder if her grandmother meant to kill her. Even if she did not, still Agnes thought she might die, and when Wrestbone twisted the knife in such a manner that she felt as if her insides were being stirred and tangled like dirty rope, she wished for it. She would have pleaded openly, if she still had the capacity to speak.

Later, she would be stunned to learn that they were all surface wounds. They had felt as deep as a sleep without dreams.

She remembered the precise moment that she stopped. When the breath went out of her, and blood sloshed from the hollow of her stomach and onto the floor. Her eyelashes were thick and daggered with tears, and she could see very little through them, only the vague outline of Wrestbone's shiny skull, rising up against the library's filmy darkness like the pale crest of a wave. She breathed in again, scream gathering in her throat, but the sound never made it past her lips.

She had chosen it, the silence. She could have kept screaming, and thrashing, and sobbing. The silence was not an inescapable fog that consumed her, nor was it even a heavy cloak she drew around herself; there was no comfort in this choice, and certainly no escape. It did not numb the pain—if anything, without the release of her screams, it made the agony sharper.

But she had realized her voice was worth nothing. No matter how loud or how fierce, it could not impress itself upon the world. And it had been worth nothing all along. Wrestbone had known she would scream and her grandmother had known she would scream and it had not stopped them, had not even made them flinch or grimace. But silence—they would not expect that. They would not know what to do with it.

And indeed, when she swallowed her screams and her sobs and did nothing but breathe softly through her nose, Wrestbone paused in his ministrations. Adele-Blanche's grip on her loosened slightly. They both peered down at her, brows wrinkling.

"You have not maimed her seriously, have you?" Adele-Blanche asked.

"No," said Wrestbone. "I did precisely as you asked."

Tears ran down Agnes's unmoving face.

"Well," said Adele-Blanche, "are you finished now?"

"Not yet."

There was another gash. Agnes closed her eyes briefly. The pain soaked into her like rainwater into the cracked earth.

"There. It is done."

She was left alone there in the library, blood drying into stagnant pools the color of rust, her bare skin sticking fast to the wood. She lay there in utter silence. Each breath was agony, but every time a sob or a whimper threatened to spill from her lips, she swallowed it down. Even her tears, after several moments, dried into stale paths of salt. Her lashes fluttered. Like susurrating moth wings, it was the only sound in the room.

The pain did not abate, but her patience with it did. Agnes sat up. She ignored the white-hot fire that laced through her veins and ran her finger gently along the wounds. The cuts were not nearly so deep as she had imagined them. The blade had not touched her insides, had not scraped her bones.

But the marks were deliberate. It took several moments for her to find a pattern beneath the drying blood and the red, taut swelling of her flesh. She traced the words underneath her left breast. NEVER SEEK THE PLEASURES OF THE BODY.

Agnes was startled by the words, and by their remarkable legibility. She followed the sequence further.

Along her rib cage: EAT NO FOODS RICHER THAN BREAD AND NO WINE WITHOUT WATER.

Across her stomach, in an arch: CONSUME ALL KNOWLEDGE OF HERBS AND PLANTS.

Below this there was a magnificently etched drawing, so detailed that it was like the craft of the sculptor who chipped away at the frieze in the basement. Agnes did not know it then, but the etching was of henbane and mandrake, their leaves unfurling down her abdomen, a flower circling her belly button.

She dipped her finger lower, tracing the skin just above her mound: JEALOUSLY GUARD YOUR MAIDENHEAD.

There were yet more words, but the cuts were too fresh to make them out, and the agony strengthened with each passing moment. Agnes lay back down. Only the softest breath went out of her.

She would learn to live by these rules. That day was the last that she had a bite of meat, the last before she knew the taste of henbane on her tongue. And it was the last that she made a sound. It was not some unconscious mode of being, impressed upon her by terror, a sickness that the pain had infected her with, a symptom that she struggled violently against, a betrayal of her mind by her body—though many, including Adele-Blanche, thought it to be so. Her grandmother believed she had stolen the words from Agnes's mouth.

It was not true. Her silence was as much a choice as any speech had ever been. It was not withdrawal, not cowering. As she had discovered, silence was not the absence of a thing. It was a force in and of itself. She brandished it like a sword. She impressed it upon the world. And in that manner, she could alter the shape of things. Perhaps only in the minutest fashion, but her screams had never done so much. They had been empty air.

The act of disappearing was a mightily visible one. A lady who spoke little could be forgotten. A lady who did not speak at all evoked, at the very least, a curiosity. And she could draw out that curiosity, mold it into embattled frustration—this by the power of her silence. It was no flimsy weapon. It was a punishment she inflicted upon any who dared to grow near.

She guarded the secret of her silence as jealously as her maidenhead. Because the truth would drain it of its power. And because Agnes did not want to admit, even to herself, that she was as cruel a creature as Adele-Blanche had made her. That beneath her silent exterior, under her frail, corpse-like beauty, she was filled with envy and a focused, sharp-edged rage.

And yet—even her silence did not belong to her alone. When at last she managed to peel herself from the table, when the blood had dried and the cuts had mostly closed, Agnes went down into her chamber and found Marozia there. Canny Marozia, who for all her faults, had a clear-eyed perception of everything that others desired. Marozia, who, as always, undressed her and helped her change into her nightgown. Marozia, who saw the wounds and, even though her chin quivered, never said a word. Marozia, who knew Agnes's secret without ever needing it to be spoken aloud, and who wielded Agnes's silence like a subtle dagger of her own.

Agnes woke from her dreams like she was surfacing from the water: gasping, panting, searching vainly for breath. She swam through the morass of sheets and clawed herself free of them. The sky was dense and black now, yet it made it easier to see the timid winking of stars. There were few of them that could be seen from her window—perhaps the most minor of constellations.

She rose, keeping her hand clutched close to her breast. The pain was more ice than fire now, though no less brutal for it. But the despair that pooled like stale water in the pit of her stomach was not because of this ache, not because of the crushing realization that she could no longer write. That was not the loss she grieved.

No, she grieved the loss of her most formidable weapon—perhaps her only weapon—and her most beloved ally. For the first time since that day in the library, her silence did not serve her. It was a false friend all along. A fragile blade, so easily shattered by the king's ravening fury.

It was a greater agony than the severing of a limb. Tears pricked at her eyes, but of course they did not fall. She had lost herself in Castle Crudele. She wondered if her silence had ever been strength at all. She wondered if perhaps she had been wrong—that it was no more than a festering wound that would not close. That her grandmother had relished it, that Marozia had relished it, and she had been the only one who was bereft, and was too dull to even realize. She felt ashamed and foolish now to ever have called her silence power.

There was a soft thudding sound. Agnes broke from her reverie, and followed the sound to its source.

Upon the window ledge there was a moth. Its antennae flickered, and its large eyes shone like two lanterns in the dark. She approached, and the creature cocked its head, a gesture that made it look curious, as if it did not know its own purpose there.

Tentatively, Agnes reached out with her undamaged hand. The moth crawled up onto her outstretched fingers. Its wings were dappled black and white, like the bark on a birch tree. The moth then ascended her arm and perched on her shoulder. It was nearly the size of a hunting hawk.

An unexpected yearning filled her—filled her in a manner that reminded her so bitterly of her own emptiness. Speckling, she remembered, as the creature nuzzled its head against her cheek, was for an apology.

XXVII
WALTRUDE IS STRICKEN

It was a terrible morning in Castle Crudele, though Waltrude had seen a great many of those. The morning after Philomel's death had been terrible, mainly for all the commotion and the soiled sheets that Waltrude had inherited the grim task of washing. How miserable, she had thought, as if the Crown could not afford to burn these and buy new ones. Was there some crippling shortage of sheets on Drepane? Her hands trembled at recalling it. A spray of white seed and streaks of fresh red blood. The same as their wedding night, she had realized with a shudder.

On this terrible morning, she had been called, too early, to the prince's chambers. Waltrude dragged her feet as she went. The scent of blood floated in a bitter mist through the corridors. There was splatter on the floor leading out from the great hall, and Waltrude hoped her task would not be to scrub it.

She reached the prince's door, the dread weighing heavily upon her. She raised a reluctant hand and knocked.

The prince's voice rang out immediately. "Come in."

Waltrude did.

A feeling of wrongness overcame her at once upon entering. It was not only that the table where the prince took his meals had been overturned, along with several of the chairs; it was not that the hearth was ashen—though it had been a cold night, it looked as though it had never been lit; it was not only that there was a smashed carafe, wine spilled across the floor. It was something intangible that hung in the air, limp and gray, as if the spirit of life had been drained from the chamber.

The prince stood at the window, facing away from her. Waltrude took several steps inside before he turned around, and when he did, she stopped in shocked horror. His hair was mussed and the top buttons of his shirt were undone. But most alarmingly, a bright, pulsing bruise stretched across his cheek, marring the lovely golden skin beneath.

"My prince!" she gasped. "What has happened to you?"

His eyes were the dull blue of a languid tide pool. "Nothing. That's the problem—*nothing*."

Aghast, Waltrude approached him. With trembling limbs, she reached up and, ever so gently, touched her palm to his bruised cheek.

The prince closed his eyes briefly and leaned into her touch. His skin was very warm. She wondered, with no small amount of dismay, if he was drunk. But the carafe was shattered and the wine was on the floor.

"You must have heard," he said lowly, "what my father has done."

Her stomach clenched. She had not wished to speak of it. She was not even certain, really, of the truth—rumors had spilled from the mouths of the leeches like a spewing of insects from a bloated corpse, but these were rumors only. Ugly, garish, and bleak. She did not want to believe them.

But Waltrude felt the aura of the prince's anguish and knew it was true. Even so, she needed him to speak it aloud—perhaps the reality would be not quite so terrible as the lascivious accounting of the leeches.

"Let me hear it from your lips, my prince," she said.

A breath went out of him, hot with the smoldering anger in his heart. "My father was enraged by the House of Blood's absence at the desecration. I told him it was a petty snub, but he could not be dissuaded from his rage. He decided to repay this slight with an insult to the assembled leeches. These dull, innocent men who could not be prevailed upon to thumb their noses at him, much less plot some sinister treachery. He served them stale bread and watered wine and then had a gross feast brought for himself. Naturally, one leech stood and gave a feeble word of protest . . ."

The prince paused, and his gaze left Waltrude's face. The anger had been fierce in his eyes, and now it had softened into an expression that was closer to shame.

"I should have prevented it," he said. "Had I stood then, myself, and tried to cow him into silence. Had I told him to recant . . ."

The prince shook his head, as if to clear it, and his eyes sharpened once more. "Of course my father could not let even the most pitiful protest lie. He went around the room and had each man swear fealty to him. Call him a true king. All the leeches he demanded this of—and then he turned his gaze to the high table."

Waltrude's chest tightened. She did not want to believe—and yet she found she could imagine it all so easily, as if she had seen it herself in a dream. The king, spitting his fury. The leeches, bowing their heads in wretched submission. And even that, she knew, would not have sated him. The Sluggard, they called him, but perhaps he should have been titled *the Glutton*. It made her ache for the little boy she had known, the one who had nursed so gently, had not even been overly solicitous of her breasts. Something vile had poisoned his innocent spirit. The world had sullied him.

"They all answered yes, of course, you are a true king." Liuprand's voice was pained. "The Most Esteemed Surgeon, the princess—even I wrenched the bitter and reviled words from my throat. But then he came to the lady Agnes . . ."

The silent Lady Agnes. The statue-girl. The living corpse. Waltrude swallowed down her own horror.

"She did not speak. He knew she would not. He knew it all along. He had arranged the moment, like a tournament spectacle. Some sort of grand joust," Liuprand bit out. "When she refused to answer, he . . ."

The flush of passion on his face vanished, and his skin took on a cast of gray. It was no less angry, but it was a cold sort of rage, laced through with anguish and disgust. The disgust was mostly for his father, of course. It was easy to be revolted by the king and all his deranged appetites. But Waltrude knew the prince well enough to know that a bit of the disgust was for himself. An arrow pointed inward, aiming at his defeated heart. This, to Waltrude, was the vilest of all Nicephorus's crimes: to make his son loathe himself for every one of his own repugnant acts. To make him believe that each atrocity occurred not because of the king's nature, but because Liuprand failed to prevent it.

"He drove his knife through her hand." Now the prince did little more than whisper. "Again and again. I could not . . . the Dolorous Guard thundered in and held me back. As I said, he had planned it. He said he would stop if she spoke, but I do not believe he meant it. He did not want her words; he wanted her blood. To prove his power—as if the torture of an innocent girl proves anything but his own barbarity." Liuprand laughed, a hollow and joyless sound. "I broke from the grasp of the Dolorous Guard and stopped him, though not before he had destroyed her hand. He has ruined it, Waltrude. I do not think she will ever hold a quill again."

Waltrude felt her own voice wither in her throat. She croaked out, "And all that time, she did not speak?"

"No. I did not see even a tear fall from her eye."

A bit of perverse, ill-timed curiosity tugged at her. She could not help it. The same question had been winding through the halls of Castle Crudele since the arrival of the princess and her cousin. It had reached the ears of every servant, every guard, every kitchen girl, and of course all the leeches, who worked their tongues as cannily and dexterously as their hands. Each one offered a different story, from the innocent to the truly depraved. Still, Waltrude tried to keep her tone mild as she spoke.

"Whatever do you think is wrong with the lady Agnes, my prince?"

As offhand as her question had been, it aroused the prince mightily. He drew himself up to his full height, shaking off Waltrude's hand, eyes narrowing to sharp points. His face regained its flush of passion.

"You should ask what is wrong with the world, that it has forced her into silence," he replied. His voice was so bitter, Waltrude regretted having spoken at all.

"Yes," she said hurriedly. "You are right, my prince. I am sorry."

But just as quickly as it had overtaken him, the vital spirit evacuated again. His shoulders slumped, and he exhaled a low, tremulous breath.

"I could not sleep," he confessed. "I could not excise my own rage."

Shame touched his tone once more. "And every time I closed my eyes, I saw her tearless face. I heard the princess's sobs. The memories would not leave me." For all his largeness, his noble beauty, the manhood that had welcomed him early and eagerly, in this moment Liuprand appeared to her like a very little boy, one she could still hold on her knee and regale with nursery rhymes about too-clever hares and grandmother's stew. "Waltrude, you must go to her."

"To the princess?"

"To the lady Agnes."

Her brow furrowed. She tried to mask her bewilderment as she replied, "To what end, my prince?"

"To see to her wounds. To offer her comfort."

It was a less ignominious task than scrubbing the blood off the floor, to be sure, but it vexed Waltrude nonetheless. "I'm afraid I am not very fit for the tending of wounds." Nor for offering comfort, though she did not say that. "Are you certain you do not want to send for a leech? It would likely be more effectual."

"*No*," Liuprand said sharply. "No leeches. In fact, do not allow any past her door."

Waltrude frowned at this odd request, but she did not challenge it.

"Go to her, treat her wounds. She will try to refuse your aid. Do not let her. She is stubborn and willful, so you must be resolved. I am entrusting this to you, Waltrude. There is no other in this castle I can depend on."

She nodded, chest swelling. "I will not fail you, my prince."

"I know." His gaze upon her was brief but tender. "Now go to it."

Waltrude knocked on the door, though of course the lady did not answer. Through the wood, there was no shuffling of footsteps, no rustling of skirts. Perhaps the lady was asleep. Waltrude would not have blamed her for falling instantly into an oblivious slumber, exhausted by the torment she had endured. Yet a fear crept into her, like frost on the first morning of winter. She could recall Philomel standing at the ledge of the window in this very chamber, howling with all the anguish of a wounded animal. Waltrude and her other ladies-in-wait approached her slowly, careful not to frighten her into slipping over the edge. Waltrude remembered how terror had lodged her heart in her throat. How she could not breathe again until they had drawn Philomel away from the window and held her, hunched and sobbing, to the floor. How after that she had been moved to a distant tower, far away from the king, who had not visited her once until that final fateful night.

Now that same terror rose and compelled Waltrude to push open the door.

The lady stood by the window, but not close enough that she could easily clamber up onto the ledge. Waltrude crossed the room briskly—moved more by her own fear than any action of the lady or any emotion she exuded—and took the lady Agnes gently by her uninjured arm. She maneuvered her away from the window, toward the desk in the corner of the room. The lady did not protest, nor did she aid Waltrude by moving of her own accord. Yet she was so thin as to be almost starved looking, and it did not take much effort to position her as Waltrude wished. Gaunt and fragile, she seemed barely to inhabit the dress she wore.

The washed-out lilac gown itself was so thoroughly drenched in blood that the scent of it, coppery and bitter, thickened the air. Still damp in some places; when Waltrude let go, her fingers came away stained crimson.

The lady had her hand wrapped up in the folds of the gown, and that was where the blood was the wettest and the darkest. She did not have the wounded-animal look of Philomel; there was no desperate, anguished bravado on her pale face, but Waltrude still thought it best not to reach for the damaged hand immediately.

"Won't you let me have a look, lady?" she asked softly instead.

Lady Agnes shook her head. Waltrude had expected as much.

"It is not a wound that will recover of its own accord," she said.

The lady, of course, did not reply.

Waltrude looked into her haunted eyes. They were the gray of granite in the rain, dark and matte, holding no light within them. Her oval face ended in a surprisingly pert chin, and though her stare was hollow, there was a bit of defiance in that chin—so subtle it could not be discerned unless one knew to look for it. Her lips had hardly more color than her wan cheeks. The purple bruises of a sleepless night were pressed like hard thumbprints beneath her eyes.

"Please, lady," Waltrude said. "Let me look. I was sent here by the prince."

At those words, something came alive in the lady's face. Her gray eyes managed to capture a bit of the window's draining light. Her nose—that, too, was surprisingly pert, upturned in illusive defiance—flared just slightly. The weakest hint of color trickled into her cheeks. And where her whole body had been taut in silent protest, Waltrude saw her muscles unclench in a very, very faint show of submission.

Seizing upon the opportunity, Waltrude maneuvered her into the desk chair. There the protest drained from her at last. She slumped down and let her hand fall away from her chest, stretching it out over the armrest of the chair.

With no small measure of trepidation, Waltrude peered at the hand. Whatever she had expected—whatever the prince's words had portended—the truth was worse. Ugly, garish, bleak indeed.

There was a gash in the center of her hand, large and deep enough that it exposed a pale slant of bone. The edges of her torn flesh were withered and white and oddly damp, like something rotten. Smaller gashes between her knuckles were not quite so deep, but those still leaked, a weak and watery red, as if even the rush of blood was close to giving itself up.

And yet the worst wound was on her fourth finger, where the flesh had been split open right to the bone. It was no deeper than the large cut, but there was less skin there to protect what lay inside, and so the crass innards were exposed: the ripped bands of muscle and sinew, the dull knob of her knuckle. This sight, at last, caused bile to rise in Waltrude's throat. She could feel the cold horror overtaking her own face, turning her cheeks as white as the lady's.

Yet she resisted showing this horror openly—if the lady did not shed a tear at her torment, the very least Waltrude could do was appear similarly unshaken. She assumed a mask of calm and patted Lady Agnes gently on the shoulder.

"There, there," she said. "It is not beyond repair."

It was an absurd gesture, false comfort and bald lies. She had expected it to have no impact on the lady at all. But Agnes looked up at Waltrude through a dense fan of dark lashes and gave the slightest nod.

Enlivened by this response, Waltrude set to work. She dabbed at the wounds with water until the blood was mostly gone. She cut the cloth and wrapped the bandages—pretending, all the while, that the labor was not foreign to her. The larger wound could have done with some stitches, but she did not have a needle or thread nor enough confidence in herself to perform the task. This was the purpose of a leech, Waltrude thought bitterly, not a wet nurse. She would merely have to hope the wound could knit itself closed beneath the protective caul of cloth.

Through all this grave effort, she was surprised to see that the lady quite frequently winced. She did not, of course, utter a sound, nor did any tears wet her eyes, but there were subtle indications that she did feel the pain of Waltrude's intruding ministrations. These flinches would have gone unnoticed by anyone who was not as close as Waltrude, or who was not disposed to wonder about this strange lady who seemed not to feel pain as others did. After what the prince had said, she had expected the lady to remain as sober as the statue-girl Waltrude had first encountered here in Castle Crudele.

But something had shifted within the lady Agnes, as faint as the rippling of water under ice. She had relented quite easily once the prince was mentioned. This, too, did not escape Waltrude's attention.

As Waltrude wrapped the last of the bandages, she noticed the glint of metal on her finger. Previously it had been hidden beneath the gruesome splatter of blood and the gape of ruined flesh, but now that the wounds were clean and covered, it gleamed up at her, like quartz in the mouth of a cave. A silver band, set with pearls.

It was the ring the prince had given her, on the eve of his wedding. The gift that had confounded Waltrude, even as she placed it in the lady's hand. The lady had not simply taken it as a trinket, worn it once out of courtesy, and then deposited it into her box of jewels, where it would lie ignominiously beneath gaudy strands of ruby and tumescent pendants of emerald. In fact, the lady wore no jewelry at all save for this small and rather unshowy ring. A ring that would only be noticed, would only be remarked upon, by the one who wore it and the one who had given it.

A prickle went up Waltrude's neck. Agnes was no longer looking up at her. She was examining her own hand, trying to make the smallest movements with her fingers. Though she of course conveyed no discomfort, it was nearly unbearable to watch; Waltrude winced in sympathetic pain. *He has ruined it, Waltrude. I do not think she will ever hold a quill again.*

It was the meager bit of hope that these movements expressed that stung Waltrude. Did the lady, beneath that imperturbable mask, still nurture a secret longing in her heart? And if she did long for this one thing—to use her hand—could she not long for another?

"Perhaps you should let it rest now," Waltrude said. "In time, your strength will return." Of course, she could not promise such a thing. A leech would be able to assess it and inject the lady with the appropriate amount of optimism or despair.

Agnes let her hand go limp on the armrest, but she watched it carefully, as though it might surprise her by moving of its own accord. Waltrude's heart winced again.

She took stock of the lady, slouched there on the chair, her bloody gown crumpled, her hair coming loose from its crown of braids, which was ordinarily so neatly bound.

"Here," Waltrude said. "Let us get you out of this gown and into something clean."

At once, the lady's gaze snapped up. Her eyes flared with panic, and she shook her head furiously. As she curled her good arm protectively around her bodice, Waltrude realized she had touched upon an area of sensitivity, though she could not guess why. It would be impossible for the lady to dress herself now, with only one hand. And she and the princess kept no handmaidens in attendance; they each serviced the other as a handmaiden would. A queer arrangement that still galled Waltrude. Queerer still was the fact that the princess was nowhere to be found. Why was she not at her cousin's side when the lady Agnes was in such peril?

I am entrusting this to you, Waltrude. There is no other in this castle I can depend on. No leeches. No princess. No handmaidens. The Lady Agnes was, in every possible manner, alone.

And Waltrude thought again of Philomel, locked in that remote tower, where she screamed herself hoarse to no avail and then at last fell silent. Even her son was not often allowed to visit. The prince was a creature of great compassion and keen observation. Clearly, he had seen the lady's lonesomeness and sought to remedy it. That was certainly not beyond the boundaries of etiquette.

Waltrude let her hands fall back. "Very well," she said. "The prince did say you would refuse all aid. Stubborn and willful, he called you."

As before, mention of the prince aroused Agnes. She glanced up at Waltrude, a sudden, shimmery light enlivening her gray eyes. She seemed to be asking a question, but Waltrude did not speak the tongueless language of mutes. So she merely returned the lady's steady gaze.

Then, with what appeared to be great effort, Agnes leaned forward and reached for a parchment upon the desk. She took it and smoothed it flat. Then she reached for a quill—all of this, of course, with one hand. By the clumsiness of her movements, Waltrude presumed she was left-handed, and unaccustomed to performing these functions with her right. But she tried. That slight defiance flared in her again. Waltrude saw then the willfulness that Liuprand had alleged.

Her writing was slow, labored. Her fingers trembled. She bit down on her lower lip, consummately focused. The letters she made were blocky and tottering, a child's scrawl. But she did not relent until she had finished writing out the two words.

Thank you.

And then, something extraordinary happened. Waltrude was overtaken by a wave of knowledge. It was not simply a sequence of facts that hardened like diamonds in her mind, but a total and encompassing awareness, one that engaged all her senses. Liuprand had impressed upon her his purpose, and now, it seemed, he had impressed upon her his total perception and judgment, as well.

She saw the lady Agnes as the prince did. She did not see a walking corpse, a ghost in a grayish gown. She saw a vivid creature, all the intricate faculties of life occurring with great subtlety beneath the surface, as roots writhe and swell underground before at last showing themselves green and tender in the dirt. She saw again the slant of defiance to her nose and to her chin. She saw the clever shifting of her gray eyes—and oh, she felt a fool for ever thinking them dull and lifeless; they were so compelling to her now, perceptive but coy, somehow both solemn and earnest. She could have lost herself in those eyes, pondering their multitudes, searching their immeasurable depths.

It was not the same vibrant life as her cousin Marozia, the ever-more-resplendent flower. Agnes was another plant, trickier in its arrangement of petals, not so easy to find within a field of many blossoms, all competing for the attention of the sun and the admiration of humans. She was a night-blooming flower that did its growing in the dark, nurtured by the moon and weaned by the stars.

Waltrude saw the contrast of her black hair against her skin, with its soft, pearlescent luminance, and was made weak in the knees. She saw the way her full lashes curtained her eyes. She saw the tender bow of her lips and felt suddenly, alarmingly, obliged to kiss them. She saw even the faint swell of her breasts beneath the bloodied bodice and felt a pull in the base of her belly.

The Lady Agnes was beautiful. And that realization filled Waltrude with a cold, infinite terror.

Very briskly, Waltrude snatched the note from Agnes. She found that her own fingers were trembling as she folded it into her palm.

"I will take it to the prince," she murmured. "I am certain it will please him."

She *was* certain—horribly, wretchedly certain. She doubted that Liuprand had betrayed his wife in body—he was an astonishingly restrained man in that regard—but in spirit, his vow was broken. With despair, Waltrude knew that his heart did not belong to the princess. And she knew, because the Seraphine were not quite human—they were something slightly greater, with an augmented and refined capacity for love—that his heart never truly would.

Was the lady Agnes afflicted with this same catastrophic sentiment? Waltrude could not be as sure. But it did not really matter. The treason of the prince's emotion was enough. Kingdoms crumbled and crowns were lost for less.

As Waltrude left the lady and began her terrible journey back to the prince's chambers, her knees wobbled, and her back ached beneath the burden of this knowledge. *You fool,* she thought bitterly. *You could well be the ruin of us all.*

XXVIII
THE DAGGER SLIPS

It was not long after Waltrude departed that Marozia emerged at last. She wore the same deep-crimson gown as the day before, though her hair was combed and fixed into a thick braid, and her red hood with biliments of gold was now a golden hood with biliments of white, which looked ever more like a tiara. Ninian was at her back, peering nervously over her mistress's shoulder. She closed the door behind Marozia firmly.

"You look a fright," Marozia said.

Agnes stared back at her hollowly.

Marozia's lips twitched. She turned to Ninian and said, "Leave us."

Ninian's face fell. She appeared deeply crestfallen to have been dismissed, but she left as she had been ordered, with only one mooning glance back at her mistress. A faint flicker of irritation went through Agnes, though it extinguished quickly. Nothing within her could remain alight.

At last Marozia's gaze fell to her hand. "You've had it wrapped. By whom?"

The question could not be answered in a gesture, but when Agnes looked over at the parchment and quill on the desk, she was overtaken by exhaustion.

It was not an exhaustion she could not have surmounted had she wished it. Though as her eyes lingered on the paper, she felt a protest harden in the root of her throat. She would not speak it aloud, of course. But it was there, calcifying with each second that passed, and it did not fade through her as the irritation did.

"Well?" Marozia prompted.

Agnes looked back up at her and did not answer.

A furrow formed in Marozia's brow, and her dark eyes danced. It was not anger—not yet. It was merely the bewildered embers of it. Her mouth opened and then closed again, lips dragging down into a frown. She could not find the words to contend with Agnes's refusal because Agnes had never refused her. Always her silence had been a weapon wielded against the world, against all but Marozia. Or—perhaps it had been Marozia's weapon, all along. But now with her own dagger turned in against her chest, it was Marozia's turn to fall silent.

She would not admit defeat so easily by getting angry. She blinked, as if to stamp out those early sparks of rage, and then said, "Let us get off your gown. It's filthy."

Agnes grew stiff in her seat. She drew her arms up around herself, but either Marozia did not notice this silent protest, or else she did not care, for she came behind her in the chair, lifted the sagging braids from the back of Agnes's neck, and began to unbutton her dress.

Shakily Agnes stood. The gown fell down in increments, baring first her collarbone, then her shoulders, then her breasts. At last, it drooped forward, exposing her stomach. The scars shone bright in the glowing pink dawn. No blood had leaked through the fabric, and her skin bore only these old, healed wounds of the past. Wounds that Marozia glanced at but did not truly see.

A part of her wanted to know where Marozia had spent the night. What had happened in the gloaming darkness while Agnes had dreamed her hideous dreams. Her hand twitched toward the quill, but she could not make herself grasp it.

Marozia perceived the question from her anyway. As the gown puddled to the floor, she said, "Ninian made up another room for me. I will sleep there until this bed is clean. Until the prince calls me to his chamber."

There was no tremor of uncertainty in her voice. Had some reconciliation occurred between her and Liuprand while Agnes slept?

Had her torture—and the king's obviously increasing madness—encouraged him to at last fulfill his marriage vows? More than ever the kingdom needed unity, confidence in this match. An heir, to mingle the blood of Drepane with the blood of Seraph.

Agnes's gorge rose. She had not once felt the urge to retch, even as the king had visited his violence upon her, even as she looked upon her ruined hand, but now she did. The very thought of Marozia in Liuprand's bed made her taste that foul bile of envy in her throat.

And Marozia—ever clear-eyed in her perception of others' desires—seemed to perceive this question from her, too. A smile touched her lips.

"I did not exchange words with the prince *yet*," she said. "But today I will. My tears moved him to a rage of his own. He was horrified by the crimes committed against his wife's house—I heard he tore apart his room in a fury! I knew he nursed a secret affection for me. This action by the king has brought it out. We are saved, Agnes. I will be queen, just as our grandmother wished it."

Agnes stared down at her wrapped hand. At the ring that glinted subtly through the bandages. Her throat burned like a bed of cinders.

Marozia combed through her hair, her ministrations rough and hurried. She undid the old braids and began twining new ones. She took silver pins and arranged the braids into a crown, held aloft from her neck. The pins were tight, pressed too close to Agnes's skull. As Agnes sat there, naked, this ordinary act—Marozia fixing her hair—suddenly seemed grotesque. So aberrant that a princess should perform such a base and common task. It was almost disgusting.

These were the freakish customs of their bloodline that made Drepane revile the House of Teeth. And the other folk of the island did not even know the whole truth of it. They did not know that the ladies of their house drank from their mothers' breasts until they were old enough to have breasts of their own. They did not know that they slept nude with their cousins and sisters and mothers until their bodies were too big for a single bed to hold. They did not know that the ladies belonged to the house, in form and in spirit, such that any act upon their person was righteous and glorious with purpose, so long as it strengthened and extended their bloodline. They did not know that Agnes had tasted the meat of an infant fresh from the womb.

The dress for Agnes was the color of a near-faded bruise. Marozia buttoned it and then jerked Agnes up by the arm, out of her seat. Two locks of hair came loose from her braided crown and fell against the sides of her face. They feathered her jawline as Agnes kept her gaze trained on the ground.

"The king has asked for our presence in the great hall," Marozia said.

Agnes froze.

"Do not be afraid. He will not offend our house so grievously again; even he is not fool enough to scuttle such a useful alliance. If anything, I believe he means to repent for his actions. I am sure he and the prince have had words in private."

Agnes looked down again at the ring on her hand. In all this time Marozia had not remarked upon it; likely she had not even noticed. And so, as Agnes had chosen her own torment before, she chose to follow Marozia out of the chamber and into the corridor, trailing the princess and the Mistress of Teeth like a tethered ghost.

XXIX
MISTRESS OF TEETH

Someone had scrubbed the floors of the great hall very solicitously, for there was no blood to be seen or smelled in the air. Agnes was filled with wonderment at how they had managed to banish even the scent so quickly. The stench of blood had seemed overwhelming, infinite and total, the running of it as thick as tar. But as she approached the dais with Marozia, Agnes was given to understand: The table was not the same table. The one she had bled upon had been replaced. Chopped to pieces, she figured, and then burned. The only evidence of her torment was the bandaged hand she kept clutched to her breast.

But there were subtler signs, which Agnes only noticed as the room began to fill. There were no leeches in attendance, and there ought to have been, for it was their task to copy down and disseminate all royal pronouncements. The Most Esteemed Surgeon was absent, as were Truss and Mordaunt. More peculiarly, there was a single member of the Dolorous Guard present, who seemed only there to help the king to his throne atop the dais. Bearing Nicephorus's weight alone must have been a toil; his armor creaked and squealed with effort. But then when the king was seated, he waved the guard away.

Something had shifted in the foundation of Castle Crudele last night while Agnes had thrashed within the dark waters of her dreams. She did not yet know what.

Liuprand stood before the dais, in his doublet of midnight blue. His bruise was faded now, but his face was otherwise a great tragedy: the violet circles of sleeplessness ringing his eyes, the alarming paleness of his cheeks, devoid of their natural golden glow. His hair was mussed, a lock of it falling down across his forehead.

And then there was the sword at his hip. Agnes had never seen him with a sword before, nor a weapon of any kind. He kept one hand resting upon its hilt, and the other curled into a fist at his side. Agnes looked for any kind of redness upon his hands—*I heard he tore apart his room in a fury*—and found it. A rosy hue, like dawn breaking over the white cliffs of his knuckles.

She saw something else there, clutched between his fingers. A scrap of parchment.

Liuprand lifted his head and met her gaze without hesitation, without contrition. He unclenched his fingers, just briefly, yet long enough for her to see the words scrawled upon the paper, her words. *Thank you.*

They were the first true words she had communicated to him, and he held them like they were the most precious thing. The scrap of parchment was so small that no one else would notice, and even if they did, it was so innocuous they would never think to inquire about it. They would look but they would not see. Agnes glanced down at her ring, which shone so brightly to her, but to no one else within the room. No one but Liuprand.

Their gaze was broken as Marozia stepped between them, nearing the very foot of the dais. She curtsied to the king, low and deep, and after a moment, Agnes did the same. From beneath the fringe of her lashes, Agnes stared up at the king, at his many chins, at his bulbous and broken nose, at his small, watery eyes, which held so little within them. No light, but no shadow, either.

Agnes would have hated him less if he had looked upon her with contempt, with revulsion. Yet she seemed to almost pass beneath his attention. And as she rose, a lusty hatred rose with her.

"You seem hardly worse for the wear, Lady Agnes," he said, amusement lifting the corner of his unappeasable mouth. "Someone has seen to your wounds."

This time, Liuprand would let nothing lie; not a word from his father would go unchallenged. He stepped forward, hand still resting on the hilt of his sword.

"Yes," he said. "I sent Waltrude to her. And if there is truly so little damage done, then she is lucky."

The king's gaze flickered mildly to his son. "Your compassion for the lady is stirring."

There was a very small sound from Marozia beside her. Just the faintest catch of her breath. Agnes glanced over at her cousin and saw her bite down on her lower lip. It pleased Agnes, in a slick, pitiless way. How easily this sentiment occurred to her was frightening. She tucked it away in a hurry.

"Stirring, too, is your commitment to resolving the matter with the House of Blood through diplomacy." The king raised his voice and looked out upon the small gathered audience. "Perhaps I was too easily seduced by the proposition of violence. I believe there is another way forward."

Liuprand's eyes narrowed. "And what way is that?"

The king leaned forward in his seat, steepling his hands over his enormous stomach. Another smile played at the corner of his wormy lips. And then, slowly, horribly, he dragged his gaze across the room toward Agnes.

"You claimed yourself, my son, that there is no stronger bond than a betrothal," he said. "What better salve for bitter wounds than love?"

Agnes merely stared at the king, uncomprehending. And Liuprand's brow furrowed in confusion.

"In the late hours of the night I devised a solution," Nicephorus went on. "A solution I believe will greatly please both aggrieved parties. Lady Agnes will wed the Master of Blood."

Silence reigned across the hall. It reigned cruelly and coldly. Its frigid grasp was so powerful that Agnes could not even think; her mind emptied instantly into a slippery black pit. Her only thought was that perhaps she had misheard the king. Perhaps she misunderstood.

It was Marozia who spoke, before Liuprand could find his voice.

"But please, Your Majesty," she said, "Agnes does not speak."

The king guffawed. "What does she need to speak for? Many husbands would prefer their wives be silent. And there are better uses for a woman's mouth."

"*Don't*," Liuprand broke in. "I will not allow you another vulgar word."

There were storm clouds on Liuprand's face, and the fury in his voice was barely checked. But the king merely regarded his son with a bland sort of amusement.

"Is the truth a vulgar thing to you? A silent wife would appeal greatly to most men, and you know the reason why. Had your mother been silent—"

"Keep her name out of your mouth," Liuprand said blackly.

Yet the king pressed on. "It has been decided, Liuprand. It is my royal decree. The Master of Blood has been alone since the death of his wife many years ago. He will be pleased and more than pleased to have a new woman to warm his bed."

Still Agnes could not think. The words slipped in through the shell of her ear, but they could not sink themselves into her brain. Nicephorus looked down at her beneficently, as if he had bestowed upon her some great gift. So many idiotic details captured her focus: the way his yellowed teeth were wedged together in his mouth, like stones built upon stones; the way grease from breakfast painted a sheen on his chin. There was a sensation of standing at the edge of a very tall cliff, and she felt the height in the soles of her feet.

To her surprise, it was again Marozia who spoke.

"Your Majesty," she said, in a tremulous voice. "I do not mean to question your wisdom, your judgment—but I fear that the Master of Blood may not think this an act of goodwill. My cousin is a lady of the House of Teeth, yes, though—forgive me—she is not otherwise a lady of great esteem. She has no title. The Master of Blood may feel you have merely sent him a hostage or a bedslave. Not a wife."

And then, to her even more momentous surprise, the king fell silent. He leaned forward and rested his chin upon his steepled hands. Contemplation danced through his dull eyes.

"You speak sagely, Princess," he said at last. "It is true: Your cousin has no title of her own. Though—did you not say that she is the elder?"

Marozia hesitated. Her gaze was uncertain. "By five days, Your Majesty. But her mother—"

"Then I do not see why she was passed over for the title Mistress of Teeth."

Silence rose like a white-headed wave and drenched the throne room. Agnes heard Marozia's breath catch again, yet this time, her hand went to her throat; to the necklace that circled it.

"That is not the way of our house," Marozia managed. "My mother was the elder, and so I am the heiress. Adele-Blanche—"

"Is dead," the king cut in. "Expired. Extinct. Forever gone. And now her blood has been woven inextricably with my own royal line. The strange ways of her house must die with her. You are the princess; you will birth the heir to Drepane's throne, so should you not follow the customs of the land? The other houses will wish it so. Your subjects will wish it so. When you are queen."

At that, Marozia could no longer speak. She opened her mouth and then closed it again, making no sound.

Nicephorus's eyes flickered to Liuprand. "Do you not think this wise, my son?"

Liuprand's teeth were gritted, and a muscle feathered in his tautly clenched jaw. His own eyes searched his father's face, as if hoping he might find some chink in the armor. The king so rarely spoke with this cool, remote reasoning, and when confronted with it, Liuprand seemed to flounder.

"I think you should take care when suspending the traditions of Drepane's noble houses," he replied after a moment. "The other masters may not be so pleased to see such a precedent set."

"Liuprand the Heedful. Always you seek the path of appeasement.

But what is the purpose of being king, if not to set the laws of the kingdom and see that they are followed?"

For this, even Liuprand could not summon an argument. The fog of bewilderment around Agnes began to clear, and in its place rose a cold, choking mist of fear. She could not be married off. Adele-Blanche had forbidden it. The words writ upon her stomach were clear. She could seek no lustful pleasures; she could not share another's bed. She was not Mistress of Teeth, but she was the secret heiress to Adele-Blanche's hopes and dreams of power. This could not happen.

Yet she could not speak in order to stop it.

All Liuprand could respond was, "A king must still take care not to estrange himself from his powerful allies." His voice was a murmur, and his gaze was no longer on his father. He was watching Agnes with a growing horror, his dark-blue eyes showing their immeasurable depths.

"Then we are in agreement," Nicephorus said. He clapped his hands together, and the sound made Agnes flinch. "The title Mistress of Teeth will be transferred to the lady Agnes. Then let us see the Master of Blood refuse such a noble and propitious match!" With a jerk of his chin, he gestured to Liuprand. "My son, will you do the honors?"

Confusion clouded Liuprand's features. Agnes, too, found herself bewildered again. It was Marozia who first understood. She uttered a small, wordless noise of protest, and her fingers clenched around the necklace of teeth.

"Go on," Nicephorus urged.

Slowly, his movements made heavy and stiff with chagrin, Liuprand approached Marozia. Her breathing was quick; Agnes saw the labored rising and falling of her cousin's chest. She even thought she saw tears springing to the corners of her eyes, glistening like shards of precious stone. Liuprand raised his hands hesitantly, but before he could touch her, Marozia reached back and swept the hair off her shoulders herself. She held her great mane of dark curls aloft while Liuprand unclasped the necklace and drew it from her throat.

It was not grief that Marozia exuded. Agnes knew her cousin as well as she knew her own hands. Anger rose off her in great waves. It gusted toward the king, but he was too far away to feel it. It blew toward Liuprand, and *he* felt it: He stepped briskly away from her, drawing up his shoulders—almost shivering, cowed by his own wife. His fingers had barely grazed her, yet this was the only touch that had occurred between them since their wedding day. The discomfort of the moment was so obvious that even the king seemed to notice; one of his pale eyebrows rose.

But most of Marozia's anger was reserved for Agnes. The cold cloud of it enveloped her, raising gooseflesh down her limbs. Agnes had not known Marozia capable of this icy type of rage—but perhaps she was finally coming into her inheritance. This was Adele-Blanche's poison, seeping through the generations. Marozia could not truly remain unspoiled. Agnes had not moved even a muscle, yet to Marozia's mind, she had marched over and yanked the necklace violently from her throat.

And this anger filled Agnes to the brim, like sips of heady, unwatered wine. The poison was in her, too. There was no antidote for one's own blood.

Liuprand stepped behind her—so close that she could feel the heat of his body. It sent fleeing some of Marozia's wintry anger. Because Agnes's hair was, as always, aloft in its braided crown, he did not have to lift it from her throat. He merely had to sweep away some of the soft, feathery strands so they would not be caught in the clasp. Or perhaps he did not have to. Perhaps he only chose to, brushing his fingers so gently across the back of her neck that she shivered.

He did not speak, nor did she. He drew the necklace around her throat, faintly grazing her jaw as he wrapped it. Agnes did not have her cousin's full bust, so the third strand hung down deep between her small breasts, low enough to nearly touch her rib cage. Despite having been pressed to Marozia's skin, the teeth were cold, and she felt her own skin prickle.

Liuprand was so close that she could hear his breathing—irregular and short, as if this small act required great effort. His fingers fumbled with the clasp. Once, twice, it caught and then slipped. He exhaled softly. Against the back of her neck, his fingers actually trembled, and it made Agnes tremble, too. Never before had he seemed at all fragile to her—not Liuprand the Golden, blood of Seraph. But as his hands shook, and as he breathed unevenly, all of a sudden he seemed as shy and hesitant as a very young boy in the presence of his paramour. She chastised herself for this thought. It was a dream she was not allowed to dream, more treasonous than any seeds she had planted or smoke she inhaled.

This whole process could not have lasted very long, but the time was somehow infinite, a tender, languid unfolding of moments. Then the clasp was fixed with a soft *snick* of finality. The necklace settled against her skin, across her collarbones, between her breasts. It was like a coiling serpent, like a prisoner's manacles. It both choked her and armored her. It was an affront to the legacy of her house and the secret wish of Adele-Blanche. Agnes had only heard her whisper it once, offhandedly, and often she thought she had simply imagined it, for the sentiment had never been repeated. But her grandmother did not ever speak without depth of meaning or height of reason.

A pity you were born to the spare and not the heir. I would rather see a clever mind on the throne than a simple pretty face.

Marozia, of course, had not heard this offhand comment. She was not invited to listen and learn at Adele-Blanche's feet. She had tutors for her harp and seamstresses for her gowns and leeches to treat the occasional blemish. And she had Agnes for every other whim or desire, Agnes to warm their shared bed. But she did not have their grandmother's esteem. And Agnes thought for the first time that Marozia truly knew that, comprehended the fullness of her dismissal. Or else tears would not right now be threatening to spill from her dark eyes.

As Liuprand stepped away from her, Nicephorus nodded approvingly.

"The bauble suits you," he declared. "As does the title. She is the spitting image of Adele-Blanche, no?"

He directed this question at Liuprand, his stare leering and expectant.

Liuprand lifted his gaze to look at her. It was a lidded gaze, tempestuous and dark. Each time Agnes thought she had uncovered him, he confounded her again; she could not read the emotion within his eyes now. Without taking his gaze off her, he said lowly, "I do not see the resemblance."

Did he mean it as an insult? His voice was not cold, though it was not warm, either. Perhaps he meant to cheer his wife's spirits by slighting Agnes, but Marozia did not even appear to notice. She had her fist clenched at her breast as if feeling for the vanished necklace, her fingers closing around empty air. Almost unconsciously, Agnes lifted her own hand. She let the teeth roll under her fingers like pebbles on the riverbank. Her grandmother's inheritance. A hope dashed and a wish fulfilled at once.

And a portent of Agnes's doom.

"Well, Mistress of Teeth," the king said, raising his mighty head, "prepare yourself for your betrothal. Pack your gowns and choose which handmaidens will attend. The House of Blood is not far, but the journey is a treacherous one. Pretty yourself, too. Some powder on those pale cheeks. I must not risk insulting the Master of Blood with my offering. A beautiful bride is essential to this mending of alliances and soothing of ills. Oh, and the Master of Blood has been alone for so long. I know he resents the coldness of his bed. He will be so happy to have a woman for his fondling, he will fall upon you with insatiable lust. I hope you are firm enough, despite that fragile shell, to satisfy these hungers without being eaten to the bone."

 # XXX
A VERY HEAVY SILENCE

Agnes sat in the half dark, a golden cage upon her knee. The metal chilled her skin even through the fabric of her skirts. But the cage was empty, and the moth was on her shoulder. It nuzzled her cheek. Its body was warm and soft, though the comfort it offered was cold.

The carriage trundled along, jostling and jolting over what seemed to be more rough stone than road. Agnes had to cling to the seat so she was not thrust against the carriage wall or hurled forward. If she were hurled forward, she would land in Liuprand's lap.

Liuprand. He had not taken his eyes off her since they had climbed together into the carriage, though he was yet to speak. His blue eyes smoldered like burning glass, giving them the quality of chiaroscuro, equal parts light and shadow. Agnes could not be entirely sure, but she suspected that the carriage's third passenger was what prevented his speech.

Waltrude sat on the bench beside her, crinkly lips pressed together. She had an overall discomfiting presence, her gaze shifting unreadably from Agnes to Liuprand and back again. She knew her place and would not speak unless directly addressed, but Agnes sensed there were words on the tip of her tongue just barely restrained.

The wet nurse was not, perhaps, the most natural choice for a companion—though Agnes had few options. Ninian would never be persuaded to leave Marozia's side, and Castle Crudele's other handmaidens regarded the strange silent lady with suspicion and unease. Liuprand had suggested Waltrude, and Agnes had no good reason to refuse him. The trust between the two was palpable, their gazes for each other tender and full of well-worn love. And at Liuprand's request, Waltrude had come to treat Agnes's wounds with great gentleness. This in turn engendered trust in her. It would have to be enough.

Agnes did not think the nurse's wizened body could survive standing between her and her betrothed, but it was preferable to having no allies in her new home at all. Well, aside from the moth. It sat placidly upon her shoulder, gray wings folded and sheathed, legs curled under itself like a cat's.

A wedding gift, Liuprand had said bitterly. Those were the last words he spoke to her before they stepped into the carriage, many hours ago.

The House of Blood was not far away, but, as the king had promised, the journey was indeed treacherous. It went down a road favored by thieves and other lawbreakers, through a forest of twisted black trees. They were mangled and ugly, as if they had each been struck down by a powerful bolt of lightning, and though the bare branches offered no concealment, the mist was thick enough that Agnes knew there were knives and clubs and greedy-eyed villains hiding within.

Yet only a crazed fool would attempt to storm the carriage. Liuprand had insisted on taking the largest retinue that Castle Crudele could spare. There were twenty-four members of the Dolorous Guard with them, twelve before the carriage and twelve behind, each with his sword unsheathed and held aloft as they parted the mist of the woods.

"I have heard no stories about the especial cruelty of the Master of Blood," Liuprand said.

The suddenness of his speech made Agnes's head snap up. She regarded him with uncertainty.

"I have not seen him myself since I was a child," he admitted. "When his wife still lived. He seemed a docile enough man. Reasonable. I do not know what has provoked his spat with my father, but his quarrel is with the king. I do not think . . ."

Liuprand trailed off, a quiet agony entering his tone. Agnes felt her heart stutter. He cleared his throat and went on, "He has no animus for the House of Teeth. Unless your grandmother gravely offended him before her death."

Adele-Blanche did not have enough contact with the other houses to offend them. Her coldness held her fellow nobles at a distance, which truthfully was better for all. Agnes shook her head.

Liuprand's eyes shone faintly with relief, though his mouth still slanted in dismay.

"My father sought to frighten you," he murmured. "I do not know how much of what he said is true. But I will not . . ." He paused, drawing in a breath. "I will not allow you to be harmed, Lady Agnes. Do you believe me?"

Desperation cracked his voice. Agnes met his gaze, and then slowly, she nodded.

He exhaled. "I will remain with you at the House of Blood until the wedding. The Dolorous Guard will protect you with their own lives. Waltrude will keep to your side, always. And if ever you are afraid, send your moth to me, and I will come. Do you believe that as well?"

Agnes nodded again. Liuprand's jaw clenched and he looked away from her, out the window, at the black trees fingering through the mist. He did not know what war was being fought behind Agnes's eyes. He did not know that she was thinking of seeds and of smoke and the vapors of her dreams. He did not know that she feared the dead more than she feared the living.

She had not even had time to harvest the henbane and mandrake before she was shuttled into the carriage. She had been forced to leave behind her mortar and pestle. And now, with each passing moment, she was carried farther away from the secrets she was meant to uncover, from the library where the forbidden spell-words lurked, from the castle where her destiny lay. She wore her grandmother's necklace of teeth, but it lay across her throat in cold shame. She was failing Adele-Blanche. And even if she beat against the walls of the carriage and tore at her hair, she could not stop it.

Agnes was too afraid of her grandmother's posthumous existence to even let sleep draw down her eyelids. The scars on her stomach burned as if they were new. She had come to Castle Crudele and squandered all her chances. What was the worth of her life now? And when the Master of Blood pinned her down to the sheets and broke apart the seal between her legs, it would not matter if she managed to find her way back to Castle Crudele, if she uncovered the words of the spell, because she could never cast it—she would be spoiled, too disgraced for her purpose.

She leaned back against the seat and closed her tired eyes, but only for a moment, not long enough for her vision to be smudged with black. If she let herself sink too deeply into darkness, her grandmother would swiftly come.

The moth on her shoulder shifted, its wing brushing her cheek. Liuprand was watching her again, and now she returned his gaze, but this summoned an even sharper pain. She could scarcely see him without imagining Marozia in his bed. Her cousin's hands tangling in his golden hair, fingers spreading across his broad, bare chest. The bruise on his cheek was nearly gone now. It was only the look of desolation on his face that made him seem less than princely. Liuprand the Sorrowful, she thought bemusedly. But why? He should not grieve her. She should be nothing to him.

Agnes looked down at her left hand. It was still swaddled in bandages, and her fingers could not move the way she willed them. But the ring glinted up from between the white fabric and the pink, swollen flesh. It gleamed more subtly than a flame, but more steadily, too. It would not burn down or be snuffed out. In fact, it would pass beneath all others' attentions. All but hers and Liuprand's.

And one more? When she lifted her gaze again, Agnes saw Waltrude was staring down at her hand, too. Her sharp green eyes reflected the soft glow of the pearls. The corner of her mouth quivered as if she wanted desperately to speak. There was knowledge in her stare, but it was a wretched knowledge, which she seemed to resent having learned. And Agnes could not quite puzzle it out. The wet nurse knew something she did not.

XXXI

THE HOUSE OF BLOOD

The mist-cloaked woods broke open at last. The black trees shuddered away. The mist itself remained, but only in thin, diaphanous vapors, which draped over the fat gray towers of stone like tattered banners. The castle was a distended thing, wider than it was tall, gorged with outbuildings and crumbly ramparts. From the vast lime-green moat, moths rose in white clusters, like souls fleeing the underworld.

All seven noble houses of Drepane were alike in one respect: However they had endured, they had endured through some manner of apathy. The House of Teeth had the advantage of its remote location, guarded by those jealous peaks. Those houses that were not fortunate enough to be remote in location had to be remote in spirit. This castle was not foreboding so much as it was, simply, indifferent. Fat and self-concerned. It did not even have guards posted upon its battlements or parapets. It knew, with an air of disdain, that even those who could brave these twisted woods would fall vainly against its stone walls or drown in its stagnant moat.

Upon looking at it, Agnes was not filled with fear. The castle seemed to impart upon her its own impassiveness. She felt more like a ghost than a body, watching with lidded eyes as the carriage clattered to a halt before the closed drawbridge.

Yet there had to be some surreptitious observer, for the moment the carriage stopped, the drawbridge began to lower. It creaked and groaned and then thudded to the earth, kicking up the hard-packed dirt and splashing the green water of the moat all about. A bullfrog leapt to safety, and more moths fluttered upward, blown like the petals of a flowering pear.

Liuprand opened the door to the carriage. Already the Dolorous Guard had arranged itself, forming an aisle from the carriage door to the open drawbridge. Liuprand offered his hand to help Agnes down, and then Waltrude, the golden cage in her arms. Each guard's hand rested meaningfully on the pommel of his sword.

"Stay behind me," Liuprand murmured. He dropped her hand.

At the loss of his touch, Agnes felt immediately bereft. She nodded.

He walked slowly down the path formed by the guards, not with hesitation, but with the leisurely deliberation of a prince; the Master of Blood would wait on him, not the other way around. Agnes followed, unable to see very much with his large body in front of her. She peered around Liuprand's elbow. He, too, palmed the hilt of his sword.

Liuprand reached the end of the aisle and stopped. A heavy, languorous breeze picked up, thick with the vapors rising from the fetid water. Agnes's skin prickled.

Then a voice rumbled out: "Your Highness."

Still Agnes could not see to whom the voice belonged. It was a throaty voice, suggesting that it was conceived by aged lungs, but through it there was a subtle rippling of vitality.

In turn, Liuprand inclined his head. "Lord Fredegar."

There was a brief moment of silence. The moth rustled in its cage. And then the voice answered, haltingly, "Let us not linger here in the dank air. Please come in, Your Highness."

The Dolorous Guard preceded them, forming a gray phalanx around Liuprand, Agnes, and Waltrude. Agnes could see, very faintly, through the gaps in the guards' arms, that they were passing by a man wearing a dark-crimson doublet. She saw his chest only, his silver belt. And then they were through the barbican, into a courtyard, and soon after delivered into the great hall of the castle.

Only when they were inside did the Dolorous Guard part, and Agnes was finally treated with the sight of the man who had spoken.

He was a shockingly large man, nearly of a height to Liuprand. He was as at least old as Nicephorus—likely older, his hair a neatly slicked-back silver—though surely not of an age with Adele-Blanche. The vitality that had been apparent in his voice was apparent in his form, too, though less subtle. Here was no Sluggard, no indolent lord well past his prime, contenting himself with only wine and feasting and women. He was broad-shouldered, well muscled, as though his days in the tiltyard were not so far behind him. And his face, though lined with years, was long and handsome. There was a particular and unexpectedly vivacious gleam to his eyes, their color a soft hazel.

The man raised his arms, and then spoke ruefully. "My deepest apologies, Prince Liuprand. Had I known you were coming, I would have made arrangements for a welcome feast. As it is, I will have to see what my servants can put together."

Immediately Agnes was bewildered. He had not known they were coming? She wondered if this was some kind of sly device by the king, but she could not puzzle out what it would achieve. He had seemed sincere in his declaration that she was to marry the Master of Blood.

Liuprand's forehead wrinkled. "My father did not send a missive?"

"No, or at least, not one that arrived in time. But regardless, you are happily received by the House of Blood and its master."

"Thank you, Lord Fredegar," said Liuprand, though his voice was strained. "Then I suppose you do not know our purpose here, either?"

"Other than a friendly visit?" Lord Fredegar quirked one of his silver brows. "No, Your Highness, I am afraid not."

Agnes drew a breath; she could not help it. She hoped it would not catch anyone's attention, but Lord Fredegar heard and glanced over at her.

"Is this your lovely wife?" he asked Liuprand. "The princess Marozia?"

A muscle feathered in Liuprand's jaw.

"No," he said. "This is her cousin, the lady Agnes. Mistress of Teeth."

"Ah," said Fredegar. "The blood of Adele-Blanche as well, then. It is always a pleasure to host a beautiful woman in my halls, and an even greater pleasure to host one of such esteem. I am sorry for the recent loss of your grandmother."

Agnes nodded slowly, and assumed what she hoped was a gracious expression.

The confusion she was well accustomed to ran across Fredegar's face. He watched her for several moments, expectantly, eyes wide and head tilted. When still Agnes did not reply, he turned to Liuprand, directing to him the silent question.

"The lady Agnes does not speak," Liuprand said tersely. And then he himself fell flatly silent.

The remoteness of his affect was beginning to greatly unsettle Agnes. She had never seen Liuprand fail to show a prince's eloquence when addressing any of his subjects, much less nobles and lords. His dignity, perhaps his pride, seemed to have taken some blow, though she did not know by what means. Perhaps he simply could not exorcise his anger toward his father. Perhaps he feared, as Agnes did, some elaborate guile.

But Lord Fredegar did not seem affronted. He gave her a gentle smile and pried no further.

"Forgive me, Your Highness," he said, "but I do not wish to offend you due to ignorance. Pray tell, what *is* the purpose of your visit here?"

It was Liuprand who drew a breath then, and raised himself up to his full height.

"The matter at hand, Lord Fredegar, is your brazen defiance," he said. "Twice now you have rejected my father's summons. First at my wedding, and then again at the desecration of the Exarch, not a week ago. You could not even be disposed to send a member of your household in your place. The king wishes to know why you have spurned him so openly."

A long silence stretched over the great hall. It gave Agnes the opportunity to look about the room. It was far from the cold vault of Castle Crudele; the floor did not seem to lurch and swell with memories of the blood spilled there; the walls did not press in tightly, as if to remind its occupants of how Berengar had built them on the bed of such garish violence. There were hunting tapestries and crimson velvet drapes, with vast, plush carpets under their feet. The chair upon the dais was constructed of simple wood, not iron or stone, though it was carved lovingly, with intricate patterns on the back and along the armrests.

To her great surprise, Agnes sensed no coldness within this chamber, and not even very much apathy. It felt warm and shockingly bright, for how little sun managed to seep through the gray mist and then through the arched windows. The Master of Blood had not been alive to see the plague, nor Berengar's conquest. And so perhaps he had never learned cruelty at the feet of Drepane's first king.

Lord Fredegar blinked and blinked, as though to clear wetness from his eyes. He opened his mouth once, closed it, then opened it again, and at last he said:

"My deepest apologies, Your Highness. But I never received any summons from the king."

Liuprand's gaze flashed. Agnes felt her heart stutter. "Do you accuse my father of deception?"

"No, Your Highness. No." Fredegar shook his head gravely. "I merely mean some miscommunication has occurred—through no fault of the king's, I'm sure. The woods can be treacherous; I wonder if the messenger merely lost his way? Or perhaps . . ."

He trailed off, thoughtfulness clouding his stare.

"Two messengers, lost in as much time?" Liuprand accused. "I do not believe it."

"I swear to you, there is no artifice at work within the House of Blood, my prince. This is some unfortunate accident of fate."

"If you never received the missives, why did your house send a wedding gift?" Liuprand's voice was ever sharper. "A single bottle of wine, left as a taunt. It came with a note in your hand."

At this, Fredegar drew a breath of reproach. "I have no knowledge of this—please, Your Highness, believe me. To speak baldly, I no longer oversee my own envoys. I have left the managing of my household largely to my son."

Liuprand's brow lifted. "Your son?"

"Yes." Fredegar raised a hand and beckoned one of his men. A leech, in spotless sepia robes. "Pliny, go fetch Unruoching. Now."

With a silent nod, the leech went. It did not take him very long to return with Fredegar's son.

He was a tall man, of a height to his father, but without his father's broadness or powerfully rolled shoulders. He was slender in a way that Agnes had rarely seen in men out of boyhood, as though flesh was yet to fill the spaces between his bones. His shoulders were narrow and sharp. His face was long, his chin pointed at the end, giving him a foxlike appearance. He was not an overall unappealing man, but he seemed out of place beside his father; Agnes would not have been surprised to learn he was a legitimized bastard, another lord's offspring. Even in matching doublets of dusty crimson, they were more different than alike, as if Fredegar were a man and Unruoching merely the shadow behind.

Unruoching dipped his head. "Father. Prince Liuprand." He did not acknowledge Agnes's presence at all. "What brings you to the House of Blood?"

"A grave misunderstanding," Liuprand replied coldly.

"The king has sent our house two missives, which I somehow did not receive," Fredegar said. "Nothing from Castle Crudele passed beneath my gaze. And yet—a wedding gift was sent, with a note written in my name. Surely you have some explanation."

Unruoching's eyes shifted. Their color was unclear to Agnes. As his gaze moved from his father to Liuprand, they looked by turns green, then blue, then gray. They could not settle. They were like pebbles turned continuously by the tide.

"I fear there is some mistake here, Father," he said after a moment. "I received no letter. Nor did I send any gift."

"That is impossible," said Fredegar.

Unruoching raised his narrow shoulders. "I am sorry, Father. But I cannot tell you what I do not know."

A beat of silence. Liuprand curled his lip. "There is something rotten at work here, Lord Fredegar."

Before Fredegar could reply, Unruoching rushed in to say, "Are you certain, Father, that the memory of these missives did not merely slip from your mind? Your wisdom is not as firm as it once was. Lately you have often acted . . . out of character. You are a great man still, of course, but your age shows in some matters. Is that not why you have left the managing of the household to me?"

The insult, couched within the safety of euphemism, made Agnes's breath catch. In the presence of a prince, what son could so openly question his father's fitness? The shiftiness of Unruoching's eyes took on a truly sinister quality. Agnes felt her skin prickle as she watched him.

But Fredegar did not respond with the defiant anger she expected. Instead he placed a contemplative hand under his chin.

"Well, I suppose," he mused, "all men must acknowledge the diminishment of age . . . and it is true, I am not the fit mind I once was." He raised his chin. "Your Highness, I accept responsibility for this terrible slight."

Liuprand's face showed the consternation Agnes felt, but it was the expression of the leech, Pliny, that caught her eye. His mouth was twisted into a scowl, his small, dark eyes narrowed to points. His displeasure was so blatant, it was almost as if he hoped for someone to notice. It was not becoming of a leech to show such base humanity— yet luckily for Pliny, Agnes was the only one to see it.

"That is well enough," Liuprand said at last, slowly, "but I do not think my father will so readily accept this resolution. He has been moved to great anger by your perceived treason."

Fredegar gave a grim nod. "Certainly. I understand. I pray then, tell me what I can do to heal the wounds I have wrought?"

It was Liuprand's mouth that twisted now. Bitter storm clouds gathered on his brow. As silence reigned in the great hall, Agnes thought—hoped—that he would defy his father. That he would accept

Fredegar's apology on the king's behalf and turn around, take her into the carriage, march the Dolorous Guard back through the wood, and return them all to Castle Crudele. The hope burned within her only briefly, but it was very warm and very bright. Her throat squeezed.

Yet it was a glance down at her hand that sealed Agnes's fate. Liuprand's gaze was fixed on the bandaged extremity, and his eyes darkened with desolation. He would not underestimate his father's rage again. There was still worse he could do, if his orders were disobeyed.

Finally, Liuprand spoke.

"My father proposed a match," he said. His tone was bleak, his voice coarse and low. "He wishes for you to wed the Mistress of Teeth, and thus seal your house's allegiance to the Crown."

The silence that came over the hall now was like a heavy quilt, and it smothered the flames of Agnes's hope. Smothered them quickly and without contrition. There was no protest from Fredegar; how could there be? The king had given him an order and it must be followed. It was only a matter of shaping his mind to accept the new architecture of his life, the walls that were now flowering up around him. Around Agnes. New, cruel structures, upon the apathetic foundation of the House of Blood.

She looked over at the leech again. He had schooled his expression into a blanker slate, more befitting his position—yet still his eyes burned.

"That is . . . a generous offer," Fredegar said at last. "Who am I to refuse such a profitable match with a woman of great beauty and great stature?" His gaze shifted to Agnes. It was a gentle gaze, bemused. "My bed has been empty for a very long time. Lady, I would gladly make you my wife."

XXXII
PLINY

As if a spigot had been turned, a flood of bodies washed out of the great hall. The Dolorous Guard, a tributary of gray, carried the prince and the lady Agnes along their course. Then Unruoching, whose vanishing was as quick and cold as a floe of ice borne down a fast-melting river. In mere moments, the hall was left parched and empty.

Save for Pliny and the lord of the castle. Fredegar exhaled loudly and slumped over, Pliny rushing to his side to support his master's weight.

"Thank you, Your Scrupulousness," Fredegar murmured.

Pliny frowned. A thousand and one times he had told Fredegar not to bother with such stilted formalities. He had pulled forth the man from between his mother's legs, wiped from him the plum-colored mucuses of birth, and clipped the fleshy cord with his own shears. They were long past this pomp and mummery.

"Would you like to go to your chambers, my lord?" Pliny asked.

Fredegar gave a tight nod. "Yes. We cannot discuss these matters here."

Thus began the journey to the master's chambers, which were not far but felt quite distant to Pliny, aware that the castle had been invaded by outsiders with their inscrutable agendas. These halls were as well known to Pliny as his brain's own circuitry, but with the intrusion of the prince and his retinue, they began to feel obscure, strange. The corners, where neither the sun nor the torchlight reached, seemed impenetrable with shadows.

Once they were within Fredegar's chambers, Pliny shut the door and his master went immediately over to the table, where his carafe of wine was waiting. He poured a glass, drank deeply of it, then set it down again with a burdened sigh.

"Truly it is incredible," he murmured, "how a man's stars can change within the span of a moment."

"For the worse?" Pliny asked. "Or for the better?"

Fredegar smiled with wine-stained lips. "I was hoping you would tell me."

Pliny flexed his fingers, the fingers that had pulled the master and his son from the womb, the ones that had performed a thousand desecrations at Lord Fredegar's heed, yet were still remarkably smooth and strong, unmarred by the blotches of age or the creases of a lifetime of labor. Because rarely did these efforts feel like labor when he knew he was performing them for his gentle master and for the noble House of Blood.

"I fear you do not have much choice in the matter," Pliny said at last. "But you are wise enough to know that. The king's orders cannot be refused." He paused. "I do wonder what his purpose is with this match. If still he is wary of your treachery and thinks binding you to the lady Agnes will keep you in check. Now that the Crown is allied forever with the House of Teeth." Again he paused. "But it is a profitable match, as you said. You could hardly hope for a wife of finer pedigree."

At that, Fredegar inhaled sharply. "You know the stories, don't you, Pliny? Do you think they are true?"

Once more, Pliny looked down at his hands. This time, he found them to be slightly more infirm. Tremulous and showing their age.

As remote as Castle Peake was, it could not hold all its secrets within. Rumors rolled down the mountains like mist. And for the oldest men and women on Drepane—older even than Pliny himself—with the longest-reaching memories, these were more than idle gossip.

"I do," he admitted. "No one can say for sure, of course—now that the old woman is dead. The truth may have perished with her. But . . ." He trailed off, then shook his head, as if not to be consumed too inexorably by this smog of ugly thoughts. ". . . for myself, yes, I do believe them to be true."

Fredegar was silent. He lifted his wineglass again but did not drink from it. At last, he said, "I had hoped you would say otherwise."

Pliny merely looked back at him grimly.

Fredegar sighed. "Such degenerate cruelty within Castle Peake. Old crimes and old sins. I never knew the man, the grandfather of Adele-Blanche, who perished under the blade of Berengar. But perhaps that one murder was just. I cannot fathom—to force your granddaughter, at fifteen, to bear your child."

"Children," Pliny corrected softly.

"Yes." Fredegar swirled his cup. "Children. The mothers of the princess and the lady Agnes. They were never married. Adele-Blanche rejected all suitors. I wonder, by what means were her daughters bred?"

"Adele-Blanche would have her title pass only through her female heirs." This fact, at least, was known by all, and had alone birthed some of the grisliest rumors. The conditions that might cause a woman to rule would, in the minds of men, necessarily be repugnant. "Perhaps she did not wish for her grandfather's crimes to be repeated. It is suspected—merely suspected, of course—that she used peasant men for breeding stock, as one harvests the seed of bulls to propagate their herd. Her daughters impregnated by nameless, faceless serfs. It is a clever solution, I must confess. Her line has remained unsullied, the power of her daughters and granddaughters unchallenged by male relatives."

Fredegar nodded slowly. The wine in his cup formed a small red tempest. "I do not see the stain of incest upon the lady Agnes. She is beautiful, no?"

"In a peculiar way, as a statue, or a corpse before its desecration." Pliny tried to inject his voice with humor, but his master did not smile. "But yes, my lord. She is lovely."

"I did not think I would ever be prevailed upon to marry again, after Eupraxia." Fredegar cast his gaze out the window, and Pliny wondered what he was seeing there. Eupraxia, dancing as she once had in the courtyard, pale flowers in her hair? She had been so young then, and so had he. "I have often wondered if my heart has become too scabrous and shriveled for love."

"Love and marriage have little to do with each other," Pliny said gently.

"True words. It will be enough, I think, to at last have a woman to share my bed. I have missed that these many years."

"Better still, the lady is young," Pliny agreed. "There is ample time for her to bear you many children, should you wish it."

At that, Fredegar's gaze snapped up. "And why should I wish it? I have an heir, and my heir has a son. My line is secured."

The sudden hostility in his master's voice was not unexpected, though it perturbed Pliny nonetheless. Lord Fredegar was a wise man, humane and genial. That he could have begotten a son so different in nature was a source of much philosophical musing on Pliny's part. Yet Fredegar was not inclined to suffer any slights against Unruoching, no matter how measured or subtle. The love of a father for his son was something Pliny admittedly could not, and would not, ever understand. It was greater than a love of an artist for his painting, a yeoman for his crop, a diver for his treasure. Pliny wondered if it rivaled the love he had for his own lord.

"I only meant that she is fertile, and a child is likely to be produced from your coupling," Pliny said hurriedly. "The lady herself might wish to be a mother. But I am not given to know."

"It may be difficult to ply such truths from her," said Fredegar, "if she is indeed as silent as the prince says."

Pliny was not remote enough from his humanity for that piece of knowledge to pass beneath his interest. He wondered if perhaps *that* was the stain of incest upon the lady Agnes, that perhaps her tongue did not work as it should, some consequence of ill breeding. But he did not think his master would appreciate these musings being spoken aloud, either.

"That does not trouble me," Fredegar said suddenly, as if he had decided the fact right then and there. "Eupraxia was near mute, at the end—do you remember? When sickness stole her voice. And then her breath."

"I remember," Pliny said.

Fredegar stepped away from the window and turned his back, so that his large body partially obscured the light. What little sun could leaked down around him, over his strong shoulders, in the gap between his arms and his torso, between his legs. There was his outline on the floor, a shadow man, carved out from these beams of light. This shadow man quivered, growing wispy at his edges. But the real Lord Fredegar had no such infirmity. He was like the proud hull of a ship, streaked with the white lashings of salt, yet hard-carved and pointing ever forward. If Pliny had not seen this shadow man stretched and shuddering across the floor, he would have feared nothing in the world; he would have believed his master could endure all.

But as it was, the shadow was as real as the man who cast it.

"Thank you for your counsel," Fredegar said, lifting his gaze to Pliny's. "It is wise as always. By the skillful shaping of the Surgeon's hands, I shall wed the lady Agnes tomorrow."

Pliny stepped out of his master's chamber and closed the door quietly behind him. The corridor still felt to some degree impure, tainted by the obscure agendas of strangers. The shadows were deeper with the waning sun, and the light had a waxy tinge of gray, as though it were infected. He wondered if he alone was given to sensing it, or if others could perceive this sickness within the House of Blood.

He was not very far down the corridor when another man's shadow stretched along the wall, warping and straining as he rounded the corner.

"Your Scrupulousness," Unruoching said. He bowed so low, and with such a grandiose flourish, it could not be anything but drollery. Yet Pliny had never known Unruoching to be droll. The humor was not meant for him, for Pliny, his father's leech and trusted adviser. It was meant for Unruoching alone. The corner of his narrow mouth twitched, barely resisting the grin his own jest had provoked.

"My lord," Pliny replied.

"How momentous the day has been," Unruoching said, rising to his full height. "A visit from the prince himself; who could have foreseen it? And now . . . a new wife for Lord Fredegar, after so many years of lonesome widowhood. What do you think, Pliny? Shall I call her Mother? I believe she is closer to my son's age than to mine."

"Gamelyn is just a boy," said Pliny. "The lady Agnes is a woman grown, and mistress of one of Drepane's most ancient and noble houses."

Unruoching's lips curled upward. Yet it was not what could be called a smile. "Father has warmed to this proposition, then."

"He could not refuse it, even if he wished. And it is a greatly favorable match. No man has ever suffered for having the confidence of the king."

"A pretty aphorism," Unruoching replied. "You are always so full of them. Yet not all kings are made from the same stuff."

Pliny sniffed. "You are safe to speak such words with me, my lord. But I would put these whispers away in the presence of the prince and the lady Agnes."

"The prince is clever enough to know what many nobles think of his father. *The Sluggard,* they have titled him. And he even wears this epithet with pride." His eyes, with their mottling of light and shadow, settled upon Pliny. "You are clever enough to know that my words are merely a *jest.* If you repeated them to the prince or to my father, they would surely see the humor in them. And they would also see the faithless leech who does not keep his master's secrets."

You are not my master, Pliny wished to say. It was not the House of Blood to whom his loyalty belonged. Leeches were not servants, not slaves, not vassals, not men-at-arms, not sworn swords. Their foremost faith was to their duties, and then to the Most Esteemed Surgeon himself. Pliny the leech served the articles of the Septinsular Covenant. But

Pliny the man served the wise and genial Lord Fredegar, and none other.

Yet Pliny was not so full of pride that he would risk the aggravation of his master's son. Unruoching's vengeful nature was nothing to be underestimated. As an infant, he had bitten the nipples of his wet nurse until they bled; he had raged at his mother until she wept; he had pulled the tails of the kitchen cats until they yowled. He had once cornered a dog from the butcher's slaughter-yard and tied one of its legs up against its body, then fell down laughing as it hobbled about, whimpering. This act had impressed Pliny. Until then he had thought his master's son as simple as an animal. This degree of cruelty required a human's wiles.

So he did not go about riling Unruoching now. He merely said, "I would never think to betray the House of Blood."

"Of course not." Unruoching's mottled eyes danced. "That is why I know it was a simple mistake that the king's missives were discarded under your hand."

Pliny could not help the strangled noise that leapt from his throat. "Pardon me?"

"An unfortunate error," Unruoching went on. "A mind of your years is not the most reliable. You have served this house since my own father's infancy, have you not? Age takes its toll upon a man's reasoning."

"My mind is as sharp as it has ever been," Pliny bit out. "I saw no missives."

"Precisely. They passed beneath your attention. It is understandable." Unruoching's voice took on a tone of gentleness, but it was as false as the eye on the wing of a moth. "And the matter has been settled now. But I expect, if the prince inquires further, that you will confess to your part in it."

Pliny met the gaze of his master's son. He still had the lankiness of a boy, but Pliny had thought he had left behind his boyhood's cruelties. He realized now that he had not. He had only grown cleverer at disguising them.

Pliny was not proud. But he did believe himself to be a reasonably clever man in his own right. At least, clever enough not to fall into a trap so clumsily set.

"Then I will confess it," he replied. "But it seems that perhaps the loss of these missives was a secret blessing. For now your father will have a new wife, and you a new mother, and perhaps, if the lady is fertile, a new brother."

There was a low, rough exhale from Unruoching. His eyes narrowed. "My father has no wish for more sons."

"So he has said. But perhaps his love for the lady will change his mind. She is from an immensely virtuous bloodline. It stands to reason that she would want to see her own line continued." Pliny raised his shoulders, then let them drop. "But who can know what works behind the lady's silent gaze?"

For a long moment, Unruoching did not speak. Unlike the lady Agnes, his thoughts were not well disguised. His anger burned right through his eyes.

"I will always be the eldest boy," he said at last. "My father's first son."

Pliny pressed his lips together—inclined, in that moment, to allow the silence to speak for him.

"You are old, leech," Unruoching snarled. "And so is my father. Too addled and frail to see that the world you have always known is breaking apart beneath you. The prince, of all people, understands the burden of a son not to allow his father to rule beyond his limitations. He knows it is to the detriment of all."

"Perhaps," Pliny said. And then he spoke no more.

With a wordless growl, Unruoching pushed past him. Pliny watched him go, shadow loping after him. It was a distorted beast, its limbs overlong, its fingers sharp at their ends. Even when Unruoching turned the corner and vanished, his shadow remained for several heartbeats after, stretched across the wall like a stain of wine from a shattered glass.

XXXIII
GRAY FOR GRIEF

There was a tall pendulum clock in Agnes's chambers. It was carved out of black bog-wood; indeed, it looked as though it could have been dredged intact from the peatlands outside the castle, the fossilized instrument of the ancient peoples who had inhabited the island well before the plague and well before Berengar. Their bodies often surfaced from beneath the lime-green waters, their skin dyed charcoal, their bodies scrolled and tiny like a fetus wrenched too early from the womb. Their hair was always the same gorgeous russet, no matter what shade it had been in life. And indeed, while there could be very little determined about their lives, their deaths were writ all over them. They were found with ropes around their necks, swords plunged through their desiccated chests. There were laws written into the Septinsular Covenant about how to deal with these corpses from the bog. They were too frail for desecration—half the houses would have been bereft of their inheritances, including the House of Blood—so instead their bodies were trampled under the leeches' feet, squelched into matter so small it could never be revived.

Agnes looked through the window, over the castle's gray wall, and beyond, to the marshes. Black trees rose from the shallow water like rain-slicked horses, dark but arrested in motion, as if someone had jerked the reins upward and then time had frozen. The air had grown too stiff around them, molding them into these poses. Everything was still. There was not even the ripple of a silver-backed fish.

She was overcome, suddenly, by the notion that it was beautiful. It seemed to come from outside of herself, this knowledge, as if someone had tugged her by the sleeve and whispered it into her ear, but of course it was only her mind supplying the thought. Her mind—perhaps she had grown too obscure to herself even to recognize her thoughts as her own. But she thought the stillness was beautiful, like an oil painting. Such a one that she could pass every day and be reassured that it would never change. Such a one that was lovelier than whatever scene it portrayed, because all the grueling little details—the white feces of birds on the dark branches, the brown of dying grasses, the flowers where there shouldn't be flowers—were taken away by the stroke of a dreaming artist's brush. None of life's painful mushrooms grew.

If I live here, she thought, *I will not live.* The epiphany was as beautiful as the tapestry of a hunt that had never been.

"Agnes?"

Liuprand's voice startled her. She turned toward him, away from the window.

He did not stand near to her. It would take him three strides—perhaps four—to reach her side. He stood near the pendulum clock, across the room from the large canopy bed. Behind a screen, Agnes could see the outline of a deep porcelain tub. This was the chamber of a lady, not just a passing guest. Her trunks had already been opened and their contents placed upon shelves and within wardrobes.

Liuprand knew that, and it cowed him. His gaze was on the floor.

"Lord Fredegar seems to be a gentle man," he said, after a moment of her watching him expectantly. "By all accounts, he cherished the wife who came before."

Agnes nodded.

"And he holds no ill will toward my father. He will not . . ." Liuprand raised a hand and ran it through his hair. "He will not endanger his relationship with the Crown by mistreating the Mistress of Teeth."

Again Agnes nodded. Her moth rustled in its golden cage.

"So the marriage will proceed."

The quality of stillness about the House of Blood made silence seem far more natural than speech. So while Liuprand said nothing more, and Agnes of course did not answer, the air did not stiffen; it did not crack; it did not grow oppressively hot.

It was Agnes's heart, instead, that cracked.

She moved toward him. One faltering step. There was still too much space between them—the abyss too vast for her to reach out and grasp whatever part of him she could touch. She stopped there, her footsteps soundless against the plush carpet.

The urge to move closer was so unconscious that it frightened her. It was no foreign emotion, like the sense of beauty, impressed on her by some outside force. It came up from the deepest reaches of her soul, or down from her soul's greatest heights. It surfaced from these depths like a whale, its great white head breaching the black water, or swooped down like a hawk, its wings slicing the blue sky.

Liuprand lifted his gaze to hers. She wondered if there was such a bird inside him, or such a fish. Now she would not ever know.

"I suppose," he said, "your husband will want to put his own ring on your finger."

Agnes looked down at her hand. From between the swaddling of bandages, the dark pearl gleamed. Just as soon as she had convinced herself to stop wondering about it, Liuprand had brought it to her mind again. She glanced back up at him, a question in her eyes.

He returned her stare with a bleak sort of humor. And perhaps he had learned a bit of her language, too, the language of mutes, because she was able to read this line in his eyes: *If you do not ask, you will never know.*

And so perhaps that had been the reason all along. Some ploy to draw the words from her throat. She had considered it, once, that she was nothing more than a curiosity to this prince, a strange insect trapped beneath glass, a beach stone lathed by the tide into an odd shape. But there was such devastation on his face. No man could grieve so deeply the loss of a stone.

The ring could not be removed without causing her a great deal of pain. King Nicephorus had sliced the skin of that finger right down to the bone. Waltrude had bandaged it as well as she could, but the flesh had not fully knitted back together again. It was pulpy and white, like damp paper, and when Agnes pulled back that first bandage, the pain went through her like a lancet. She had to bite down hard on her lip to stifle a gasp.

But Liuprand had known her now long enough that he would not miss this subtle indication. He frowned, the corner of his mouth trembling, as if he wanted to speak but could not work up the nerve. Instead he merely watched. Watched as she was subjected to this torment, so small in scale compared with what had wrought the wounds in the first place—though she herself was the perpetrator this time. Agnes wondered if he was thinking of how she had looked pressed to the high table, his father's knife in her hand. Liuprand looked as though he, too, was being subjected to some small-scale torment, his features held in a stricture of pain.

At long last, the ring was off. Her blood was smeared across the silver band. She had studied the engravings, written in the ancient tongue of Seraph, but she could not read them. Agnes had wanted to learn the language, once. She had hoped she might teach it to herself in the library of Castle Crudele. But then Adele-Blanche's ghost had wriggled its way into her mind like a white worm, reminding her that she had one goal in the castle and one goal only. She had no reason or no time for such frivolity, for learning a language that was long dead and had never been spoken on Drepane anyway. Such a shallow yearning it had been on Agnes's part. The desire of a child to know something merely because it was unknown.

What was her goal now? Adele-Blanche had poured so much into Agnes, but it was a spill of water into the dry-cracked earth. It was all gone and she was still as barren and dead as she had ever been. Her grandmother was expired, extinct, her blood in Fredegar's stores, her bones girding Amycus's torches, her teeth ringing Agnes's throat. And Agnes had not known, until this moment, how terribly alone she would feel when there was no ghost left to haunt her.

She reached out, stretching her arm to its limit, and dropped the ring into Liuprand's hand.

He let it sit there for a moment, a gleam of silver upon his flesh of gold. Then he closed his fingers around it. Agnes could sense their warmth even from a distance; his skin radiated pure illustrious power, like the heat from a fire. She remembered how his touch on her chin had chased the winter from her veins. The ice had frozen back over now. Nothing else had the power to melt it. She felt she would never be warm again.

"In Seraph," he said softly, "there are laws governing marriage and laws governing love. They are not one and the same. Perhaps they cannot even be reconciled with each other. But I do not know the laws. I have never touched Seraph's shores or seen the precise shade of its great lagoon. I do not think I ever will."

Agnes regarded him questioningly.

"Seraph is finished with us," he said. "With this island. It has been nothing but more bulk upon a sinking vessel."

She had suspected it, as all the great houses of Drepane had. But Agnes had not known it was so official, this severing. His marriage to Marozia was more essential than she had thought—essential to all who lived upon this sickle-shaped island, no matter if they were a peasant or a king. It was the union that would save Drepane.

It could not be violated, could not be threatened. Even the smallest fissure in its foundation would mean ruin. Agnes stepped back and let her arm drop to her side.

Liuprand squeezed tightly the hand that held her ring. And then, with his other hand, he reached into his pocket and retrieved a small scrap of parchment. It was creased very deeply, as though it had been folded and then unfolded a great number of times. He unfolded it once more so Agnes could read the words, written in her own halting, sloppy penmanship.

Thank you.

"If I accomplish nothing else in my tenure as prince, or in my reign as king, at least I will have this," Liuprand said. "I will have proof that the lady Agnes deigned to deliver two words to me."

A smile lifted the corners of her mouth; she could not help it. She could feel his warmth even from a distance now, even through the space between them, the still air that seemed to fix them in place, like carvings in a marble frieze. Agnes turned on her heel and vanished for a moment behind the screen, where her belongings had been placed. She searched among the shelves until she found parchment and ink. Then, with immense difficulty, and several false starts, she took her quill and wrote something down.

Returning to Liuprand, she held out the paper.

He took it, squinting down at the words. Her penmanship with her right hand was as clumsy as a child's. But when a smile overtook his face, Agnes knew he had been able to read it.

Now, four.

Liuprand exhaled softly. "Another great triumph to my name."

She almost laughed then, and was surprised that the urge even rose in her throat; she could not remember the last time any sound had come so close to spilling from her lips. Agnes swallowed it down, and it dissolved in her belly. But the smile remained. There was no power within her to revert it.

Liuprand folded up both papers and slipped them into his pocket. The ring he still held in his closed fist. She wondered what he would do with it. Would he clean her blood from the band? Would he toss it into a fire to be melted? Would he let it gather dust in some forgotten corner?

Agnes would never know that, either, because Liuprand left her without speaking another word. When he was gone, she went behind the screen again and sat before the table where the moth's cage had been placed. It was rustling ceaselessly inside, but she could not tell if it was from agitation, from a desire to be free, or merely from some base animal instinct. As intelligent as the creature was, she could read no emotion in its solidly black eyes. She only knew the language that Berengar had impressed upon it. Gray were its wings; gray for grief.

Agnes lifted the cage into her arms and carried it over to the window. She set it upon the ledge and then unlatched the golden door.

The moth shifted, but it did not move toward the now-open door. It simply stared ahead at the sudden gap in the bars. Some feeling she could not discern was working behind those animal eyes. Agnes did not know what she hoped for as she watched it. That it would flutter out into the hazy white air, its sudden, palpating motion despoiling the stillness, blemishing the oil painting? Or, as soon as it flitted free of its golden cage, would it freeze mid-beat of its wings, captured in an instant by the stroke of that dreaming painter? A smudge of gray that the brush's bristled end blotted once against the canvas, then dried and sealed with varnish.

Agnes could imagine it. The painting. But just as easily she could imagine its spoilage.

Yet the moth did not leave the cage. It only sat, like a cat upon its haunches, its antennae vibrating softly.

XXXIV
WITH FLOWERS IN HER HAIR

The gown had been worn to one wedding before, though it had not been her own. A very pale lilac, closer to gray than to purple, with silver stitching up the bodice and sleeves that fit tight to Agnes's thin arms. Only now her throat was not bare. The pendulum of teeth dangled between her small breasts. And now there was no golden gown, no golden princess-to-be, making her look dull and unremarkable by compare. Within the House of Blood, Lady Agnes was the only bright thing. Her gleam was softer, subtler than her cousin's, but here, where there was no sun, the moon was an object of greatest worship. With Marozia's light gone, Agnes was aware, for once in her subservient, ignorable life, she could shine.

The revelation was more poignant to her than she expected it to be, as Waltrude clasped her final button. In the long, narrow mirror, Agnes regarded herself. The mirror's gilded edges closed her in, but not like a cell. Instead they framed her, as though she were a painting. Perfectly still, as all things within this house were, the varnish giving her an opalescent sheen. Her paleness was not that of a corpse or a statue—how could she have ever been convinced of such a thing? Her skin glowed like a pearl. Her eyes were not the gray of rain-damp stone—they had depth, a light behind them! Her blue veins were glistening, like rivers under the winter starlight.

She was overcome. She had to look away from her reflection, for this realization filled her with a grief that was just as poignant as the epiphany itself. All the years piled on her like snow. Years that she had spent as a servant, dusting Marozia's skirts. Years she had spent as a reflecting pool, vaunting Marozia's beauty. Years she had spent as a cistern, being filled with Marozia's outpouring of passions.

"Are you well, my lady?" Waltrude asked.

Agnes blinked. She was shocked and horrified to find that wetness was gathering at the corners of her eyes. She looked over at Waltrude and nodded.

"Do not grieve this union, lady," Waltrude said softly. "Lord Fredegar is a good man."

But Agnes was grieving the past, not the future. Waltrude patted her gently on the shoulder and then, with one gnarled hand, adjusted the necklace around her throat. Agnes stole a glance back at the mirror. It was all perfectly arranged now. Her hair, in its braided crown, black as the ocean at night. No strands came loose to tickle or caress her cheeks. Her cheeks! There was color in them: the faintest rosy hue. Her flush had risen at last. The House of Blood had compelled it.

"Your bandages," Waltrude said suddenly. "Let me change them before the ceremony. So they are clean."

Agnes nodded again, and Waltrude vanished behind the screen to search for new cloth. Agnes turned back to the mirror.

The bride within the frame was no longer grieving. The wetness had disappeared from her eyes, yet they gleamed still, from within, as if a match had been struck in her mind. The light trickling in faintly from the window pooled in the hollows of her throat; it gathered along her cheekbones. Her shoulders were narrow, but she did not slouch. She stood with her head aloft, chin inclined.

Some rich and powerfully strange metamorphosis had occurred while she slept. A dreamless sleep it had been, matte and black, with no mists rising, no cold sweats breaking, no Celeste with the masticated babe at her breasts, no Adele-Blanche poking her hoary eel's head through the hallucinatory reeds. The weight of her grandmother's posthumous existence had lifted. Her ghost had been exorcised.

Agnes did not fully understand how it had occurred. Was it that, for the first time in her life, she had not slept with Marozia? Adele-Blanche had planted them together, twin seeds, their proximity as essential to her purposes as any elixirs or dreams. Every custom of the House of Teeth was arranged to her aims. Their lives were joined, though those lives were only preexistent deaths.

But Nicephorus had given her no time to rest before leaving for the House of Blood, no time, even, for a farewell. Even as she dressed and packed to go, Marozia had not come to her. She did not know if the king had prevented her, or if it was Marozia's own heart that kept her removed. Did it still beat with anger over her reduction in status? Or did it sense, somehow, that the distance between them had grown intractable? Marozia had a sharp-eyed vision of such things; she was brash but not a fool, and she knew Agnes best of all things in the world. Even blind and deaf, she would have perceived the treasonous splitting, the treasonous growing.

Had Agnes finally been permitted, in her cousin's absence, to bloom within that bed of dark earth? Or perhaps some great shears had been at work for a long time, sawing slowly at the rope between them, too subtle for her to notice, and it had only just now snapped. And where the grief had been, something new flowered up within her. Something so foreign she could not even name it. But it filled her, like a gulp of unwatered wine, and made the emptiness of her soul feel like a distant memory.

Waltrude returned with a new length of cloth. While she unwound the old bandages, stained rusty with blood and yellow with pus, Agnes watched her own hand. She still could not move her fingers as she wished, but they would occasionally twitch of their own volition. Looking down, she felt a prick of loss again. The absence of Liuprand's ring. Her hand seemed wrong and even more foreign to her without it.

"Does it pain you still?" Waltrude asked, her voice low.

Agnes considered the question, and found it impossible to answer. But before she could consider whether to nod or shake her head, there was a knock upon the door.

Waltrude left her hand unbandaged and went to answer it. She opened the door a crack, suspicion in the high pinching of her shoulders, and then suddenly doubled over in a deep curtsy. The wet nurse moved swiftly aside, and Lord Fredegar, Master of Blood, entered the chamber.

He was dressed in his house's favored shade of crimson. His doublet was velvet, with obsidian buttons that shone like small dark eyes. But these deep colors enriched him, rather than making him look weak and pale by compare; here was a man fit to wear the title Master of Blood. His hair was more gray than silver, like iron, and it lent him an overall steadiness, as though he had strengthened with age rather than withered. If Agnes threw herself against him, he would not even stumble. He was as sturdy as the motte and bailey of his own castle.

Yet his great stature was offset by the gentleness with which he held the object in his hands. Broad hands, darkened by the sun and only faintly stippled with age, carrying a delicate wreath of white flowers.

"My lady," Fredegar said, with a low bow. "You are beautiful."

The simplicity of his words made them feel to Agnes more sincere. The Master of Blood was not a poet or a bard; she would rather a man show himself for what he was than wear a false face. She smiled at him.

"I would not be so arrogant as to say that this will augment your beauty," said Fredegar, looking down at the wreath. "You are fairer a bride than a man like me has any right to expect. I merely thought you might wear it as a token of my affection, a symbol of my great confidence in this union. My late wife Eupraxia often wore a garland like this in her hair."

Hesitantly, with her good hand, Agnes took the wreath. It really was quite lovely, and intricately fashioned. Sprigs of infant's breath joined together fragile moonflowers, their petals still soft and scarcely crinkled, suggesting they had not been plucked from the earth more than a day ago. He must have sent a servant out to the garden last night, picking the petals of these night-blooming flowers by the shimmery light of the moon. Perhaps he had even done it himself. She imagined Fredegar, with his large, solid body, wading through evergreen shrubs and stalks of milkweed in the darkness, everything shaded in silver and black, like a charcoal sketch. She held this image in her mind, and it filled her with a fondness that made her smile grow wider.

"It is a kind and generous gift, my lord," Waltrude said. "If it please, I will put it on the lady now."

Fredegar dipped his head. "Of course. I will leave you to finish your preparations."

He departed then, leaving Agnes and Waltrude alone. Agnes ran her fingers along the velvety petals of the moonflowers, just barely grazing the frail infant's breath, not wanting to take the chance of crushing them. But her hand—her good hand, at least—seemed capable of such gentleness. She was no longer a child, clumsily squashing insects in her fist. She would not spoil every delicate thing in her grasp.

After Agnes nodded her approval, Waltrude took the crown of flowers from her. Agnes bent down so that it could be placed upon her head. And Waltrude did so quite solicitously, careful not to ruin the flowers, and careful not to tug too hard on Agnes's hair. She wove the flowers into Agnes's braid until it almost looked as though they were blooming right from her skull, as if her hair was the earth itself, darkened with rain and made rich and fertile for seeds.

When it had all been arranged, Agnes stood. Waltrude's fingers danced around her face, tucking back any errant strands of hair, smoothing the soft black fuzz at the nape of her neck. Waltrude had now known her long enough that she could read Agnes's face—what little she offered the world with her expressions, the subtlest shifts of her mouth and eyes and brow. And so perhaps she could read the emotion of her countenance before Agnes even found a name for it herself. It was a lucent feeling, softly bright, like morning dew on a daffodil, the dawning sun gathered on those drops of moisture and making them shine.

It was an emotion so foreign to Agnes that her mind stammered and tripped over the word. It was the opposite of hunger, the yawning pit in her stomach, the scraping of bone against bone. There could be no such harsh ugliness when this other emotion existed within her, all around her. This thing of nascent, glowing beauty, this hope.

Agnes saw the great hall through the mesh of her bridal veil. The veil was thick; Waltrude held her by the arm and led her down the aisle and to the dais. Given the hurried, almost clandestine nature of their betrothal, there had not been time to marshal up guests to fill the seats. The other great houses would hear about it through missives and messengers. The joining of the House of Teeth with the House of Blood. They would hear that Adele-Blanche's strange, silent granddaughter had finally been taken to wife.

The seats were occupied by several members of Fredegar's household, some names Agnes had not yet learned, but faces that would soon be familiar to her when she was the mistress of this house. In the front row there was Unruoching, his brow dark with simmering storm clouds, his eyes narrowed to knifepoints. Curiously, he did not wear the colors of his house; instead he wore a doublet of powdery black, like ash in a cold hearth. At his side was a young and rather beautiful woman, striking mostly for the bright, fox-red color of her hair. It shone in the torchlight, fire to her husband's cinders. Agnes knew she had seen this precise shade of red before, though she could not place where.

At the woman's other side was a boy—old enough to begin training in the yard, but not old enough to use real steel in the place of wood. His hair was a coppery color, darker than his mother's and richer, as if it had settled somewhere between the hues of his parents. His eyes were darting all over the great room—more, Agnes suspected, out of childish boredom than true curiosity. But when they landed upon her, they lingered there, his brows arching upward. Momentarily, she had cured his boredom, or perhaps sated his curiosity. He had the noble, appealing features of his grandfather; there was nothing within him of Unruoching that Agnes could see. She looked away from the boy.

On the other side of the aisle, sat alone, was Liuprand.

It was a futile effort to try not to stare at him. Even in his doublet of grayish blue—a curiously diminished color; she had never seen him wear such a shade, and it did not suit him—he was still the brightest thing in the room, his puissant aura radiating from him like heat from sun-warmed stones. Liuprand the Golden. Thinking those words choked her. Her throat constricted and she faltered, just one small stumbling, perhaps not noticeable to anyone but Waltrude, who tightened her grip on Agnes's arm.

Yet Liuprand noticed. He always did. He always had. When she had still been a wilting flower, a statue-girl, the ghost to Marozia's warm body. Now she saw him tense, the muscles rippling beneath his doublet, as if he was restraining himself from rising to his feet.

A thought skipped over her like a flat rock across the water. *I wish he would.* So quickly had the words come to her mind that Agnes flushed with shame.

She shoved them down and yet—steps away from the dais where her true husband waited—more treasonous words rose within her.

Stand. It was almost beseeching, a silent plea. *Stand and stop this.*

The vision even played out, in front of her eyes. Liuprand rising in a ripple of gray-blue and dark gold, his powerful form planted between Agnes and the dais where she would be wed. The vision did not merely layer over the real world like a thin onionskin paper; it replaced the real world entirely. It was clearer and sharper than any memory; it was like a waking dream.

But this was Marozia's husband and Drepane's golden prince, and she was promised to another. Agnes had never been one to allow herself impossible dreams. So she blinked furiously, and the vision was cleared away, like a hand wiping condensation from glass.

Yet ahead upon the dais was another future she had never allowed herself to imagine. A husband, kind and noble. A life that was not lived in Marozia's shadow. Days that were not spent breathing in treasonous smoke. Nights that were not stitched through with noisome, pestilent dreams. No more shadows rippling like fetid water at the edges of her vision. Adele-Blanche's posthumous existence, banished as if by a prophet's incantation.

As Agnes stepped onto the dais, she joined Lord Fredegar and his leech in their still-life portrait. She felt the air go stiff around her, freezing her in place. She felt the boar bristles of the artist's brush. She felt the cool coat of varnish, both holding her in timeless suspension and making her gleam. It was the perfect scene for a painting: bride and bridegroom mounted high above their guests and arranged neatly, facing each other, the leech in his sepia robes a bridge between them. The flowers planted in Agnes's hair would never blow, for the wind was absent in this sacred place, and they would never rot, and never grow.

She could not help but wonder if Liuprand managed to see it: the beauty of the world when all its ceaseless motion was, for a moment, arrested. But Agnes could not bring herself to look at him. She did not trust her mind not to dream.

Instead she looked at Lord Fredegar, through her veil, and smiled. He looked back at her in surprise, then pleasure. For a bride to smile on her wedding day was a rare thing.

The leech, Pliny, began to speak.

"This noble lord, Fredegar, Master of Blood, and the lady Agnes, Mistress of Teeth, have gathered here today to be wed." He had a high and clear voice, as if age had not shriveled his vocal cords or wizened his lungs. "We call upon the hands of the Surgeon to anoint their union. If anyone in attendance has cause to protest it, let them speak now or hereafter hold their tongue."

No sound spoiled the air. The stillness had caught them all, like flies drowned in honey. Agnes could not have shifted her gaze from Fredegar even if she wanted to.

"Then I endlessly seal these two in lawful union. This binding is absolute and can be broken only by the cruel artifice of death."

The ring that Fredegar produced was a thick band of gold set with a smooth black stone. Agnes had no name for such a stone, but it drew in the torchlight and glittered, iridescent like the shell of a beetle. Fredegar did not comment on the state of her hand as he drew it toward him; he merely frowned, perturbed, and slid the ring on with great gentleness. Agnes was aware of the pain as the metal scraped her tender, unhealed flesh, but it was a disembodied awareness, known rather than felt. Such a vulgar and common thing as *pain* could not exist in this moment, on this idealistic artist's canvas, in this house where even blood stood still.

A few more words from the leech and the ritual was done. Hand in hand, Agnes and Fredegar turned toward the small crowd of guests. There was Waltrude, who watched with her canny green gaze but did not show any sentiment, pleasure or otherwise. There were the members of Fredegar's house, whose names Agnes was keen to learn. There was Unruoching's son, who looked eager to be done, his leg jiggling with anxiety. His mother had an arm braced around him, as if to fix him in place, her long red hair tumbling over her breast. And then there was Unruoching himself, whose lip was pulled back into a silent grimace, who nearly shattered the stillness of the room with such brusque and obvious disgruntlement. He must yet mourn his mother, Agnes thought. Or perhaps, petulantly, he mourned the loss of his father's attentions.

And then there was Liuprand. At last Agnes turned to him. His marine-blue eyes were more cloudy than clear, as if a heavy fog had overtaken their waters. But Agnes saw the fog for what it was, as she had those same mists within herself. It was a dream, sepulchral and deep, impossible to realize but just as impossible to disillusion.

What a perilous thing to do now, to dream. Agnes broke their gaze and allowed Fredegar to lead her off the dais and away, into the feasting hall.

So few guests were in attendance that there was room for all at the head table. Fredegar sat in the center, of course, with Agnes at his left. But Liuprand was a prince, and so he was sat in a place of great honor, next to the bride. Even with such a small number of attendants, the fit around the table was tight. Liuprand was close enough that their arms nearly brushed as they sat. Nearly. There was still an abyss between them that might as well have been the breadth of the ocean.

On Fredegar's right was Unruoching, and then Unruoching's wife, whose name, Agnes had learned, was Ygraine. She fussed over her son—the boy Gamelyn—smoothing his hair back from his face, cutting his meat for him, even arranging the bites on his plate. Agnes saw that he took little heed of his mother's attentions. He was as restless as he had been during the ceremony. Here was a boy whose mind was in the tiltyard, whose fingers ached to hold a sword. His grandfather was in him, Agnes thought. The lanky arms and legs of youth would grow into limbs as sturdy as an oak's. His restlessness at the banquet table would serve him well in his battle.

Agnes would come to know him well, she realized. She would be witness to all of this blooming. The House of Blood was her house now.

This epiphany was a simple and obvious one, childish almost, but it filled her with a frantic sort of joy. In this house, Adele-Blanche's ghost did not dare tread. The artist would never paint such a gruesome event as death. And so Agnes's good hand moved to the platter of roast boar in front of her. She speared a piece with her knife. A dark spurt of oily blood welled up around the blade.

She lifted the meat to her mouth and ate it. For the first time since Adele-Blanche had torn her infant brother's limbs asunder, Agnes tasted the flesh of another creature. Rich, steaming, the half-burnt skin crackling on her tongue, her teeth tearing through the rubbery ring of fat. They felt soft and dull, her teeth, but as she worked the meat in her mouth, one tentative chew at a time, they seemed to sharpen within moments, as if whetted against a stone. This was their very purpose, and they had been deprived of it for so long, like a soldier starved of fight, a monk forbidden from prayer.

It tasted of gristle and salt, flavors foreign to her, so when Agnes swallowed she half expected the meat to come immediately back up and choke her. She would have been humiliated to spit up the masticated food onto her plate. But she need not have feared this; it was her throat's purpose, too, to swallow. Her stomach welcomed the boar's meat as a parched tongue welcomes water.

Water, she thought. And then—no. Wine. She reached for the carafe on the table.

She became suddenly aware that Liuprand was watching her closely. He spoke no words, but his gaze was steady, unblinking. She poured the wine, that gleaming, ruby-hued elixir so long forbidden to her, and then swirled it in her cup until the sediment was distributed evenly, until it was absorbed into the liquid. Then she raised the brimming cup to her lips and drank.

Her first swallow was sweet, her second bitter, then her third sweet again. With each sip, Adele-Blanche's ghost screamed and rioted; it rattled the cold manacles of death. But the chains were adamant and could not be broken. And Agnes closed the dungeon door in her mind, and then she walked away down the long gray corridor, until her grandmother's delirious, phantasmal protests were lost with distance.

The ball and chain broke from her own ankle. The corridor broadened, and the walls themselves fell away. Agnes walked farther, and then she was free.

And somehow Liuprand had seen it all, had seen the prison in her mind, the chains, the smothered screams of the ghost. She knew he had seen it because where there had been grief in his gaze, there was now a soft varnish of joy. She did not know how he saw these workings inside her, or how she could perceive this knowing from him, but Agnes was sure, as sure as a seasoned warrior's blow, that the walls of her cell were shattered. And the felicity of her freedom was Liuprand's felicity, too.

He nudged a platter of soft cheese drizzled with honey. "Here," he said. "Try this."

She did. The rest of the table was oblivious to the ecstasy of her feasting; they did not know this was an ascetic's first indulgence, her first brush with the sumptuous pleasures of the world. She shared this euphoric moment only with Liuprand. His golden aura touched her, and her rapture touched him, even if their bodies were still separated by that unbreachable chasm.

This bliss was interrupted by the sound of a scraping chair. Fredegar's leech, Pliny, stood, holding his cup of wine aloft.

"If you will permit a few words from a humble leech," he said, "then I would offer my most redoubtable and sincere congratulations to my lord and his lady wife. May their marriage be joyous, and their union be fruitful."

There were scattered murmurs of agreement from the table, and Fredegar nodded at his leech and smiled fondly. But there was one face among them that did not smile, one mouth that did not utter a glad word. It was Unruoching, sat beside his father, who twisted his lips into a scowl and did not speak.

This was exceptionally untoward, beyond what most men would tolerate, but Fredegar did not appear even to notice. He was looking at Pliny with a misty gaze, deeply moved by the leech's words. The love between the two of them was clear. It was beyond the love of a servant for his master; it seemed to Agnes a true and equal affection, one of friend to friend. She had seen a similar fondness between Liuprand and Waltrude—a love so bold and lasting that it had stretched to encompass Agnes as well. She was happy to know that, even when Liuprand was gone from the House of Blood, this enduring love would keep Waltrude at her side.

Unruoching took a long sip from his wine and then set the glass down with much greater force than necessary, making the dinnerware on the table all clatter and tremble.

"Are you well, my son?" Fredegar asked. There was no ire or provocation in the question; he was sincere in his concern.

Unruoching lifted his eyes. They were lidded, their color endlessly shifting, and there was a slight sheen on his face that made Agnes wonder if he was too deep into his wine. After a long moment, he said, "I feel a bit fatigued. From all the excitement of the day. It is best if I retire early."

"Yes, do not tire yourself needlessly," Fredegar said. "Sleep well, and return hale tomorrow."

"I will, Father," Unruoching said, and the words came out of him strained, as if his tongue were too thick in his mouth. He was wine-weary, Agnes decided. She had not been paying too close attention over the course of the meal, but he had drained that last glass so quickly.

Unruoching rose from his seat. "Good night, all. My prince. Lady Agnes." He nodded to each of them in turn, but his gaze lingered on Agnes for an uncomfortable beat. "What a joyous thing, to welcome such an esteemed lady to this house."

Yet his tone held no joy at all. Agnes could well imagine why he would not be pleased with this union. If a child were to be produced, it might threaten his status as his father's heir, though the obvious love Fredegar held for his son made Agnes doubt very much that this would come to pass. Still, he had reason to be wary of her, not least because she was Adele-Blanche's blood.

Yet curiously, when he spoke to Liuprand, his voice filled with reverence.

"It has been an honor to host you, my good prince," Unruoching said, eyes glittering beetle-bright. "I hope that with this union, you will look even more favorably upon the House of Blood, both now and in the future. As my father's heir, I promise to serve you most loyally."

So cloying were the words that Agnes felt compelled to look down the table for the reactions of the other guests. She did not understand Unruoching's grasping plaudits. Surely he should resent Liuprand, the architect of this union, of his new, more precarious life.

Fredegar regarded his son, as he always did, with a father's uncomplicated affection. Liuprand appeared unnerved, but it was so subtle that only Agnes, who knew him well, would notice that faint furrow in his brow, the slight narrowing of his eyes. Yet it was Pliny whose expression captured her attention. His displeasure was not subtle. He stared up at Unruoching with immense chagrin on his wizened, rather jowly face.

"Your loyalty is most welcome," Liuprand said. "Good night, Lord Unruoching."

"Good night, my prince."

And then, with a deep bow, Unruoching was gone. His footsteps were hurried, and their sound was lost quickly to distance. There was only a short beat of silence before Fredegar clapped his hands together and said amiably, "Please, do not cease the festivities on my son's account. A man of my age must make the most of every moment of gaiety."

There was scattered laughter, genuine and jubilant. Dinnerware clinked; wine was imbibed once more. Conversations resumed. Agnes could not help but let her gaze linger on her husband, this broad, gentle creature beside her. His walls, the solid, still walls of the House of Blood, were flowering up around her as the bars of her prison flaked away with rust and crumbled.

It took her several moments to notice that Liuprand was watching her. She turned to him, the fond smile for Fredegar still on her face.

"You will be happy with him," Liuprand said. And his own smile was fond, too, though it did not touch his limpid blue eyes.

Agnes nodded.

Liuprand drew a breath. A swallow ticked in his throat, that great muscle flexing. And then he rose to his feet, wine cup aloft in his hand. His ascent immediately quieted the table, all heads turning toward their golden prince.

"A toast," Liuprand said. "To the health and happiness of Lord Fredegar and Lady Agnes. May their lives be long, and their love be eternal."

XXXV
THE MUTE TONGUE MOVES

The torches were burning low by the time the feast was done, when all bellies were filled near to bursting, all cheeks flushed with wine. The fullness in Agnes's belly made her body feel alien to her, but it was not unpleasant at all; she had merely pared away the aching, banished the vestiges of pain from her mangled hand. What remained was the essence of a real girl, red-blooded, warm-skinned, sated, even happy. A bride. A wife.

As the servants cleared away the plates, Fredegar reached out and took her undamaged hand, lacing their fingers together. She felt no prickle of heat, no shivering of anticipation, but she did feel his softness and steadiness, his uncalloused palms. Hand in hand, they rose from the table.

There were no words passed between them as Fredegar began to lead her from the chamber. Agnes had not thought she would look back, but some force deep within her soul compelled her. She glanced briefly over her shoulder, gaze skimming over Waltrude, whose eyes were narrowed with unease, and Pliny, whose face was open, at peace. And then Liuprand.

He watched her, and suddenly Agnes was hurled back into a memory. It was the memory of their first meeting, Adele-Blanche's body being squelched into the dirt, Marozia smiling hopefully, exuding her charms. He had regarded her quizzically then, already bemused by her silence. Then he had turned to go, leaving Agnes overcome by his obvious beauty, his golden aura, as if she had encountered the sun itself.

This time, it was Agnes who turned away from him. His beauty still burned behind her eyes. But so did his final words, whispering through her mind.

You will be happy with him.

And she knew that she would. She did not look back again as Fredegar guided her into the corridor.

Now that they were alone for the first time, Agnes felt a brisk flush of shyness. They paced on for a few moments in silence before Fredegar halted and turned to her.

"I must thank you, my lady," he said, "for humoring me by wearing these flowers. They suit you as well as they did Eupraxia."

Eupraxia, the mistress who had come before. There was a faint tinge of grief in Fredegar's voice, but it did not shame Agnes, did not make her envious of the dead woman or fear that her husband was overly loyal to a ghost. It only made her feel safe in the knowledge that Lord Fredegar, Master of Blood, was such a man to honor his wives, even when they were gone from the world. Agnes would not be misused.

"She was mute, too, for a long time," Fredegar said suddenly. "The sickness closed her throat and burned it raw. So for many months she did not speak. But it did not trouble me. I loved her without the ornamentation of words. I must confess I have never been an eloquent man, not like our prince." He paused and let his gaze rest upon her poignantly. "So your silence will never trouble me, lady. If you wish someday to speak, I would be pleased. But if you do not, it will not gall me. Our union will not be strained or burdened by it."

A great swell of emotion gathered in Agnes's throat. There were no words for it, even if she had wished for them. Instead she merely smiled and felt the corners of her eyes grow warm with water.

Fredegar smiled back. Then he raised her hand to his mouth and very gently kissed it.

"Come then," he said in a low voice. "Let us rejoice privately the joys of the day."

They walked together down the corridor, their pace unhurried. The walls of stone were solid around them, adorned with little more than torches and the occasional tapestry, simple yet undeniably lovely. It was warm in those orange pools of torchlight. And as always, it was very, very still.

As they turned a corner, one long shadow stretched across the floor in front of them. A narrow shadow, rheumy at its edges, the shape of a wiry and slender-limbed man. Unruoching.

"My son," Fredegar said in surprise. "I thought you had retired for the night."

"I had," said Unruoching. "Yet as I lay in bed, sleep could not find me. I was plagued by the grimmest of thoughts."

Fredegar frowned. "What such thoughts?"

Unruoching took a step toward them. Agnes was perturbed by his assurance, his graceful prowl. As he had left the great hall she had seen him too deep into his wine, tired and ungainly. But there was no clumsiness to his stride, no muddled quality to his eyes. They were clear and sharp in their kaleidoscopic color. And when he stood before his father, he did not slouch or quake.

"To speak truthfully," he murmured, "I have been plagued by these dark thoughts for quite some time. I have seen you grow infirm and less than wise in your age, Father. Yet you persist in ruling this house as you once did. You have even taken an unsuitably young woman to wife. I fear you do not see your own deficiencies. I fear it will be the ruin of the House of Blood."

Fredegar blinked in bewilderment. "How long have you harbored such concerns? You have not spoken honestly to me; you have shown a false face. Yet I swear I will hear you, at another time. These are matters for the council chamber, not for my wedding night, not in the presence of the lady."

"Ah," Unruoching said, with a cluck of his tongue, "but the lady is precisely the audience I desire."

"Why?" Fredegar stiffened, standing up straight and shifting slightly so that Agnes was now behind him, shielded by his broad body. "Speak plainly now, Unruoching."

A very faint smile toyed at the corner of Unruoching's mouth, but it was humorless, and it was even cruel.

"I cannot allow a child born of your union to usurp my place as heir," he said. "And *now* I shall speak plainly indeed—the time of Lord Fredegar is over."

His next motion was so quick, Fredegar could not even gutter out a noise of shock. Unruoching's hand went to his belt and unsheathed a dagger. There was the sharp glint of metal in the torchlight. It gashed the air and then, fast as it had been drawn, it was buried in his father's chest.

Fredegar did not raise an arm to defend himself. He merely looked at Unruoching, confusion and sorrow clouding his gaze, and then down at the wound, which was curiously bloodless, and perhaps even more horrific for that fact. The stillness of the air now seemed perverse.

But then the knife was drawn out, and all that was still in the air became frenzied and mad.

Blood spurted from the deep gash; it splattered on the front of Agnes's dress, her face. Her mouth was open in shock and she even tasted it, oily on her tongue. But this was not the end. Unruoching drove the blade again, deep into Fredegar's stomach, and here blood came more dramatically, a torrent that could not be quenched, closer to black than to red. The wound was long, and something slippery showed through—his intestines? They spilled out and piled on the floor.

Astonishingly, Fredegar stood. A corpse with a still-beating heart. He turned, wobbling, to face Agnes, something childlike in his expression. In death all men became children again, for it was something that no human could truly comprehend.

Then his knees began at last to quiver, and he reached up, grasping at Agnes for purchase, to keep himself upright. He found it on her necklace of teeth, but it broke easily in his scrabbling fingers. The chain snapped. The teeth went scattering all over the floor.

Unruoching reached around his father's shoulder and made one last cut. Fredegar's throat opened under his blade. The blood was like a geyser, and Agnes was drenched in it.

And then, at last, he fell.

Agnes looked down at her husband, crumpled in a heap on the floor. Blood poured out, stretching in all directions, like shadows lengthening as the sun cached away its light. It lapped at the hem of her dress, over her slippers, a dark and slimy tide. The life went out from him. His eyes were like smoked glass, matte and opaque, nothing to be seen behind them. He did not even moan or otherwise protest his exit from the earth. It had all been too quick.

Slowly Agnes lifted her gaze to meet Unruoching's. He stood as still as his father lay there at his feet, his face blanched like naked bone. The fury was all in his eyes; they were wet, and whetted, and sharp. And he breathed heavily, shoulders rising and falling, like a man in the throes of finding his pleasure, moments before the crest of climax. The dagger was held limply in his hand.

Blood soaked her shoes, and something else died in that corridor. The beautiful, immortally frozen canvas, the work of art she had imagined her new life to be, was torn up, ripped from its frame and shredded into irretrievable pieces. Set alight, then stamped into ash. And that bauble of light, the gleaming object of loveliness that Agnes had polished within herself, that shattered, too. Hope misted out of it, like perfume from a broken bottle, and then was dissolved into the air.

With trembling fingers, Unruoching raised the blade.

And Agnes screamed.

It was at first a wordless shriek, high and thin, and it burned as if her throat were blazed through with fire. The agony was beyond what she could have imagined, the dredging of her voice, at last, from its cold tomb within her. It was so loud and so sudden that the knife fell from Unruoching's hand and clattered to the ground, shock making him stumble back.

She screamed and screamed. It turned into a broken and bitter howl. Gray moths rose from her and took flight, their wings beating a thousand furious beats. Terror lifted in a palpating scarlet mass. The corridor was glutted, the air was thick; Unruoching shrank down then, arms braced over his head, as if to shield himself from the fluttering legions of grief, of fear, and to muffle the terrible, animal sound of her howling.

Agnes chose these screams just as she had chosen her silence. Her silence broke apart, like ice in an avalanche. She screamed Liuprand's name.

The hallway thundered with footsteps. Armor clashed as the Dolorous Guard rounded the corner, and metal hissed as they drew their swords. Agnes saw no more than flashes of steel, metal-plated limbs whirling about her, forming a circle that pressed her within.

She dropped to the floor then, exhausted by the agony of such vicious wailing. She knelt in the puddle of blood, her legs and arms boneless, as weak as jellied broth. Tears ran scorching paths down her cheeks. What rose was not a scream but a sob, wretched and guttural, mucus clogging her throat and half obstructing the sound.

Agnes bent over, and then she could not keep herself aloft at all. She collapsed upon Fredegar's chest. Her cheek was pressed to his doublet, the velvet turned sticky with blood, dyed a darker and richer red. She clung to him like a child. Her sobs ran through her; her whole body convulsed with them, as though she were being tossed and tossed again by a vicious current.

There was so much of this hideous red liquid. It sank into the floorboards, into the stone, absorbed into the very foundation of the castle. She imagined the walls woozy with blood, bloated, swaying like a drunkard. She imagined the castle itself, falling.

And then, through the clashing of metal and the furor of her own sobs, Liuprand's voice cleaved like a sword.

"Make a path," he said.

Armor clattered as the Dolorous Guard stepped aside. Liuprand knelt down; she heard the sloshing of disturbed blood as he did. He slid his arms under her, gently, one beneath her shoulders and the other beneath the crook of her knees. She clutched at Fredegar's doublet, but her fingers were too weak to keep hold. So when Liuprand rose to his feet again, he lifted Agnes with him.

Tears had turned her vision into something like rain-streaked glass. She pressed her face into Liuprand's shoulder and sobbed.

"Take him to the dungeon," Liuprand said. His voice was as black as midnight. "Clap him in as many chains as you can find. Tie the rope tight."

Helmets clanged; the Dolorous Guard were nodding in collective assent. Agnes heard Unruoching babbling incoherently, more gasps than words, as the guards closed in on him. She squeezed her eyes shut as the very last of her sobs drained out of her. Her tears had soaked into Liuprand's doublet, turning the fabric soft with water. She clung to his chest, the fingers of her good hand clenched so fiercely that her nails scraped and broke his flesh.

There was nothing but darkness behind her eyes, limpid and gauzy. She felt Liuprand turn. Away from the thick brine of the shuddering air, the blood besmirching the floor and the feet of all those who stood upon it, and Fredegar's body, already growing stiff and cold, gripped by the cruel rictus of death. Her sobs had quieted to small whimpers, her mouth full of spittle and salt, but she was not silent. It was Liuprand who held her without speaking, his grip both firm and tender, and carried her down the corridor, until the smells and sounds of the carnage behind them were lost to distance.

The water folded over and under her limbs, soft as skeins of silk. It rose up, brimming like the tide, covering her breasts, leaving only her collarbones and her shoulders exposed. Without the time to heat it above a fire, the water was cold, cold but clear, pooling with the golden torchlight.

Until the blood poisoned it. The solid crust of red was scoured from her body, turning to a thin mist as the water lifted it and spread it about within the tub. Now the water was hot and thick and smelled of copper, of brine. It was red, and red, and red. Though her skin was clean, all around her, Fredegar's blood pulsed and rippled. It was diluted, translucent as the tail of a fish, but not gone. It engulfed her still.

"It will all go down the drain," Waltrude murmured. "Down the drain. Down the drain."

She could not stop repeating this phrase, as she combed her fingers through Agnes's hair. The pins were pried out. The braids were undone. Her hair, now loose, floated around her, buoyant in the water, like the dark tendrils of a squid.

The flowers were scattered on the floor. The white moonflowers, the infant's breath, splattered with blood and crushed like paper as she had buried her head against Fredegar's chest. His body had still been warm, his flesh soft. It was impossible that he could be gone. But the House of Blood had taken what it was owed from its very own master. The foundation was soaked with it and the articles of the Covenant had been fulfilled, Berengar's cruel laws followed to the letter. And so it had to be true.

Waltrude lifted Agnes's arm a moment from the water and scrubbed at it, expunging the blood from the clever places it had hidden, between her fingers, in the crook of her elbow. One arm and then the other. Her limbs felt heavy and foreign to her. *She* was not dead, but her body did not seem to know it.

"There's a good girl." Waltrude's voice was so soft and low, it was almost a coo. "In a moment it will all go down the drain."

Agnes found she could not close her eyes, though her body was limp in the water, unwound and as tranquil as a bird briefly stunned by its collision into glass. Instead she stared ahead, taking in the screen of the chamber, the writing desk, the stone wall and the unlit fireplace, her belongings still scattered about, placed on shelves; the wardrobe door was open and her dresses were hung within, all but the bridal gown, which was puddled on the floor, soaked in red like a gored pig.

The sensation that it was ugly washed over her. All the beauty of the House of Blood had drained out with the lifeblood of its master.

What remained was a gruesome and shuddery dream, a scene set on the dark floor of the ocean, scattered about with huge-jawed fish and quivering purple kelp, curled mollusks the size of men, crabs so bulbous with barnacles that they could not lift their claws, sanguine-colored sharks that had never felt even the feeblest slant of sunlight.

Waltrude lifted Agnes's hair and gently scrubbed the back of her neck. She whispered, but not to Agnes, "Down the drain. Down the drain."

There was a sound outside the door. Waltrude's gaze snapped up and she let Agnes's hair fall and spread out again in the water.

It was the scuffling of footsteps, the faint clanking of armor as the guards posted outside the door stirred. There was the murmur of voices, but it was too quiet for any words to be discerned. Then, slowly, the door opened.

Waltrude rose to her feet, sponge clenched in her fist. A fearful but defiant expression crossed her face. But it dissipated at once, upon her seeing Liuprand.

The wet nurse did not speak, did not even acknowledge his presence with a deferent dip of her head. Yet her eyes had the steadiness of secret knowledge. At a distance, in the half-light, Agnes could not easily perceive the expression on Liuprand's face. She only saw the soft golden gleam of him, which repelled the dark. It spasmed off him, like arrows deflected from a steel breastplate, and these weapons of shadow fell dully onto the floor.

As he stepped toward her, toward the tub, she saw the blood staining his doublet. It had dried into a deep shade of rust. Some of it flecked his throat, his chin. There was even a streak along the left side of his jaw, where one of her dyed-red fingers must have brushed. He wore her husband's blood on him like a second layer of livery.

Waltrude stood for one moment longer, the damp sponge dripping in a steady rhythm. Then, without speaking a word, she crossed the room and went out through the door. There was more faint clanking as the retinue of guards broke apart to let her pass.

Then Liuprand stood before her at the foot of the tub, alone.

"Unruoching has been imprisoned," he said quietly. "He will never again breathe free air." He paused, and his eyes gleamed like the moonlit ocean. "He will never so much as look upon you again."

"Yet he will live always within my thoughts," Agnes said.

The shock that overtook Liuprand's face was not fast and bright, a sudden and short-lived flicker, but rather a slow burning—embers, not flame. His aura smoldered a darker gold. And it was her voice that set this fire within him.

So delicately, almost painful in his deliberation, Liuprand stepped toward her. He knelt beside the tub, near where her head rested against the marble.

"I would give my life," he said, "to turn it back. To have the knife buried in my chest instead."

"No." The word lifted from her like a pale moth, taking flight. "I would never wish for such a thing. This I may survive. But not that."

Liuprand drew a breath. "Agnes," he whispered. "I cannot exorcise you from my mind. I have tried—but I think of you always. In sleeping, in waking, and especially in dreaming."

She looked upon him. His beauty was immeasurable. It could break a thousand hearts down their center. But she saw beyond that, beneath it, as one can glimpse the wondrous creatures of the sea below the surface of clear and sunlit waters.

Her friend, who had seen her when no other had cared to look. Who had urged her to speak when the rest had ignored or rejoiced in her silence. Who had taught her the language of rustling wings. Her protector, who had aided her in so many ways she could only recognize now. Who had sent the girl Ninian, so she did not have to labor any longer at Marozia's feet. Who had ordered Waltrude to bandage her wounds and keep the leeches and their hungry mouths from her door. Who had tried, even, to stand between her and the king.

The water rippled, and she saw still more. She saw the man who read with her in quiet companionship, Liuprand the Scholar. She saw the man who spoke with such eloquence always, wise beyond his years, Liuprand the Silver-Tongued. She saw the man who was gentle to all his subjects, even to those far beneath him, Liuprand the Good. And she saw, of course, the man who had entered a bleak and loveless union for the security of his kingdom. Liuprand the Confessor.

Her companion, her guardian, and her beloved, who had hoped and waited for her in anguished silence.

Agnes lifted a hand from the water and touched his chin with just one finger. Warmth flowed into her skin.

"Liuprand," she said softly.

He exhaled, a tremulous sound. With both hands he clung to the edge of the tub, knuckles white.

"Say it again," he whispered.

"Liuprand." She brushed her thumb over his bottom lip. "Liuprand. Liuprand—"

He grasped her around the shoulders, pulling her into his chest. Then he lifted her from the tub. Water streamed down her naked body; she rose from it, like a naiad cresting the waves. One of his arms braced around her hip, the other around the backs of her thighs, holding her so that their eyes were level. Her own chest heaved against his. Her breaths were shallow and her blood was hot.

He kissed her, fiercely, desperately, without contrition. Her fingers scrabbled for a moment then found purchase in his hair, the golden hair that was somehow softer than she had imagined it would be—and she had imagined it, imagined this, in flashes of shameful desire that made her skin prickle and her stomach twist with longing.

Yet she had never dared to imagine this: his lips trailing along her jaw, down her throat, as her head fell back and stars clustered behind her eyes. She felt fragile in his arms, but there was no fear in that. If anything she felt a surging of relief, the knowledge that she *could* fall apart, and he would hold her and not let her break. He would hold even the broken pieces of her, she knew. This epiphany was so powerful that it encompassed her soul itself, and her whole body ached with love for him.

Liuprand carried her across the room with great ease and then laid her down gently upon the bed. She was bare before him, long, damp hair spreading out across the coverlet.

Even the reaching shadows could not disguise them: her scars. His gaze ran over the raised white lines, from the words inscribed across her rib cage to the etched flowers on her stomach, down to the instruction, the warning that spoiled and defaced her mound. She would not have been surprised to see his face twist in disgust.

Yet no repulsed grimace ever came. His eyes only gleamed, both dark and luminous at once, that night-ocean blue.

"You are more beautiful than even my imagination could conjure," he said at last.

"*You* imagined this?" she asked.

"Yes." The word was so low, so deep in his throat, it was almost a growl. "And this."

Then he surged forward, onto the bed, his lips on her lips and his arms sliding under her still-wet body. When he pressed against her, it made his clothes wet, too, and it made the blood look new again, but she did not care—she could not care about anything, not when his mouth trailed down her throat and found her breast.

Agnes was barely able to stifle a moan; it hardly even occurred to her that she should. She knew the guards were posted at the door and that they might hear, but Liuprand was reckless with his desire and all her reason was undone by his mouth. His tongue worked her nipple gently, and the pulse of longing between her legs was so powerful it was almost painful, and she wanted to tell him, to beg him to attend to that part of her, too.

She did not have to. His mouth left her breast, swollen now, and laved its way down her stomach, over her scars, which flared like signal fires at his touch.

He kissed her center just as he had kissed her lips, his tongue caressing her, his teeth grazing that hard nub that made her gasp and arch into him. Her fingers tangled in his hair, urging him closer, yet his palm pressed flat against her stomach, pinning her down onto the bed so that she could not see him; she could only writhe there among the sheets as he visited pleasure upon her again and again and again.

Agnes cried out, and she clapped a hand over her mouth to muffle the sound. Her vision flashed with white.

Then Liuprand rose over her, his hair mussed, his lips and chin glossy with her spend. He breathed hard and so did she, their chests pressed together so their hearts pulsed in tandem, beat for beat, as if they were linked by some invisible cord. With infinite tenderness, Liuprand swept back the hair from her face. His fingers trailed through it, from root to end.

"I dreamed of seeing it like this," he said. "Of seeing you like this, undone. It pained me some days, to keep from touching you. And even when the agony of it did not leave me sleepless, you invaded all my dreams."

"Did I speak?" she asked him. "In your dreams?"

He shook his head. "No. But you moaned, when I did this."

And then he stroked a hand between her legs, so expertly that she moaned indeed, hips straining upward into his touch. Her mind was so broken down by this onslaught, her limbs quivering like saplings in the wind, though she still had just barely enough sense within her for the question to come tumbling from her lips.

"Does Drepane's golden prince have a hundred secret lovers?" she managed.

He laughed, pausing for a moment his ministrations and leaving Agnes suddenly, horribly bereft. "Not even one. I did not even know what it meant to want until I first laid eyes on you."

Her chest tightened with fondness. She cupped his chin in her hand, and he stroked her again, making her writhe and abruptly grasp at his face, fingernails digging into his cheek. She swiftly took her hand away and hoped she had not hurt him.

What *she* wanted then was to please him in the same manner, to see *him* undone at her touch. He had endured so many weeks of restraint, and even now, she could tell he ached from it. She ran her fingers down his chest, feeling the damp and bloodied fabric of his doublet (an unforgivable oversight that he wore it still) until she reached the swelling in his breeches.

She did no more than brush against the cloth there and he groaned, with relief and with need.

Agnes pried the buttons loose and freed him. Her heart skipped—he was large, larger even than she had expected, given the sheer size of his body, the Seraphine build and its pulsing power. But he quivered under her touch like a supplicant before God.

The taste of him was salt and skin, and apostasy. Whatever obedience, whatever duty was left within Agnes fell away from her, crumbled, as a pedestal beneath a statue that had become too fragile to shoulder the weight of its idol. She was no ascetic, no scrupulous, shrinking virgin, no longer slave to the posthumous existence of Adele-Blanche. Her grandmother's cold and sepulchral power had been diminished. Dissolved into nothing. It vanished like mist in the summer morning, expunged by the stunning light of day.

Liuprand's fingers tangled in her hair, and then he wrested himself free. His chest was heaving, the enormous length of him throbbing and taut with blood.

"Lady Agnes," he said, between breaths, "will you have all of me?"

She was panting, too, and could not find words. She merely nodded.

Finally the doublet came off. He loosed the buttons and then peeled it away, that livery stained with her husband's blood, damp with her wetness, and let it crumple to the floor.

She could not have imagined the beauty of him, what lay beneath his clothes. The corded muscles of his chest were as firm and thick as the branches of an oak. She ran her palm across them, past his navel, and down to where he was achingly hard and still damp from the ministrations of her mouth. He groaned again and then surged forward, his huge body arching over her.

Their faces were close. He brushed his lips against hers, kissed the tip of her nose. She shivered, trembling with need.

"I do not want to hurt you," he said. "Will you tell me if I do?"

Again she nodded.

With agonizing slowness, he began to thrust himself inside of her. His entrance was eased by the slickness of her channel; she was so wet and needful for him that there was hardly any pain at all. What little pain did occur to her was so twined with pleasure that she could not bear to tell him to stop, the loss of such pleasure would have destroyed her.

Still, his restraint was remarkable, and it was almost as great as his need. He did not increase his pace until he was fully hilted within her, their bodies joined most inextricably. Then he paused and looked down at her questioningly.

Her face was so flushed, her mouth ajar with the beginnings of a gasp; how could he question her desire? But there was a wry tilt to his lips, a teasing glimmer in his eyes. He would make her speak it.

"Liuprand," she said, her voice strained with desperation. *"Please."*

Would he make her beg more piteously for it? She would. But then he began moving within her, gently, so gently she could have cried out in frustration—instead she lifted her hips and wrapped her legs around him, pulling him even closer.

This was all the urging he needed. Liuprand increased his pace until she was jostled across the bed, nearly up against the headboard, though his arm shot out to keep her from knocking into it, curling around her skull protectively. Yet still Agnes sensed restraint from him. She wondered if his strength was such that the world around him took on a terrible fragility; did he fear that if he unleashed himself, he could inflict some grievous harm upon it? Upon her? The Seraphine were heaven-kissed, imbued with power beyond that of humble humanity. It seemed to her more curse than boon, to live in a world too flimsy for your unshackled touch.

The notion grieved her so deeply that Agnes suddenly pushed herself up. Liuprand halted at once, stricken, but she did not allow even the half-formed thought to pass through him, the fear that he had hurt her. She braced her arms around his neck and pulled him up with her, until she was spread open in his lap, her back against the headboard.

She hoped this would undo him, undo all his careful restraint. Even without speaking, she hoped she had made her intent known. A silent vow that she would indeed take all of him. That his need did not frighten her; she would never cringe before his true face.

Black desire was in his eyes, and she was almost brought to climax by this look alone. He grasped her thighs, her flesh swelling up from between his huge fingers. His restraint fell away from him at last, and he thrust into her so powerfully, so uninhibitedly that she cried out in a broken sob when her release finally came. Her vision blistered with stars.

And then, as if fevered by the sound of her climax, he spent himself inside her. He muffled his own cry against her throat, kissing her there messily. He gave two last, shuddering thrusts and then went still. His mouth slipped from her neck.

Rather than collapsing upon her, he pulled himself out and, with one fluid motion, flipped their bodies so that she lay on top of him. His arms curled around her; she was bastioned against him. His heart beat as if it might crack through his chest. She felt every pulse of it reverberating through her like it was an organ of her own. And the beating of his heart, so raw, so close, banished every last drop of coldness from her veins. His seed, pooling warm inside her, melted the frost of Agnes's eternal winter.

She took Liuprand's hand by the wrist and guided his fingers across the scars on her stomach. Slowly, so that he could read them with his touch.

"You are my ruination," she whispered.

With his free hand, Liuprand tipped her chin up, so that she could see his face. The look in his eyes was pained.

"Do you regret it?" he asked. "I would have never—"

"No," she broke in. She guided his hand down farther, so he could feel the slickness of their coupling between her thighs. "I begged for it. Just like in your dreams."

He stroked her there, once, and she twisted against him, biting her lip on a moan. Then he leaned down and kissed her, briefly but deeply.

"Your ruination is the most beautiful thing I've ever seen," he murmured.

Those were the last words that passed between them for a long time. She merely lay upon him, breathing, exhaustion weighing down her eyelids. His grip on her never slackened, and Agnes was glad for it. She thought she might die—truly—if he ever let her go.

They did not speak because they both dreaded the words that hardened in their throats. The truth, as bitter as the core of an apple: that this had not been Agnes's ruination alone. That all of Drepane would fall if ever their clandestine coupling came to be known. And then there was the truth within the truth, which was as poisonous as it was sweet, the secret at the heart of it all—that not even the threat of the kingdom's ruin would make them regret what had been done.

XXXVI
THE CASKS OF LORD FREDEGAR

The House of Blood did not see its greatness diminished by its dungeon, as so many houses did. It was no forgotten, moldering niche, no rat-filled hole in the earth. The door was that of a vault, gridded with iron and then limned in gold, and the wood did not swell or sag with moisture. There was a dampness, of course, and mold that could not be warded off even by the most devoted of servants, who came down often to scrub the walls and the floors. No cobwebs frosted the corners or draped between the slats of the wooden banister, and the steps down to the dungeon were softly worn with many centuries of footsteps.

The guard who sat within had his legs propped up on a table and a book open in his lap. Cendrillon, he was called. Yet his book contained no poems of courtly love, no mythic sagas of the ancients, wrung out through generations. Rather, it was a ledger book, an accounting. And all within the dungeon had been most scrupulously accounted for.

Cendrillon's marginalia also decorated the page. He had drawn a rat king and a series of comic sketches wherein rabbits hunted men with crossbows and spears. The drawings were quite good. The rat king seemed to undulate there on the page, and the rabbits had perceptible vengeance in their eyes. A rush of envy flooded through Agnes, who would never create anything so poignant with a quill again.

Bordered by the marginalia were neat rows and columns. In one column, which read PRISONERS, Unruoching's name had been penned in floral script.

"Bring him out," Liuprand said.

The dungeon-keeper was a rather lovely man. He could not be many years Liuprand's elder, yet there was a softness about him—not just youthful but infantile. His pink, fleshy face could have been fresh from the womb. He walked with a delicate, prancing gait, his white-gold curls rippling in the torchlight, as though the dungeon were a field of flowers and he a storybook maiden within them. He wore a cream-colored doublet, and the subtle but inevitable grime of the dungeon had not sullied it. The keys that jingled at his waist did so musically.

With a nimble flick of his wrist, Cendrillon unlocked the door to the cell. His airiness, his lissome graces, were almost enough to make Agnes forget her purpose there. The dungeon was a sublime place with Cendrillon inside it. It was only Unruoching, as he emerged slouch-backed from his cell, who at last defiled it.

The Dolorous Guard had not failed to follow Liuprand's directives; Unruoching had been bound and bound again. The chains wrapped all around his body, from his throat to his knees, so tightly that he stumbled forward rather than walked. His arms were fixed to his sides, and his fingers were purple at their tips from the stricture of the chains.

Still he wore his father's blood upon him. It had darkened nearly to black, and stuck to his skin. Flies that had landed and gotten caught there as the blood dried twitched feebly, their filmy wings flicking as they tried vainly to free themselves. Their buzzing was mournful. Agnes watched them die one by one.

"Your Highness," Cendrillon said with a supple bow as he presented the prisoner.

The torchlight flickered across Liuprand's hard-boned face. "Lay him down."

This order was not for Cendrillon (who could think of burdening this comely man with so ugly a task?) but rather for the Dolorous Guard, who crowded into the dungeon behind Liuprand. Two of them lurched forward at once, seizing Unruoching about the arms.

Two more descended on Cendrillon's table. Cendrillon quickly snatched up his book, clutching it to his chest with an appalled gasp. The guards maneuvered the table to the center of the chamber, and then Unruoching was laid upon it, on his back, like a roast boar wrapped in twine.

Until now, none of the gathered audience had dared to make a sound. And still Unruoching was silent, his expression one of gelid shock, as though he had been turned one moment to stone.

The sound came from Ygraine, who stood at a distance, ringed by red-clad members of the household. Their names and faces were still unknown to Agnes and would be, always. But Ygraine would not be obscure to her. Agnes would remember the broken sobs that wrenched violently out of her, as if they were living things, maggots erupting from the fetid body of their host.

Her sobs were wordless, and they went unacknowledged. Not even the members of her own household moved to offer her comfort, a warm hand upon her shoulder, or even a look of sympathy. Their gazes were limpid with shame.

Only her son, Gamelyn, gave any notice to his mother's tears. She leaned upon her son heavily, arms braced around his shoulders, face buried into his neck. She had to hunch over to do so, and her long red hair draped over his crimson doublet like a cloak. Its vulpine color was made dull by the dungeon's dearth of light.

Gamelyn held on to his mother, but he did so stiffly, almost unconsciously, as if it were a fulfillment of quotidian duty. It was not unloving, however. It was only that his attentions were elsewhere: His green eyes were fixed on Liuprand, and he did not so much as blink. His expression was so remote, so chillingly bleak that Agnes had to avert her own gaze, for no child's eyes should look this cold. This single night had piled years of anguished bitterness upon him.

Liuprand approached the table in fluid steps. He peered over Unruoching's prone form for several moments before speaking.

"Have you any words to offer in your defense?" Liuprand asked. His tone was cool—more restrained, Agnes knew, than he felt. "Choose them carefully. I will not invite your speech again."

Unruoching swallowed audibly. His throat pulsed, straining beneath the rope, the skin rubbed raw and red.

"Please, Your Highness," he gulped out at last. "I acted only in the best interests of my house. My father—though I loved him dearly—was weakened by age, his wisdom dried up, and he would no longer hear sense! He was past the point of reason and would not step down from his post, not shift his title to his son, as *any* man of wisdom would. The king's missives were lost beneath his inattentive eye! What more vital things could be dismissed by such an addled mind? Surely, my prince, you can understand—sometimes a son must move against his father, for the greater good of all."

Liuprand allowed several more moments to pass, and the chamber was silent but for Ygraine's sobs.

Then, very quietly, he asked, "And of the lady Agnes?"

All the eyes of the dungeon turned toward her.

"I would not have harmed her!" Unruoching's voice cracked with desperation. "I aimed my knife only at Lord Fredegar. I never would have lifted a blade against the lady."

"Liar," Agnes whispered.

Her hair was still damp from the bath, and it flowed loosely over her shoulders. She had wanted to wear her wedding gown, bloodied and ruined as it was, but it was so wet that it made her shiver when she had tried to clothe herself in it again. Her skin rose with gooseflesh she could not banish on her own. And so Liuprand had laid upon her his own heavy blue cloak. Sheltered within its folds, she staved off the dungeon's chill. Yet beneath the fine cloak, she could not forget she was still a widow robed in her husband's blood.

At the sound of her speech, several in the room uttered gasps of shock. Liuprand, even, looked surprised to hear her voice. His gaze was tender when he regarded her, though his lips pressed thin with the fury he could barely check.

"Go on, lady," he said. "What occurred in the corridor?"

"He lies." Agnes bit out the words. "The moment his father's body fell to the floor, he turned his dagger on me. He said he could not allow any offspring birthed of our union to usurp him."

More scattered gasps came from the audience, and anger flared in Liuprand's eyes. He turned back toward Unruoching.

"So you are not only a kinslayer, but a false face as well," he murmured. "You would have struck down an unarmed woman, all for your crazed and petty jealousies." With each word, color rose in his cheeks. "You are a greater danger to the world than your father ever could have been."

Unruoching was weeping now. Fat, garish tears, mucus running silvery paths from his nose and into his mouth. It was pathetic to watch a grown man weep in the manner of a child, but Agnes could not wring from herself even a drop of pity. Her heart was cold.

"Please, Your Highness," he whispered. "It has always been your faith I have sought. Not your father's. I would urge the House of Blood to champion the reign of Liuprand, the golden prince of Drepane, Liuprand the Great, Liuprand the—"

"Enough," Liuprand said. "Let me hear no more from you."

Unruoching sniffled, spittle pooling at the corners of his mouth. These showy tears perhaps worked their alchemy upon the members of his house, who began to turn their gazes to the floor and wipe at their own eyes, but Agnes felt nothing. And his own son, Gamelyn, only stared unflinchingly at Liuprand, with that frigid and surpassing hate.

Liuprand left Unruoching there upon the table and walked back farther into the dungeon, approaching the entrance to one of the tunnels. He felt along the wall for a moment and then pulled something out from a shelf within it.

It was a wooden cask, smaller than any Agnes had ever seen, hardly any larger than an ordinary bottle of wine. Liuprand hefted it easily in one hand. Agnes now knew the strength of those fingers, which had last night left bruises of passion on her hips and along her thighs.

He turned the cask over, squinting at some faded script written across its side. Then he raised his other hand and beckoned Cendrillon.

"You," he said. "Bring that ledger book and tell me whose lifeblood I hold."

Cendrillon hurried over to him, his gait made clumsy by his fear. His nymphlike graces had suddenly evaporated. He stopped before Liuprand and paged through the ledger book, pausing after a few moments and pointing his finger at a page.

"There," he said, in a high and tremulous voice. "Montagu, of the House of Lungs."

"Noble blood," Liuprand said. "A fine vintage. Lord Fredegar was so fastidious in his accounting."

It took a moment for Agnes to understand. Just as Adele-Blanche had ordered the great frieze to be built in Castle Peake's dungeon, and the teeth of their house's inheritance set within it, Fredegar had turned his dungeon into a vault inside which the blood of every corpse was bottled like wine. *Clever,* she thought dimly, and then dismissed the word, for it pained her to praise her dead husband, whose blood would never be bottled and treasured, would only ever be an inglorious stain upon the floor.

Liuprand returned to Unruoching, holding the cask. There was no spigot for him to twist, so instead he thrust the heel of his hand against the wood, and it splintered. Agnes thought she had finally come to know the heights and depths of his strength, but clearly she had underestimated him still, because the wood fell away so easily, and blood came pouring forth.

It poured down over Unruoching's face, dribbling into his eyes, into his mouth. He gasped and choked, spitting out what blood he could, only for more to come gushing in. He thrashed there on the table and tried to cry out, but his screams were strangled by the ceaseless flowing of red. It drenched his doublet and the table beneath him. Even his ears were flooded, like cisterns filling with rainwater.

"*Please!*" Ygraine's desperate howl broke the air. "Please, my prince, *please,* give my husband a different death. Or please at least let my son not bear witness to it."

She had clapped a hand over Gamelyn's eyes, but her fingers were splayed such that he could still peer through them, and his gaze was unrelenting. Agnes felt her skin prickle at seeing it.

Liuprand's head snapped up. He set down the cask, leaving Unruoching to writhe and desperately splutter out what blood he could, moaning weakly.

With measured steps, Liuprand approached Ygraine. He looked down at her sympathetically. Kindness touched the planes of his lovely face.

"You beg mercy for your husband," he said, and his voice was gentle. "You are a loyal wife, even now, and I hold such a virtue in high esteem. Do not believe otherwise."

Hope brimmed in Ygraine's green eyes.

"And yet," Liuprand said, "mercy precludes the possibility of true justice. What recompense will there be for the lady Agnes's pain? For the bride who saw her hours-old husband struck down in front of her? Who wears his lifeblood upon her still?"

The heads of the audience once more turned to Agnes. Ygraine's tearful gaze caught on her as well, and she bit her trembling bottom lip.

"I am sorry, lady," she whispered. "I never wished for this. I loved Lord Fredegar as I do my own father. And now I feel your pain, the pain of watching your beloved's torment."

Ygraine paused and waited for Agnes to speak. She did not. Her throat felt like a burnt tree, curdled and black.

"Go on," Liuprand said. "Beg your mercy from the lady Agnes."

Slowly, Ygraine crossed the room. She left her son, whose green gaze shifted at last to follow her. When she reached Agnes, she lowered herself to her knees, pale, pretty face turned upward, the shimmer of shed tears on her cheeks. She clasped her hands before her chest with all the penitence of a prayerful monk.

"Please, lady," she said. "You did not deserve to witness such a thing. In all of this you are innocent. But surely—perhaps—you can say the same of me. That I do not deserve such a fate, either. That at least my son and I are also blameless."

Agnes looked down at her, yet she did not see her, not truly. Instead Ygraine's blanched countenance became as shuddery as a pool of clear water, and in this water, Agnes saw her own reflection. Not the reflection of a woman grown, loose black hair flowing over her shoulders, wrapped in the prince's cloak; rather she saw herself as a girl, spread out naked upon her grandmother's table. It was not a memory, for she had not witnessed the event from afar, as though watching a scene in a masque; it was something her imagination had conjured on its own. She saw her crazed, wheeling eyes, their whites shot through with red. She saw the spittle dripping from her lips and her own cold sweat soaking the wood beneath her. She saw the blood—so much, more in her imagination than there had been in reality—transforming her flesh into no more than a mangle of white and red. She saw the slit between her legs, dripping with desperate, protective arousal. She saw her mouth, opening and closing as it worked out its vain pleas.

A thin bile of disgust pooled within her. Agnes placed a hand on Ygraine's shoulder to feel the warmth of her skin, banish these visions of her putrid girlhood, and return to the woman her face.

"Would you have begged your husband for mercy, had you been witness to his crime?" she asked quietly.

Ygraine's brows drew together. "Of course. I would have fallen to my knees in the corridor. I swear it."

"It would not have done any good," Agnes said, "just as it will do no good now."

At first there was only bewilderment in Ygraine's eyes; it darted like minnows through those pools of moss green. It was not until Liuprand lifted up the cask again that she cried out, cried as if someone had thrust a knife into her own belly, and then fell forward onto the floor, quaking with sobs.

Agnes took a step back so that Ygraine's lamentable form did not brush against her skirts.

Blood poured from the cask in hot, heavy gouts onto Unruoching's already profaned face. He gulped and gasped still, but these sounds were muted now, and where before he had writhed and thrashed in protest, now he merely trembled. His own life was leaving him in slow and agonizing increments. The knowledge of this grew Agnes's heart with pleasure, though it was not the sort of pleasure to make her smile.

"Lady?"

The suddenness of this voice startled Agnes. She turned to see the leech Pliny standing before her.

Her mind understood that he was quite an old man, for he had been present at Lord Fredegar's birth, but the sight of him did not accentuate this understanding; in fact, it undermined it. The skin about his face was loose and silver-stubbled, giving him the appearance of a hoary tomcat, but otherwise he stood impeccably straight, his posture not remotely diminished by age. He was a good deal taller than Agnes, though not of a height to Liuprand. He had a large forehead, intimating that he was bald beneath his leech's hood, but the flesh of it was taut and shiny, and bore none of those brown splotches of senility.

Agnes acknowledged him with a nod, thinking he merely meant to make a show of his deference, but he did not nod back. Instead he reached into the folds of his robe and retrieved something, which he then held out to her in his open palm.

"If it please you, lady," he said, "I have had it repaired."

It was the necklace of teeth, her house's ancestral totem, but it was not the same bauble that had been torn off her and scattered across the floor. He had retrieved all the teeth—Agnes counted them swiftly—but he had reset them, in a silver chain instead of gold. Between each tooth he had even added a small pearl, which transformed the piece of jewelry from something primeval and gruesome into something new and delicately beautiful.

Agnes reached out and took it.

"Thank you," she said softly.

She imagined the leech kneeling on the floor, kneeling in Fredegar's blood, carefully plucking up each small tooth as though he were sifting through sand. He had treated the teeth so lovingly, as if they were his master's own.

Pliny nodded. And then a new cacophony of sounds called their attentions back to the table.

Unruoching's coughing was renewed in strength, and now there was bile seeping from the corners of his mouth. There was yet more writhing, though it seemed a less conscious action, as if he were a puppet with its strings cruelly tugged by a child. A child of Death, who watched over the whole proceeding, a gathering of shadows along the wall. His cruel white hands were reaching, and he would strike out with them soon.

But it was here that Liuprand paused and set down the cask. Unruoching groaned feebly.

"Your words have moved me, Lady Ygraine," he said—suddenly, as if he had only decided it at that very moment, and bewildered himself with the knowledge. "I shall give your husband a different death."

Ygraine looked up through a tangle of red hair. Yet there was no more hope in her eyes, only hollow despair. "You will?"

"Yes," said Liuprand. "I shall give him a death that your son will not have to witness. In fact, no one will bear witness to his death at all."

The crowd mumbled with confusion. Agnes glanced over at Pliny; a frown pulled down his mouth. He had relished watching Unruoching's torture, as had she. The red thread of love stretched from his finger to Fredegar's corpse, which still awaited desecration. He was loyal even in death, and her chest tightened with fondness for him.

"Where are your masons?" Liuprand asked, directing his question toward the crimson-clad staff of the House of Blood. "Summon them."

Still, confusion reigned, as one man pulled himself from the throng and departed up the dungeon stairs. He brushed past Cendrillon, who still clutched his book against his chest, as though he feared it might be snatched from him. The ethereal qualities had vanished from his face; it was a mask of quotidian, human horror.

The man was gone for a long stretch of time, during which no one dared speak. Ygraine pushed herself up onto her knees, breathing hard enough to make her shoulders rise and fall heavily.

At last the man returned with three masons, their hands hard and yellow with calluses, the years of labor showing on their furrowed brows and slouched backs. Their long arms hung limply at their sides, giving them a rather simian look. They arranged themselves in a half circle before Liuprand and gave low bows in deference to their prince.

Yet rather than addressing them, Liuprand turned to the gathered crowd.

"The casks of Lord Fredegar are well kept and well treasured," he said. "I would not waste any more of them. And I am sure, for whatever time Lord Unruoching is given to live, he will not be inclined to indulge in any more of these fine vintages."

His words did not make sense to Agnes, nor to those around her, who looked among themselves in bemusement. She began to feel removed from the room, from the chill air of the dungeon, from the coppery odor of blood, all her senses becoming obscure. And as she stood there, a ghost slipping from its frail human shell, another world shuddered to life before her, layered over the first. It was the world of strange vapors, of spectral mists, miasmas of silvery gray. The phantasmic vision played out before her eyes.

A mason, laying bricks. Her dream had been drivel to her then, but now she knew it was prophecy. For the flesh-and-blood masons began to heft down wagons of stone, the carts clattering heavily against the steps as they descended. And Liuprand began to beckon the crowd away from the table, toward the door of the dungeon, where they all became audience to this prophecy made manifest. It was only Agnes who did not move, struck dumb by the way her vision turned corporeal before her eyes. And if she had once dreamed the future, what of her other slumbering fantasies? Were they prophecy, too?

Liuprand approached her, a gentle hand on the small of her back. "Come, Lady Agnes," he said softly. "Soon there will be nothing to see here."

Agnes allowed herself to be led toward the steps, but she did not look away. She watched on as the Dolorous Guard untied Unruoching, thrusting him from the table and onto the floor, where he crumpled into a heap on his hands and knees. They shifted the table back toward Cendrillon, though it resembled less a table and more a butcher's block, so thoroughly drenched in still-wet blood. The nymph of a man shuddered.

Without Agnes particularly noticing, Ygraine had fainted. She was borne away by two crimson-clad men, her body held by the ankles and wrists, swaying between them like a pendulum. Thus Gamelyn was alone now, watching without blinking as a wall flowered up around his father, stone upon cruel gray stone.

Agnes looked up at Liuprand. "How long will it take? For him to perish here?"

"Mere days." Liuprand glanced at Unruoching's quickly vanishing form. "A man cannot go much longer without water." Then he cast his gaze around the room, over Cendrillon, over the small audience that remained. "I shall leave some men from the Dolorous Guard here, to ensure that the wall is not broken and Lord Unruoching is not rescued. And when he has died of thirst or hunger, I shall expect to receive a messenger at the castle gate, bearing his teeth."

The masons were efficient at their work. They were even swifter than the ghouls of Agnes's dream. And though Unruoching faded from her sight as the walls grew like mushrooms after a rainstorm, she found that he continued on in her imagination. She imagined that he would throw himself against the bricks, again and again, howling pitifully for release. She imagined Ygraine, pressed against the wall's other side, whispering to him through the stone. Reassuring him, perhaps, as his tongue thickened in his mouth and death carved at his body like a lathe. *Mere days.* So short a span of time, yet so long.

As Liuprand guided her up the dungeon stairs, Pliny followed closely behind. She cast one last look over her shoulder. First her eyes landed on Cendrillon, who still grasped his notebook tightly, and she felt the familiar stirring of envy within her. She knew he did not think of it as a blessing, that his hand belonged to him, that he could move it as he wished, that it held such force within its working muscles and tendons.

At last, she looked upon Gamelyn, and found with great unease that he was staring back at her. Their eyes met for the briefest moment, green into gray. Agnes could sense herself becoming a specter within his mind, such a one that would live always in his thoughts.

She did not wish to swallow this truth. And so she left the boy alone with his ripening ghosts.

XXXVII
SEQUELAE

The mist and the twisted trees slipped by them, as if the world were moving rather than the carriage. The stillness had long since gone from the House of Blood and its environs. Now the white vapors swirled, the black branches swayed tremulously in the wind, and a number of birds darted from perch to perch, small flecks of color against the forest's monochrome canvas. Agnes's eyes followed them. A red bird. A brown-bodied sparrow. A cone-headed jay. A nightjar.

"What works within your mind?"

Liuprand's voice was nervous. Yet it was a shallow and trembly sort of nervousness, as a boy might speak for the first time to a girl he had long been besotted with. It gave the scene a luster of absurdity, for surely he should be feeling a grown man's fear.

Agnes turned back toward him and smiled faintly. "Nothing especially interesting."

It was impossible, in these circumstances, for either of them to speak freely. They were not alone in the carriage. While Agnes shared a bench with Waltrude, Liuprand shared the bench on the opposite side with Pliny.

When she had asked the leech to come with them back to Castle Crudele, it had been a genuine entreaty. She worried he would no longer be safe within the House of Blood, having shown such obvious and enduring loyalty to Fredegar even after his death. Unruoching would soon follow his father's fate, but Agnes was not innocent enough to believe that he had been the only one to harbor treasonous sentiments toward the old Master of Blood. The rest of Fredegar's house might seek vengeance against his remaining loyalists. And Pliny was shrewd enough himself to know this.

And Agnes did not want to return to Castle Crudele as alone as she had been when she departed. Bereft of any friends, save Waltrude; she had even lost Marozia's confidence and was not sure how she could earn it back. She was not sure if she even wanted it. The leeches at the castle were all sworn to the king and to the Most Esteemed Surgeon. Truss and Mordaunt had been the only accessories to her torment, but any leech would have leapt at the chance had the king asked. So to have her own loyal leech only seemed wise.

Yet now she felt pricked with a small needling of regret, for she would have to choose her words carefully in Pliny's presence. He did not know—he *could* not know, or else he would forsake her. Such a steadfastly faithful man might believe she had dishonored her husband by taking another man to bed mere hours after his murder.

But Waltrude.

The wet nurse knew. Even if she had not seen Liuprand come to her chamber that night, still she would have guessed; she was as canny as a weasel and as perceptive as a carrion bird. Yet more than that, she loved Liuprand. Their souls were twined in some strange sense that Agnes could not fully comprehend, and that meant she could feel the love he felt for another, like a tugging on some invisible thread within her. Perhaps the same thread was now wrapped around Agnes's wrist. The weaving had become so intricate, so complex, that Agnes's mind struggled to work over all its tangles and knots.

"Your thoughts are always of interest to me," Liuprand replied.

This reply made her heart leap—first with fondness, then with fear. Every friendly word that passed between them might now be prodded and racked, wrung out for evidence of perfidy. Could she bear it? She had spent so many years in silence that it was accustomed to her, and she to it, but it was not the easy slide of a knife into its sheath; it was the thrust of a blade into giving flesh.

"I was wondering if you remembered the nightjar," Agnes said. "The message it bore to you those many months ago."

Liuprand smiled. "A clever little bird. Yes, I remember."

Months before they had finished all their business and departed Castle Peake. Months before he had slipped a ring on Marozia's finger.

She wanted to touch his hand. A simple touch, one that might have been within the bounds of propriety once, but not anymore. Even though she now knew what he felt like inside her, the small space between them was as unbreachable as ever. The ache of longing in Agnes's chest was so great that she almost imagined it could be *seen*. A dark gash, exposing her blood-fed, anguished heart.

In the eye of her mind, she saw that same wound within Liuprand. Black, depthless, dripping lifeblood. He reached out, hand open, but before he could close that space, he retracted his arm. He clenched his fingers, folding them into his palm.

Agnes looked down at her own hands. One was fisted in her lap; the other was limp at her side, for still she could not make its fingers move of her own accord. The days-old bandages were yellow now, stained with Fredegar's blood as well as her own.

When she glanced up, she saw that Pliny had been watching her steadily, perhaps for quite a long time.

"If I may, lady," he said, and it took a moment for Agnes to understand that this was a question.

She nodded permission, and very gently, the leech took her damaged hand in his. With the most delicate of ministrations, he turned it over. He peeled back the bandages to examine the wounds beneath. He tapped softly against the tips of her fingers, as if trying to urge a response. To even Agnes's surprise, her fingers twitched, some reflexive action disconnected from her mind.

"I believe I could help restore some of its function," Pliny said. "And at least soothe some of the unpleasantness of the injury. You must be in a great deal of pain."

Agnes met the leech's eyes, which were warm and densely brown, like some furred animal in a coil of hibernation. Slowly, she nodded.

In their returning, Castle Crudele occurred to Agnes as a marvelous thing, not for its size, which she had long since comprehended and come to peace with, but rather for its majestic, appalling coldness. The House of Blood had been warm—as blood freshly spilled—but Castle Crudele had been built on long-ago horrors, a foundation of naked bone, the flesh eaten by maggots, the organs and entrails liquefied through the unerring compression of time, the white feet of death crushing the bodies of Drepane's old nobles like grapes for wine.

These ancient horrors were what floated up around the castle now. Agnes had at first attributed them to the mists of the crashing waves, but those were briny, deep with the scent of sea life. These vapors were boreal, remote, and bitter as the castle they enveloped.

The disembodied helmets that lined the path to the barbican clanked and juddered in the wind. Their emptiness did nothing to assuage Agnes's mounting terror. She wished again to reach for Liuprand, but she could control at least one of her hands, and kept it fisted obediently in her lap. She did glance over at him, and saw the same glassy fear in his eyes.

The carriage, of course, rattled on. It stopped only when it had reached the courtyard, white sand stirred by its wheels. The Dolorous Guard dismounted their horses and came around to open the door. Liuprand stepped out first, then Agnes after him. Here, at least, there was good cause to touch his hand. He helped her down from the carriage, the warmth of his skin sending the green shoots of spring through her veins.

Three more guards waited at the entrance to the castle. They stood as still as draughts tiles, faces hidden entirely behind the grates of their helmets, and only when Liuprand approached did they speak, without even turning their heads to look at him.

"The king is waiting in the great hall," one said, in a toneless voice.

Liuprand gave one stiff nod and nothing more. He swept his arm forward chivalrously, allowing Agnes to pass first into the castle. But he was not far behind, and Waltrude and Pliny were not far behind him. And when the corridor began to open into the great hall, Liuprand put himself in front of her again, powerful muscles tensing beneath his blue doublet. One hand was held in a tight fist; the other rested on the pommel of his sword. Agnes wondered if she would ever see him unarmed again. Even with his own retinue of guards at his side, would he ever risk it? And who would the Dolorous Guard fight for if there came a final schism between Liuprand and the king? They were sworn to the royal house of Seraph. But what if the house was divided?

And against all odds, she nourished the most fragile of hopes within herself: that the king might allow for the marriage, still unconsummated, to be annulled. That Liuprand might be permitted to marry another lady of the House of Teeth instead.

Agnes had no more time to ponder these questions, nor entertain these hopes, for they were now before Nicephorus. He sat upon his throne, on the dais, wearing a white tunic and holding a bright goblet of wine. His largeness occurred to her with no small amount of alarm. He was Liuprand's father after all, the blood of pure Seraph. The goblet looked like a child's toy in his hand.

And Marozia. Agnes's breath caught within her throat. Her cousin stood before the dais, hands clasped at her waist. It was a more docile pose than Agnes could ever remember seeing from her. But there was no obeisance in her eyes. They burned like the vivifying oil within dark lanterns. After so many days absent from her—more days than Agnes had ever passed without Marozia in her entire life—her cousin's beauty was as astonishing as a sudden spilling of blood. Red, she wore, deep and dark, with a matching hood that held back her long hair, caught now within a single thick plait. She had replaced the necklace of teeth with a great golden choker, one that nearly obscured the whole column of her throat. Agnes need not have wondered who had procured the necklace and who had braided her hair. The girl Ninian was at her side, regarding her mistress with slavish love.

Marozia's eyes lifted to regard Agnes, and Agnes knew what she saw. First she must have seen the flowers she wore in her hair, white flowers, to honor Lord Fredegar. She must have seen the way her hair was not held up in its customary crown but rather flowed over her shoulders and down her back, like a pour of water. And she must have seen, of course, the new necklace, the elegant bauble that reflected the graces of modernity rather than the garish horrors of the past.

Agnes met her cousin's gaze without blinking. A white foam of guilt crested within her, but it was not guilt alone. Beneath it, the water of her defiance was dark. These two forces were not opposed; they were twined inextricably, a single wave that crashed and rose and then crashed again. She looked down at the ring on Marozia's finger, and this vexing tide grew in power and ferocity.

The king's voice jolted Agnes from the inner workings of her mind.

"The House of Blood's messengers preceded you," Nicephorus said. "I know all that occurred within its walls."

Liuprand regarded his father but did not speak. It was not fear that drove his silence, but rather the same waters that churned within him, words lost in their tumultuous foam.

"For all your high-and-mighty talk of diplomacy, of peace . . ." Nicephorus's throat rattled with mucus as his pitch rose. "You have destroyed any rapport between the royal line and the House of Blood. It is expired, extinct, forever gone."

Liuprand tilted his chin, undaunted. "The House of Blood destroyed itself. A son, slaughtering his own father on his wedding night—you would have me leave this crime unpunished? You would let a kinslayer wear the title Master of Blood? I would not have imagined you to take patricide so lightly."

"So now you are aghast at the thought of a son betraying his father!" Nicephorus's voice boomed through the mostly empty hall, and a cruel, humorless laugh followed. "Always you have thought yourself too clever. But now you have shown your true face. There could have been a swift death for the betrayer, but you insisted upon the utmost depravity. Had justice been served with a mundane, expeditious hand, perhaps the Crown would not now find itself bereft of the confidence of *two* Houses."

"Two?" Liuprand echoed. "Why two?"

The king let out a breath of contempt. "Because, foolish boy, the House of Blood and the House of Eyes have long been bound by marriage. Lady Ygraine's father is Master of Eyes."

That vulpine color of her hair. Now Agnes knew where she had recognized it. A woozy feeling of dread rose within her.

"Now Thrasamund is roiling with fury at the gross crime inflicted upon his daughter. He has forsaken all amity between his house and the Crown."

Liuprand's face had paled very slightly, but he did not quiver as he spoke. "Justice had to be done. Not only for Lord Fredegar, but for the lady Agnes."

Nicephorus's watery eyes flickered to her. Agnes flinched, and a sudden, revived pain shivered from her hand through her arm. Yet the king's gaze did not linger; he turned swiftly back to his son.

"Liuprand the Just," he said, tone full of dripping mockery. "Is that the epithet you seek? You have plunged Drepane into greater turmoil than ever with this act of barbarous *justice.*"

He allowed the hall to grow quiet for a moment, eyes still trained on his son. He expected a rejoinder, but Agnes knew that Liuprand would not grant him such satisfaction. He regarded his father in stony silence, his lips pressed into a thin line and his jaw taut with trembling pressure.

"Luckily for you," the king went on, coolly now, "I have come to a solution that will assuage all wounds."

Liuprand was quiet for several moments more, reluctant to indulge his father, before finally asking in a half-strangled voice, "And what is that?"

Nicephorus smiled. It was a resplendent smile, almost beautiful, yet perverse as it crossed his hideous face. And even before he spoke, an icy, infinite horror was clambering up Agnes's spine, like vines made of pure winter cold. For as much as she had scarcely permitted herself to dream of Liuprand's fetters broken, his love for her surmounting all, she had not allowed herself to imagine that there might be a worse fate for him still.

"You have yourself said many times that marriage is the most potent method of forming alliances. So I have proposed exactly that. You will make your union with the princess Marozia fruitful at once. She will bear a daughter, and that daughter will be betrothed upon birth to Lord Gamelyn, the boy who is now master. When she is of age, they will marry. The House of Blood has agreed to these terms, and even Lord Thrasamund's anger has been abated. Are you not pleased, sweet son, at such civil diplomacy? It is your seed, sown within the princess, that will preserve Drepane."

BOOK II

I
WHAT CANNOT BE REVERSED

Of all the commendable traits possessed by Pliny the leech, the one that brought him the most secret pride was, perhaps, the most unshowy of all. Punctuality was a virtue overlooked by most others, but he cherished it in himself, polishing it like an amulet, and he valued it greatly in others, as well.

Which was why, to a great degree, the lady Agnes had quickly endeared herself to him. She was never a second late to their meetings.

He had expected her, like all the noble ladies he had known, to be frivolous with time—the other women of Castle Crudele slid languidly through moments, as sluggish blood through a too-narrow tube, lingering over their lunches, plucking indifferently at their harps. But of all the traits possessed by the lady Agnes, frivolity was not one. A serious creature, she was. Not as solemn as she had once been, when she was silent, no longer the castle's dour statue-girl (Waltrude's epithet, not his), yet still she was sensible in her manner.

This, too, appealed to Pliny tremendously. Perhaps more so because, in their meetings, he managed to see the occasional slipping of this sober mask, each of her subtle smiles like a secret shared with him and him alone.

And so she came, as she always did, with the noontide tolling of the bell. The library door cracked and then shuddered closed behind her. Her slippered footsteps were measured and almost musical upon the floor.

"Good afternoon, Your Scrupulousness," the lady Agnes said.

Like his old, beloved master, she persisted in this formal mode of address, despite the duration and intimacy of the time they had spent together over the past months. In moments like these, he grieved Lord Fredegar more acutely, imagining what a fair and sympathetic match he and the lady would have made.

"How is the pain today, lady?" he asked.

Frowning, Lady Agnes flexed her wrist. There was still a distinctive tremble to her fingers, though the visible wounds were long healed and showed only white scars. The inner wounds, however, the damage done to her veins and nerves, the spreading, rootlike nexus of sensation—

"There is more numbness than pain," she said. "And I am all the worse for it, I think. I have not been able, since our last meeting, to hold a quill."

That had been her stated goal since the beginning of their sessions: The lady Agnes wished to write again. Pliny disguised his consternation; he did not wish to sadden her, though neither did he wish to fill her with false hope. Nine months later and still her fingers could not be persuaded to do so much as form a fist to crumple paper. No progress had been made in relearning the delicate, minute tasks of maneuvering a quill. It was difficult for Pliny not to feel as though he had failed her.

At least she was no longer in such a great deal of pain. Sighing to himself, he said, "I have thought of a new activity for you."

Agnes arched a curious brow. She allowed herself to be led over to the table, where Pliny had placed a large pot of uncooked rice. Beside it, there was a tray of glass beads, most of them polished amber, yet a few among them that were blue. He had plied the beads from the castle's metalworker, which had been a more vexing task than receiving the rice from the chef, a very sweaty yet still gregarious man named Gower.

The metalworker had glared at him with knifepoint eyes. "You queer leeches," he said, tapping ash from his poker while Pliny stood in the hostile light and heat of the forge. "What use are you when there are no corpses to desecrate? Why should the king let you roam the castle of the living?"

"It could be said that today's living are tomorrow's corpses," Pliny replied.

With a phlegmy noise of disgust, the metalworker thrust the beads into his hands. Pliny left, his legs sticky with sweat under his sepia robes. Now, having recovered from the ignominy of the encounter, he was optimistic about showing Lady Agnes his new clever device.

Eschewing a preamble, Pliny lifted the tray of beads and poured them into the vat. With his own hand (dexterous, unmarred), he stirred them about until the beads and the rice were a novel concoction.

"These are the prettiest, shiniest weevils I have ever seen," Lady Agnes said.

Pliny smiled. "No, my lady, it is not that the rice has been polluted, nor the beads diminished—they are an elixir all their own. A healing tonic, though not one to be consumed. Sifting through and retrieving the beads, these inanimate little weevils, will help to recover the delicate finesses of your hand, the agile graces of your fingers."

Agnes had the decency not to appear skeptical. She gave a rather steely nod and said, "I will try."

She sank her hand into the vat, her pale, slender wrist vanishing into his unorthodox draught. Pliny could no longer see the motion of her fingers; he merely heard the scrabbling of them among the rice on the edges of the vat. Her brow creased with concentration. With her right hand, she reached over and rolled up the sleeve of her wine-colored gown.

Increasingly, since their return to Castle Crudele, Pliny had observed the lady Agnes wearing richer and richer colors. Plums and violets, dark orchids and indigos. She could even be persuaded into amethyst or iris. Slowly, too, these gowns began to reveal more of her skin, her narrow shoulders jutting out, bare, from the low neckline. Somewhere along the way, her hair had come down, falling in a glossy sheet to the small of her back. Occasionally she still wore it half up, in the accustomed crown of braids, but more often it was simply loose, kept back from her face with only a pair of modest silver clips.

Yet two things she was never without: the pearl-and-tooth necklace that Pliny had recovered and remade for her, back in the House of Blood, and a cluster of white flowers, woven through her black hair. In this way, she honored her title as Mistress of Teeth, and she honored her late husband, too. With these accoutrements, no one could fail to appreciate her noble pedigree—nor her widowhood. She had made both essential to her person.

Having watched the lady's metamorphosis from its very inception, over these nine months, Pliny had spent no small amount of time ruminating upon it and the feelings it provoked in him. He had observed her come into awareness of her own beauty, tentatively at first, and then without inhibition. As her voice lifted from her throat, some of her modesty had been shed, a newly winged insect shucking its outgrown husk. The façade of her statue had been broken apart, revealing the living girl within.

It sent Pliny into deep thought. He was not so cruel, so bitter as to hope that widowhood would diminish her, that she would shrink and languish in Fredegar's absence as a flower in a rainless winter. So why should he begrudge her sudden flourishing? After much consideration, he realized that this metamorphosis was not to do with his old master. And once he realized, it seemed so clear—that, quite simply, the lady Agnes was no longer deigning to live in the coldness of her cousin's shadow.

Stumbling upon this epiphany was like overturning a stone and finding a writhing mass of serpents beneath. Pliny wished he had not uncovered such a thing. Yet the stone could not be set down in the same place, just as his elixir could not be returned to its unblended state.

Marozia's shadow—and what a shadow it was. Agnes was not the only one who had changed tremendously in these intervening months.

Pliny watched the lady's fingers, trembling as they sifted through the rice, seeking the amber beads that turned over and over, slipping from her clumsy grip. She could cup her hand and let the rice pool there in her palm, but she did not have the dexterity or control to pinch a bead between her fingers. They rolled and rolled in a seemingly endless gyre, catching the golden light of the library when they surfaced, like flotsam in the tide, and then were buried once more, sunken treasure on the ocean's white-sand bed.

After several moments, Agnes lifted her head. "Do you think I might try holding a quill again?"

Half of Pliny was relieved, for it was sad for him to watch these earnest but futile efforts; the other half feared that she would only be disappointed again when she found her fingers could not come around the quill or manipulate it to form legible words. But he nodded, and she withdrew her hand, and he moved the vat away, relegating his impotent elixir to an inglorious spot beneath the table.

Pliny set out the parchment, the inkwell, the quill. There were always ample writing supplies in the library, for he and the lady Agnes were only two-thirds of its regular visitors, and the other patron was not impaired as Agnes was.

She sat down, her hair slipping over her bare collarbone. In the streaming of sunshine from the library's single high, circular window, the hair was not pure black, as it appeared in less beautifying lights. It was dark brown, like peat, like petrified bog-wood dredged up from centuries-long interment. In no other aspect did Agnes particularly resemble her cousin, but this color was, Pliny concluded, the mark of the House of Teeth, as legitimizing as a signet ring.

Her quivering hand scooped up the quill. It shifted between her fingers as they spasmed desperately to grasp it, and Pliny could not bear this, could not bear to witness the shame of her struggle, so with an uncharacteristic impetuousness, he leaned over her shoulder, closed his hand around hers, and maneuvered her fingers into position.

Agnes swiveled her head to look up at him. And then he was bestowed one of her secret smiles.

"Perhaps this is the more practical endeavor," she said. "I do not think I will have much occasion in my life to sift through rice."

Pliny offered her a small smile and nod in return. "Tell me, lady, what you wish to write, and I will help you."

The lady paused, rumination furrowing her brow again. She made to open her mouth but, before a word could fall from her tongue, the door to the library opened and the last of its regular visitors appeared in the threshold.

His golden aura could be seen, almost felt, from a distance, like the warming glow of a hearth.

Pliny straightened, his hand leaving the lady's, and then he bent at the waist in a bow. "Your Highness."

"Your Scrupulousness." Drepane's prince crossed the room in a mere three strides, his gait powerful and assured. "I hope you do not begrudge the interruption."

"Of course not, Your Highness."

Lady Agnes rose then, a bit of color coming into her pale cheeks. This did not pass beneath Pliny's notice. The prince—Agnes always had many a secret smile for him.

"Lady," Liuprand said, with a dip of his head. "How is your work coming this afternoon?"

"Well enough," Agnes replied. "Pliny is a great help to me. The pain is nearly gone."

The smile that broke apart the prince's face was for Agnes, but Pliny could not help feeling it was a gift to him, too, such was the beauty and the charisma of the man who would be king. To even stand in his proximity was to bask in a vivifying light. Pliny felt this in his creaky knees, in his once-broken elbow, in the marrow of every one of his old bones.

"I am gladdened to hear it." Liuprand looked away from her, to Pliny. "Forgive me, Your Scrupulousness, but I must speak to the lady alone."

The dismissal was not unexpected, though it slightly rankled him, only because he did not like losing the time of their sessions together. The metalworker, for all his acrimony, had been right in the sense that leeches did not have much to fill their hours when there was not flesh to be pared or blood to be drained. Death had not touched Castle Crudele in the nine months that Pliny had been here. And so his service to the lady Agnes formed the shape his days.

He refused to partake in the ignominious little amusements of the other leeches, like Truss and Mordaunt, who could be occupied for hours over knucklebones or spinning tops. Games of chance held no appeal for him. Nor did the company of Truss and Mordaunt. If he had one friend within the castle, it was the wet nurse, Waltrude.

So with one last bow to the prince and a nod to the lady, Pliny set off to find her. He left behind the pleasantly heavy air of the library for the cold, thin atmosphere of Castle Crudele's corridors, and felt the loss acutely, just as acutely as he felt that, had he stayed, he would have borne witness to something else he did not wish to know, something that ambivalent time could not prevent or reverse.

II
THE JUST

Each day Agnes entered the library it felt new again, not for the room itself but for how she could freshly perceive it. Since she gave up the pursuits of her grandmother, her vision seemed to have shifted irrevocably. The gray veil over the world had lifted, and nowhere was this more evident than in the library.

One day it was maze-like, all the spiral staircases and the shelves that curved in and around endlessly, like a conch shell, and she wondered, *How will I ever escape this labyrinth of knowledge? How will I ever be satisfied to leave?* And in those moments, Agnes searched for books of philosophy, the musings of old men from Seraph long expired, arguments of law and matter and mathematics, such that her grandmother would have disdained and forbidden her from.

And the next day the library was a comfort, and she returned to it as an animal to its den, a bird to its nest, knowing the spine of each book so intimately that it was as if she had constructed the library itself. She read accounts of the adventures of great men, soldiers and kings, that were half true at most, knitted through with the fantastic, dragons and ogres and vengeful, squabbling gods. She read only of their lives, not their deaths.

Agnes was one day jubilant, one day fearful, and yet she never hesitated to enter, because she could not be dissuaded from the hope that her work with Pliny would restore to her the faculties of her hand. Such dear hope was both enlivening and miserable.

Yet it was not half so dear as the secret hope she nursed within the recesses of her soul. The hope that Liuprand would appear to her as he had today.

He stood before her in his doublet of midnight blue, the rich aura of Seraphine blood around him, brilliant and gold. His beauty, which was never anything less than a revelation, was a force that emanated from him as well, though beneath it—well cloaked—Agnes recognized exhaustion. No one else would see it, because no one else would think to look; no one wanted to perceive any weakness in their prince.

But Agnes saw it—the dull gleam of his ocean-colored eyes; the daubs of sleepless gray beneath them. And in that moment she was glad her left hand was useless to her, for she wished so desperately to raise it, to cup his cheek, to stroke her thumb across his weary face.

Liuprand's gaze met hers steadily, within it a thousand unspoken words. And then it skirted down to the arm that hung limply at her side.

"You said there has been an improvement in the pain," he murmured.

She nodded.

"But no progress made in restoring its function?"

"Little progress," she admitted. "It is not for lack of trying. Pliny has devised many creative schemes. But I fear it will not be enough. He does not wish to deflate my hope, of course, by speaking such a thing aloud—though I think he, too, believes the inner wounds are too grave to be remedied."

Liuprand drew a breath. The tremulous rise of his shoulders spoke to Agnes of fettered anger. The vengeance he craved upon his father was a glass that he drank from and then filled again and again.

"Perhaps I am being too precious in my wishes," Agnes said with a sigh. "I wish to write again. I do not care about sorting beads from rice or threading needles for sewing. But perhaps I should be satisfied that I still have a hand at all."

"No," Liuprand said firmly. "Your wishes in this matter are so modest. And your desires . . . they are not aberrant. Do not let yourself be convinced otherwise."

Agnes gave a faint shake of her head. "Whatever I would write has no great value to the world."

"That is not true."

She lifted her good arm and swept it out, indicating the masses and masses of books around them, the staircases of books that climbed to the high circular window, spiraling up endlessly toward that aperture opened to the sky. "Is each of these tomes of equal value to you?"

There was a tug at the corner of Liuprand's mouth; it was almost a smile. "You always have the quicker rejoinder, lady. Yes, of course some books are more essential to me than others. And even if I live another century, there are some I will never have the occasion to open—for sometimes I would sooner return to the same book for comfort than seek out a new one. Does that make me a coward of the mind?"

"It makes you human. There are other reasons to read than for the sake of acquiring knowledge." Agnes had to bite her lip to keep her own smile at bay. "Which book do you return to most often?"

"Such an intimate question." Liuprand lifted a brow. "Perhaps I shall have you guess."

"You must give me a hint," Agnes protested. "This library is large enough to fulfill the appetites of a hundred sages."

"My mother would be pleased to hear that," Liuprand said, a note of melancholy in his voice. "Here. I will lead you to the proper section. Within that, you will have to pick it out yourself."

No small task, as every discrete section of the library was a cobbling of at least a dozen different cabinets, the books crammed tightly against one another on every shelf, hardly leaving room for dust to gather. Liuprand made his way toward the rear section, farthest from the door, where the space between the shelves grew so narrow that he had to twist his enormous body sideways to fit through them. Agnes followed, pulse twinging in her throat.

Where Liuprand stopped was not particularly remarkable; they were hemmed in by shelves on either side, cast in the rather aqueous gleam of sunlight from the very distant window. There was a sense of great stillness here, but not the stillness of death, of blood stopped suddenly within its course, of a body seized in rigor mortis. It was the stillness of the seafloor, where the water lay gently over the white sand, and the sand lay gently over the crabs in their shells and the pearls in their oysters and the buried doubloons in their chests. It was a stillness that held the hope of life within it.

Liuprand watched her expectantly, a pleased gleam in his eyes. Agnes looked around. Up to the tops of the shelves where the books were stacked in perilous, tottering piles, and then to the floor. Her gaze caught on one pale spot, where the carpet had been rubbed to whiteness by the repeated planting of feet. She approached it, and stood upon it. Then she rose up onto her tiptoes, as far as she could manage, holding on to the shelf for balance. She could not, of course, fully approximate Liuprand's height. But her fingers could reach up and brush the spine of the book that, she imagined, would be at his eye level.

Still pushed up on her tiptoes, Agnes looked back over her shoulder. Liuprand was smiling. A secret smile, for her and her alone.

"You are terribly perceptive, my lady."

"I think perhaps you are not quite as enigmatic as you hope."

His smile deepened to form dimples in his cheeks, and he approached her. They did not touch, but Agnes could feel the warmth and nearness of his body, and her heartbeat quickened. He reached over her shoulder and took down the book from the shelf. He gave it to Agnes.

As an object of art, it was nothing exceptional. Agnes had bound books for her grandmother that were more ornate, even when constructed with her clumsy child's hand. (How she longed for that clumsy hand now!) The cover was brown leather, worn around the spine, with gilt peeling away in long stripes from the page edges. She passed her palm across it and felt the embossing, the slightly raised symbol—a sun, its feathery rays extending nearly to the corners of the cover. Touched by curiosity, Agnes went to open it.

Yet before she could, Liuprand's arms came around her. The suddenness of this movement made the book fall from her hands and thud to the ground. He gripped her tightly, one arm across her middle, the other over her breast and her bare shoulders, and his cheek brushed the column of her throat as he held her there against his chest.

His need pulsed from within him, like a second heartbeat. Agnes could feel it, thudding through her, heating her blood and the very marrow of her bones. She was made a hollow drum, his desire beating against her taut skin.

The sensation it provoked in her was almost beyond words. Her body remembered every moment of their coupling, the dragging thrusts of him, which were now echoed in the intangible aura of want. And so he ground her *own* need into her—the ache between her legs terrible, as her channel clenched and clenched around empty air.

"Please," he rasped, lips brushing the shell of her ear.

She could not move; she was bound to him as a martyr to her pyre. Her arms pressed tautly to her sides. Her throat was not similarly subjugated, yet she could not speak. The words only inked themselves into her mind. *Call me by name, I beg of you, say Agnes, not lady, do not act as if we are strangers—*

Somehow—perhaps she should not have been surprised—he perceived this need from her. He dipped his head lower until his lips grazed her nape, and he whispered, "Agnes. Agnes—"

Her head was not subdued, either; she could turn it, and she did. Slowly, so that their noses touched, and their mouths were so close she swore she tasted him already, and with her eyes shut, she could pretend for a moment that this was not the greatest and most faithless of treacheries.

Unaccountably, a prick of reason jabbed at her. Agnes opened her eyes and recoiled only slightly, as much as she could when she was so firmly bound against him. Liuprand flinched.

"We cannot do this," she said brokenly.

"No, I cannot do without it." Liuprand's voice was low and rough, and it laid bare his pain. "There is not a single moment that is empty of my need for you."

Her stomach contracted upon itself. Weakly, she said, "You must be a master of your body . . ."

Liuprand shook his head, which brushed his cheek against hers again. "It is not the desire of my earthly form that torments me. I would want you even if I could not touch you. I need your clever counsel. All your secret smiles. Your gentleness and sensibility . . . I need the one person in all the world who can tend to the feeble creature beneath the epithet."

At last he had been marked with one. Liuprand the Just, he was called, after the news of what had transpired at the House of Blood made its way to the ears of peasants and nobles alike. It would not be penned into Drepane's annals until he died—one could gain or lose an epithet over the course of one's life—but for now men drank toasts to the prince who had proven patricide could not go unpunished, that such a savagery would be repaid a thousandfold. To the prince who promised a reign of brutal righteousness when finally he came into his crown.

Agnes could see very well the creature beneath the epithet. It was the epithet itself that gave the eye of her mind trouble. Justice meant violence, and this was incongruous with the character she knew, the one who held her now, the one who tended moths and preferred books to jousting or merrymaking, the one who had martyred his own pleasure for the health and longevity of Drepane while his father the king consumed whatever was in reach of his hands. But a man would not prostrate himself for Liuprand the Gentle, or Liuprand the Wise, or Liuprand the Learner. These virtues held no honor on Drepane.

It was certainly not Liuprand the Just who embraced her. This creature was perfidious, and so was Agnes.

"I would give you all you wish for," she whispered, "if there were not half the world between us."

His lips pressed to her ear again. "I feel nothing between us now."

Agnes felt herself dripping for him. "You are reckless with your desire, and all my reason is undone by your mouth."

He groaned softly and ground himself against her. Her legs were weak, and had Liuprand not been holding her, she might have dropped to the ground, a wobbly wreckage in purple silk. He was crumpling the white flowers in her hair, and she did not care—she cared nothing until she felt his mouth fix to her throat, just barely grazing the necklace of teeth there.

This rocked the reason back into her. Agnes wrested herself free of him, breathing hard.

Liuprand's chest was pumping, shoulders rising with each ragged, heavy inhale. His eyes still gleamed with desire, but as he regarded her, they shifted and grew matte with despair.

Though he opened his mouth to speak, Agnes's tongue was quicker.

"You are the prince," she said. Each word was wrung out from her painfully. "You are bound to another . . . to . . . ." She shook her head. It was pure cowardice that she could not speak the name. "I will not be your ruination."

"*No*," Liuprand broke in, reaching for her. "You are the only thing that will save me."

But Agnes could bear no more. She fled the library, fled the treachery of her desire, though her heart ached with love for him and she was still slick between her thighs.

III
NINIAN

First came the bandages. She had boiled them, and they were clean again. White, pure, befitting her mistress's faultless flesh. The princess was standing, though she should have been sitting, for her own sake and for Ninian's. They were of a height, but in her heeled slippers, the princess Marozia was taller. And so Ninian had to push up onto her toes to wrap the bandages around her swollen breasts.

Marozia made no sound that indicated pain or pleasure. In fact she stared past Ninian, at nothing in particular at all. But her eyes were not glazed or listless. They were as sharp and cunning and bright as ever, and they were beautiful, an almost pure black, like obsidian beads polished to wear around the throat of a queen.

Perhaps she would like such a necklace, Ninian thought. The princess's throat was bare. It was a form of protest. She would not replace that garish bauble of her inheritance, and its absence would remind all of what had been stolen from her. *Stolen.* The mere thought, the memory, made Ninian's stomach form dark storm clouds of anger.

The handmaiden finished her wrapping and hurriedly went to the wardrobe to retrieve her mistress's gown. The princess did not like to be naked for long. Her new form repulsed her.

Marozia stood as still as stone, her arms at her sides, as she waited to be robed. Ninian had to maneuver her hands through the sleeves, for her mistress remained limp, giving her no help at all. Yet the more difficult part was to draw the front of the gown up over her stomach. That distended, tumescent thing that held the spawn of the prince.

Ninian did not so much like to look at it, either. Her mistress's skin had been stretched so tautly that her blue veins showed in a stark, bright nexus, and across them there were garish red streaks, like the claw marks of a mountain cat, and the flesh itself had grown dimpled and furrowed in places, as one's fingers shriveled in warm water.

None of this detracted from the princess's beauty, not in Ninian's mismatched eyes. Her beauty was like marble; nothing could corrode it, not even this blight, now hidden beneath the crimson velvet of her gown. It was a fever that would pass, a gangrenous limb that would be amputated, a cancerous lump that would be excised. It was a foreign thing that had infected her mistress, not something that had been engendered by Marozia herself. And it was the prince who had spread this pestilence.

At his father's orders, yes. The fault did not lie with Liuprand alone. He had been as unwilling a participant as the princess herself, both of them so rudely forced by the brute machinations of the king. They had shared a bed only once. Ninian knew this because it was she who shared the princess's bed on all other nights. One brisk and joyless coupling, one that had left Marozia in a state of unnatural stillness and silence, like a victim of the unspeaking plague that had once gripped the inhabitants of the Outer Wall.

(In those months, Ninian had passed countless slumped bodies on the street—not dead, but not quite living, either, merely stunned and stupid as the sickness ate away at their minds. Her mother had passed in this manner, and her brother. She had spooned water into their mouths until the moment that their empty, unfixed eyes closed for good.)

This unhappy coupling had sent the prince into some small self-exile. Weeks went by before he revealed himself again in the feast hall, and even then he ate little, drank more, and spoke in short, bitten-out words. He did not deign to even look at his wife, though his cheeks flushed in shame as her stomach swelled and swelled, the child desired by no one growing within it.

Ninian did not pity this unborn creature. She could not. It was a soulless thing, to her. It felt more like a machine, a device made solely for her mistress's torture. More than once she had ached for a scalpel. More than once she had woken at night, gently pressed a palm to her mistress's belly, and yearned to carve out this ugly instrument from within her.

"Ninian," Marozia said. "My rings."

"Yes," Ninian said, blinking from her reverie, "of course, my princess."

She went to the jewelry box and retrieved them. She knew which three her mistress wished to wear, and she cringed as she placed them in her palm. They were beautiful but hateful. Most loathsome of all was the wedding band, with its bulging, blood-red ruby, that seemed another device of torture, especially now. Ninian paused before Marozia.

"Are you certain you wish to wear them, my princess?" she asked. "I can have the metalworker stretch the bands—"

"No," Marozia snarled. "Put them on and do not question me again."

Ninian ducked her head, cheeks pinking with shame. At least the princess did hold out her hand and splay her fingers, so it was not as difficult a task as it might have been otherwise. Still—she struggled and her brow dewed with sweat as she tried to force the rings down her mistress's swollen fingers. All the while sympathetic pain scraped at her. But Marozia did not even flinch.

"The child will be born soon," the princess said, more softly now, "and the swelling will go down."

Ninian nodded. The fingers were not the only thing that gave her trouble. There were her feet, bloated to a vulgar size, which Marozia still insisted on cramming into her same slippers. At night, when Ninian removed them, her mistress's poor toes were mottled blue. She insisted, too, on being buttoned into stiff gowns of velvet, unforgiving of her new girth, bandaging her breasts so they would fit and so the leaking of milk would not show through.

At least in this she acquiesced—Ninian was allowed to bundle up her long, thick hair and enclose it in a golden hairnet. But the more she considered it, the more she thought it was perhaps not an acquiescence but another dagger aimed at her husband, making more obvious the bare column of her throat and that brusquely poached title.

Yet perhaps not a dagger? That was too common and too flimsy a weapon. And it could pierce only one heart at once. The princess had blades for many in Castle Crudele. Her eyes were always shining like their sharp ends.

Then came the heavy earrings, solid gold and large as figs, which pulled down her mistress's poor earlobes. Then the rouge, which gave some color to the flesh that had grown wasting and pale, as if the princess's lifeblood were being siphoned by the foul parasite within her. All this finery lay over Marozia with a stiffness, transforming the princess into something like a painted doll. Nothing like the straw dolls Ninian had played with as a child, rough and crude. The princess—whom Ninian handled just as gently as she would a child's toy—was the loveliest thing within the castle. No object, no bauble could be more beautiful or more treasured.

Ninian allowed her finger to rest too long on the princess's cheekbone. Marozia twitched, but it seemed an unconscious seizing, like a clamshell or a poisonous plant snapping itself shut.

"Enough now," her mistress said. "I am awaited in the great hall."

Marozia made to leave the room, and Ninian rushed to follow her, plunging ahead so she could open the door for her mistress. The princess went past her down the hall, Ninian loping after, and they walked for several moments in silence—other than the faint, granular sound of the bandages rubbing together and against Marozia's flesh, which only Ninian's ears were trained to hear—before Marozia turned and said, "I have no need of you tonight."

Ninian's face burned, and her stomach twisted with horror. The words were not unexpected, yet to be separated from her mistress for any length of time was torturous. Ordinarily Ninian would lie in their shared bed, face pressed to the princess's pillow, smelling the salty dew of her body, the oils of her hair, each moment they were apart dragging past painfully, like the scrape of a paring knife against bone.

But Marozia did not like to always be attended, not even now; especially not now. She did not wish to be perceived as weak, leaning upon her handmaidens as her pregnancy dragged after her like a sodden dress . . . yet more, Ninian suspected, she did not wish to accentuate in any way her husband's benevolence, his generosity. After all, Ninian had been a gift from the prince. Ninian knew her mistress would sooner drink poison than let him think her grateful.

"Shall I ready a bath for when you return?" Ninian asked hopefully. "Perhaps a balm for your feet? I can seek the counsel of the leeches—"

"I do not care what you do." Marozia's lips were thin, and because Ninian had not painted them, they were as white as marble. "I wish only for my labors to come and to be finished quickly."

Chastened into silence, Ninian merely nodded.

Marozia turned and did not look back at Ninian again; her gait did not falter, not even in the too-small slippers, in the starched confinement of the dress. She stopped only a single moment, placing one hand flat upon the top of her swollen belly, and Ninian knew she was feeling the gyrations of that miserable creature, its writhing, like a worm inside the unwilling flesh of a lovely red apple.

Ninian watched until her mistress turned the corner and vanished from her sight. Her heart was filled with longing and with hate.

Like a beaten dog, Ninian walked glumly through the halls of Castle Crudele, the image of her mistress and her mistress's traitorously swollen belly grinding on and on in her mind. Always she had been prone to florid imaginings. Maleagant, the wise woman of the Outer Wall, said that her mismatched eyes had gifted her with second sight: blue for what was, and gray for what was to come. She had so far manifested no talent for prophecy—much to the dismay of Maleagant, who wished for a successor—but she could so easily envision things that were impossible, things that would never be.

Now she imagined a device of torture, so large and multiform that it could not be real, though it *was* real—Ninian tasted on her tongue the blood this machine would draw. It had a long but narrow blade, rather like a sewing needle, but what it lacked in girth it made up for in sharpness, filed to a point that could pierce flesh with barely a prick. And as the victim lay strapped to a rack, the machine moved on its own, as if manipulated by the hand of God, to scrawl words into the sinner's skin.

Horribly, she could see her mistress on the rack, and the words on her skin were Liuprand, Liuprand, Liuprand, and Ninian clapped a hand over her mouth so she would not scream. She screwed her unnatural eyes shut. And then, through their eerie power, she saw the prince strapped to the rack instead, and the words on his skin were scourge and ruin and plague.

Maleagant had taught her how to read and write, and this was its profit.

She could not share these visions with another soul, for how vulgar they would think her. Yet she could not be idle when her mistress was by moments pricked and pricked again. And so Ninian's feet carried her down the stairs, farther down the stairs, through the twisting halls, past the statue of the youth with broken hands, past two hissing kitchen cats that swiped at her skirts, and to the leeches' bay, the small, stuffy chamber in the cellar where Truss and Mordaunt sat.

"Good afternoon, Your Scrupulousnesses," Ninian said. She curtsied.

"Shh," Truss said. "I am trying to concentrate."

He was shaking a closed fist; Ninian could not see what he held within it. Mordaunt snorted.

"This creature thinks he can wish a favorable roll into being," Mordaunt said. "He thinks that his mind is so powerful a thing, it will affect the course of the world."

"Shh," Truss said again. Then he opened his hand and let the knucklebones spill out across the table.

Mordaunt peered over at their array. "It appears that your focus was all for naught."

"Naught?" Truss echoed. "You will play for naught? I shall take those odds."

"You are an idiot," Mordaunt said. "Put those away. What are you here for, girl?"

Ninian glanced about the room. All around there were cots with stained linens, for when a servant or a messenger or an attendant or a soldier of Castle Crudele fell ill. There were saws and shears hanging on the walls for surgery, their blades flaking with rust. There were jars of herbs and vials of liquid, in all shades from sanguine to black bile, and rolls and rolls of bandages, which was where she had procured those for her mistress. A shiver ran through her. Had she remained in the Outer Wall, and been apprenticed to Maleagant, she would have known the use of all these materials; perhaps she could have even crafted the potion herself.

"If it please Your Scrupulousnesses," she said, "I seek a tonic for my mistress."

Truss was slipping the knucklebones back into their pouch; he did not look up at her. Mordaunt's wrinkled brow wrinkled further.

"For the princess? What is her affliction?"

Ninian shifted anxiously and drew a breath before speaking. "Her affliction can be seen easily with the naked eye . . . she wishes to be progressed from this unpleasant state to the next."

Truss did not appear to understand her, and his brown eyes were cloudy and dim. But Mordaunt did. Slowly, he rose to his feet, his overlarge leech's robes seeming to hang off his bony frame as if he were an ill-dressed scarecrow. He was not especially tall, but his gauntness gave him a falsely augmented height.

"Such tonics are not easily fashioned, nor easily swallowed," he said. "The princess is far from the first woman to seek one. I would have her know that it may taste like poison. I would have her know that a woman of weak constitution may not survive its effects."

Heat rushed to Ninian's face. "My mistress is *not* weak."

"Of course not." Mordaunt walked to one of the shelves and began plucking down jars. Ninian wished she could recognize the herbs within them—if only Maleagant had not been so protective of her ways! She would have no chance to learn such an art now, as women could not be leeches. Yet still she watched intently as Mordaunt began to grind down a purple-leafed herb with a pestle.

"The princess looks prepared to burst already," Truss said from his seat at the table.

Ninian's cheeks flushed even more brightly. "My mistress is *not* a pustule."

"Of course not," Mordaunt echoed. "Be quiet, Truss. Fetch me the mandrake."

Mandrake. Ninian made a note of this herb in her mind. Truss rose at last and, with heavy, plodding footsteps, made his way into some darkened alcove, where Ninian could barely glimpse his sepia robes in the shadows. When he emerged, he was holding a white, maggoty-looking root in his open palm.

Ninian wished she could have asked Mordaunt to describe the process, but the leeches kept the secrets of their art close. Instead she could only look over his shoulder, trying to appear as innocuous as possible, as though this were of no great interest to her. Mordaunt did not seem to notice. He continued on with his duty, grinding and mashing until what remained within the mortar was more liquid than solid. He then managed, with dexterous fingers, to pour this liquid into a minuscule vial. He stoppered it and shook it, and as Ninian watched in both awe and revulsion, it turned a viscous shade of charcoal.

"The taste and scent are like sulfur," Mordaunt said. "It will be hard, I expect, for the princess to stomach it. It must not be mixed with wine to dilute the flavor. Such an amalgam would be deadly. A true poison. It would turn black the blood in her veins and stop the heart."

Ninian nodded. "And she must drink it all?"

"A drop will suffice." Mordaunt held the vial out to her. "It depends on how quickly she wishes for her state to progress. The more she consumes, the faster her labors will come—and the more violent. It is not for a woman of infirmity, as I have said."

Ninian took the vial. It was warm, burning even, as though the liquid within was exuding an unnatural heat. Could it burst through the glass? As the pads of her thumbs began to prickle painfully, she slipped it into the pocket of her shift. There it still hummed with that perverse warmth, radiating through the fabric and to her flesh.

"Thank you," she said. "I will make sure the princess calls upon you when her state becomes . . . changeable."

Mordaunt gave a stiff nod. His expression was, as always, one of stoicism, yet some indiscernible emotion made the corner of his mouth twitch. He glanced from Ninian's face to the pocket where she had placed the vial. He appeared to be mulling something over.

At last, he said, "The tonic is a powerful one, and it does not affect the mother alone. There may be some risk to the child within her. It may be born cold as a stone. It may be born grotesque, mutated by the elixir spread through its mother's veins. I have seen all and more in my time. Make sure the princess understands this price and is willing to pay it."

There was a flutter in Ninian's stomach. Visions were flowering up behind her eyes. She blinked to banish them and then said, "She is."

"And is the prince willing to pay it? Is the king?"

Ninian set her jaw. And she did not reply.

The elixir had been made; it could not be undone, and she would not be buffeted from her course. She departed the leeches' bay, leaving Truss and Mordaunt to their squabbling and their games of chance, and passed through the icy corridors of Castle Crudele. When she was alone, by the statue of the handless youth, she reached into her pocket and removed the vial. The glass was hotter than before, and it burned a red mark into her palm.

Her mistress would not take this tonic willingly, Ninian knew. It would be treason, to endanger the life of the heir that turned in her belly like a worm—let the price of that treason fall on Ninian's head instead. *She* would pay it. She would lie on the rack and welcome the machine to carve BETRAYER and BUTCHER and VILLAINESS onto her skin. She would allow herself to be carved down to the bone.

There, in this secret corridor, Ninian unstoppered the vial. She poured a bit of the liquid onto the pad of her finger—oddly, the potion itself did not scald. Then she smeared the tonic onto her lips. Let her mistress think she had merely eaten something foul . . . let her believe that there was no craft, no perfidy, when Ninian gave the princess her nightly kiss on the mouth.

IV
THE MUMMERS

Agnes was not forced to confront Liuprand again until supper. She had thought to take the meal in her chambers, for the mere notion of seeing him, especially under the scrutiny of others, threatened to desolate her—how could she maintain this farce of remote civility?

Once, perhaps, they could have been companions, with nothing but the amity of common interests between them. Who but the king could tell the prince which company to keep? But they had poured themselves these gushing goblets of passion and drained them both in a single gulp. And now neither could be satisfied with the bland waters of *companionship*. It left them both so weak and wanting these past nine months. Either Agnes was always thirsty, or she thought she would never be thirsty again.

But Waltrude came to her door and said, "The king requests your presence tonight, my lady."

Agnes tried to appear unmoved. Waltrude knew her too well by now, however. The wet nurse's brow arched.

"Do not tell me he has found another act," Agnes said wearily.

Waltrude pressed her gummy lips together.

Agnes sighed. So supper would not be a simple affair, and she could not go in her current state. Waltrude picked through the gowns in her wardrobe, holding each one up for Agnes to affirm or to reject. There were gowns of lavender and lilac and gray, but Agnes passed over those, not for their color but because she did not fit them anymore. In these nine months she had eaten meat and drunk wine, and flesh had begun to fill the empty spaces between her bones. She would never have Marozia's lush figure, but her breasts now strained the bodices of those old gowns and her hips split the seams of their skirts. It was not that she had had a child's body before; it had been a corpse's. She was now not only a woman but a living creature after all. Her cheeks could even be persuaded to fill with color.

So new gowns had been ordered from the seamstress in shades of deep violet, rich plum. These gowns had necklines that Agnes would have once considered daring—which would have scandalized her grandmother and which not even Marozia would have deigned to wear—and she chose them not despite this, but because of it. Adele-Blanche was dead and gone, and so was the silent Lady Agnes who had always seemed halfway to joining her. The Agnes who spoke, and smiled, and sometimes even laughed—she bared her collarbones and her shoulders and the necklace of teeth, refitted to suit her coloring and her coloring alone. *Mistress of Teeth* was a title she had made new, with the help of Pliny's craft.

But Agnes's form was not without its faults. As Waltrude laced her into an orchid-colored dress, Agnes looked down at her hand. Compelled the fingers to curl, the disloyal fingers. She could get them halfway up, but she could not cajole them to touch her palm. And again and again the quill slid out from her flaccid grip.

"It will come right," Waltrude said. "Pliny knows his art."

"Perhaps." Agnes then clenched and unclenched the fingers of her right hand. "But I think that if I wish to write again, I should start learning with the other. I cannot wait forever."

Waltrude sniffed. "You are so young, to think that nine months is forever."

"Nine months is all it takes for a mere thought to become flesh and blood."

At that, Waltrude fell silent. She used the excuse of crossing the room to fetch Agnes's slippers. When she returned and knelt to slide them onto Agnes's feet, she said, lowly, "I know it causes you grief."

Agnes felt ice flood her veins. She did not allow her mind to turn, to truly consider Waltrude's words, to let the panic spread its cold roots through her. With a short breath, she replied, "It causes me grief to know that the union between the prince and the princess is not a peaceable one."

Disdainfully, Waltrude said, "I was never fool enough to believe it might be peaceable. This castle has not seen a peaceable union in all its years standing."

Agnes's skin prickled. She did not like to feel as though her world were the execution of some prophecy. Yet so often it did. Despite the articles of the Covenant, despite all the swords that had broken to banish bitter death from Drepane's shores, the bones of their ancestors were the castle's foundation and the past was always pulsing under her feet.

Perhaps it was not so horrible a thing to consider, the legacy of the royal line in this respect. Widsith had his squires, and Nicephorus had his whores. Agnes could only assume that even Berengar had his overt indiscretions. It was no sin to seek pleasure outside the marriage bed. But to seek love?

I would want you even if I could not touch you.

If a sickness could not be seen, could it ever be cured?

As if intentionally, to break Agnes from her reverie, Waltrude jabbed a pin to the hair near her temple. The wet nurse was never especially gentle, and Agnes flinched.

"I suppose you'll want your flowers," Waltrude said.

Agnes nodded.

At least in this, she never had to go wanting. As soon as they had returned to Castle Crudele, Liuprand had ordered a new plot dug and a new garden planted. A garden of white flowers, in every species, lilies and camellias and infant's breath and yarrow. The garden had its own cadre of servants to tend it, and more than once Agnes had glimpsed Liuprand there himself, cupping the flower heads in his palm to examine their fitness, even lowering himself to the ground to test the dampness of the soil. And each time her heart broke, and then mended itself, and then broke again, harrowed by this terrible affliction of loving him.

She wondered what the other inhabitants of Castle Crudele thought when they saw their prince among the white flowers, in the garden he had built for a woman who was not his wife. It was close to treachery because it was close to love. Would they see the gentleness beneath the epithet, the tenderhearted creature upon whom the crown and the title rested so heavily? Or would they only squint their eyes and wonder if it was truly *just*, to behave so devotedly toward the lady Agnes, when it was her cousin who wore his wedding band? Such thoughts could drive one to madness.

As Waltrude picked the crushed petals from her hair, Agnes flushed to recall how they had been so mangled. If she tried, she could summon the memory of his body pressed against her, his warmth and his hardness, his yearning made physical and driven into her. When Agnes had returned from the library, she had slipped her own hand between her thighs and brought herself to release with thoughts of Liuprand in her mind, but it was a hollow pleasure, a shade of what he could do with his fingers and his mouth. Her flush deepened. She hoped Waltrude did not notice.

"There," the wet nurse said, stepping back. "You are fit for supper with the king."

If only it were just supper and nothing more. Agnes's stomach ground against itself. And then she departed for the great hall.

Agnes heard the jangling of bells before she even reached the chamber; the performance had begun without her. Dread still knotted her insides, but she pushed through the door and entered. The feasting table was set out on the dais, but the other tables had been cleared away to make room for the mummers.

Their silk ribbons twirled in endless red gyres, and their slippered feet slapped the floor in a tuneless rhythm. They seemed to take no notice of Agnes's arrival, and she gave them a wide berth as she passed.

She climbed the dais and took her seat. The art of silence was still one she knew well, and it was only Liuprand who stirred when she sat. King Nicephorus was chewing on a leg of lamb and enraptured by the performance of the mummers. And Marozia—

Marozia. She sat at Liuprand's right and stared straight ahead—not at the mummers but past them. Yet her eyes were not glazed or hollow or empty. They were as sharp as they had ever been, flashing like the beaks of carrion birds, and her jaw was held taut. Her focus seemed to be on not looking at her cousin, on not acknowledging her presence.

A certain grief entered Agnes at this cold neglect. Marozia had been many things, but she had never been a creature of ice. Never heir to Adele-Blanche's legendary apathy. Now a strange reversal had occurred, one that Agnes half feared and half hoped would never be undone: Agnes wore the necklace of teeth and bore the title, but she no longer shared her grandmother's pitiless temper; Marozia had lost her inheritance yet now seemed more than ever Adele-Blanche's successor.

"Good evening, lady," Liuprand said. "I'm glad you have joined us."

"Thank you, my prince. I am glad to be here."

Pure lies and they both knew it. Agnes feigned great interest in her plate. Anything to keep her focus off Liuprand, and off the mummers.

They were mainland mummers, actors of farce, the faint aura of Seraph pulsing from them and turning the air in the great hall a very pale gold. As Agnes had recently learned, not all those of Seraphine blood seemed to equally inherit its gifts. These mummers were not especially beautiful; their hair was a dull shade of yellow, and though their eyes did gleam blue, Agnes could not recognize Seraph's lagoon within them. She knew this particular hue well, for how long she had spent looking into Liuprand's eyes.

She did not understand the language of Seraph but it did not matter, for the mummers did not speak. They went through the motions of their act in silence, with great, exaggerated gestures, swooning dramatically or stomping in feigned, sensational fury. The plot was a simplistic one and could be followed even without speech. There were no heights or depths. Two men fought over a woman (who was really a man in a gown and a wig, for mummery was a profession prohibited to the fairer sex), and the woman died. The men raged in grief and stuck swords in each other's bellies. Yet they played it all with humor. The king chortled as the mummers shook their fists at each other; when the woman died, he laughed so heartily that he dribbled wine down his doublet.

These acts were the new fancy of Nicephorus, whose former amusements had worn thin. It was whispered that he had grown too indolent to even welcome his favorite whores to his chamber. He had tasted every flavor of pleasure on Drepane. It all turned to ash in his mouth. So now he must import his merriment from Seraph.

Always the acts were excruciating, and none but the king enjoyed them. Perhaps he derived some pleasure from this—the small torments he inflicted upon his court by forcing them to watch again and again these dull charades. Agnes picked up her wine and took a sip, but it was as thin as water and as sour as bile. It did not fill her; it only reminded her of her own emptiness, how she had not felt Liuprand's lips on hers for nine terrible months.

Marozia had touched neither her food nor her wine. It would not have been an easy task, anyway—her chair was pushed far back from the table to accommodate the swelling beneath her gown. That sorrow swaddled in velvet. Agnes's throat grew tight as she stared at it. Since she had returned from the House of Blood, they had not shared a bed. She had not seen how her cousin's stomach had grown; she had only been able to perceive it as a stranger.

And yet its grotesqueness was not lessened for that; it was even augmented, perhaps. If Agnes had been able to touch her cousin's flesh as she once had so commonly, she might have managed to glean some fondness from it. Yet as it was, there was only limpid horror.

"You must eat something," she said, softly. "To keep up your strength."

Marozia's gaze snapped to hers immediately. "I will eat when and what I please."

Agnes felt a pricking at the corners of her eyes. "Perhaps just some bread?"

Marozia did not acquiesce, but she did not refuse, either. Her gaze was still fixed ahead. Agnes took the bread from her own plate and began to butter it. This was not the easiest task, given the limited use of her left hand, but she had been training her right to compensate so she did not make such a terrible mess of it, did not clumsily mangle the bread. She then cut the bread—with her right hand, again, in uncertain motions—and held out one small piece of it to her cousin.

As she did, Agnes's fingers were shaking. She was afraid Marozia would not take it, but she was equally afraid that she would. Marozia's head turned toward her, and in the dark mirrors of her eyes, Agnes saw herself not as she was but how she had been—the corpse-like figure with odd-jutting bones, her flesh more gray than white, the statue-girl, the silent lady. She saw her mouth as that unused, parched, ugly thing—the lips that had not ever been kissed, the tongue that had never tasted wine.

It would be so easy to fall, she thought, to slip back into that creature like a ghost returning to its body. She was filled with horrible terror, horrible dread, which made her want to drain her goblet and crunch the gristle of meat in her teeth to remind herself that she was *not* that creature, not anymore, though her flesh remembered all its abuses and her belly remembered its scraping emptiness. *Please, please, do not let me go back, I cannot return to that—*

Gingerly, as a cat laps at a bowl of milk, Marozia bit off the smallest chunk of bread. She chewed, chewed, and swallowed. Agnes grew as still as stone. When Marozia took another bite, Agnes felt her teeth graze the very tip of her index finger, and her tongue slightly rasp her thumb, and she was falling then, not into an empty abyss, but rather into a smothering warmth, almost a womb, a place that was so familiar to her that she nearly keened. She nearly fed her thumb into her cousin's mouth.

Marozia had a handmaiden now to share her bed, and Agnes had not held or been held by her in nine months. In this moment, she realized she missed it, missed it the way a whetstone missed its blade. And so Agnes lapsed back into silence as Marozia ate the bread from her hand.

Yet her gaze wandered as she did. Wandered to Liuprand, who was watching this act unfold intently. His ocean eyes were a maelstrom, but Agnes could easily imagine the thoughts turning behind them. He was willing her, in his mind, to stop this. He could see how it both comforted and diminished her. He was wishing that he were the hand, and she were the mouth, that he could feed her endlessly, that he could take her fingers into his mouth. This was the part of him whose shoulders trembled under the weight of the crown.

And then there was Liuprand the Just, who saw his wife being attended, who saw the ripening of his seed in her belly. The child who would mend these gashes his actions had left upon the island, turn those wounds to stiff blue scars. He had told her in haunted, miserable tones how the child had come to be conceived—and Agnes had listened, beaten by each word like flotsam caught in a snarling tide.

She came to me in my chambers. She was escorted by the Dolorous Guard. Flanked, on either side. They said my father had given them orders not to leave until it was done. They stood outside the door, and when they heard nothing but silence from within my bedchamber, they sent in those two leeches—those hideous creatures Truss and Mordaunt. The tall one came to me and the other to her. He stroked me roughly until my body betrayed my mind, and the princess's legs were pried apart and held there—and I was guided by their crass hands . . . when it was done, the stained sheets were taken to the king.

Agnes had then lapsed back into the agony and safety of silence, as her mind supplied her with a single thought: *I cannot bear this manner of existence for a moment longer.*

The mummers' act was done, and they bowed deeply. Through a mouthful of meat, the king ordered applause to be given. Agnes did not clap; her hand was occupied. Marozia was eating from it, but the bread was nearly gone. When it was, Agnes would miss it.

"There," Agnes said, softly. "Would you like any more?"

"No," Marozia whispered. "Just water, to wash it down."

So Agnes lifted the goblet in trembling fingers, and Marozia drank deeply of it. The mummers proceeded out of the hall, their feet slapping the stone floor. She wondered if they could feel the coldness through their slippers. And all the while Liuprand watched Agnes with a steady gaze, as if they were the only two creatures in the world, when in truth the world was crushing them inward, like grapes mashed for wine.

V
LIFE AND DEATH

Waltrude knew the sound of a woman greeting her death. It echoed throughout the halls of Castle Crudele that night. She woke to it with a start, as it reverberated like bells gonging within her ancient bones. She rose and followed the sound. She was too fixed in her course to even be afraid of what she would see when she found it, to even be haunted by the howling of ghosts. They were following her, but at a distance. Iphigene. Philomel. Pale-haired wights, held aloft in the air like ornaments fixed on an invisible string.

The sound led Waltrude to the princess's chamber, and she did not hesitate before swinging open the door.

She was not first to come—that was Marozia's handmaiden, the queer-eyed girl Ninian. She was holding her mistress's hand as her mistress writhed and twisted in the sheets, her sleeping shift pulled up over her breasts and her gruesomely distended belly. Her sweat had turned the bedclothes damp and dewed her forehead, but there was no blood to be seen yet.

Waltrude approached the bed briskly, sparing no moment for her own upset. She had witnessed and aided many a violent labor before. The only shock to her was how swiftly this labor had come. The princess had complained of no pains; Waltrude had not even noticed her wincing as she walked. Despite her thrashing, Marozia's legs were wrapped together, the muscles in her thighs clenching and taut. This was no good. Waltrude took one of her knees in each hand and began to wrest them apart.

"No!" the princess screeched. "Don't touch me!"

The viciousness of her protest made Waltrude recoil, but only briefly. "The child will not come if you are blocking its path, Princess," she said. To Ninian, she said, "Fetch some rags and hot water. Quickly."

Her queer eyes wavered and her chin quivered. "I should not leave my mistress's side . . ."

"This bed will become her deathbed if you stand there like a dumb statue," Waltrude snapped. "Go. *Now*, you useless girl."

Still, Ninian hesitated. With a deliberation that seemed to cause her physical agony, she untwined her fingers from the princess's. Marozia gasped at the loss, but then she was racked with a great pain that made her howl and writhe again, swollen breasts leaking.

She did not—perhaps could not—protest now as Waltrude pried her legs open. The oils of birth shone on her thighs. Already the child had begun to breach the exit, horribly stretching the flesh of its mother with the overripe plum of its head. There came now the trickle of blood, madder red.

Marozia shrieked again, fingers scrabbling for purchase in the sheets. When Ninian returned with the rags, Waltrude would put one in her mouth for the princess to bite down upon, which was as much for her own sake as for Waltrude, whose ancient ears were beginning to throb at the sound.

Yet it was not Ninian who came through the door then. It was the lady Agnes.

Unlike Waltrude, she hesitated there, just past the threshold. She, too, wore her nightgown still, suggesting she had been roused from her slumber and come running—her hair was loose around her, glossy yet mussed with sleep. And her eyes, her stone-gray eyes, were flung wide in horror, the color having already drained from her cheeks.

When it became clear that Agnes was frozen there, Waltrude jerked her head toward the princess. "Come now. Hold your cousin's hand. She will need a vessel for the pain."

Agnes came, but her steps were wobbly, halting, as if she were being yanked rudely forward on a rope. She paused at the edge of the bed, her gray eyes round and huge, and then, after another moment's hesitation, she found Marozia's hand amid the sheets and laced their fingers.

Marozia clamped down upon Agnes's hand at once, nails clawing at the flesh with such violence that it made even Waltrude shudder. The lady Agnes did not flinch. Instead she glanced up at Waltrude and in a small voice asked, "Is there nothing to give her for the pain? We should send for Pliny. He will—"

"No," Marozia gasped, and with a sudden surge of strength, she pushed herself up to a near-sitting position. "No leeches. Swear to me there will be no leeches."

Waltrude raised a brow. "Then you will endure the pain baldly?"

Tears broke from the princess's bloodshot eyes as she looked down at herself, at the swollen, undulating belly, at the open space between her thighs. "I do not care," she rasped. "I do not care, I do not care— only get it out of me, get it out of me *now!*"

On that final word her voice crested into a scream. Her face contorted into a grimace of anguish, the whites of her eyes flooding with yet more red.

Waltrude dipped her head between Marozia's thighs. The child's head had made no noticeable progress forward, and her stomach twitched with alarm.

"You must push, Princess," she said. "Else the babe will die half stuck within you."

A strangled sob wrenched from her throat. As she pushed, she howled and howled, and Waltrude could see, in her mind's eye, the sawing and scraping of the princess's vocal cords, which would steal her voice for days after her labors were done. Agnes's hand grew a blotchy purple, so mangled it was by Marozia's unrelenting grip.

Yet still—the babe's head did not proceed. There was another twitch in Waltrude's stomach. Before she could speak and urge the princess on, the door opened and Ninian came through. She carried a heavy bucket of water, which slouched her shoulders and slowed her steps to an awkward stumble, and under her arm was a bundle of rags.

She approached and set them down before Waltrude, shaking all over like a sapling in the wind.

"Is she well?" the girl asked, in her pitifully quavering voice. "Will the child be born soon?"

Waltrude did not answer. Rather, she said, "Damp the rags now and wipe the princess's forehead."

This was not essential and would not help along the labors, but it would keep the girl busy. Agnes's hand was still being crushed and mauled. Still the princess screamed. And still the babe would not come.

It was not yet the moment for a new course, but it would be soon. Waltrude waited and watched. When moments passed without progress, she said, to Agnes and to Ninian, "Get the princess to her feet. And then down onto her hands and knees."

Marozia protested, but it was a wordless, mewling sound, which only dribbled spittle down her chin. Her eyes still twisted shut, she allowed herself to be maneuvered—more hauled—out of the bed and onto the floor. Waltrude thought to cushion her knees, but this concern blew over and past her, for there was no opportunity to worry over small comforts. They walked now within the shady membrane between life and death.

In these circumstances, time bore down on Waltrude like a lathe, grinding and grinding. The princess no longer screamed—she whimpered, and wept in blurry gouts, but all her exertion was for nothing, and so were her tears. The babe would not budge.

Waltrude found her own hands shaking as she moved to wipe sweat from the princess's brow. Strands of hair were plastered to the skin, like kelp to a sunken statue, and she did not feel feverish but rather cold, and this frightened Waltrude to such a degree that she snatched her hand away.

Would this castle be so cruel as to claim another wife? Was Berengar's line so bitterly cursed that all who were yoked to it—who merely brushed against it—were doomed, too? These were questions for mystics and prophets. They were beyond the purview of a wet nurse. So was the saving of a life.

Two lives: the princess, and the infant stuck half inside her. Marozia was mangling her cousin's right hand, such that it grew to resemble her scarred and ravaged left. Yet Agnes did not flinch, did not move, only knelt there on the floor beside her, in a pose that was almost penitent, if anyone on the island of Drepane knew how to pray.

The girl Ninian had slumped over against the wall, her lashes fluttering. *Good,* Waltrude thought savagely, *let her faint and be done with this sniveling.* But she did not faint. Her knees were pulled to her chest, arms wrapped around them, and she rocked herself back and forth, whispering, "I'm sorry, I am so sorry, I never meant for this, never, never, never . . ."

On and on she went. Anger smoldered within Waltrude. Her mistress was in the narrowing gyre of death, and the girl thought only of herself. She should never have been plucked from that hovel in the Outer Wall. What a vain and stupid creature.

"Waltrude," Agnes whispered, interrupting the course of these cruel thoughts, "we must send for Pliny."

The princess was too mired in her agony to overhear. She had sunk to the floor and tipped onto her side, other hand pressed to the freakish swelling of her stomach, which seemed somehow—impossibly—larger than it had before. Waltrude gave one quick, stiff nod.

"Yes," she said. "We must."

Agnes's throat bobbed. "I will go."

"If she will let you." Waltrude indicated their joined hands.

At that, Agnes's gray eyes began to shine. Tears glistened at their corners, and her lips pressed into a thin grimace as if to keep from expelling a sob. Waltrude was alarmed, as she had never seen the lady weep before. By the time she had come to her after Lord Fredegar's death, her eyes were flat and dull, the tears as dry as the blood on her gown. The look of these coming tears filled Waltrude with dread.

Agnes bent over, lowering herself to her ground beside the princess, so that their heads were at a height. Their long hair—the same smoky-black shade precisely—twined and tangled. She pressed her cheek to her cousin's cheek, her lips to the shell of her ear, and whispered something that Waltrude did not have the privilege to hear.

Whatever these brief, secret words, they moved the princess. Her fingers slid limply out of Agnes's grasp, and her hand now rested like a dead thing on the floor. Agnes pushed herself to her feet and left the room without another word, her nightgown shuddering after her.

Alone now with the princess—except that useless lump rocking herself in the corner—Waltrude sat back on her heels and let out a breath. Before her was Marozia, wife of Liuprand the Just, the once-heiress of the House of Teeth, the great beauty of Drepane. But also before her was Iphigene, that golden child of Seraph, stiff as a doll in the white sheets that had been her death-shroud, and Philomel, the screaming queen, the lioness in chains, her throat crushed under her husband's brutish hands. All these others, whom Waltrude could not save.

VI
SPARE

Agnes had started her journey at a walk and then quickened to a run. Yet still this was not fast enough. The halls seemed to unspool before her, gray and endless, and her bare feet throbbed from beating over and over against the cold stone floor. She hated to be aware of any of it, to even be aware of the tightness in her chest, the burning of air in her throat. She hated to think of anything but Marozia, dying.

She will not. She cannot. I will not let her. She reached the arched entrance to the leeches' bay.

Agnes did not care to look around, nor did she have to—Pliny rose from his cot at once and came to her. He flipped his brown hood up over his head, covering the pits and the spots of age, and when he met her at the threshold, he merely said, "The princess?"

She nodded.

No more words needed to pass. This was good, as her voice was lost to her. Agnes turned back to the corridor and Pliny followed, and when she broke into a run again, the old leech roused his ancient muscles and ground his ancient bones and ran, too. Time clenched and then flattened. Within minutes, they were at Marozia's chamber again.

There had not been blood when Agnes had left but there was blood now. The salt of it curdled the air. It broke cold beads of sweat across Agnes's forehead, this weighty atmosphere, these red mists, and for a moment she was stopped in her tracks. Stopped as she breathed in Lord Fredegar's death. As she felt the briny tide of his blood rise and rise around her.

"No," she whispered. "This is not then."

Yet her own mind did not submit to her. She could not walk; she felt mired as if in a mud pit, and her lashes fluttered and her knees grew weak and all she saw was red, red, red.

"Lady?"

It was Pliny, touching her arm. Pliny, who reminded her, *Yes, this is not then.* He had seen Lord Fredegar's blood, too. Had crawled on the floor with it. Agnes tried not to see it, oh, she tried, but she had never been good at banishing ghosts.

She blinked through the haze, through the miasma of red, and saw Marozia on the ground. The spewing of her own blood was around her, up her swollen and pulsating belly, staining the white nightdress that had been removed to reveal all of her, her milk-heavy breasts and her nipples, grown stiff and taut from being exposed to the air.

Agnes felt her legs tremble under her. It took every ounce of her withering strength to cross the room. To kneel beside Marozia, in the spoiling pool of her blood, and press her hands to her cousin's cold cheeks. They were like two gray stones.

Her voice rose within her, out of her mouth and then to a pitch that grated her own ears. "Help her!" she cried. "Help her, do something—"

Swiftly, Pliny dropped to his knees. He pulled Marozia's legs apart; she was too far past the point of being able to protest. He dipped his head between them, examined her for a moment, then raised his head again. In a grave tone, he said, "Turn her over."

This was not an easy task. Marozia had gone entirely limp. And the handmaiden Ninian was of no help; she had curled into a fetal pose on the floor, hands clasped to her ears. But with difficulty, Agnes, Waltrude, and Pliny managed to flip her onto her back.

Though the rest of her body was still, Marozia's belly seemed to pulse and ripple. Agnes did not dare look between her legs, from where the blood was draining steadily. She focused on Marozia's face, on her faintly fluttering lashes—the beautiful face that Agnes had by turns desired and envied, loved and hated, now turned ashen and dull. The lips were odd, stained black. When Agnes brushed her finger across them, it came away with a faint charcoal-colored smear. As if she had drunk strange dark wine.

"You must keep her awake, lady," Pliny said, "else the babe will not be born naturally. It will be—"

"I know," Agnes bit out. She could see the scalpel flashing, that cruel and remote surgeon's tool. She would not let it happen. Not such barbarity—the smell of the blood was making her woozy, and an even more peculiar odor was lifting from Marozia's mouth.

Still, she pressed her forehead to her cousin's. She spoke and let the mists of her words drift down onto Marozia's cold-fevered skin.

"Be strong," she whispered. "You have done so well already. Do not be silent—do not give up your screams. Let your pain be known to all. Let it echo through every corridor in the castle. Punish the world with your agony. I know you have the strength for this. In my dreams, I have seen you survive it."

Very faintly, Marozia's lips parted. Her eyes remained yet shut, though she said, in the lowest rasp that even Agnes strained to hear, "Get it out of me. Please."

Agnes smoothed back the hair from her sweat-dewed forehead. "You must push. Only a little longer. I swear this trial is almost done."

Of course, she could not swear such a thing, but her own desire to believe it was at least as powerful as Marozia's. Her cousin's brow furrowed, her lips twisting into a grimace, and she reached out and grasped for Agnes's hand as she indeed gave a brutal, wrenching push.

Pliny's head bobbed there between her legs. "Good, Princess. Now again."

She obeyed, and this time a howl broke through her gritted teeth. Agnes let her hand be crushed in her cousin's grip, let Marozia press her pain into Agnes, let it pour into her like a cistern filling with rainwater. She allowed the smallest pearl of hope to glisten inside her. And then—

The door swung open, with no subtlety or gentleness. In the threshold stood the leech, Truss.

Marozia's eyes grew wide, her agony and her efforts momentarily forgotten. When she saw Truss, she screamed wordlessly.

The leech's face went pale. He looked as though he wished to flee, and Agnes wished he would, but before he turned in cowardice, he said, "The prince waits outside the door."

At this, a serpent within Marozia woke. She pushed herself up onto her elbows and shrieked, *"Get out!"*

Truss fled.

But Waltrude, who knelt on Marozia's other side and held her knees apart for Pliny to work between them, glanced up at Agnes.

"Go to him, lady," she said quietly. "The prince must know what comes of his wife and child. He must be consulted—better him than the king."

Agnes's stomach twisted. Words she wished to speak became dammed within her throat. So rather than reply, she gently extricated herself from Marozia's grasp—her cousin seemed hardly to notice, now within the fog of rage that Truss's presence had provoked—and rose to her feet. Unsteadily, as if bloated with wine, Agnes walked toward the door. She opened it.

Liuprand was pacing the corridor, his head turned down as he stared at the nothingness of the cold gray floor. When Agnes emerged, he looked up at once. The turmoil on his face was beyond description. Yet another crack went through Agnes's brittle and scabrous heart.

"The babe will not come," she choked out. Her vision swam with tears, though some ancient pride within her refused to let them fall. "She will not survive much longer in this state—Pliny will turn to the scalpel soon. I cannot—"

A sob rose from her chest and tumbled, still tearless, past her lips. Liuprand stood with perfect rigidity, his arms at his sides and his fists clenched, as though he was restraining himself from reaching for her. Agnes wanted the comfort and warmth of his body, but she could not bear what it would mean—the treachery, the perfidy—to be embraced by him.

Instead she exhaled a shuddering breath.

Innamorata ~ 317

"You must tell them," she said. "The leeches—your father. You must tell them that the princess's life is paramount. That she should not be sacrificed for—"

Agnes could not go on; another knot of tears had coiled in her throat. She smelled it, even here: the blood, the blood, the blood. It was all the same. Fredegar's, Marozia's. It was all brine and red. It would rise in its heavy swells and drown her.

She saw Liuprand swallow. That muscle, feathering in his jaw.

"My father slumbers still," he said at last. "It will take more than a woman's screams to wake him. He has slept through that and worse before. If anything, it is a lullaby to him. He . . ." Liuprand's voice broke off for a moment. His gaze swept to the ground.

Agnes only watched him, strung halfway between despair and hope.

Liuprand lifted his gaze again. Where they had been blurred before, like window glass in the rain, now his blue eyes were sharp and clear and burning.

"I will keep him from the door," he said. "Him and his leeches both. But I cannot promise how long." He cast a quick glance over his shoulder, down the long corridor where Agnes presumed Truss had fled. "Were I stronger—"

"No," Agnes cut in. Her heart was beating a fierce but jagged rhythm. She pressed her finger to his lips, silencing him. "Not here. Not now. There is no *time*."

And then she turned and went back into that bloody chamber before Liuprand could speak again. Her limbs were trembling, and she was filled with remorse. She had dismissed it too quickly—his turmoil, his pain. It was his child, after all, caught half inside its mother, dying before it would ever take its first breath of air. But she knew he had little love lost for the creature sown of this wretched union.

At that, Agnes felt her breath catch a bit in her throat. Even if this babe was born, if it lived . . . it would be hated for the hellish circumstances of its conception, hated for the pain it had wrought upon its mother and father both. *The Sorrowful. The Ill-Made.* Half a dozen cruel epithets Agnes conjured as she watched Marozia writhe and scream.

Ninian had been roused at last, and with her help, Waltrude and Pliny had lifted the princess back onto her bed.

Pliny's robes were drenched in red up to his elbows, hands still working between Marozia's legs. Upon hearing Agnes's entrance, he paused his ministrations and looked up. Ninian and Waltrude, too, let their gazes leave Marozia and land upon Agnes.

Her silence was terrible, in that moment, in the blood-humid air, with Ninian's tear-streaked face and Waltrude's grave, green eyes and Marozia's dazed, desperate keening. Only Pliny appeared unshaken—after all, he had seen so much blood before.

Somehow the silence had ensnared her again, that all-but-forgotten little noose. It had been her armor once and now it was her shackle. So Agnes had to swallow hard, and swallow again, until she tasted the burn of salt in her own mouth, until the words at last were freed.

"The prince has ordered that all measures be taken to preserve the life of the mother," she said.

Still they stared on. There was only Marozia's shallow panting to beat back the silence.

"*So do it!*" Agnes shouted, and she surprised herself more than anyone with the force of her words.

Flustered, the leech and the two women immediately returned to their task. Agnes joined them at the bed and saw at once that indeed some progress had been made in her absence. The head of the infant was now fully cresting into the world, plum-colored, smeared with the mucuses of birth—yet underneath those fetal oils were its eyes, the translucent lids showing a nexus of tender blue veins, and its lashes, which fluttered so very faintly, proving there was life within this yet-unborn creature. Agnes's heart skipped.

Ninian was now the one who held Marozia's hand, the girl's fingers turned blistery red and throbbing with the pressure. But her pain was a trifle to her; Ninian's tears were all for her mistress. She leaned down, close to Marozia's ear, and whispered apologies, which were odd for Agnes to overhear. She did not know what the girl had to be sorry for. And she did not think that Marozia would care to hear them, either.

But this left Agnes to stare down at the branching of her cousin's legs as she howled and thrashed and pushed and, at last, *at last,* the screaming of her child mingled with her own. It slipped out of her like a minnow, greasy and blood-dark, and Pliny caught it in a bundle of clean rags.

The denouement had come so suddenly, after these interminable and excruciating hours, that Agnes could only stare in blank shock. Pliny handed the infant to Waltrude, who began to wipe off that blood and grease, and he snipped the cord with a small pair of shears that seemed such a quotidian tool, better suited to embroidery or gardening than to the weighty tasks of life and death, and Marozia fell back limply on the bed, silent and still at last.

The infant's cries warbled through the air, tremulous yet strident. Waltrude had managed, in a matter of mere moments, to bundle it up, to pin down its tiny limbs. She rocked it once in her arms, then carried it past Agnes to the side of the bed. As she laid the swaddling on Marozia's chest, she said, "A girl, my princess."

Weakly, Marozia opened her eyes. "A girl?" she echoed in the lowest, hoarsest tone.

Waltrude nodded.

With quavering arms—yet with a strength that surprised Agnes mightily—Marozia reached up and embraced the writhing white bundle. Agnes had yet to see its full face, and still she could not imagine it as anything but a vaguely formed creature, more a dream in her mind than a living thing. She could only watch as Marozia pressed the infant to her breast, as she lowered her lips to the crown of its head, weeping heavily, now in symphony with her daughter.

Her daughter. If already an unbreachable rift had grown between them, now Marozia had left her in the most permanent of ways. Within moments, the second-greatest metamorphosis of all had taken place—birth and life, second only to death—and Marozia had become something Agnes never would. A mother. This transformation was irreversible. Both she and the infant were wound around the spool of time, in endless coils of red thread. There would be no unwinding; the thread could only be cut by a single pair of shears, the shears of death itself.

Yet just as the infant began to quiet, as Marozia learned the first trick of soothing her child, Pliny said, "You must prepare for the other, Princess."

Marozia's head snapped up, her gaze swimming with weary bewilderment. "The other?"

"Yes. The second, your daughter's twin."

That horrible, weighty silence blanketed the room yet again. There was only a sharp inhale from Ninian, a gasp of shock, and that selfish little breath filled Agnes with fury—why should even a moment be spared for the upset of some common-born handmaiden while the princess of Drepane had just brushed fingers with death? Yet the fury vacated her as quickly as it had come, replaced with a stretching, frigid dread. It spread its coldness through the marrow of her every bone.

"No," Marozia managed, her voice a rasp. "No, there cannot be . . ."

"There is." Pliny's tone was gentle, yet it left no room for further protest, for disbelief. "Push, Princess. Else the child will die before it can make its way into the world."

Marozia's arms, curled protectively around her daughter, began to tremble. Her voice rose beyond a whisper. "No. I do not want another."

This should be the end, Agnes thought. The princess should give her order, and no one should rebel against it. She was Drepane's future queen; her word was close to law. But the laws of humanity did not—could not—govern the course of nature. It would all grind on—time, birth, life, death—and not even the most preeminent of men could stop it. In the face of such relentless yet indifferent power, even Marozia was cowed. She was made as small as the cringing handmaiden, as the stoop-backed leech, as the wet nurse with wrung-out breasts. And Agnes felt herself crushed like a mason's brick.

It was Waltrude who spoke.

"The second will be easier," she said softly. "It is nearly here already. Nearly here, nearly here." She turned these words into a chant, and Agnes was reminded of how she had crooned to her, *Down the drain, down the drain, down the drain,* as she sat in a bathtub of Lord Fredegar's blood. These recitations were as close to comfort as the wet nurse had ever come.

A sob broke past Marozia's lips.

"No, please, no," she cried. "I don't want to. I do not want to do it again. *Please.*"

Agnes should have tried to soothe her. Ninian had become useless yet again, standing with her mouth hung open like a gutted fish. Waltrude patted Marozia's bent knee, as Pliny ducked back down between her spread legs, and the princess was riven apart once more by a new chorus of contractions. Her belly, still swollen, began to ripple and warp again.

Marozia howled. The infant on her chest—who of course could not be ignorant of her mother's agony—began to howl as well, her cries thinner yet no less passionate. Agnes felt their reverberation in her bones. Marozia pushed one moment and protested the next, her second labor a staggered, halting thing that made Agnes's gorge rise. She still could not move, could not speak. She could only wonder how this could be so. How, for all these months, could Marozia not have sensed the movement of two creatures inside her?

Where the chamber had once been overly warm and overly red, now it felt gelid and remote, as cold as the silver flash of a scalpel. Yet to her relief, Pliny never brandished one. Perhaps it was that the first child had eased the second's passage, or perhaps Marozia felt even greater desire to be rid of this babe than she had its elder, but the labor indeed progressed more quickly—and within what felt like mere moments, another minnow-like creature slipped from between her legs.

This one did not weep. From Agnes's vantage point, she could see only brief flashes: the infant's mottled blue skin, its sylphlike limbs, its overwhelming stillness, the mouth that did not draw breath. She saw Pliny rub his fingers furiously against its tiny chest, while Waltrude took up the shears this time and severed the stiff infant from its mother. Marozia fell back limply once more, only able to keep one arm bracing her daughter to her chest.

Agnes, too, felt she could not draw breath. She stared blankly at the spare child on the bed, the enormous hands of adults working over it, trying to grind life into its unmoving form. They worked out of instinct, out of the base human obligation to banish death wherever they could. They did not work for the infant's sake, for Marozia's sake, even for the prince or the king. They worked because it was distasteful to watch anything die.

And then, impossibly, came the very weakest of cries. The infant's blue-tinged lips moved.

Before it could even begin to thrash its diminutive limbs, Waltrude wrapped it in clean cloth, binding it within a cocoon of white. The pallor of bloodlessness faded slowly from its skin. Waltrude dabbed at its face, wiping off the sticky mucuses of birth, and its features revealed themselves—the tiny bulb of a nose, the pale fringe of lashes. Agnes wondered for a moment until Waltrude proclaimed, "A boy."

She moved to lay the child on Marozia's chest. But Marozia jerked upward in a frenzied spasm and shouted, "No!"

Waltrude halted. "It is your child, Princess—"

"*No,*" she wailed. "Get it away from me; I do not want it."

Her legs were still spread open and her bed was a slaughter-yard, doused in red and sticky-black clots. The infant squirmed in Waltrude's arms, opening its small wet mouth to show soft, toothless gums, but it more panted than wept, as if it struggled to draw enough breath for screams.

"I will take it," Agnes said. "Give it to me."

She had not been aware of the words gestating in her mind; they seemed to have been born fully formed on her tongue. Waltrude furrowed her brow and looked between her and Marozia for permission, but Marozia's attention was only on her daughter, kissing and nosing her head, as Agnes imagined a mother-wolf would her cub. After another beat of hesitation, Waltrude shifted the baby into Agnes's arms.

It gave another hiccuping breath, still mostly soundless. Its form was featherlight, but the warmth of its small body thrummed through Agnes's skin. Uncertainly, Agnes adjusted her grip, positioning the infant against her own breast. Mistaking her for its mother, the baby began to suckle against the bare skin of her collarbone. Persistent was this suckling, as if the baby did not—could not—know that the endeavor was fruitless, that Agnes was as barren as a salt flat. Yet she did not try to release herself from its latching.

When Agnes raised her head, she saw that Marozia was watching her. The look in her glazed black eyes was hateful.

"Get out," she rasped. "Get that creature away from me; I do not wish to look upon it."

Her voice was still weak from all her previous screaming, so Agnes did not perceive it as an order, did not at first understand how serious her cousin was. She merely stared back, as Marozia's son sucked a red mark into her skin, trying to find words but failing. Surely, Marozia could not mean—

"Get *out!*" Marozia shrieked. "Get out, get out, get *out!*"

Jolted with shock, Agnes staggered backward. Marozia's shrieks did not abate. Tears tracked down her cheeks, and spittle down her chin, and her teeth flashed and gnashed, and she even managed to push herself up onto her elbows, grasping for the candleholder on her bedside table. With perverse and freakish strength, she hurled it toward Agnes.

Agnes ducked, and the candleholder shattered against the wall. The white wax broke into pieces, like fragments of bone. The babe at her chest began to squirm and fuss, unlatching its mouth at last so it could give that same low, wheezing whine. Agnes righted herself, blood boiling with adrenaline.

Marozia screamed again, this time a wordless howl. And so Agnes turned and fled the chamber, leaving her cousin alone in her thrashing rage.

VII

WANTING, WHICH LIES LIKE SLEEP

It occurred to her only when she had exited the room and stood alone in the corridor that Agnes held Drepane's future king in her arms. Liuprand had gone—to fend off his father, she guessed—so he did not know that his seed had sprouted two children, that he now had a daughter and a son. One to wear a bridal veil, and the other to wear a crown. In a single labor, the alliance between the king and the House of Blood had been guaranteed, and Drepane's royal line had been secured. Such grand and weighty things, to rest upon these tiny infant shoulders.

Agnes had seen a newborn babe but once. She wished she did not remember the flavor of it. When she recalled this, she felt her throat fill with bile and her stomach turn sickishly empty. It was hunger and disgust, both at once. She was not fit to hold such an innocent creature; she was tainted by what she had done; she would never cease to taste newborn flesh on her tongue. Her hands trembled around the infant, her arms turning limp. Perhaps she should let it fall—perhaps the cold stone floor of Castle Crudele was a safer place for the babe than the lady Agnes's depraved grip.

Yet she held on, perhaps only out of instinct, the predisposition of a woman to succor a child even if she was not and never would be a mother. Adele-Blanche, with her concoctions of herbs, had made sure Agnes's womb would remain forever empty. The thought had not brought her particular grief until now, when she clasped Liuprand's son to her chest. His blood and Marozia's, mingled irrevocably, their union manifested in flesh and bone. She might have Liuprand's love, but it was an intangible thing. This that she held in her arms was solid, real. It could be seen and felt. It breathed; it lived.

She could have hated it, she supposed. It could have borne the burden of her grief and her dearth. But as Agnes examined its softly suckling face, she found that she could not summon up any such emotion. The opposite, in fact—Agnes found that she loved it. So simple and base was this epiphany that it seemed almost childish. Yet here was a creature upon which the world had so far left no mark, who held no ill feelings in its heart, whose mind was too unformed for thoughts of malice or vice. A fear clutched at her then, a terror that the world would sully it. That her arms would never be protection enough.

What had her arms even done, before she held this child? What had her soul done with this surfeit of love? Agnes wished so terribly and so bitterly that her breasts were not as barren as her womb, that she could at least nurse it—but that job would fall to Waltrude, she knew.

And Waltrude would come soon, either chased from the chamber by Marozia's roiling rage, or of her own accord, to see to the future princeling Agnes had stolen away. Soon this brief time of solitude between them would be done. But for the moment Agnes merely clutched the infant in her arms, its mouth still searching for purchase against her lacking breasts, and imagined that this time might stretch on forever, time in which she was not the hollow creature Adele-Blanche had formed from the red clay of her own wrath.

It then occurred to her that she should take the child to meet his father. She had gotten him, the little princeling, to stop fussing, though Agnes paced the halls of Castle Crudele with excruciating slowness, so very careful not to disturb the bundle in her arms. It slept now, but not deeply. It was restless with its new embodiment, with the first breaths of worldly air. Agnes paused often to stroke the soft crown of its head. With the oils of birth wiped away, she could now see the very pale blond fuzz there; he would be a golden prince one day, just like his father.

She had never been to Liuprand's chambers before—she had never dared, afraid that her passion would overtake her and she would commit yet another act of treason there—but she found her way eventually. She knocked quietly once upon the wooden door. There was no answering voice from the other side.

Agnes was then gripped by a nauseous sort of fear, fear that, in his grief and confusion, Liuprand had gone to enact some punishment upon himself—or perhaps he had not gone anywhere and was instead engaging in private torment in his chamber. It was this thought that eclipsed all her better judgment and urged her to push open the door.

She stepped inside, and the chamber was empty. Yet she could see Liuprand everywhere: in the gold-and-midnight-blue livery in the wardrobe, in the half-gulped carafe of wine on the table, in the bed that was unmade, suggesting no servants had been allowed inside, and in the books that were stacked in a perilous manner all over the floor.

Had it been anyone else, had Agnes not known Liuprand down to the soul, she would have been alarmed, would have seen this all as evidence of a disordered mind. As it was, she could imagine how the anguish and turmoil of these months had reflected themselves in the state of Liuprand's chamber. She wandered over to the pile of books and began to examine the spines; still the infant slept against her chest.

In the midst of this prying, Agnes heard the door to the chamber open. She whirled around, and the infant began to mewl at its sudden jostling.

The ember of hope in her heart was immediately snuffed, for it was Waltrude who entered the room, not Liuprand. The wet nurse's hands had been cleaned, her fingernails even scrubbed, yet the dark blood still dried in blotches on her white shift. When she saw Agnes, her ice-green eyes grew wide.

"What are you doing here, lady?" she demanded, in a voice far too rough for her station. But Waltrude was not just a servant here; she was too ancient for that, and too beloved. "Are you mad?"

"No," Agnes said, though her shoulders rose defensively around her ears. "How is Marozia? Is she well?"

"Well enough to hiss at me like a she-cat when I offered my breasts to the babe," Waltrude said. She clucked her tongue. "She insists on nursing the child herself. I am to understand this is a custom in your house, but it is unbecoming of a princess."

In half hope, half fear, Agnes asked, "Has she not demanded to see her son?"

Waltrude shook her head grimly. "She has demanded the opposite. She does not want the second child anywhere near her chamber—nor anyone else. She banished me; she banished Pliny. She wishes only to have that dull sparrow of a handmaiden at her side."

Agnes's stomach clenched. The princeling stirred again, searching its small mouth along her chest.

"Give the child here, lady," Waltrude said. "And leave this chamber at once. You cannot be seen here, much less in this state of undress. It is indecent."

Instantly, a flush rose to her cheeks. For all these months she had convinced herself that Waltrude did not know—could not know—yet it was hollow comfort now; she could no longer make herself believe it. But she was safe in her knowledge that Waltrude would never betray Liuprand—even if she did not love the thing he loved. And still, no crime had been committed beyond that single night in the House of Blood. A man could not be punished for the secret thoughts in his mind. Agnes swallowed.

"Unless you believe your breasts will begin to leak within several moments," Waltrude said dryly, "pass me the infant so he may eat. *Lady.*"

Every muscle of her body resisted the act of letting him go. She was awash again with the grief that her breasts could never nourish another, that she was such a deficient woman in that manner. She petted the babe's head. She wondered, with anguish, whether she would ever be permitted to hold him again. But she swore forever and ever she would not be the covetous creature Adele-Blanche had been. So with painful reluctance, she shifted the princeling into Waltrude's arms.

The wet nurse had warmth enough for the infant, and she rocked him gently against her chest. "There's a sweet boy," she whispered. "Already he is a picture of his father. He will be a strong king one day."

Agnes felt the weight of this expectation on her own shoulders, and she pitied the child. Already the world was beginning to press itself cruelly upon him. She wished he could have remained cached in her embrace. She wished such a great many things that it was like a knife, jabbed within her and twisted endlessly, stirring her organs and tangling her intestines. Once she had been able to elide this pain. But swallowing the poison of love had made her weak, and she could bear it no longer. Agnes left the chamber, her deprived heart beating brokenly.

VIII
A THOUSAND CANDLES BURNING

Agnes returned to her chamber, hating both its emptiness and her own. She stripped off her nightdress, irrevocably sullied with blood and sweat and the oils of barbarous birth. She flung it onto the ground, and it fell like a ghost bereft of its vessel. She stepped over it, the bodiless, soiled white, and went to her wardrobe.

She chose a deep-violet gown, the darkest she owned, the richest in hue, almost pure black. Violet for victory? Or black, for mourning? Her emotions were too multiform to be communicated through the limited language of rustling wings. There were not enough colors for all that she thought and felt. This was the gift of speech, which Liuprand had worked so meticulously and lovingly to draw out of her. And now she could not find him, her companion, her guardian, her beloved, the creature beneath the epithet whom she cared for so immeasurably that it had healed the broken pieces of her.

The flowers in her vase were wilting, but she had neither the time nor desire to go down to the garden and pick more, so she plucked the two least shriveled and put them in her hair, held there with a pair of silver clips. The necklace of teeth was fixed in place around her throat. And when she regarded herself in the mirror, she saw the lady Agnes, Mistress of Teeth, a rose-pink flush in her cheeks, made vivid and bright and even beautiful by the strength of the desire coursing through her. She could be all—she could be so much—except she could not be a mother and she could not be Liuprand's bride.

Agnes pushed these thoughts from her mind. To find him was paramount. She would feel irreparably lost until she did.

First, she made the journey back to his chambers. The floors of Castle Crudele felt exceptionally cold at this early-morning hour, but perhaps it was merely because her feet were so warm. Her body was overall warm, almost feverish. *Please,* she thought, as she reached the door, *please let him be on the other side.*

But when she pushed it open, it was only Waltrude there still. She sat now, holding the child to her breast. The princeling was finally suckling, and the scent of milk filled the room. Agnes's stomach twinged with grief.

"He has not yet come?" Agnes asked. "The prince?"

Waltrude regarded her with reproach. "No, he has not come. And you should not have returned here, lady. It is unbecoming." The wet nurse sighed. "Yet at least you are properly clothed now."

Heat prickled across Agnes's cheeks, but she did not reply to Waltrude's chastisement. Instead, she began to pace the room, trying to appear innocuous and incurious, as Waltrude continued to look at her with disdain. She let her eyes graze the half-gulped wine, the unmade bed, the crumpled livery. And then they landed upon the stack of books.

Waltrude let out a huff, but Agnes was undeterred. She walked over to the stack and lifted up the first book. It was the one she had picked out from the library herself—Liuprand's favorite—the worn and rather unremarkable tome with the embossed sun on its cover. She ran her fingers gently across it, feeling the raised rays of solar fire. The spine was creased with a hundred openings and closings. When she opened the book herself, it fell open to the most accustomed page. It had been marked so many times that the corner was permanently creased.

Agnes did not know the plot of the book at all, so she could not guess at why it was so beloved to Liuprand. It would take hours to read in its entirety, and she did not have the time. So she merely skimmed this single page, all while Waltrude let out contemptuous sighs, and the soft suckling of the infant gave the chamber a warm and peaceful chorus.

Innamorata ~ 331

At the bottom of the page, her eyes stopped. She read the final line. *And wing'd, sure-foot'd Tisander went to beg from the gods forgiveness for his father's crimes*—and Agnes knew where Liuprand had gone.

It was the very highest room, in the very tallest tower, and Agnes's calves were straining by the time she reached it. The chapel. She suspected that few in Castle Crudele even knew of its existence, and those who did would never care to visit, especially since the Exarch had passed. What reason would they have? God had long been banished from Drepane. Whatever holiness still lurked behind these doors was invented by the chapel's visitors, their mind supplying divinity where none existed. The mind, which itself could fathom the sea into a desert, and an oasis into a wasteland.

The door was heavy and gridded in iron. Agnes could not push it open merely with her hand; she had to thrust her whole body against it—once, twice, three times—and then it scraped open.

She had expected darkness on the other side, a filmy, smeared gathering of shadows. But instead there was, all around her, smoldering golden light. It pulsed from the altar in the very center of the room, where what seemed a thousand candles were burning. It pulsed from Liuprand himself.

He turned at once when he saw her, his face bathed in that heady glow. What might have been disguised in shadows was now thrown into harsh relief: the gash along his cheekbone, the blood trickling from the corner of his mouth. Agnes's heart stuck in her throat.

No words passed; she merely hurtled toward him. She managed to stop just before they touched, and her hand felt for the altar, gripping the stone to steady herself. The candle flames juddered with her movement, her intrusion upon the room's stale air.

Liuprand did not even reach up to wipe the blood from his face. He let it drip down his chin. A moment or two passed. And then he said, in a hoarse voice, "She lives?"

Agnes nodded.

"And the child?"

"Children," she whispered. "A girl and a boy."

She watched his eyes fill with horror. He, too, had been made into something against his will. He had been sculpted from the clay of the king's malice into this new creature, and it was a metamorphosis that could not be reversed. One might die, but one could not be unborn. And so Liuprand the Father now stood before her. The blood trickled past his chin and down to his throat.

"Agnes," he said, so softly. Then he stopped and spoke no more.

He had stood between Nicephorus and Marozia and had suffered these wounds for it. Endured them to save the wife he could not be persuaded to love, the wife who loathed him down to her marrow. Liuprand the Just. Was it the fate of a just man to ever be confronted with such impossible choices—mother or child, bride or heir? Was it the fate of a just man to ever make small his own desires? Agnes's heart beat with grief for him, with love, with longing.

"Would I were your wife instead." Her voice broke. "Would that my womb could bear your child . . ."

Liuprand gave his head the smallest of shakes. "Do not speak such rapturous dreams to me. My greatest weakness is my wanting for the impossible."

Pain embedded itself in her skin like splinters. "But it is not fair—it is not fair that we are doomed to only dream—"

She lifted a hand to his face. It was treason, she knew; it was perfidy, it was sin. Liuprand at first remained as still as stone, but then he leaned almost imperceptibly into her touch so that she could run her thumb along the gash on his cheek, so very gently, such that he did not even flinch. Agnes could imagine the force of the blow that had caused it— only a man of Seraphine strength could wound another creature of Seraph so facilely—and it made her skin heat with further defiance, with further abandon. The sight of this wound could almost convince her that she acted with justice. That the evil deeds of the king deserved to be repaid with treachery.

Yet this was not why she acted. Not truly. She acted because her wanting for the impossible was more potent than any sense of justice or reason.

Agnes pushed herself onto her tiptoes, to the greatest height she could reach. Still it was not enough, not until Liuprand dipped his head to meet her. To touch his blood-tainted lips to hers.

It did not even begin gently; it could not. They could not stand among these flames without being consumed. Liuprand drove his mouth against hers, relentless, ignorant to—perhaps uncaring of—how he further opened and aggrieved his split lip. Agnes tasted his blood on her tongue, and it was salty like his seed.

He groaned, hands roaming against her breasts, grasping her hips through the skirt of her gown. Without breaking the kiss—and with such swiftness and ease that it was a shock even now to Agnes, who thought she had accustomed herself to his strength—he lifted her.

There was a small swath of stone on the altar where no candle burned, just large enough for her to be seated upon it. Liuprand set her down carefully, on the very edge, so that if she leaned too far forward she would fall. Yet the position was in fact twice as precarious: If she leaned too far back, her hair would catch fire, and she would be truly consumed.

Liuprand did not bother fumbling with the stays of her corset. He grasped the front of her bodice and tore it open, exposing her breasts to the cool and gloaming air. His thumb dragged across her nipple, stiffening it, and she moaned. Already she was slick for him, dripping through her skirts and to the stone of the altar below. Their coupling would leave its mark here.

Agnes had thought at first to be tender with him. Since last she had touched him, he had been handled roughly, by those cruel and detestable leeches, and she did not wish to make him recall those moments when his body had not been his own. But he did not want her restraint.

He wanted to know that his yearning was not unanswered. That he was not alone in this doomed and desperate desire.

So she tore at his breeches, feeling the hard swell of him beneath the fabric that made her throat go dry with need. He drew in a rasping breath, his lips against the shell of her ear and then the column of her throat as she divested him of the breeches and then the underclothes, and took his length in her hand.

Liuprand let her hold him for no more than a moment, and then wrested himself free and knelt before her. He shoved up her skirts and fixed his mouth to the sweet place between her thighs, the place where she had so often stroked herself but could never manage to find even a shadow of the pleasure he had impressed upon her. Agnes's eyes squeezed shut and her head rolled back, the ends of her hair dangling mere inches above the leaping flame.

All her reason was, indeed, undone by his mouth. Yet just as her release was mounting within her, Liuprand pulled away. Panting, he looked up at her, lips painted with a smear of her spend and his blood, blue eyes holding the light of these thousand candles.

"Will you have me?" he asked in a voice as deep as a dreamless slumber.

"Yes," she whispered back, "please—"

He rose and caught her mouth in his. She grasped at his shirt, tugging it until she bared his collarbone and his shoulder, though she could not manage to get it off all the way. For now it was enough to touch even a modest expanse of his bare skin, after so long having not more than a glance from afar. She felt him nudge at her entrance, and she pushed her hips upward, coaxing him inside her.

In all these months, she had almost forgotten the magnificent size of him and how he seemed perfectly formed just to fill her. She had been so horribly, bitterly empty, and now she was sated at last—almost glutted, as her channel stretched and stretched to accommodate him. His thrusts were hard, and ruthless, and nearly bruising—though any pain was pain she welcomed, pain she craved, pain she would have even begged for.

Liuprand crushed her against his chest, holding her taut there so she would not slide back and be eaten alive by the flames. He fisted her hair, dislodging the clips and scattering the white petals about the altar. Some of them caught alight; she smelled their burning. With his other hand, Liuprand clutched and kneaded at her breast, her terribly deprived breast, which ached, too, at its emptiness. She wondered if he was thinking it—that it would never swell to feed a child. She wondered if the thought struck him as grievous and unjust. But as he thrust into her, angling his hips to reach that exquisite place within her, Agnes could think no longer.

His climax was near; she felt his breathing grow rougher and his thrusts more desperate. Agnes was making high, keening sounds that she should have muffled against his shoulder, but they were in such a secret and remote place that she knew no one would hear. This was not like before, in the House of Blood, borrowed space and borrowed time. The moments stretched and warped around them, accommodating their act of perfidy.

Her short, sharp gasps filled the room, as did Liuprand's throaty groans. His mouth caught hers in a kiss, hasty and heedless of his own pain, or hers, teeth grazing her lip and then her tongue.

He caressed her nipple just so, and then she was undone. Her head tipped back, her mouth unlatching from his so that she could cry out with her release. Pleasure rolled through her in one great wave, and then another, as she felt Liuprand spill himself inside her. He muffled his own cry against her throat, but the sound of it echoed through her, making her skin hum like a harp string. When she felt the warmth of his seed rush into her cold and barren womb, she came to climax once more, imagining the impossible, that it might take root.

Liuprand remained that way, inside her, holding her flush against his chest, until he grew limp and slid out. Agnes let out a whimper as his seed leaked down her thighs. Tears gathered along the line of her lashes, and she pressed her face to the fabric of Liuprand's doublet to keep them from falling, to keep him from noticing that their coupling had stirred within her a certain grief. But he did notice—how could he not, with the warmth and salt of her tears seeping through his shirt? He pulled away, one hand on her thigh to keep her steady upon the altar, and the other under her chin, tipping her face up to his.

"I hate to watch you weep," he said. "What have I done to you, Agnes?"

It was a question as much to himself as it was to her. Agnes merely shook her head. The tears doused her cheeks.

"Tell me." He spoke with a prince's tenor. His thumb stroked over her lip. Moments fell around them, sand through the siphon of an hourglass.

"I did not wish for this," she said brokenly, at last. "Who would wish for this—for love that burns only in the dark?" She took him by the wrist and guided his hand down, over her stomach, bony and scarred, and pressed his palm flat against it. "To be mistress at best, never bride, never wife, never mother."

Liuprand inhaled, sharp and tremulous. His fingers splayed across her belly, tracing the words Adele-Blanche had etched there. JEALOUSLY GUARD YOUR MAIDENHEAD. Well, that was over, and Agnes was glad for it to be done. But the very deepest wounds, the ones that could not be seen, remained. The wreck of her womb, stabbed and shriveled. A sob tumbled past her lips.

"Would that I could take it back," he whispered. "This miserable union that writhes within us all like a maggot. I knew from that earliest moment. From the moment I met your eyes above Adele-Blanche's desecrated body. I knew that I would die a thousand deaths waiting for you."

The gash on his cheek was still fresh and red. Many halls and chambers away, Marozia lay stiffly in her bed of blood. And Agnes's tears spilled and spilled, half defiance, half sorrow, and all for what she could see but never hold, for what she could hold but never have.

"At least let me go then," she said, her voice choked with bitterness. "As you would have done with Lord Fredegar . . . make me another match so that I must not always be tormented with the sight of you." The words were perhaps harsher than she meant, but her tongue felt loose in her mouth, and her tears had slicked the path for such stinging retorts.

Liuprand's face hardened. "Is that truly what you desire?"

No, she thought, and then yes, and then no again. Agnes let her hands fall into her lap, into her crumpled skirts. Her bare thighs were two shocks of white against the altar's dark stone. Her fingers, spidery, pale, laced with the memory of Nicephorus's knife. She thought of Marozia's thighs, painted with blood, of Marozia's hands, knuckles straining under her skin as she clawed at the sweat-damp sheets. None of this could be undone.

Agnes reached through the flame-daubed dark for Liuprand.

"We may never dance at a masque," she said, "or hold each other in the light for another pair of eyes to see. But I will not be your secret shame." That word, *mistress,* was like a rotten piece of fruit in her mouth.

"I will never be ashamed." Liuprand sounded almost angry. "You are my secret joy, my secret comfort, my secret passion and need." His voice grew low. "Tell me what you wish and I will do it. Make me your disciple; I will kneel for no other."

This, perhaps, was true—he had knelt before her at the altar, and she had never seen him yield like this before. But Agnes did not wish for a disciple, for a slave. Painstakingly, she pushed her skirts back over her naked thighs. She drew her torn bodice up to cover her breasts. She began to slide down from the altar, and Liuprand immediately moved to help, lifting her into his arms and then setting her gently upon the floor.

"Not disciple." Her fingers ghosted across his cheek; even when she touched the wound, he did not flinch. "I would have you be my equal, my matched half." She closed her eyes, and a single tear painted a path down her face. "But it is impossible. The dead would sooner wake."

IX

WHAT MIGHT BREAK APART THE WORLD

"Princess? Princess?"

His words fell upon the limp body in the bed like leaves from a dead tree. They lay across her but did not penetrate. Marozia was on her side now, the child swaddled in her arms and held near to her face so that she could brush kisses against her daughter's red cheeks. The sheets were soaked with the mucuses of birth, sweat, and blood. Her nightgown was tangled about her tired limbs, which lent her the look of a mermaid caught in a sea-net, having yet given up its desperate thrashing.

She did not seem to even hear him at all, so Pliny gently touched her arm.

At that, she came alive, flinching and then jerking up to shake off his grip. The babe stirred, but only yawned and then returned to sleep. Marozia flashed her teeth.

"Get away from me," she rasped. "Leave me alone with my daughter. You foul little worm."

"I will, Princess," Pliny said. He was well accustomed to the mistrust many on Drepane harbored toward leeches, but such a slight directly against his person was enough to prick at him. "But first I must ensure that you and the child are sound."

"I am sound enough to claw your robes to ribbons and your heart to shreds."

Pliny retracted his hand. He laced its fingers with those of his other and held them across his middle. He did not care for the princess at all—he much preferred the nature and manner of her cousin—but he could not help feeling a begrudged tug of admiration. She had survived what most other women would not. Such a violent labor he had never seen, and so unprovoked. He had not been given a chance to examine her during the pregnancy; Nicephorus had his own leeches perform this task, but nothing about her general condition suggested to Pliny that she would be so wrung through so brutally as her children were delivered into the world.

At that moment, as if summoned by his thought, Truss and Mordaunt came through the door. Pliny stifled a sigh.

These two leeches—the favored of the king and the Most Esteemed Surgeon—were not, to Pliny's mind, shining paragons of their order. He had observed them spilling tonics, shattering bones as they were bundled up to be sent to Lord Amycus, and playing inane games of chance in the leeches' bay. This could occupy them for hours. Once, Pliny had asked the short one, Truss, what had inspired his interest in surgery and ceremony, such that he would take the leech's somber vows. Vows that would put one always in the reach of death's white arms. Truss had replied that he enjoyed the company of men who spent their money on gambling instead of on whores.

"Princess." Mordaunt, the taller and slightly wiser of the two, bowed his head. "Congratulations on the birth of your children."

Marozia's dark eyes narrowed to slits and she did not reply. She only clutched the infant closer to her chest.

"Where is the other?" asked Truss.

"Gone," Marozia hissed. "I do not wish to see it. Do not even speak of it."

Truss and Mordaunt exchanged dumb glances.

"With the wet nurse, Waltrude," Pliny answered in Marozia's stead. "Your daughter will be hungry soon, Princess. I shall call Waltrude back—"

"*No!*" Marozia cried out, this time with less vitriol than grief. "I will nurse her myself . . . it is the custom of my house . . . she will not spend a single night in another's arms."

Pliny drew in a breath. Truss and Mordaunt still regarded each other in doltish bewilderment. A heavy and discomfiting silence filled the room, and it was broken only by a small, soft voice from the corner by Marozia's bed.

"If it please, my princess," Ninian whispered, "let me, I beg, at least give you a fresh gown and sheets."

Marozia's mouth dragged down into a grimace of pain. Yet she did not protest; she did not even speak. Evidently her handmaiden knew that this silence was assent, for she then moved toward her mistress and began removing the sheets from the bed. A difficult task, as Marozia still lay within it, stiff as a stone, but Ninian persevered.

After watching her labor for several moments, Pliny stepped forward. Silently he withdrew his shears and began to cut the bloodied sheets until mere strips of fabric remained, which could then be slipped out easily from beneath the princess's unmoving body. Truss and Mordaunt, of course, watched this all without even the subtlest indication of wanting to assist.

Her nightgown was still plastered to her limbs with blood, drying as dark as oil. Gingerly Ninian began to peel back the fabric, but it stuck on her mistress's skin, and Marozia gave a grunt of displeasure.

"You will need a sponge and water for that," Pliny said quietly. His gaze flickered to Truss and Mordaunt. "Go fetch them at once."

Mordaunt gave a haughty sniff, but if Truss chafed at being ordered by a leech of no special stature, he did not show it. The two went obediently, their sepia robes hushing across the stone floor. Once they were gone, Marozia went limp against the bare mattress.

"Please," she whispered. It was nearly too low for Pliny to hear. "Please, leave me. I wish to be alone with my daughter."

To hear a princess beg was appalling to Pliny. Her desperation was a tangible thing, a gray miasma in the air. It touched him, and his heart flooded with grief and with pity. No princess should be in such a state that she pleaded mercy from a leech. It almost disgusted him.

He should have stayed, to ensure that she—and more important, the child in her arms—was firm enough to survive. It was his duty, as he had sworn when he took his leech's vows. But Pliny tasted the brine of blood on his tongue, and his arms were soaked with it up to the elbow. That alone would not be enough to dissuade him—he was a surgeon, after all—but when it mingled with the princess's despair, he felt as if he might be sick all over the floor.

So with one last dip of his head, Pliny obeyed the princess and vanished.

What was his duty now? He had been dismissed by the princess; he had not even been granted a moment to examine the infant clutched so jealously in her arms. His duty was to surgery, to easing and prolonging life, to beating back unyielding death. If the princess or her child died under the inept care of Truss and Mordaunt, Pliny would not endure the guilt. This was the mark of a good leech, he thought. To shame oneself for failing at one's paramount task. Death sweeping in, beneath his notice, and stealing away the breath of Marozia and her daughter.

Perhaps he should have insisted on staying. Perhaps he should have fought. Pliny turned all of this over in his mind as he paced the corridors, until he remembered—*There is another*. He could redeem himself in this matter by seeing to the second child. The poor, rejected princeling, smaller and weaker than his sister, turned away from his mother's breast before he could ever feel her warmth. *Waltrude*, he thought then, *I must find Waltrude. The princeling will be with her.*

He first checked her chambers and found them empty. Had she gone to the leeches' bay, seeking a tonic to bring forth her milk? This was possible; probable, even. Pliny chose this as his next destination. By now dawn had come, and it lit the hallways of Castle Crudele with pale and powerful beams of sun, shrinking the torch flames within their sconces. Yet for all this light, the stone floors never grew warmer; they were as cold as ever beneath Pliny's feet.

Pliny was approaching the long spiraling staircase to the cellar when another thought entered his mind. The prince. Waltrude would have gone to him, would she not? Liuprand was her dearest love, the singular joy of her shriveled heart. She would have wanted to show him his son.

So Pliny turned abruptly on his heel and headed backward to the prince's chambers. He had been summoned there twice, maybe three times before, to treat Liuprand's minor ailments—a headache induced by a greedy gulping of wine, a bruise or a cut that he claimed was from a tiltyard tumble, though Pliny had never seen the prince take up a spear or a sword. He had no squires, and seemingly no love for hunting or sport. His only true passion appeared to lie within the conch-shell spiral of the library.

When he reached the door, Pliny rapped once upon the wood. There was a shuffling, and a haughty breath he recognized, and then Waltrude called out, "Come in and do it quickly." As if she could scent him through the threshold.

He entered and found the wet nurse seated with the princeling in her arms. He slept now, a tranquil bundle of white, though the red blotches of birth were still risen across his cheeks. Otherwise he was a handsome infant, though Pliny would not expect anything less from the joining of the prince's blood with Marozia's. The baby's beauty could only increase as he grew—or so Pliny thought. This was the first time he had seen the product of a union between Seraph and Drepane.

"The child," Pliny said. "He is well?"

Waltrude nodded. "He ate fulsomely and rests now. Already he is the picture of his father, in face and in nature. A quiet, unobtrusive infant. A boon to Castle Crudele."

Pliny inched closer. The child's face was indeed turned blank with sleep; there was no scowl or grimace or furrow in his brow as he dreamed his first living dreams. "Has he yet been named?"

"No. The prince cannot be found. Still he has not laid eyes on his son."

"Still?" Pliny inhaled, breathing the lingering scent of milk in the air. "Where do you suspect he has gone?"

Waltrude examined the infant's face very closely. She hummed a tune, wordless and brisk. Then she looked up at Pliny and said, "I have sent the lady Agnes to find him."

Her voice had the charge of the sky before a storm, dense and taut, with the promise of cruel white lightning. Pliny shifted, made uncomfortable by this sudden transformation, which turned the whole room into a place of ill omen, of warning. He was silent for quite a long time, considering how the mere mention of Agnes's name had engendered this change. Waltrude's lips were pressed into a thin line. Pliny did not even bother to ask, because he knew she would reveal nothing on this matter.

Instead, he chose a more innocuous question.

"Do you think the prince has gone to see his father?"

Waltrude gave him a dour look. "That is the last place he will have gone."

The last place, indeed. No one went to pay a visit to the king unless it was on pain of death. These past months had warped and mangled Nicephorus so repulsively. Now, Pliny thought, the king was lucky to only wear the epithet *the Sluggard,* for he could invent far more fitting titles that were far less flattering.

Pliny considered this all heavily. Not the king's chambers, not the tiltyard—nowhere he would expect to be easily found. He did contemplate the library, but if the prince was indeed hiding, he would not be in one of his daily haunts. He would cache himself within the castle's most secret place. Where not a soul would think to look because they did not even know that such a place existed. But Pliny did. And so that was where he went.

What a grueling journey, to Castle Crudele's tallest tower. Pliny's muscles twinged with agony and his very bones seemed to tremble, age and exhaustion loosening them at the joints. Only torchlight thrived here, flickering boldly against the windowless dark. No sun could pass through solid stone. Pliny put one hand upon the wall to steady himself as he climbed, acutely aware of his own labored breaths, how his panting made the mucus rattle in his throat. Yet undeterred, he climbed.

When he reached the landing, he stopped to regain his strength, and was suddenly overcome by a sensation of ill ease. It did not press in on him as some atmospheric augury; rather, it was summoned from within his very own being. There was a heat that began in his chest and then stretched its tendrils outward, until the tips of his fingers and toes hummed like beating wings. The bones of his sternum seemed to rattle as his heart leapt and juddered with impossible ferocity. His mouth filled with saliva, which threatened to foam and spill past his lips. His lips! They were aflame, puckering and curling, though not of his own accord—shaping themselves for some action, to fit some form.

And most perturbing and foreign of all was the pull between his legs, the bunching, like a fist curling into fabric. A second pulse began there, and he was filled with desire that was beyond desire, a cloying and desperate need, which he had not felt since boyhood, long before he had taken his leech's vow. So aberrant it was that Pliny nearly guttered out a noise of shock.

Under it all was revulsion and terror at his body betraying him. At his mind, which could not keep dominion over these unsanctified urges. At this age, Pliny had long since shaved down his cravings to the bone, to the barest essentials of humanness: the want for food, for water, for occasional companionship, for an afternoon spent in the warmth of the sun. These modest desires he allowed himself, and nothing more. Yet now another need was building upon him, adding muscle and sinew and voluptuous flesh to the bare skeleton of his asceticism.

What had happened to fatten his form so lasciviously, and so suddenly? Pliny was alone on the landing, in only the bare glow of the flickering torchlight, his feet and hand against cold stone. It could not be the castle itself, the castle built upon the blood of those struck down by Berengar's needle-thin blade. Rather it was something that existed *within* these cruel walls, a strange flower that bloomed despite the dark and the frigid air—a night-blooming flower, perhaps, that opened its petals only beneath the obscurity of the black sky.

Could such a thing be born here? Something so fleshy, so full? Pliny's mind could not conceive it; his body could only feel it. His bones knew that a secret lurked within these walls. His heart propelled him forward, almost unconsciously, toward the chapel's heavy stone door.

He felt possessed, too, by a preternatural strength, and a stealthiness that better befit a mountain cat than an ancient leech. So when he pushed open the door, it opened for him immediately, and without a sound. No scrape of stone upon stone; even his footsteps did not hush against the floor. Every thought seemed to have vacated his mind, so Pliny had no expectation of what he would see when he crossed the threshold. He was more a spirit than a body; a figment, not a form.

So perhaps it was no surprise that his entrance did not shift the air within the chapel or alert those within it to his presence. The prince was indeed there—Pliny had been right to expect this—but what else he saw shocked him to stillness, and made all the moisture dry up in his mouth.

The prince was standing at the altar, where every candle had been lit, forming one large swell of flame, greater than its discrete parts. He was half clothed, his breeches shucked and his doublet tugged down to bare one shoulder. And there before him, balanced precariously on the edge of the altar, her hair dangling down in dangerous proximity to the flame, was the lady Agnes.

All the breath was stolen from Pliny's lungs. Agnes's gown was pushed up around her hips, and the bodice was ripped—violently, almost, as if passion had prevailed over tenderness. Her breasts were released to the cold air, her nipples two stiff peaks, and they shuddered with each of the prince's savage thrusts. Yet there was no cruel edge to this savagery; Pliny saw only desperation, the rough and crude abandon of reason, of reluctance. Agnes gasped and moaned, and the prince twisted his hands into her hair, tipping back her head so the sounds could pour out of her, unobstructed, something else for his senses to feast upon.

This scattered the silver clips about the floor, and the white flowers, those petals of stubborn mourning, were shaken free and cast into the fire. Lord Fredegar's hold upon her, released. Pliny watched it as though it were the most stunning of metamorphoses, a butterfly cracking open its cocoon, an infant breaching its gray birth caul. The prince's love—could it be called love?—was changing her in such an astonishing way that it would have beggared his belief if he were not observing it now with his own eyes.

The prince's thrusts deepened as he grew close to his release, battering his hips against the lady's. He groaned, a low sound of pure need, and Agnes seemed to answer with her own whimper. His hand found her juddering breast and kneaded it, coaxing another moan from her mouth. His lips moved along her jawline and down her throat, in a manner almost worshipful.

Pliny was then possessed by the notion that it was beautiful. This highest of treasons, this act of perfidy, which could break all of Drepane and sink the island into the sea—both Agnes and the prince were wise enough to know this, and yet they feasted upon their own pleasure as though it were a banquet upon an endless table. And Pliny understood that it was more than lust, for they both could have satisfied that need elsewhere and not risked the very order of the world. He knew, down to the marrow of his austere and ancient bones, that what he saw before him was no less than love.

And for being love, the danger was immeasurable. This cold fear clutched at Pliny, like the grasping of ghosts. Liuprand spilled his seed within the lady and choked—nearly sobbed—with relief. Agnes collapsed against him, shoulders rising and falling, as if she could not breathe around the knowledge of her treachery, as if she were being strangled, slowly, by her apostate heart.

X

TANTALUS

Never had Agnes been summoned to the king's private chambers before. There was no reason for her to expect it and, even now, she was surprised by the request to join him there. She was further surprised to learn that these chambers were so far from the other apartments, those occupied by the prince and Marozia and herself. He was nearer to the servants' quarters and the leeches' bay, one short stone staircase above the great hall. When she considered this, it made a good deal of sense. Even in these past nine months, the king's mobility had been greatly reduced. He could not ascend steps without assistance from at least three attendants, and of course he would not wish to be very distant from the kitchens.

Yet—when she entered the chamber, Agnes was impregnated with the heavy scent of ripening fruit. It made the room thick and damp like the air above a scummy pond. She choked on her first inhale and put a hand decorously over her mouth. She felt that *she* was the one to rudely penetrate this perversely hallowed place, that her presence was the infection and not the reverse, that this was an environment that could not foster burgeoning and tender life; it could only spread about decay.

Her senses had not misled her. Piled about the chamber were bowls and bowls of fruit, most of them past ripe and into rot, softening and blackening. They overfilled their vessels and tumbled onto the floor, where they leaked their putrid juices. The carpet was spongy, like moss thick with rainwater, and each step wet the soles of Agnes's feet.

Nausea slicked through her. She should not be here. Her hand throbbed, those dormant nerve endings flaring like signal fires, alerting her to the danger of being alone with Nicephorus. And, too, there was a less cerebral fear within her: the base and animal fear of entering a world in which she did not belong, a world she could not know, could not love, and that could not love her in return. She was in it like poison in a vein. Like a worm in an apple. Her vision shuddered.

"Come. Come here," the king rasped. Agnes could not see him, only his shadow; he was behind a thin screen. "And bring me a bowl."

Agnes recoiled at such a request, her shoulders pinching. How could she touch—she should not touch—and yet it was an order, which she could not refuse. So with no small amount of reluctance, she reached for the nearest bowl. The fruit within was so far gone that its rancid juices sloshed about when she grasped it. The bowl was copper, and heavier than she expected. She had to draw an arm around it and hold the vessel to her breast as she approached the king behind the screen.

He was half reclined upon a velvet chaise, his doublet unbuttoned to show the stained shift beneath. It stretched and pulled tautly across his tumescent belly, turned as thin as onionskin by such strain, translucent enough that Agnes glimpsed through it to see his dimpled flesh. Blue veins bulged gruesomely on his neck, pulsing a sluggish beat. Past his shift, he wore nothing at all. His legs were bare and mottled purple. Several toes, Agnes noticed, had been removed, and some not-so-clever leech had badly cauterized the incision, leaving the scar tissue lumpy and gnarled as a knot on a tree.

Every step must cause him great pain, Agnes thought. She wished this realization pleased her. Yet no sensation could slither through her disgust.

"Here," Nicephorus snapped. "Give it here."

Glad to be rid of it, Agnes held the bowl out. Yet she had not grown close enough, and when the king reached for it, he merely swiped at the air. A low growl of frustration rumbled in his throat.

Scattered about the floor around were empty bowls, overturned, and the mushy black rot within them spilled and seeping into the carpet. Standing there, Agnes contemplated such a tormented existence. The fruit was all around him, yet he could not reach it without help. The rot was not the sickness itself; it was a symptom. For the king would have consumed all the fruit, quickly, if he were simply able to grasp it in his own hands. But because he could not, this world was a torturous one. It was water running over him, yet nothing he could drink.

Pity, at last, wriggled its way through her revulsion.

Agnes stepped closer, and the king successfully grabbed the bowl. He fished through the slime and pulp for the most intact fruit and bit into it. Rancid juice, dark as ink, ran down his chin. Agnes's stomach rippled and churned.

King Nicephorus ate the fruit down to its core before he spoke again.

"I am told I have two grandchildren," he said.

Agnes frowned, wondering why she had been the one summoned to relay this information. "Yes, Your Majesty."

"And are they hale?"

Her frown deepened. "Perhaps, Your Majesty, you might speak to a leech. I do not have their art; I am not fit to judge—"

"All my leeches are imbeciles. They prefer knucklebones to setting bones and gambling coin to stitching wounds. I am asking you, Lady Agnes. Did you not witness the princess's labor?"

"I did," she replied slowly. "It was not an easy one. The princess survived, but barely." The king's expression did not shift; it was as if the words had not been heard at all. "But as best as I am given to know, the children will live."

The king gave a mere grunt of acknowledgment, neither pleased nor displeased. An ember of rage burned within Agnes. All of this garish suffering, all of this blood, at his orchestration—yet now he could not even be persuaded to feign joy at its happy outcome? *He* had done this, he was the architect of her agony, and Marozia's, and his son's. She recalled the gash on Liuprand's cheek, his swollen lip, and the ember of rage grew to engulf her, flushing her cheeks and quickening the beat of her heart. She would do it, she thought, she would speak, or otherwise make her fury known—

Before she could act upon this urge, there was a knock on the door.

"Come in," the king called out in his throaty bullfrog's rasp.

Agnes turned and watched his chamber fill with bodies. First came Waltrude with the child in her arms. Agnes's heart winced to see it again, that white swaddling that held so much lovely innocence within. Then, to her surprise, came Pliny, and to her even greater surprise, Liuprand. Yet she could not have expected the last to enter: Marozia, her handmaiden attending her, and her daughter asleep against her breast.

A lump swelled in Agnes's throat and almost choked her. A mere day had passed since the labor that had nearly killed her, and Marozia somehow looked as preeminent as she ever had. The bulging stomach made impossibly flat again; her face, drained so cruelly of blood, now flushed prettily. Her dark curls were gathered neatly into a golden hairnet; her bare throat, as slender as a white-gloved hand. Her breasts were milk-swollen, straining the bust of her scarlet gown—yet this did not detract from her beauty; it amplified it, swanning the proof of her sumptuous fertility.

Agnes tasted it again. The sour bile of envy. No word, no blow, could wound her as grievously as the sight of her cousin, lush and flowering, with her daughter in her arms. Liuprand's child. Despite the lack of sympathy between husband and wife, here was a thread that bound them to each other, inextricably and mysteriously, forever obscure and forbidden to Agnes. She wanted to howl her sorrow, but it was an invisible thing. Absence could not be seen.

"Your Majesty," Marozia said. Her voice was clear and bright as ice melt. "I present my daughter for your viewing."

"I can view nothing from here," the king said. "Come closer."

Marozia did. Her heeled slippers sunk into the damp carpet, and thus her footsteps were soundless. She leaned over and showed the infant's face to King Nicephorus. The infant stirred, but only to give a sweet whimper. From her vantage point, Agnes could glimpse the loose, soft coils of golden hair. The petal-pink, toothless mouth. Yearning and more yearning filled her.

"She will be fair," the king proclaimed after several moments' inspection. Marozia gave a nod of pride and drew the infant to her breast again. She stepped back to her handmaiden's side.

A subtle gesture then, which was not observed by any but Agnes: Marozia allowed Ninian to rest a hand on the small of her back, steadying her. Agnes could not place why, but it sickened her to see this. In that moment she hated—and she was shocked by the force of her own loathing—this mousy handmaiden with her queer, mismatched eyes.

"Now bring the other," Nicephorus said.

Obediently, Waltrude now stepped out of line and approached the king. When the infant was held out for inspection, he did not stir at all; within his swaddling, he was as still as a stone. Agnes's stomach clenched nervously—was he in truth a sickly child, infirm? She could not bear it, if it were so. But the king's brow furrowed as he examined the princeling's face, and then at last, he proclaimed, "A handsome child."

Agnes suppressed an exhale of relief. Such gore and madness, yet against the odds, all was well.

"Leech," the king said, jerking his head toward Pliny. "Tell me—are they hale?"

"Yes, Your Majesty." There was an odd hollowness to Pliny's tone. Perhaps the horrors of Marozia's labor had left a mark upon him. But that would be strange—had he not seen worse before? Had he not witnessed his own master's brutal slaying, the total emptying of the Master of Blood's noble veins? "To the best of my judgment, both will grow strong."

Pleasure spread across the king's red-blistered face. No, perhaps not pleasure. It was satisfaction, which was not quite the same thing.

"Then all will proceed according to my design," he said. "The boy-child is heir. One day, he will wear the crown. It is good to have the line of inheritance secured so early. And the girl-child will be wed to Lord Unruoching's son as soon as she can walk and talk—ha! Would that she could be wed before she gains the faculties of speech; the line of Lord Fredegar does so like its silent brides."

The air seemed to crackle, to prick against Agnes's skin. She heard Marozia draw a sharp and uneven breath.

"Your Majesty," she said in a voice that was no longer clear, no longer shining, but that twisted and strained, "it is the custom of my house that the first daughter of the first daughter be named Mistress of Teeth and be given all the rights afforded to the head of a great house."

Nicephorus's damp, reptilian eyes narrowed. "And is the child not, equally, the blood of Seraph?"

Marozia's mouth quivered. Against her breast, the babe shifted.

"She is," Marozia replied at last. "But—"

"Then there is no more to be said," the king cut in. "The child has been promised to Lord Gamelyn since before her very conception. She will be wed as young as the House of Blood will have her. It is done."

Again the chamber was utterly silent, and yet, when Agnes turned to Marozia, a shuddering transformation took place that froze the marrow in her bones. She saw her cousin not as she was now, rigid and upright with her daughter in her arms, but rather as she had been a mere day ago, prone on the cold stone floor, blood pouring from between her legs. The sweat-soaked and soiled nightgown, the plum-colored head of her daughter cresting forth. This image of Marozia shrieked and howled, yet it was silent. Her mouth opened to a chasm, and no sound came out. Her body convulsed. Her mute tongue thrashed.

And for this, Agnes wanted to scream until her vocal cords withered to nothing.

But Marozia did not speak. Her chest heaved, and the color drained from her face, and then without a word she turned and fled the room. Ninian gaped in shock and then scuttled after her. In her haste, she overturned a bowl of fruit, and its rotten contents scattered all over the floor.

Agnes dared a single peek at Liuprand. She had not laid eyes on him since their disloyal tryst in the chapel. The blood on his cheek had dried black and jagged and harsh; his pride had not allowed Pliny to treat the wound as he should. The swollen lip was only swollen now with the memory of her kisses. It seemed to her both debauched and tragic, her love as ruinous as his father's hate. Liuprand's throat pulsed as he swallowed.

"Is this all you wish to say?" he asked curtly.

"Only a faithless son grows weary of his father's voice and counsel." Nicephorus dropped the empty bowl without ceremony, and it fell soundlessly to the soaked carpet. "The boy shall be brought up as a prince, trained in all the arts befitting a future king of Drepane. And take him to the tiltyard the moment he is old enough to hold a sword. I'll not have him grow up a milksop with his nose in a book." He looked with a shining eagerness at Liuprand, as if he hoped the words would rile him.

Liuprand's expression remained unmoved. However, in a flat voice, he replied, "Every wise and humane father wishes for his son to be greater than him."

Nicephorus's jaw twitched. Fear entered Agnes—she wished Liuprand had not said such to provoke him. But she suspected the king could not rise to his feet without help, and none of his attendants were about. No revenge would come, for now.

"That is all," he said lowly, at last. "Every one of you, go now. Let me see no more of you."

XI

ASUNDER

Agnes was the first to leave the king's chamber, in the hope that she would not be followed. Indeed, she took a long and meandering route through the twisted corridors to vex any who might try to chase after her. She was accompanied on her journey by only her shadow, that black and wispy twin that brushed the white walls of Castle Crudele like dark lashes against a pale cheek. It oozed and slid alongside her.

As Agnes walked, she had the heaving sense that she had failed, even now, to perfectly exemplify all of her grandmother's teachings—she had spurned Adele-Blanche's posthumous orders and given up the pursuit of mystic power, though she had still believed herself as clever and clear-sighted as her grandmother had trained her to be.

Somewhere in the time that she had stopped dreaming of the dead, Agnes's earthly vision had begun to blur around the living. Nicephorus, brute she had long imagined him to be, had in this instance honed his cruelty like a finely tempered blade. She should not have thought him limpid and dull—Adele-Blanche had taught her better than that. With one decree, he had cowed the princess, ended the glorious and horrible traditions of the House of Teeth, and regained the favor and loyalty of two more great houses. And he had dealt his son, writhing so painfully within the stricture of this detested marriage, another mighty blow. Two children, burdensome and unwanted, forever and ever a reminder of how he had been so brutally forced that night in bed.

She could not afford to believe that this was all incidental. Might she one day find herself trussed up by hands she had once believed were too clumsy for such maneuvers?

Silence had suited her, had oiled the wheels of her intellect and perception. As much as it frightened her to think it, when Agnes's tongue had stirred to life, a part of her mind had died.

Agnes stopped before the door, sickened to stillness by her failure. *I will resurrect that clever creature,* she vowed, *that sharp-eyed, venom-mouthed thing, no matter the cost. That thing that flourishes grotesquely in the quiet.*

Armored by this resolve, she pushed open the door and stepped into Marozia's chamber.

Her cousin sat in the chair that was ordinarily posed by the window but had, without Agnes knowing when or how, been moved to the dim, airless corner of the room. Marozia was lit not by the sun but by a contorted, half-melted mound of candles, like orphaned chicks in their aeries. Flames danced on the side of her face, warring with the murk of shadows.

Alerted by the sound of Agnes's entrance, Marozia lifted her gaze through the gloom.

"What are you doing here?" she asked, without inflection.

The bodice of her cousin's dress had been drawn down, her breasts exposed to the shadows. The child was clutched to her chest, the wet sounds of its suckling as steady and rhythmic as a needle through embroidery cloth. Standing beside her, in gray observation, was her handmaiden, Ninian.

"What are you doing here?" Marozia repeated sharply.

Agnes flinched, yet a part of her—that malformed, freakishly growing thing—loved the catch of her cousin's voice, how it nipped at her with kitten teeth. Slowly and solicitously she approached, apology in her posture.

Marozia drew a sudden breath, like a dress snapping in the wind. As Agnes grew closer, she recoiled, shoulders rolling back and long, supple neck straining to its full extension. A muscle throbbed in her throat.

"You don't have to be here," Marozia said, quieter this time, yet all the more bitter for it, somehow. "I have no need of you."

Agnes thought to reject the words at first; she knew her cousin was brash and impulsive, and so aggrieved as to be beyond reason—yet as she looked on in silence, Marozia's gaze did not falter, nor did she blink, and there was only the sound of her daughter's suckling, more vigorous now, filling the room with the warm and sensuous scent of milk.

Her daughter, who should have been heiress to the House of Teeth, who was meant, by Adele-Blanche's edict, to wear the necklace around Agnes's throat. Agnes saw the anguish in it, in the plundering of her birthright. She could understand Marozia's malice and pain.

And perhaps once Agnes would have taken the pain, and even the malice, too, gently between her teeth and then swallowed. But now her treasonous mind reeled on, generating words that she knew she would never speak aloud.

I made you princess. I made you powerful. I made you miserable. Her throat soured with bile. *I placed that child in your arms.* In some manner, she might as well have impregnated Marozia herself. Agnes thought of the other infant, the girl's twin, half Liuprand and half Marozia, but really more of Agnes than both, for she had arranged it, arranged it all.

Not a mother, she thought miserably, *never a mother, but something worse. A creator.*

Yet now Marozia looked at her as if she were nothing.

Her gaze slid to the handmaiden, Ninian. Though all this time she had not spoken, her hostility sat around her like a cloak. She bristled with it. Agnes felt antipathy rise in her, but more powerful than that was the sense of disgust. Agnes almost wished the girl would speak; she wanted to hear the pitiful, wheedling tone of her voice, the dull and simple words of her commoner tongue, and revel in her own superior silence.

But Ninian said nothing, and neither did Marozia. The infant shifted and mewled in her arms.

And then Agnes turned. She was almost unaware of herself doing it. Her limbs moved seemingly of their own accord. By the time she reached the door there was the faintest perspiration on her brow, the prickle of cold dew, but that was all—in another beat she was through the threshold and gone.

XII

A STONE TURNED

Agnes stood outside in the corridor, her mind as empty of thoughts as her mouth was of words. She leaned back against the wall, her head thudding softly on the stone. Sensation returned to her in slow increments, first humming at the tips of her fingers and toes, then crawling up her limbs until she felt—finally, again—the aching brag of her heart.

It ached because she lived. Each beat, like the pulse of blood behind a bruise, reminded her of that fact, reminded her that she was not some statue, not some cold, stiff corpse. And because she was alive, because she was a lady, mortal, warm, soft, vulnerable, and free, she could speak. Agnes felt her lips part, and she gulped down air as if she were drawing the first breath after drowning.

But instead of speaking, she laughed.

It was such an inappropriate, unexpected sound that Agnes clapped her hand over her mouth, stifling it. She froze, listening for any movement on the other side of the door, any indication that Marozia had heard. But there was nothing.

Agnes pushed off the wall and paced down the corridor, farther and farther from her cousin's chamber with each step. She pressed her other hand over her mouth, too, even biting down on a knuckle to be certain she would not make such a sound again. But she could not help it. She rounded a corner and another laugh slipped out between her latticed fingers, like a newt wriggling free from its arrangement of river stones.

Suddenly she cared no more for what might be thought of her illicit, deranged glee. She let her hands drop, arms falling to her sides, and she laughed once more, openly and unashamedly. The sound darted about the corridor with the frenzied dexterity of a rabbit, spasming off one wall and then the other.

"Lady?"

The voice was Pliny's, and it jolted Agnes out of her crazed reverie at once. With a flush warming her cheeks, she turned to see the leech standing there in the corridor. His hands were clasped and held at his middle.

Agnes blinked, wishing he had not heard her manic laughter, that she could take it all back. When she recovered herself, she said, "Yes, Your Scrupulousness?"

Pliny was, even at the most joyous of times, a sober man and a paragon of his order, a leech who embodied every virtue of stoicism and patience. It was something that Agnes found a great comfort, under ordinary circumstances.

Yet now—and this unnerved her greatly—Agnes witnessed in him an especial seriousness, almost grief. He had not even looked so grave following the murder of Lord Fredegar. He had been less solemn when wading through the ocean of his old master's lifeblood. Agnes's marrow chilled to see it.

"If it please," he said, in a low tone, "I would have a word with you in private."

Stunned into silence by such seriousness, Agnes merely nodded. There were a number of unoccupied chambers down this corridor, those that had once belonged to queens and their ladies-in-wait, back when Castle Crudele had been stuffed full of settlers from Seraph. That tap had been turned off, and the flow from the mainland had stopped; no more golden-haired beauties would grace Drepane's shores unless they were born from the bloodline of the prince.

Pliny led her into one and shut the door with firmness behind them.

"What is your concern, Your Scrupulousness?" Agnes asked once they were alone. Worry had begun to shiver through her; for the first time in months, she was moved to pick at the beds of her nails.

The leech drew a breath. It was a tremulous one, pregnant with unspoken meaning. And then, rather than say a word, Pliny reached into the pocket of his leech's robes. He retrieved something from within and held it in a closed fist. He hesitated for several more moments before opening his hand.

There, lying flat on his palm, was Agnes's silver clip.

Her body understood before her mind could comprehend—her body, itself, flaring like a torch in the dark, crackling with warning. *Danger*, it said, *danger*, and her belly grew slippery with nausea and her throat tightened in a vise and finally, the memory unfolded in the theater of her mind: the coldness of the altar against her bare thighs; Liuprand's hand fisted in her hair, dislodging the clip, which she had then forgotten there on the dark chapel floor.

Agnes was drawn within the frigid mantle of her silence.

"I did not intend to see what I have seen," Pliny said. His voice was a whisper. "Yet I cannot continue on as if I have not."

Moments trickled past her, like water from a chipped bowl. Reason, wisdom, humaneness—all these virtues occurred to her, and then were spurned. Perhaps, were she still that gray lady, she would have remained silent and done all her pleading with her eyes. But Castle Crudele had touched her; she had been poisoned by its barbarity. And so when she did speak, it was with a vicious edge that she did not truly feel—a vicious edge that was fragile armor for her fear.

"You will not be believed," she said hoarsely. "You speak treason; the prince could have your head . . ."

Yet this cruelty did not suit her. And Pliny, enlightened and sagacious leech he was, knew it to be so. He looked at her with a steady gaze.

Words spilled out of her in a desperate flood. Confession—she might as well have dropped to her knees.

"I mean no disregard to your old master," Agnes said. Even now, the memory of his blood soaking her gown was torrid and fresh. Could Pliny not see the haunting in her eyes? "I honor him, still. I will, always. I . . ."

How could she explain that what had begun with Liuprand—what could not be reversed—had been set into motion long before she had even known Lord Fredegar's name? How could she explain the yearning that was in her marrow, in her veins, in every tough strand of sinew and throbbing muscle that constructed her personhood? Would a man such as him understand? Were his leech's vows too tight a binding for his mind or his heart to break?

"You misconstrue me, lady," Pliny said at last. "It was your secret, and now it is mine."

Agnes merely stared, for so long without blinking that her eyes began to water. The physical sensation of shock, of ebbing horror, was beyond what her intellect could put to words. When tears dampened her lashes, Pliny saw this and closed his fingers over the clip again. It was obscured from view.

"I did not wish for this," she managed. "To be so undermined by my own soul, which seems to forget all reason . . ."

Pliny gave a single, stiff nod.

"It is not my place to advise you on how to discipline the cravings of your soul. Nor, I think, need I remind you of the dangers that accompany such unshackled desires." Around the clip, his fingers tensed. "It is not *my* wish, lady, to see you writhe and suffer more within the prison of vows and laws."

Vows and laws that she had broken so recklessly. A fool, she thought; she was a terrible fool. Yet the true prison was of her own construction: the desires that kept her on this brazen and perilous course—invisible walls, invisible floors, such that could not be broken down because they could not be seen.

"Your Scrupulousness," she choked out, "I must tell you the very worst thing, which is that I love him."

This did not unmoor Pliny at all.

"I can see that," he said. "Or else you would not risk such that you have. If you allow me a moment of bluntness—the betrayal of a marriage vow, on its own, is not so unforgivable a crime; a thousand princes and kings before have shucked these hastily made promises, and done so openly. But should the prince father a child beyond the bounds of his marriage bed, death is the price. Neither child nor mother would be suffered to live."

Agnes swallowed.

"Your fear is for naught," she said. "In this matter, at least. Nothing in my womb can take root." To speak the word *barren* would have been pure agony, a blister upon her tongue. She found reprieve within the cushion of euphemism.

Once more, Pliny nodded. A strange look came over his face, clouding his dark eyes. She imagined it might be grief. Grief for her? She did not know.

"If you would allow me," he said slowly, "to offer my counsel."

Agnes realized she had picked the white band of flesh around her nail to a bloody strip. "Yes, Your Scrupulousness."

"I am not so green and so pitiless as to tell you to give this up—though perhaps I ought, at least, to try." Pliny the leech never smiled, and so it chilled her blood now to see the corner of his mouth quiver with cold and humorless humor. "So I will say only this: There is, in Seraph, a bond that surpasses all earth-made vows. It is the bond between a soul and its matched half, and every rote human law withers to nothing in its face. At least, such is the custom on the mainland. It is not within the limits of my art to declare when such a bond is found—but I have come to know the prince well in these months, and I do not believe he would risk all for anything less."

A bond that transcended all earth-made vows. Agnes recalled the words from Liuprand's wedding ceremony—the vows he had sworn, falsely, because Marozia was not his soul's equal.

I would have you as my equal, my matched half.

"I have heard tale of such a bond before," was all Agnes said. "It is the inheritance of any who carries the blood of Seraph."

"Yes, lady."

The leech really was such a clever man. Not for the first time, Agnes felt grateful that he was loyal to her and no other. Grateful that she had his confidence, his wisdom, and his discretion. He was as faithful as the strange-eyed girl who stood at Marozia's side.

So faithful that Agnes shucked her own trepidation, her own inhibitions. The urge to laugh was gone, but it had been replaced by another equally brazen sentiment. Love, which was more dangerous than the sharpest blade, and sweeter than the last fig on a branch.

Let me taste it, she thought. *Let me cut myself on it. I do not care.*

She lifted her gaze to Pliny's again. Lowly, she asked, "Then will you perform the task?"

XIII

INNAMORATA

The candles would not go out. Pliny had seen to that. Just enough wax remained that they would stay lit for as long as they needed, and offer enough luminance by which to read. It would be better if he knew the words by heart, but this was not a ceremony he performed often. The last had been, of course, for the lady Agnes and his old master. And in that, his memory was pitted with black holes, like termite-eaten wood. Small details had been lost. Jettisoned, like ballast, to preserve the soundness of the vessel that was his mind. Because it could not comprehend so much tragedy and injustice; absolute reality was too much for any human to bear.

So he had arranged the candles, as was his task. He had read the lines in the book, murmuring them aloud to himself, until he could replicate their rhythm. He was not fluent in the tongue of old Seraph, and the vowel sounds demanded quite a lot from his untrained mouth. The Lady Agnes would not understand, but, he suspected, the prince would. He was a learned man. An honorable man. Just.

Perhaps it would be only Pliny who saw this act as one of honor. But it did not matter. Because no one else would ever be given to witness it.

The prince came first, his golden aura beating back the bleary darkness of the chapel. His clothes were not especially fine—Surgeon forbid he be stopped on his way, and his ceremonial dress questioned—but the beauty of his form was infinite, regardless of how he was robed. One concession he did make was the small golden circlet, which he only placed upon his head within the chapel's dim safety, for Pliny's eyes alone.

What was the significance of the circlet, what was its provenance? It was not quite a crown, and it seemed both old and new at once, both tarnished and gleaming. A relic of Berengar's? But Pliny imagined that the king would guard such an artifact jealously. What meaning did this piece of hammered metal hold for the prince?

Pliny never learned.

No words passed between them. They waited, but not for long. The door opened, and the sudden shift in air made the candles gutter, flattening and then leaping upright again, revived. A shaft of pale light patterned the floor.

The Lady Agnes entered. She wore a gown of gray so pale, it was almost silver—it *was* silver, in fact, in the borrowed glow of a thousand candles. The white flowers were in her hair, and the necklace of teeth around her throat. She, like the prince, was not adorned in any especial finery, nothing that might reveal their purpose if they were encountered on their way to the chapel. Her dark hair fell to her waist, and Pliny realized that he loved her. She was his new mistress. His devotion slid into place like a wheel finding its groove.

Agnes did not come alone. Pliny was surprised, though perhaps he should not have been, that she was arm in arm with Waltrude. The wet nurse did not smile—he would not expect her to—but there was a ripple of fondness radiating from her, something invisible to the eye, something Pliny could only perceive with his mind. Or was it his heart?

Waltrude led Agnes through the chapel, footsteps hushing against the stone. She maneuvered the lady before the altar and placed her, as a draughts tile, across from the prince.

Liuprand's eyes were the precise shade of the ocean under a midnight moon. Pliny had heard the other leeches whisper that this was the color of Seraph's great lagoon—but he could not confirm or deny this himself, having never touched the mainland's shores. The gash across his cheek had still not been attended, and so it would heal crudely, into a thin white scar. It would be the first blemish upon the golden prince's beautiful face.

It was said that no creature born from the marshy soil of the island could ever equal the beauty of pureblood Seraph. Pliny had always accepted this to be true—why not? Beauty was not a virtue that moved him either way. Yet now, when he cast his gaze over the lady Agnes in the half-light, he was astonished to find that she looked for all the world like Liuprand's matched half. Her beauty was a secret thing, perhaps best perceived in the darkness.

Waltrude still did not speak, though her mouth quivered, as if she wished to. Instead, she reached up and drew a veil of lace over Agnes's hair. The only concession she would make to the specialness of the occasion. It was a thick veil, not gossamer, and it hid the white flowers well beneath it. Pliny's throat grew unaccountably tight.

The prince and the lady Agnes joined hands. Pliny opened the book, which was new to him, but also unfathomably old.

He spoke the sacraments in the tongue that had died, and only he and Waltrude were witness as the prince and the lady repeated them, stammering a bit with their strangeness. From his pocket, the prince produced a ring. It was a rather simple one, such that would not call particular attention to itself when the lady wore it. A black pearl was set in its center, cushioned by two smaller pearls of white. The band was silver, engraved subtly. Words that, from this distance, Pliny could not make out.

With difficulty, the lady flexed the fingers of her left hand. Outstretching them, she allowed the prince to slip the ring onto her trembling and blemished fourth finger. Pliny felt a sting of failure against his skin, like the lash of a whip, but the pain was driven out by the poignancy of this moment. All his senses gathered to him, as soldiers called to arms. He smelled the burning wax and the candles' cringing wicks. He felt the paper rasping under his palms. He saw Waltrude's lips pressed into a thin and sober line. He heard the prince exhale softly as he admired the ring on his lady's hand—no, not his lady, not any longer. She was more to him, in secret. She was *all*.

Pliny tasted his own perfidy, which was as sweet as it was strong, like wine without water. He gulped it down remorselessly.

The vows themselves had been spoken. Pliny closed the book, which gave a soft thudding sound, and the candles flickered and revived themselves yet again with the disturbance in the air. This moment would return to him often, in waking and in sleeping—especially in dreaming—with all its accompanying senses. But none would be more clamorous, more forceful, and more evocative of emotion within himself than this: Liuprand raising his hands and, so very gently, cupping Agnes's face.

"My love," he whispered.

BOOK III

I
AGNES IN LOVE

Tisander was grown. He walked—if unsteadily—without his wet nurse's abetting hand. Waltrude was ever more distant from him, watching only from afar as he stacked blocks and tugged his horse-on-a-string, or plucked flowers and menaced the moths in the garden.

Her milk had dried and withered, as did Tisander's need of it. Now it was the lady Agnes who doted upon him. And endlessly she doted upon him, with the passion of a nun at prayer. She held the boy to her breast and whispered stories of her own invention, stories in which his horse-on-a-string was a horse of flesh and blood, and he was a knight and a hero; she fed him honey from her fingers; she carried him through the castle halls even when he was large and solid enough to make her arms quiver around him, no longer a babe but a boy. And he loved no one better than Agnes—she was sure of it. It was the greatest pride of her life.

Their most common retreat was the library. He had been no more than ten days old, his eyes still gummy with the slime of birth, when Agnes had first brought him to that great golden-lit chamber and raised him high in his bundle of blankets, both revealing to him his domain and flaunting him to the lurking spirits. He had an aura about him like his father's, the pulsing, hereditary gleam of his Seraphine blood, and the ghosts all fled in his presence, banishing themselves to cobwebbed corners, or else dissipating where they floated, like tide pools dried to salt in the sun.

Agnes smiled then; she had at last put to rest those silent, lurking specters. Tisander's birth had cleansed her world of its ghosts.

Tisander had talked before he could toddle, in a clear voice, like a pour of freshest water. His hair grew in lush curls of dark gold. His eyes were the deep blue of Seraph's great lagoon. In nearly every possible respect, he was his father's son—and in the small ways he was not, Agnes told herself that it was her doting, her love, that had made him so. She refused any niggling hint that he was the profit of the woman who had birthed him.

And yet he was a peculiar child. Agnes could not deny it, even if she was the only one who saw his strangeness. As soon as he could speak, he said in that sonorous voice, as eloquent as any man grown, "Are these stories true and real?"

Agnes had stiffened, her arms growing taut around his small body. "What do you mean, my dearest love?"

"Stories of knights and heroes," Tisander replied. "Did these knights ever draw breath? Do these heroes have statues raised in their honor?"

"Only within the pages," Agnes said. She ran her finger hesitantly along the edge of the parchment. "Does that displease you?"

"No." Tisander looked up at her with the steady gaze of the waveless ocean. "But please, tell me a story that is true."

And so Agnes shucked those books of knights and heroes, of their romances and adventures, and spoke instead from her own memory, from the tales that had been told to her by Pliny the leech. She hoped they were indeed true.

"We sit within the castle of Nicephorus the Sluggard," she began, "and before that it was the castle of Widsith the Precious, and before that, Berengar Who-Fights-Alone. This is the exalted line to which you are heir, my sweet dove. But Berengar was not always such a great man—or perhaps I should say he was once only a man of great confidence. His house in Seraph was a humble one, a merchant's house, rather new in its nobility. He had only smelled the perfume of the Dogaressa at a distance. He had a modest number of ships. His stores of wealth were small—yet his nerve was boundless.

"When the plague struck the island and its revenants began to ravage the shores of Seraph, Berengar seized his opportunity. He saw the broken vessels of his fellow merchants and heard their groans of calamity. They beseeched the Dogaressa for aid, but she did not deign to answer, glutted as she was on wine and sweets and the flattery of her many suitors. And so it was Berengar alone who took up his sword."

Agnes paused there; Tisander was tensed with attention in her lap. She wondered how she might recount the garish violence that followed. There was no telling of this tale—no *truthful* telling—that omitted it. Perhaps a different child would not be able to detect euphemism or falsity. But Agnes suspected that Tisander would sense the way her tone shifted uneasily with a lie.

"Berengar sailed to Drepane with a small army," she went on, "and found that the island had gone to chaos, to madness. Revenants roved, mindless with hunger, feasting on the dead and the living alike. The clever nobles shut themselves up in their castles, safe from the savagery of these monsters. The cleverer still were those who managed to exert some control over the revenants, who could use them for their own ends."

At that, Tisander tilted his head up, eyes questioning. "And how did they do that?"

"I do not know," Agnes confessed. "That wisdom has been lost to time. All those who did know perished under Berengar's blade. He could not allow such dark practices to continue, or to stretch beyond Drepane's shores."

Tisander was silent a moment. "Why would he not claim such power for himself?"

"Because," Agnes said, and looked out over the glorious library, with its staircase that spiraled upward like the inner curl of a conch shell, with the spines of the books that gleamed gold in shafts of sunlight from the high, recessed windows, this great treasury of art and knowledge that had been built upon a bed of torrid blood, "because . . . he was too noble. Berengar knew that this power was beyond what any mortal man would possess. It was a danger, and so he slaughtered this wisdom as he slaughtered the revenants and the nobles who had borne them up from their graves."

There was a sudden tremor as she spoke the words that had once been treason to her. As surely as the necklace of teeth lay around her throat, Agnes was still the heiress of its ancient bloodline, once glorious, now shrunken and diminished. These were not tales that her grandmother would have permitted within the cold walls of Castle Crudele. Adele-Blanche mangled truth; she chewed it like meat.

But her grandmother was expired, extinct, forever gone, and the necklace Agnes wore was as much pearls as teeth.

If Tisander indeed detected the shift in her voice, he did not remark upon it. He merely snuggled closer to Agnes, his cheek pressed against the velvet bodice of her dress. The warmth of his skin pulsed through the fabric, heat leached from his body to her breasts, and she felt—cursing herself—that old, revived sense of bereftness. Waltrude had nursed the boy, not her. Agnes was still, and would be always, as barren as a shining-white salt flat.

Yet she did not have more than a moment to mourn it. The door to the library creaked open, and Pliny the leech appeared in the threshold.

Immediately, Tisander scrambled off her lap, and in his rather clumsy physicality, he appeared to Agnes as an ordinary child again. Indeed, when he reached Pliny, he grasped the leech's robes with tiny fists and excitedly cached himself among them—a little game Agnes had seen him play over and over again. If he loved Agnes best, then his father, and then his wet nurse, Waltrude, in this ranking of affection it was Pliny who followed closely behind.

The leech rested a gentle hand on Tisander's head. "It is time for your lesson, my lord."

Eagerly, and still half ensconced in Pliny's robes, Tisander followed him from the room. He paused only once, to peer back at Agnes. His gaze was bright and shimmering now, like the ocean made lively with the leaping of fish.

"Goodbye, my dear heart," Agnes said.

And Tisander waved at her as he vanished through the threshold.

The library was not Agnes's only place of refuge. Her days had become rote, though not unpleasantly so—time seeped slowly past her, like amber from oak-wood, each moment a luminous, treasured droplet. Her footsteps were slow, measured, the low hush of silk upon stone. The windows gridded the floors with squares of deep-orange evening light. Agnes passed through them, feeling the brief brush of warmth against her bare shoulder.

She did not need to hurry. He would wait until the death of the world, and perhaps even his soul would wait when his mortal form was desecrated and gone to nothing.

It was only her own eagerness that quickened her steps, as Agnes reached that final, narrow stairwell. She climbed it and pushed open the iron-heavy door.

At once she was soaked in the light of a thousand burning candles. The domed ceiling was dappled with it, as were the hoary stone walls, and in the very center, by the wax-coated altar, stood Liuprand. He was lighting the final wick.

When he saw her, he turned at once, and her name came from his lips in a soft whisper. "Agnes."

"My love," she answered.

The door shut behind her.

Agnes joined him there by the altar, as she always did, and together they looked at the lit candles in silent vigil. It was a ritual that had come to pass unspoken, grown at first from their shared sense of guilt, which bloomed outward, tinging the air with a sourness like smoke.

But Agnes was beyond shame now. She had shed its heavy husk. And as the flames leapt and the candle wicks curled and blackened, she reached up, undid the clasp, and shed her necklace of teeth, too. The chain slipped down between her breasts a moment before she caught it in a clutched fist.

Liuprand let out a shuddering breath.

"You know I would come to you already bare, if I could," Agnes said. She lay the necklace on the altar, in that one small space that was not occupied by candles.

But the chapel was not the bleak and dreary place it had once been; with the passing of years, it had evolved to meet the needs of the two lovers who met there every evening. There were sprigs of lavender to perfume the air, tapestries to adorn the walls, and most important, a velvet couch, upon which Liuprand bore Agnes down.

Their coupling was not so frenzied now. There was time and more time for tenderness, for words of devotion whispered between kisses. Gently Liuprand swept back Agnes's hair, fingers slipping through smooth black strands, baring her nape and her throat. As he trailed his mouth across her skin, down to the swell of her breasts, he murmured, "You feel new to me each night, as if I am born again in your arms."

Agnes turned his chin up with one finger, forcing him to pause his ministrations. "You are my first thought upon waking, and my every dream in the dark."

Liuprand smiled tremulously, almost shyly. He looked boyish to her sometimes in these secret moments, though he was now a man nearing thirty.

She kissed him on his earnest mouth, working at the ties of his breeches, while he pushed up the skirt of her gown to her hips. Even after all this time, after all their countless couplings, Agnes was left breathless by the size of him inside her, how he filled her so completely.

His thrusts were slow, dragging, the most exquisite torture. Agnes gasped as each one touched that place of pleasure within her. Liuprand lowered his huge body so that their foreheads were pressed together, and he stuttered around his release as she came, keening, too.

But *these* were Agnes's most treasured moments: when the feverpitch of climax receded but the fog of bliss still remained, as heavy and sweet as incense. Liuprand shifted so that he lay on the narrow couch beside her, arms circling her waist, pulling her flush against his chest. She felt the staggered beating of his heart, thrumming unevenly until, with time, it grew steady again.

Agnes let her lashes flutter shut, sleepy and content. She could have drifted then into her dreams, but she was interrupted by Liuprand, who reached out and grasped her hand.

He held it up to the light, carefully extending all her fingers. The scars that laced her skin were a faded, shimmery blue-white, scarcely visible to the eye. Agnes recalled the event that had caused them only at odd and banal times, when she made to pick up a quill but found it slipping from her clumsy, trembling grip.

Though her left hand was not reduced to complete uselessness, Pliny had not succeeded in restoring most of its more delicate functions. Yet now so many years had passed that she had trained her right hand to do all the tasks she had once done with her left. Her quill raced nimbly across the page again. And the memory, the agony—all banished, like the rest of her ghosts.

But Liuprand did not mean to make her look at the scars. He turned her hand over so that the band of pearls showed around her ring finger.

"It shames me," Liuprand said softly, "that this is the only thing I have ever given you."

"You have given me more than can be put to words."

Liuprand shook his head—it was not what he meant and Agnes knew it. But she also knew that they were edging closer to a precipice of danger. It was not such a simple thing for him to give her a gift. Should courtiers or servants notice that the lady Agnes wore a new brocade or jewels while the princess was bereft, it would cause whispers, which could grow into suspicions, which could grow into threats. Anything Liuprand gave to her would have to be subtle, unnoticeable to the perfunctory eye, or something she could treasure only in the privacy of her chambers or the darkness of the chapel.

Once, Liuprand had been a creature without indulgence, and Agnes had been a creature without greed. But now that they had given in to the desires of their hearts and their flesh, new needs had flowered up within them both, red as poppies, quick as marigolds. Why should a noble lady not want for fine jewelry and fine dresses? Why should a husband not want to lavish such bounties upon his wife?

"I have been thinking," Liuprand said, twining their fingers, "that there is something I can give you after all. Something that will bring us even greater joy here in the dark. We have created a few small comforts here, but there is more that can be done, with a bit of aid."

Alarmed, Agnes sat up. "No one else can know of this place. Only Pliny and Waltrude, who keep our secret."

Liuprand rose, too, pushing himself onto his elbows. "Do you not trust that I can force someone into silence?"

There was a faint prickle of cold on the back of Agnes's neck. When Liuprand's arms were around her, she felt safe in their strength, and his largeness was a comfort to her. But when she recalled that moment in the dungeon of the House of Blood, his size and his power, the boons of his Seraphine heritage, felt vaguely sinister to her. It seemed the natural order of the world that everyone who encountered Liuprand should shrink from him. That the people of Drepane should cower before him, just as they had all once succumbed to Berengar's blade.

"No," she said, swallowing, "I only mean that . . . it is a risk."

"It is not a risk that should trouble your mind." Liuprand shifted her with near-inhuman dexterity into his lap, her thighs spread about his hips. "I will never let harm befall you. Never, ever. Of all the vows I have sworn, you must believe this one, above all others."

Slowly, Agnes nodded. "I do."

Leaning forward, Liuprand kissed her on the mouth, on the throat, and bowed his head to the valley of her breasts. He was stiff again already and slid inside her, and she was so slick that there was only pleasure, heady as summer wine, not even a glancing pain at his intrusion.

Agnes buried her face in his shoulder, muffling her gasps and mewls. In the fevered haze of passion, it was easy to forget, but just as easy to remember, the one gift Liuprand could never give her, no matter how forceful and prevailing his love. No matter how often he filled her with his seed, it would never take root. Never, never. The ghost of her grandmother was gone, but this relic of her cruelty remained.

And yet, despite that, Agnes was not lost to her bitterness and grief.

Joy pervaded her. She could scarcely even fathom that Castle Crudele had once felt savage and inhospitable. Now when she walked its halls, shadows fled, phantoms dissolved into dust, and warmth, which radiated from her proudly bragging heart, chased away the coldness of iron and stone. The violence that constructed this great monument was less real than a dream. All because of this—Liuprand panting into the curve of her throat, whispering his devotion between breaths.

Agnes was in love: with the boy who regarded her as mother, with her husband, who had wed her by secret rite, and with her world, which seemed to enclose her in its gentle embrace, like the velvet petals concealing the bud of a rose.

II
HUMANITY'S OTHER INHERITANCE

In the east wing of the castle, there was no silence that could not, at any moment, be broken by a howl or a scream.

These were the discordant, ear-piercing sounds of a child of great need and even greater greed. If she was not attended to at once, her pink-cheeked, cherubic face cracked open with sobs, and tears rushed to the corners of her limpid blue eyes, brightening them further, like the ocean in the blistering midday sun. And if she could not muffle her cries in her mother's skirts, she grasped handfuls of her own golden hair and bit them, masticating the curls until they were ragged and soaked with spittle. Her name was Meriope, and she was to be married in sixty-six days.

It was not clear, at least to Ninian, whether the small girl understood what fate awaited her. Certainly her mother did not speak of it, at least in so many words. Once, the castle's tailor had come to their chamber with orders to measure the child for her gown, and the princess Marozia had slammed the door so hard in his face that bits of the wooden frame had splintered. Then without even a glance at Ninian, she returned, expression pale and impassive, to her daughter's side. They had been in the middle of a story.

This was no dull tale from a book, bloated with noble knights and virtuous maidens, dragons and romances and quests for grails. This was a story that came rolling off Marozia's tongue, and though she had told it more times than Ninian could count, it was always the same, down to the number of breaths she drew at each pause and which syllables she stressed. The story never, never changed.

Marozia took her daughter onto her lap and kissed her three times: once on each of her soft temples, and then on the top of her head. Meriope wriggled with happiness and anticipation. And Ninian busied herself with the ordinary chores of a handmaiden, but all the while she had her ears pricked, listening.

"The House of Teeth was not always the House of Teeth." To her daughter, Marozia always spoke quietly, in a voice so sweet it almost tinged the air with the scent of flowers. Ninian breathed deeply of it. "Our ancestors had another name, though it has been lost now. And when the plague came, they were wise enough to shut themselves up in their castle, remote in Drepane's dark mountains. While the other houses suffered and some ancient lineages were struck wholly from the earth, our venerable and noble house remained such—potent, pre-eminent."

Surely Meriope could not really understand such adult words; what did a child even know of mortality? While her mother spoke, Meriope sucked vigorously and noisily on her thumb.

"And then, when the plague had spent itself, there came another age, when the remaining noble houses of the island seized heretofore unknown power for themselves," Marozia went on. "The conquerors claim this was the magic of death, but really, it was the magic of life. Bodies rose from their graves and walked the earth again. Mothers were reunited with their children; sisters with their brothers; lovers with their lovers. The conquerors will tell you this was a time of darkness. But it was a time of joy."

Ninian, who was cleaning out a chamber pot, paused in her ministrations to listen more closely.

"And of all the houses, it was ours who made greatest profit from this magic," said Marozia. "My great-grandfather, your great-great-grandfather, raised whole armies of the dead. Bravely he fought against the conqueror's cruel blades. We were stronger than the rest. And we were the very last to submit to Berengar, the last sword to crumble."

At this, Ninian shivered. Meriope gnawed on her thumbnail.

"This is your inheritance, my sweet one," Marozia said, and stroked her daughter's hair. "Such power. Such glory. It is said that even the conqueror's knees trembled. Berengar the Boneless, they should have called him. For while he was mighty on the field of battle, he was a dastard in the feasting hall. He had to trick the lords of the island into acquiescence. And then he killed them, in the traitorous manner of a coward, slitting their throats over their goblets of wine."

Marozia let out a breath that was shuddery with fury. For the briefest moment, silence reigned in the princess's chamber. Ninian held the heavy pot aloft, afraid to interrupt this rare interlude of quiet with her scrubbing.

"What do you think of that, my dearest?" Marozia asked, dipping her head to look her daughter in the eye.

She was a beautiful child, Meriope, with the best features of both her parents—Liuprand's azure eyes and hair of gold, her mother's curls and dimpled chin and pearlescent skin. Her beauty might one day surpass that of Marozia, Drepane's bright-blooming rose. Every nobleman in the kingdom would clamor and humble himself for her hand—that is, if she were not already promised to another. If her fate had not been fixed before she was even a dream in her mother's mind.

Meriope removed her thumb from between her lips and wiped the spittle on the front of her blouse. "I'm hungry," she said.

So Marozia unlaced the front of her gown, baring her breasts to her daughter's waiting mouth. The room filled with the sound of suckling. And Ninian returned to her task.

Ninian finished with the chamber pot as Marozia tucked her daughter into bed. The single bed was large enough to fit the three of them, though just barely—when Meriope grew into her girlhood, there would not be room. Except Meriope would not grow into her girlhood here in Castle Crudele. Her time within these cold walls was nearly through.

Marozia perched on the other end of the bed as Ninian undressed her, first unlacing her slippers and sneaking a feel of her soft, supple calves. These past years had not drained even a drop of her mistress's beauty. The bitterness in her heart did not show on her face. The rage within her was kept fettered, invisible to the errant eye. Only Ninian was able to see when it raised its fierce, blood-red head.

As Ninian slid the princess's gown from her shoulders, Marozia said, "Go to the leeches' bay. Fetch me the potion."

Ninian stilled, the gown held limply in her hands. Her mistress's linens were stained with milk, sticky and translucent. For six years they had been such, her breasts full and heavy, her nipples bitten and sore. It pained Ninian to see. She remained silent for yet a moment more, and then said, softly, "Perhaps it can be deferred for tonight."

At that, the sanguine maw of Marozia's fury reared. The princess jolted to her feet and seized Ninian by the front of her dress.

"Do not defy me," she rasped, "else I will banish you to the kennel to sleep with the dogs."

Ninian flinched. "Yes, my princess. I am sorry."

"Go now. I will finish disrobing myself."

Marozia released her, and Ninian—so in love, even now—shivered at the loss of her touch. Brusque as it was, Ninian longed for it, suffused to the brim with need. She tried to quash this desire as she left the princess's chamber and walked the halls, footsteps nearly soundless, a seizing, throbbing sensation between her thighs. Later, she would tend to herself later, after she had serviced her mistress.

It was evening, and most of the leeches in the bay were resting on their cots. The stench of herbs and poultices was so strong that it made Ninian's eyes water and her nose itch. She traveled between the cots, most of the beige-robed men not even bothering to lift their gazes as she passed, until she reached the very back of the chamber, which was mostly cloaked in shadow.

There, Truss and Mordaunt sat. Even in the half-light, she knew them, if not for their faces, then for the ever-present rattling of dice. They scattered across the upturned barrel they were using as a table and showed on one Seraph's winged lion, and on the other a skull and crossbones.

"I'm here for the potion," Ninian said, lifting her chin. "For the princess."

It was Mordaunt who leaned forward, into the light. The years did not show on his face. He had looked gaunt when Ninian had met him, and looked gaunt still now. And Truss was still flabby above the belt.

"Here again," Mordaunt said, shaking his head. "When will your mistress abandon this ghoulish practice?"

Ninian's spine straightened with a jolt of anger. "It is the custom of her house. The most noble and most ancient house in Drepane."

Truss wheezed a laugh. "The most noble house in Drepane is the House of Berengar."

"Quiet, you," Ninian bit out.

The years might not have changed these leeches, but Ninian had grown both bitter and bold with time. Almost beautiful, too, she thought modestly. The princess had her robed in fine gowns of pale violet, lavender, and gray, and her hair, though still the dull shade of muddy straw, was done up in a crown of gleaming braids. Her skin had lost its rough, peasant ruddiness and was nearly as pale as her mistress's now, for she, too, spent all her days in the east wing of the castle, never stepping, even by accident, into the light of the sun.

"Come now, girl," said Mordaunt, in a pitying tone that only made Ninian hate him all the more. "You are doing your mistress no favors by maintaining this charade. In sixty-six days, Meriope will be wed. She will be taken to the marshes and tumbled into the Master of Blood's bed. The princess would be better off preparing her for this fate than pretending she is still an infant in need of her mother's milk."

Fury seared through Ninian. She would have smashed the leech's face into the barrel if she could. "You are a *leech,*" she hissed. "You are lower than a worm. You have no right to question the will of the princess." Her face was as hot as an open flame. "And besides—you give this tonic to Waltrude without trouble."

"We have not given it to Waltrude in years," Truss broke in. "The princeling is far past the need for a wet nurse. And it is her only task in this world to wring out her breasts in service of the Crown. A princess has greater purpose. She should not debase herself in this vulgar way."

"The only thing my mistress wishes to be is a mother," Ninian said. Her voice had grown soft against her will.

Truss lifted a shoulder. "Pity, then, that her daughter will be taken from her so soon."

"Give me the potion," Ninian whispered blackly. "Else I will make mincemeat of you."

Her threat was idle, a shout flung down an empty hall with no returning echo. But the leeches had no convictions and little strength of character. It was why they had joined this order of rote tasks and banal labors. They moved through the world like fish carried through a current, never so much as flicking their silver tails or turning their open-mouthed faces toward the sky. They mostly grumbled over their little game of luck being interrupted.

After several moments of sulky preparation, Mordaunt handed Ninian the tonic in a glass vial. She took it and left the leeches' bay without another word.

Back in the princess's chambers, Marozia was already undressed and tucked under the covers, but she was not sleeping. Her eyes were wide open and stiff in a manner that suggested she had not blinked in quite some time. When she heard Ninian enter, she lifted her head arduously from the pillow.

"Bring it here," she whispered.

On the other side of the bed, Meriope was sleeping, limbs flung out to her sides, except for her left arm, which was laid over her chest so that her thumb could remain in her mouth. Dried spittle crusted the front of her nightgown. But her sleep looked consummate and dreamless. Ninian approached.

Marozia pushed herself up onto her elbows as Ninian lowered herself carefully onto the bed. The princess parted her lips. Ninian uncapped the vial and poured the potion in. She watched, with a tremulous heartbeat, her mistress's throat pulsing and bobbing as she swallowed.

Ninian's gaze lowered to the collar of Marozia's sheer nightdress, and then lower still. She could see the way her mistress's breasts swelled and stiffened, the tonic taking hold at once. Her own stomach clenched, desperate with desire.

"Go on, then," Marozia said quietly.

Ninian tried to restrain her eagerness as she bore her mistress down on the mattress. She climbed upon her and straddled her hips. With shaking fingers, she pushed up Marozia's nightgown, baring her round and aching breasts to the air. A strangled moan escaped Ninian's lips.

She was mindful, however, not to drink too much, for there needed to remain enough to feed Meriope when she stirred from slumber and demanded her mother's milk. Even as pleasure rolled headily through her, Ninian took care not to scrape Marozia's nipples with her teeth, and to save some of her strength. It was not long before her mistress shoved her head beneath the covers and made her taste the sweet juice that ran between her thighs.

Marozia whimpered and keened, but never loud enough to wake her daughter, who, though mere inches away, slept obliviously through it every night.

Ninian was in love. Wretchedly, torridly—with her mistress, and with that small girl who shared their bed. And yet she hated the savage and unjust world that pained the princess so, and that would tear them apart, as vicious as a wolf feasting on its fresh kill, when these sixty-six days were through.

Time fell mercilessly past them. Ninian, for all her love and all her hate, could not arrest it.

III
LAVENDER AND WAX

Pliny the leech was such a creature who did not mind overmuch the passage of time. As he walked, hand in hand with Tisander, to the small boy's chambers, he allowed his thoughts to stretch back to the first moment he had stepped through the barbican of Castle Crudele, still raw from the death of his former master. All that blood. The stench had remained with him for days, for weeks, and grew tangier whenever he was near the lady Agnes. He saw her and tasted copper on his tongue.

Now such sentiments were embarrassing to contemplate. He was glad that time had made him a more stoic being, not so moved by the passions that did not befit a leech. It helped, of course, that everything around him had changed a great deal in these past six years, even the structure of Castle Crudele itself.

Pliny had the opportunity to glimpse some of these rather unfortunate changes as he led Tisander along the parapets and felt the whisking of the sea's salt air. It ruffled Tisander's golden curls, and the boy turned his face into the wind, closing his eyes and smiling in a serene way that did not at all befit a boy his age. In Pliny's experience children were wriggling, impatient, impulsive things—more like the little princess Meriope, who, admittedly, Pliny rarely had the occasion to see.

They came to a corner, and here was one of the rather unfortunate changes to the castle: a bit of the stone floor was beginning to crumble, the lashing of wind and rain and the slow spread of rot making this length of the parapet treacherous. Pliny had to press himself and Tisander close to the castle wall and inch along it carefully to avoid stepping on this undependable stone. Luckily, Tisander was such a patient and self-possessed child that he never gave Pliny any reason to fear a sudden movement, a reckless lurch. They crossed safely.

If Nicephorus was aware of this new deficiency, he kept his feelings secret. There was not much that could rouse the king to action these days. Pliny might have said that the years had not been kind to Nicephorus, but in truth, it was not time that was to blame.

When they at last reached the princeling's chambers, Waltrude was waiting for them. Tisander let go of Pliny's hand and ran into his wet nurse's embrace.

Waltrude swung him up into her arms, though not without difficulty, her thin limbs trembling like saplings in the wind. Who could blame her? By Pliny's estimation, she was entering the ninety-first year of her life. It would have been stranger to see her lift the boy without trouble.

"Here for your lessons, my little lord?" she asked, as though every day were not the same.

Eagerly, Tisander nodded. "I have learned all my letters."

"And soon you shall be wiser than a great horned owl."

Tisander laughed, a high and tinkly sound. He slid from Waltrude's grasp and went to the table where all of Pliny's books and papers were arranged, ink still drying on his quill-tips. As Tisander pulled himself up into the chair, Pliny was, against his will, assaulted by an arrow-volley of memories. Each one struck him, and the accompanying pain left him momentarily breathless.

He saw, in the gaze of his mind, his old lord Fredegar sitting before him in place of Tisander. Fredegar's hair had been dark and his eyes a nondescript hazel, but he had had the same serious face as the young prince, showing a queer wisdom beyond his years.

The memory rippled and shifted, and Unruoching sat there instead, indolent and distracted, picking at his nose. It had taken Pliny the better part of a year to teach him his letters. He had protested their meetings; he had raged at his mother's bedside—poor, dying Eupraxia. And half the time he had snuck off to play cruel tricks on the stable boys or bait the cats in the kitchen.

With one last ripple, the memory changed once more: Pliny saw Gamelyn perched at the table. He had not been a much more biddable pupil than his father, though for different reasons entirely. He did not complain or fight, but he jostled endlessly in his seat, eyes darting, his body never at ease. He was a clever boy and learned his letters fast enough. But it was clear that his inclination was not toward any cerebral pursuit. He belonged in the tiltyard, not the schoolroom.

The memories were sucked away like a whirlpool with the sound of Waltrude's voice. "My leech," she said, "your lord is waiting."

Tisander, with his mature mind and consummate focus, completed his lesson within the hour, when the purple haze of evening settled over Castle Crudele. The boy yawned and rubbed his eyes, and Waltrude, as she did every night, set about dressing him for bed. Pliny, meanwhile, rested in his chair. Tiredness was upon him like a heavy old cloak. In these moments, he felt his age, the sagging of his skin and the wasting of his bones. His blood seemed to run colder and more sluggishly even by the moment.

If the rest of his days followed as this one had, Pliny decided, he would be content.

Waltrude left Tisander's bedside and came to him, carrying only a candle. Its dim orange light filled all the lines on her face, like molten steel poured into a mold. In a soft voice, she asked, "Did you have occasion to see the lady today?"

"Briefly," Pliny replied, "in the library. She was reading to the boy as she always does."

"No." Waltrude shook her head. "The other lady. The lady in the tower."

"The princess?"

Waltrude stared at him unblinkingly.

"No one sees her," Pliny said. "She does not leave her chambers—nor does that girl of hers, Ninian, but for some handmaiden's errands. I wonder if her daughter could even name the color of the sky."

Waltrude bristled. It was strange to see this old porcupine put up her ancient quills. She said, "A fox run to ground still has its sharp teeth."

Yet before Pliny could reply, the door to the chamber opened, and Liuprand entered. He nodded once, fondly, at each Pliny and Waltrude, and then strode in silence to his son's bedside. He sat on the edge, leaning over, and pressed a kiss to Tisander's temple. Low, soft words were spoken, each to each. Pliny could not hear them at this distance, though he marveled, as he always did, at the impressive size of the prince, his hand so large beside his son's very small head, large enough, Pliny felt, that he could crush his skull to dust. He did not know why the thought occurred to him, why such an image rose, for there was nothing but tenderness between father and son.

With one last kiss, Liuprand rose—the bed creaking with his weight—and came to Pliny and Waltrude.

"Good evening, my prince," Waltrude said. And Pliny echoed: "Good evening."

"Tisander is well," Liuprand said. "He is happy. In his life he has never known a moment of grief."

It took both Pliny and Waltrude a moment to realize that this was not a statement but a question. When he did understand, Pliny nodded fervently, and said, "Yes, Your Highness. He has joy and no sorrow. And he is deeply loved."

Liuprand smiled, a truly breathtaking thing. His Seraphine beauty was immense, its gloriousness infinite, and when he was pleased, it showed itself best. Pliny felt as if he were standing in the path of a strong beam of sunlight, and he was lucky to be there, lucky to feel the warmth on his skin. Such was the soft power of Seraph's superior people.

"Relieve yourself for the night, Waltrude," Liuprand said. "I should like to sleep with my son."

Waltrude dipped her head. "Of course, my prince."

She turned to go, and Pliny, assuming his own dismissal, followed. But he did not reach the door before Liuprand's voice rang out, calling after him: "Pliny, stay a moment."

Pliny turned back. As he approached the prince, in the incomplete darkness, his senses were suddenly assaulted: He smelled lavender and wax. It wafted from Liuprand's body like a strong perfume, and the closer Pliny got, the stronger the scent. By the time he was at the prince's feet, he nearly choked on it.

That was how Pliny knew, beyond all doubt, that he had been with the lady Agnes. He had come directly from their tryst. He and Waltrude alone had been given to witness their secret love; Pliny himself had performed their clandestine marriage rite. And in these intervening years they had kept this love hidden to great success. Pliny was impressed by how they were able to conceal such passions. He had seen, with his own eyes, just how fervent these passions were. Fortuitous that there could be no fruit produced from their unions, no matter how much they were in love. Fortuitous that the lady's body prevented such a terrible and ruinous crime as a bastard child would be.

Liuprand leaned close to him, bending down so that their eyes were level. The lavender and candle-wax scent was as thick as incense.

"I need you to perform a task for me," Liuprand said. "It is of the utmost importance and the utmost secrecy."

"Yes, Your Highness," Pliny replied. And then he leaned even closer, to hear what treasons the prince whispered.

IV

MALEAGANT

"Are you frightened?" she asked. "Don't be frightened."

The young girl did not answer, but her teeth were chattering and her forehead was slicked with cold sweat, as if she had the pox or a fever. She was not suffering from either; Maleagant would have known that at once. Her left calf bone would have started to throb the moment the girl entered her hut.

She was also not, as Maleagant was dismayed to realize, suffering from the portentous visions that would have made her a valuable apprentice. If she were, Maleagant would have known in an instant by looking into her eyes. This girl was just a fearful, fluttery thing, like a pigeon fit for pie. She was not simple—Maleagant's left temple did not ache, and so she knew that—but she was too jejune, too vapid to perform the services Maleagant would require of her.

Perhaps she could chop herbs. Maleagant closed her eyes a moment, but she was greeted only with a star-pricked blackness. No, this girl was not even good for herb chopping. Maleagant released her arm, and the girl stumbled backward, her bare feet stirring the dust of the dirt floor.

"May I go now?" she mumbled. "Please?"

"Go," Maleagant said. "Please."

The girl staggered out of her hut as if she had suffered a blow to her head and also was being chased by wolves. Maleagant sighed. She leaned back in her wicker chair and stared up at the thatched ceiling of scratchy yellow hay. *Another failure,* she thought bitterly. *Another girl who will not rise to take my place.* The closest she had come was that pretty little maiden Ninian; her mismatched eyes had given Maleagant cause for hope. But she had been as insipid as the rest. And then she was gone. To the castle, where she scrubbed chamber pots and serviced the princess in the manner of a back-hall slattern. Maleagant saw it all, in the vaporous landscape of her dreams.

Yet she must keep trying. The Outer Wall needed a wise woman. Not so much for what she knew of the future, but for what she knew of the past. Maleagant alone was able to recall Drepane before the conquest. Such knowledge was more precious than all of Adele-Blanche's gold. Another dead noblewoman, Maleagant thought idly, whose grandchildren had given up mourning her. For all her cruelty and her wiles, she was expired, extinct, forever gone, her body desecrated, her spirit too weak to even visit Maleagant in her sleep. What an undignified end for a woman who had once fancied herself the sole sovereign of death.

Maleagant might have sat there a long while, hearing the hot breeze rustle among the thatched roof yet feeling none of it through the hard clay walls of her hut—yet suddenly there was a wincing pain in her hip bone. Someone was coming.

Someone from the castle, which she knew even before the leech's shadow darkened her doorway. His sepia robes were finer than those of any leech who lived in the Outer Wall, his posture straight and proud. He was quite tall. He kept his hood up as he entered, though as Maleagant waved him forward, his features came into view: a ponderous brow and keen but steady eyes, in fitting with his scholar's nature. Here was a leech of great esteem. Here was the leech kept by Prince Liuprand the Just himself.

"Good morning," the leech, whose name was Pliny, said.

"Good morning," Maleagant said. She leaned slightly forward in her chair but did not rise.

"I have need of your services."

Maleagant did not tell him that she already knew why he had come here; why deprive herself of a bit of amusement—some color to daub upon her dull gray days? Serenely, she answered, "And what services are those, Your Scrupulousness?"

Pliny regarded her in slight indignation, as though he was aware he was the subject of some secret jest. "I know what arts you perform here," he said. "What ancient, mystic powers to which you lay claim . . . that is of no import to me. I have come with a far more mundane purpose."

"Well," Maleagant said with a soft smile, "do not leave me to guess."

"I need an individual of a very particular nature. Someone whose absence will not be accounted for among the people of the Outer Wall, whose presence will not be missed. Someone who is clever enough to follow orders yet not wise enough to question them. Someone who will do hard work for simple pleasures in return. And someone whose words will never be taken as more than mad ramblings, should they find an ear to listen."

Maleagant's left eye twitched. Her afternoon was getting off to a rather thrilling start indeed. Very slowly, and with the audible creaking of her ancient bones, she rose. "Yes," she said, "I have just the creature for you."

He made his home in the gutter outside the butcher's shop, though when it rained, he sought shelter inside an overturned barrel, where he could hunch and fit himself tight, like a blood clot in a vein. The summer air was thick with flies and a heavy, hazy heat, so Offal-Eater was slumped against the side of the shop, wearing a stained and tattered loincloth that exposed more than it kept hidden. His gaze lifted as they approached.

Pliny did not speak to the creature in the gutter. Instead, as he regarded him with a curling lip, he said to Maleagant, "Who is he?"

"Offal-Eater," she replied.

She jerked her chin and the man scrambled to his feet, scratching what lay beneath the too-small loincloth.

"Madame Sosostris," he said, in his thin, cracking voice, "have you come for meat?"

It was all he would ever call her, Offal-Eater, though Maleagant reminded him of her real name every time they had the occasion to meet. This time, however, she did not bother: This meeting would be their last.

"No," she said, "I've come for you, who would make a rather paltry meal."

"Basket of bones, the butcher says. When I am in my barrel. He says he will slit my throat and sell me to the little man-boy-lord of Abysswatch."

The butcher meant Lord Amycus, Master of Bones, though it was impossible that Offal-Eater would know that. He stood there, trembling even in the still, hot air, a skeleton wrapped in sallow flesh. His eyes were a bleary, nondescript color, always bloodshot, and the skin of his cheeks sagged like the jowls of an old house cat. His hair had been pulled out in clumps, leaving only odd tufts, and all along his emaciated limbs he bore the tiny, raised red marks of rat bites, picked and then scabbed and then picked over again.

Pliny was observing Offal-Eater with undisguised revulsion. The leech's nostrils pinched and flared. "He smells rather strongly."

"He will improve with a bath. You may wash him down in the stables, like a horse."

"I told you I need a creature who can perform hard labor," Pliny said. "I doubt seriously that this man is up to the task."

"His appearance belies his strength," Maleagant said. "He is named Offal-Eater because he fights with the dogs for the butcher's scraps. He fights so viciously that, indeed, most of the dogs now retreat when they see him, tails between their legs. He slit open a mutt's belly once with only his teeth."

"Fond of dogmeat," Offal-Eater said. "But pigs taste better, and snakes taste best, and then comes the forbidden meat, the condemned and detested feast—"

"Can he be silent?" Pliny cut in. "If not, my master might take his tongue for it."

"He can do most anything," Maleagant said, "should he be given the proper reward."

Offal-Eater nodded fervently and wordlessly. Pliny drew in a breath.

Maleagant could have looked, could have seen, if she chose, the leech's true motive here. But without focusing, she caught only glimpses. Thin visions, like wisps of smoke, while the real world still ground on before her.

This second world, layered over the first, showed her such a scene: the golden prince, in a dark chamber that made him gleam among the shadows like treasure from a sunken wreck. His body was bare and strong, what little light there was gliding along the muscled planes of his chest. A woman was caught up in his embrace. Black of hair she was, and pale of face, her long, white limbs as bright as bleached bones. They tangled with the prince's in an impregnable knot of passion; he and the woman were one gasping, panting mass there in the murk and gloom.

All Maleagant was given to know was that this woman was not the princess.

"Very well," said Pliny the leech. "Come with me, and if you complete your task you will be rewarded with a great deal more than gutter scraps."

Offal-Eater began to shake all over with excitement, rubbing his hands up and down his emaciated arms. Without another word, Pliny turned and jerked his head for Offal-Eater to follow. He galloped enthusiastically after the leech, teeth chattering like a distressed horse. The leech walked into a thick swarm of flies and then was lost within moments to distance.

But Offal-Eater hesitated a moment, then looked back. He met Maleagant's eyes, her all-seeing eyes that, at the moment, were offering misty visions of his future. A protest formed in the base of her throat, like a clot of phlegm, and perhaps if she were of greater courage, she might have shouted it out. She might have said to this decrepit creature, *Wait, stop, don't,* for what she saw within the haze behind her eyes was terrible. It was almost too terrible for her to believe, though her visions had never been wrong before. If Offal-Eater had any romantic notions about what was to come, hopes for an elevation in status, for a meal that at last would fill his ever-hungry belly, these illusions would soon be shattered, like a bright glass goblet against the floor.

Offal-Eater raised his hand and gave a rather frenzied wave. "Goodbye, Madame Sosostris," he called to her. "Goodbye, goodbye."

Would Maleagant regret this moment? When she stood by in silence rather than trying, with what little power she had, to prevent the horror that was certain to come? It was not only Offal-Eater who would suffer; she saw that, as well. She saw untold terrors. She saw the red spurt of blood alongside the white streaking of seed. She saw the cruel flash of a blade in the dark. She saw that much and more.

Yet she did not speak. Perhaps it was fear. Perhaps it was something bitterer and deeper, a grudge that had hardened within her, grown thick and rough with time. The line of Berengar had taken from this island, had burned and pillaged and razed. Could these horrors, these unspeakable atrocities, rebalance the scales? Could the old order of the world be restored?

These questions, to Maleagant, had no clear and simple answers. She raised a hand and waved back to Offal-Eater. He gave her one final, yellow-toothed smile, and then he scampered on, disappearing into the swam of flies and sliding neatly into the groove worn by the turning wheel of fate.

V

AN ENCOUNTER IN THE TOWER

She had passed her ninety-second name day, though there was no one alive who knew that. Waltrude was the oldest creature on the island, save perhaps for a tortoise. She had only heard of such an animal; she had never seen one. They did not live on the pebbly beaches around Castle Crudele—there were just the seals that occasionally sunned themselves on sharp outcroppings of rock. But Pliny the leech had brought with him from the House of Blood an astonishing encyclopedia, a fat leather tome that showed, on each page, a different plant or creature that existed on Drepane. It was the accumulation of all his life's work, and the work of many leeches that preceded him.

So Waltrude had learned of animals like tortoises, which lived longer than mortal men, and plants like henbane that, if consumed, would infect the eater with strange delusions and terrible dreams until they sweated the poison from their system. She traced with her thumb the ink drawings of these flora and fauna, feeling almost as giddy as a girl again, delighted, after nine decades on this earth, to find that there was still something new to her in the world.

But these vivifying discoveries could not turn back time, and they could not erase what was ancient and eternal. The halls of Castle Crudele were still gray and cold. Ghosts still lurked in corners and down empty corridors, like pale accumulations of cobwebs. Her bones still cracked and ached and her flesh still slipped about loosely, sagging further with each passing day, soft as rot on a log. Her twisted nipples still pained her, each pang reminding her of the four children she had nursed, two princes and two kings.

Never a princess and never a queen, though these ghosts did not cease to haunt her. In fact, the phantoms of Iphigene and Philomel trailed after her as she climbed the stairs to the east wing of the castle. Their golden hair floated out around them, translucent as a jellyfish, another creature of whose existence she had newly learned. Their eyes were wide with fixed horror, and while they did not vocalize, they spoke to Waltrude anyway.

Save me, Iphigene whispered.

Avenge me, Philomel said.

Waltrude could not. She could only aid the living. And so, as she raised a trembling hand to knock on the princess Marozia's door, her old bones grew suddenly stiff and taut with determination.

There was some scuffling behind the door, and a bitten-out stream of words, mostly unintelligible. Waltrude waited. There was another thud and then a whisper. And then, moments later, the door opened to a narrow crack. The sliver of a face showed through.

It was not the princess. It was her handmaiden, Ninian, peering at Waltrude with her mismatched eyes. Suspicious eyes, almost hostile. Waltrude had grown used to their strangeness, but now they regarded her as if she were a most unwelcome intruder.

"Good day," Waltrude said. "I am here to see the princess Marozia."

Ninian's gaze narrowed. "She does not wish to speak with you."

"Well, nevertheless," said Waltrude, "tell her that I am here."

Ninian did not move. Her stare remained cold; she bristled with silent anger. Once Waltrude had wondered if she were simple—but oh, she had been a fool to think it. There was nothing simple about this girl, and her naïveté had been shed long ago, within months of serving at Marozia's feet. What Waltrude had mistaken for idiocy was merely love. A handmaiden in love with her mistress was far from an uncommon thing. It was only Ninian's feral passion that surprised her. She had brought with her some of her peasant roughness and animal-like aggression. It was instinctual and without true malice, but Waltrude was sure, at least in that moment, that she would scratch out the eyes and bite out the throat of any whom she perceived to threaten her dear princess.

But clearly she did not perceive Waltrude—diminished, stoop-backed Waltrude—as too much of a threat, for after staring at her a moment longer, she vanished from the doorway, shutting it behind her. There was more shuffling from within the room, more snarling whispers. Then, with heavy footsteps, Ninian appeared in the threshold again. She opened the door just wide enough for Waltrude to enter, and wordlessly waved her through.

Given the circumstances of the princess's self-confinement, Waltrude had expected to see the chamber in disarray, perhaps reeking of unwashed chamber pots and musty, moth-bitten clothes. But it was impeccably neat, from the velvet coverlet to the drapes, which were matching in their deep-red color, to the dark wooden furniture, which did not show even the faintest veneer of dust. The hearth was swept and there was no ash, only bright, snapping blue flames. And the princess stood in the very center, her posture perfectly straight, her neck as long and white as a swan's. Her black hair was bound up in a gold hairnet, and she wore rubies at her throat. There was nothing to betray a mind addled with grief.

And that made it all the more vulgar to Waltrude, all the more chilling and dreadful and dire. Here was a great lady, most noble in her pedigree, most surpassing in her beauty, clever of wit and strong of spirit. And yet still everything could be taken from her at the wave of one man's hand.

Marozia lifted her gaze to meet Waltrude's. Her eyes were as black as tide pools at midnight, and Waltrude saw no resemblance between her and her cousin. Her heart-shaped face, her taut cheeks like two fresh figs, and the natural flush that painted them, even now after countless days without seeing the sun—so different from the lady Agnes with her eerie, unworldly beauty. She almost could not fathom it that the two could be related by blood, that the two had once been so close as to be almost a single being, a symbiotic creature that fed on itself so that it was both always feasting and always starved.

The princess's voice was stilted as she said, "Waltrude."

"Good day, my princess."

"There is nothing good about it, or any other," said Marozia dispassionately. "What brings you so imprudently to my chamber?"

Waltrude's skin prickled; she had never been described before as *imprudent*. She had always done precisely her duty, no less and no more. And she remembered then her very first impression of the princess, as a vain and ungracious girl, and she was, perversely, cheered to see that she had retained some of that brazen spirit. So very different, Waltrude thought again, from the lady Agnes. So very different indeed.

She was not such a one that could have ever pleased Liuprand, aberrant as she was to the prince's tastes. Now that Waltrude knew what stirred his heart, she realized that Marozia had been doomed from the very start.

And so, filled with a pity so forceful that it was almost love, Waltrude said, "I have come to offer you my sympathy, Princess, and all the services at my disposal, modest as they may be."

Marozia opened her mouth to reply, but before she could, a tiny figure bounded into the room. Her golden curls were long and loose and a bit unruly, and her shift was wrinkled in the way of a lively and active child. She ran to her mother and leapt into her arms, clinging to her like a kitten. Marozia took a moment to cup her daughter's face, kissing each cheek and the little button of her nose, while Meriope wriggled and squirmed.

She was Tisander's twin, grown together in the womb, though if not for their physical features, Waltrude would never have known it. They had their father's Seraphine coloring, dark gold and ocean blue, and their mother's cherub face and dimpled chin. Yet in all other respects they could not be more dissimilar. And it struck Waltrude that this distinction was quite obvious, and devastating in its simplicity: Tisander was a strange, precocious being, too knowing for his years, and Meriope was an ordinary child.

Marozia turned to Waltrude, her daughter in her arms. Her brow had grown suddenly pinched with suspicion. "And what services are those?"

Waltrude drew a breath. It was difficult to speak, with the little girl now as her audience. She did not know how much Marozia had told her daughter of her fate. She searched the princess's face for clues, and then Ninian's. The handmaiden was standing a few feet from the princess, hands clasped in penitent obedience. Her expression was unreadable.

"I may look nothing more than a withered crone," Waltrude said carefully, "but I have passed more than half a century in service of the Crown, laboring for the house of Berengar. I nursed King Nicephorus at my breast. And so I believe that I may still have some influence over his thoughts."

Marozia's gaze flashed—those crow-black eyes. Her grip on her daughter tightened. A moment passed, and then she said in a low voice, "You are too boastful for a wet nurse."

Waltrude stood in silence, waiting.

"Nothing holds sway over the king save for drink and feast," Marozia went on, bitterness cracking the words. "I would be better off enlisting the aid of a kitchen wench." Still Waltrude did not speak. "And do you think I am a fool? You are slave to my cousin's whims. Why should I trust your intentions here?"

Perhaps Waltrude had not appreciated, until that moment, how very lost to each other Agnes and Marozia had become. It was not a cord that had been withered by time and strained with distance. It was a string that had been brusquely cut.

"I am a wet nurse," Waltrude replied, lifting her chin, "not a slave. I serve the House of Berengar, as I have said. And your daughter has the blood of Berengar within her. I have cause to care for her, as well."

Something in Marozia fractured in that moment, a small fissure in her façade. Her mouth quivered, the right side turning slightly down in a grimace that, Waltrude feared, might presage tears. She did not know if she could bear to see such a great and beautiful lady cry.

But instead she looked down at her daughter in her arms. "Go play with Ninian now, my sweet one," she said. "I'll be back with you in no more than a moment."

Obediently, Meriope slid from her mother's grasp and toddled over to Ninian to take her hand. The girl was dressed finely, in pale-violet silk, her hair in a tight crown of braids. Without words, she guided Meriope into one of the east wing's farther rooms. Waltrude knew every detail of every chamber here. The tower's remotest room, small and tight and dark, which locked from the outside like a vault, was where Philomel had been kept in her latter years. A queen in captivity, like some trapped lioness. Waltrude felt a sudden draft of cold, though the room with its shut windows was airless.

Slowly, Marozia approached her. She had a leonine look, as well, and stalked toward Waltrude as if closing in upon her prey. But she paused before she was in reach of Waltrude's arms.

"If you truly wish to help me," she said in a low voice, "then you will tell me what horrors await my daughter in the House of Blood."

Waltrude's swallow was audible in the silence. Her wattled throat, which felt suddenly quite exposed, juddered and bobbed.

"My princess—" she began.

And then Marozia was upon her. She clutched the front of Waltrude's dress with surprising strength, clenching the fabric in her ring-studded fingers. She was made briefly powerful in her desperation. Her lips were pulled back to reveal white flashing teeth.

"Spare me no detail," she bit out. "I am not a wilting lily. If my daughter must bear it, then I am fit enough to hear it."

Waltrude inhaled. The princess's nails were sharp, and they dug into her skin through the thin summer linen. In little more than a whisper, she said, "I am not given to know every detail, my princess."

"You said yourself you have served here for half a century. You have seen all facets of men's natures and all that women must bear because of them. The House of Blood is no different from Castle Crudele in this manner, and indeed no different than even the lowest hovel of the Outer Wall. Tell me, Waltrude. *Speak.*"

Waltrude looked down at her frock. The princess's fingers were shaking.

"I have indeed seen the nature of men," Waltrude replied softly. "Not all are the same, but in this matter, they must fulfill their duties just as their women do. I know little of the character of the Master of Blood, save that he is a young man who prefers the wind in his hair to the stuffy stillness of the council chamber. He will certainly hold your daughter in high esteem—she is of the most glorious lineages, from her mother and father both. He will not risk the ire of the Crown or the House of Teeth. But yes, he will perform the functions of a husband. If he is of gentler nature, he will wait until your daughter's first blood. If he is not, then . . . the greater burden your daughter's body must bear."

A sheen had appeared on Marozia's brow, like the misting of a fever. Her fingers trembled more fiercely. And her dark eyes flashed with half a dozen emotions within moments: hatred, terror, grief, revulsion, anguish—and then deepest, blackest hatred again.

And then the princess's grip loosed. Her hand fell, and Waltrude was released. Silence came swelling like an orchestra's chorus.

All Marozia said was, "Very well."

Waltrude regarded the princess and was struck once again by her graces and her beauty. Even now, in her unimaginable turmoil, neither quality had abandoned her. Yet—there were horrors that she still was ignorant to. She did not know of her husband's most perfidious indiscretion and her once-beloved cousin's cruelest betrayal. She *could* not know. This great and terrible secret, this great and secret terror, which could tear apart the realm like a body at its desecration . . . no matter her sympathy for the princess, the truth would never fall from Waltrude's lips.

In that same stiff, flat tone, Marozia said, "You may go."

With a nod, Waltrude turned, but halfway to the threshold, she hesitated. Marozia was no longer looking at her; she was staring blankly into the middle distance, her fingers clutching at the necklace of rubies around her throat. Fat, lush rubies, like the most exquisite drops of spilled blood. Waltrude's old jaw opened, to speak, to say—what? Words fled from her.

She was only a wet nurse. She could not stop the gyre of time. As she pushed through the door and began her dismal, solitary walk down the stairs from the eastern tower, all she could think was that she had saved nothing, and avenged no one.

VI

MILK, TEETH

Agnes was alone in the library today. Tisander had gone with Pliny to the beaches outside Castle Crudele, where, barefoot, they would walk carefully along the sand and see what creatures they could find. Pliny knew of every plant and animal on the island, all carefully accounted in his encyclopedia. Agnes had pleasant visions of Tisander, crouching before a tide pool, tracing his finger gently over the piebald shell of a crab or pointing in delight as a cormorant took flight from the rocks. Smiling to herself at this thought, Agnes took a book down from the shelf and settled in at her usual place at the long oaken table.

But she read for no more than a quarter hour before she was disturbed. The library door opened, and there was Liuprand.

She half rose from her seat in shock. "You should not be here," she said, in a thick voice that could not disguise her true pleasure. "It is a risk—"

"One I will take," Liuprand said. He walked toward her through the path of a beam of sunlight, which lit up his hair and each gilded tassel and button on his jacket. Agnes knew every contour of his body beneath it, but even observing him covered completely, her breath caught at his beauty. An impossible beauty, fed from the blood of Seraph. "I must see you."

"Will we not see each other tonight?" Agnes asked. "In our usual place?"

"No," Liuprand said. "Not tonight."

He reached the table and stood before her, and though their distance was small, it felt infinite in this unsafe place, where anyone might enter at any moment. The library was not often visited, but it was not *unknown,* not like the chapel. To muffle the instinct to reach for him, Agnes instead stroked nervously through the ends of her hair. "Why not?"

"I cannot say," he replied, "for I wish it to be a surprise. But when we convene there again tomorrow, I hope you are pleased. More than pleased." He leaned forward, and the ghost of a kiss brushed her cheek.

Agnes's skin prickled with both desire and danger. "Not *here*," she whispered, unconvincingly, for she could not bring herself to rebuff his touch.

"No, you are right." Liuprand pulled away and Agnes instantly was bereft. "But I have come to you about another matter as well."

She arched a brow. "Oh?"

Liuprand pulled out a chair and sat, while Agnes lowered herself back into her seat. They were just far enough from each other that she could not touch him, even if she extended her arms. She suspected it was for both his benefit and hers, that they might resist the temptation to fall upon each other, as they did in their secret meeting place.

"As you know," Liuprand began then, "the other houses will arrive in sixty-four days to celebrate the marriage of Meriope. Preparations are already under way among the servants, of course; we expect to host retinues of twenty for each master, and more for the House of Blood. It will be the first time in near a decade that all the houses will be gathered beneath one roof. It would be a shame for this moment to pass without putting it to full use."

Agnes frowned. "How do you mean?"

"All through my father's reign, the royal family has held the nobility of Drepane at a distance," Liuprand said. "Little effort has been made to promote true unity among the houses and the line of Berengar. *Some* effort," he admitted, a flush tinting his cheeks, and Agnes looked away, for she knew that he hinted at what they both dared never speak of aloud. His marriage. "But as we are witnessing yet another yoking of the Crown to one of the noble houses, I thought we might make of it a special celebration."

Agnes looked down at her hands in discomfort. She did not know precisely what her cousin thought of this marriage, because they no longer spoke. Marozia kept to the east wing of the castle, and Agnes to the west. But it did not take great wisdom to guess. Her beloved daughter, summarily removed from her arms and carted off to a distant house to be made a strange man's wife. Or—perhaps not entirely strange. Agnes remembered the boy Gamelyn had been, the green eyes she had gazed into while they stood in Fredegar's cellar. She remembered, with a chill, how hateful those eyes had been.

She did not know, however, if or how he had changed in these intervening years. He was a boy no longer. Would he be as kind a man as his grandfather? Or as cruel a man as his father? And would he ever forgive the Crown, the House of Berengar, for what had been taken from him? The father slain, the childhood stolen?

Agnes looked up to find Liuprand watching her intently, brow furrowed with concern.

"I am well," she assured him, swallowing hard. "Now go on."

"I propose this only because I believe you are fitted to the task, and that it might bring you joy," he said. "I thought perhaps you might be persuaded to write and prepare a masque, to be performed before our gentle guests. The subject of this theater would be, of course, the joining of the royal house with the nobility of Drepane. It would celebrate unity and promote a hopeful vision of the future."

As Agnes looked upon her lover, she was suffused with pride and affection. Liuprand the Just, he had been named, but he could just as easily be called Liuprand the Good or Liuprand the Wise. Generous, he was, clever and kind. She was glad to be his wife, even in secret. A smile pushed itself onto her face.

"Yes," she said. "Yes, of course I will do this. It is a great honor that you would think me suited for the enterprise."

"Why should I not? Your mind is sharp, your imagination colorful, your knowledge immeasurably vast. You will write something superb, such as those stories you scribbled as a girl; I know it."

It required all the strength of Agnes's will not to take Liuprand's face into her hands and kiss it. Yet she need not feel entirely bereft, for what followed was one of her most treasured occurrences—a small and humble thing, but vivifying nonetheless. Liuprand relaxed back into his chair while Agnes rose and began searching among the shelves for a book that might inspire her masque. She returned with an armful, spreading them out across the table. She picked up one, Liuprand another.

And then, as they had once before, a long, long time ago, when Agnes was still silent and Liuprand yearning against all hope, despite all odds, they read together. Not a word needed to be spoken between them. Their love was an airborne thing that could be felt, like the mists of the Dogaressa's perfume, a gift from one of her many suitors. It was the scent of roses, sweetest just before the moment of rot.

Agnes could even be contented not to reach out and take her lover's hand. His nearness was enough, the pulse of his golden warmth. In the midst of this moment, which seemed to stop time itself—or at least make it roll slowly, languorously past—Agnes managed to half convince herself that it would last forever.

That night, when Agnes returned to her chamber, her mind was abuzz with ideas; her thoughts spread out in all directions, like dark-veined rifts racing out across an expanse of cracked ice. Below the surface of that frozen water, so many creatures lay in wait: a calico shark, a blood-red squid, a whale as black as midnight. Whimsy, passion, death. Every element, every facet of existence, would make an appearance in Agnes's masque. As Waltrude undressed her, she found herself shivering in anticipation.

But still, she sensed the wet nurse's distraction. Her motions seemed almost too rote, bordering on brusque, and she kept her gaze lowered to the floor. Agnes's gown fell away from her body, and Waltrude did not quite catch it in time, leaving the deep-purple silk to drift to the ground, like the blown petals of an orchid.

Innamorata ~ 409

"Apologies, my lady," Waltrude said, bending to pick it up.

Agnes, standing nude before the mirror, saw herself frown. "You seem ill at ease," she said.

"No. I am not."

Stubborn as a carriage wheel in the mud, Waltrude was not one to argue with in such a manner. Agnes instead regarded her reflection. There had been a time when she had looked in the mirror and loathed with every aspect of her being the creature that looked back. But that was long ago. That gray, silent, wilting flower of a girl had been coaxed to blooming life by Liuprand's hands.

If she had been a girl then, she was most certainly a woman now, near thirty herself. When she had come to Castle Crudele she had come pale, her skin stretched tautly over her bones, her rib cage pressing upward through her flesh. Now fat had filled her once-sunken cheeks, and love had painted them with the most delicate flush. Her breasts had grown to pert and modest peaks. Agnes came to appreciate her own beauty—as though she were seeing herself through Liuprand's eyes—and her frown lifted into a smile.

Waltrude was not smiling. She was folding Agnes's dress with the same brisk ministrations and placing it on the chair to be washed. With the wet nurse's attention averted, Agnes plucked her own nightgown from the wardrobe and put it on, the gauzy silk gliding across her bare, supple skin.

"Where has your mind gone?" Agnes asked, approaching Waltrude. "*Speak.*"

There was a subtle rising of her shoulders, like the bristling hackles of a cat, and then Waltrude turned. Her lidded eyes were watchful and too knowing. Agnes remembered how, at their first meeting, she had been surprised to see how lively they were, how clever, for a woman so old and otherwise weary looking. Now she sensed again that Waltrude knew too much.

"Did you see the prince today?"

Agnes, not expecting her question to be answered with yet another question, furrowed her brow. "Yes," she said. "In the library. Not in our . . ." She trailed off, heat rising to her face.

Waltrude stared at her impassively. The corner of her mouth twitched, then froze, then twitched again. At last, she said, "And did you see the princess?"

The heat rose from Agnes's cheeks to her scalp. It made her hairline dampen at once with sweat. "No," she replied. "I did not."

"Hm," was all Waltrude said in response, though it was a very solid and heavy *hm*. She turned away from Agnes yet again to bundle up laundry.

"She does not wish to see me," Agnes added hurriedly, in her own defense. "She does not wish to be seen."

Waltrude's tone was pregnant with indiscernible emotion as she said, "And why is that, lady?"

Agnes could have scolded her, she supposed. She was only a wet nurse, and an unused one at that, as Tisander had long outgrown his need of her. And Agnes was a noblewoman of great esteem: the Mistress of Teeth, secret bride of the prince of Drepane. Waltrude spoke so boldly out of turn. A crueler mistress might even raise a hand for it.

But instead Agnes said, "Because she is as stubborn as you are, and as bitter as an old shrew. What privilege, what joy, has she ever been lacking in her life? The most profitable marriage any lady could hope for, a surfeit of children, the inheritance of the wealthiest house in Drepane. She is princess; one day soon she will be queen. If indeed she suffers, it is only because the world is not enough for her. It has never been enough."

Waltrude was silent a moment, and Agnes felt briefly, perversely pleased that she seemed to have prevailed in their argument. Then the wet nurse turned back to Agnes, laundry held to her chest.

"Her husband lay with her but once, against his will, and now dishonors their marriage vow every night," Waltrude said. "She has lost her title. She has one child she holds dearly, who will soon be taken from her. And she has no friends in this castle save her handmaiden. She has gold and jewels and fine silks, yes, but what is their use, when she cannot leave the confinement of her tower?"

"She is free to come and go," Agnes bit back. "She is free to do as she pleases."

"Free is not always free," Waltrude murmured, and Agnes could not deny that she knew well what that meant.

Feeling, unexpectedly, a rush of cold, even though the windows of her bedchamber were shut, Agnes wrapped her arms around herself and shivered. The risen, aged white scars brushed against the silk of her nightgown. Just as with her hand, the damage was grievous enough that Agnes lacked sensation in various places across her rib cage and her stomach, the undersides of her breasts, her mound. These days she rarely thought of it; the memory was fuzzy, like a half-faded ghost. But now—

"I will not be shamed," Agnes said in a whisper, "for seeking my own freedoms, my own passions and pleasures. You know what a deprived creature I was once. You have seen the permanent etchings on my person that time will never erase. You, of all beings, Waltrude, should not place judgments upon me. You should understand my reasons and my cause . . ."

"I have said nothing to shame you, lady." Waltrude's voice was even. "You are the one who flounders and rambles in your guilt."

"No," Agnes said forcefully. "Not guilt."

She had decided, the evening that she wed Liuprand in the dark, that she would not feel it. She would forbid that emotion to blaze its path within her. She had chosen her course; she would not be blustered from it. It was the only way she could live—to lock her guilt behind a great stone door, within an impenetrable vault. It was a cursed object, like a talisman imbued with black magic centuries old.

Waltrude merely lifted one shoulder and then let it fall back again. "Very well, lady," she said. "I will bring your cold milk from the kitchens."

Later, when she was alone in bed, Agnes sipped her chilled milk—the summer was nearing its apex, and its hot, gusty breath even managed to penetrate the walls of the castle, ordinarily so cold as to bastion its inhabitants against such heat—and she thought.

She thought of Adele-Blanche, who had long since ceased to visit her in her dreams.

She thought of her mother, and the taste of infant's flesh.

She thought of Marozia, and the musky slide of juice in her mouth.

But in the end, her thoughts always returned to Liuprand. It was not only passion she felt for him, the torrid, desperate longing that slicked the place between her thighs; it was exquisite and immeasurable tranquility, a peace and safety she had never thought possible. He had vanquished all of her ghosts. His embrace was a blessed haven. A refuge. She had yearned for it all her life and had not even known her own loneliness until she had seen his face and felt his kiss.

There was no force greater in the world than this. Than love. Nothing could dissuade her—she did not dare to give it up. She was the lady Agnes, Mistress of Teeth, Liuprand's bride in the dark, queen by the candlelight. She curled up beneath the covers and pressed these thoughts of him into her mind; the theater behind her eyelids was a riot of light and color.

And yet, when she did find sleep, her dreams were of Marozia. Her dreams were sweet milk and sharp teeth.

VII

A REWARD BESTOWED

Truss was fanning himself rather ineffectually with a bouquet of lemongrass when the man entered. At least he seemed like a man at a distance. And if he had kept his distance, Truss would have thought nothing more of it. But as he approached in an awkward, loping gait, Truss came to realize that this creature was either more than a man or less. He was *something* aberrant, something different, something peculiar, and this alone was enough to make Truss perk up with interest.

He scrambled from his cot into a sitting position and nudged Mordaunt sharply with his elbow. The other leech stirred, and Truss leaned close to his ear and whispered, *"Look."*

Mordaunt blinked fiercely—he had been roused not from rest but from slumber. "At what?"

"That thing," Truss answered. "Over there."

The creature wore a ragged tunic, hem falling just above his knobby knees. He looked blankly about the room, his gaze filmy, as if still with the mucuses of sleep, and then gave two very loud, persuasive sniffs. He inhaled creakily. And then his eyes found Truss and Mordaunt.

"Hello, Your Scrupulousnesses," he said, in a throaty voice, as he hobbled toward them. "Hello, My Superiornesses."

Truss and Mordaunt exchanged glances. Mordaunt, irritable at being woken, tugged up the hood of his robe and asked, "Who are you? And what is your business in the leeches' bay?"

"Business," the thing repeated. "Business . . . I have performed my labors already. I am seeking the reward my master promised me. But this castle is a labyrinth and I cannot find the kitchen. Please, will you help me?"

Truss gave the man a once-over, from the balding, misshapen head to the bare toes with their blackened nails. He was thin, painfully so, his collarbones jutting out like two sharp blades. His waxy skin was more yellow than white, and even as he stood still before them, he was occasionally racked by full-body tremors that made his scrawny limbs jerk upward, as if attached to erratically tugged puppet strings. Truss also noticed something peculiar about his hands—they were coated in a thick layer of dust.

"Your master," Mordaunt repeated, and he got to his feet. "What master? The king?"

The creature scratched his belly. "No, no king."

"Then who?"

He grimaced, making even more dramatic the sloped hollows of his cheeks. "I have been forbidden to say. Else I will lose my tongue for it, and how then would I enjoy my reward?"

Mordaunt frowned. He was displeased that this queer creature had interrupted his sleep, but Truss was now enthralled in this peculiar matter. It was the most exciting thing that had happened to him in years. It was like discovering a new species of animal. Or learning a new game of chance.

"What is your name, man?" Mordaunt demanded.

"I am the eater of offal and entrails, of pluck and spleen, of tripe and head cheese. Trotter and udder, suet and tongue—"

"Your *name*," Mordaunt cut in.

"Offal-Eater, I am called." Once again he scratched his belly, which, like his cheeks, sloped inward dramatically—as though, despite his name, he had not indulged himself in food or drink for weeks. Truss rose to his feet then, as well, beguiled and more beguiled by this strange beast.

"You eat all of that?" he asked. "Truly, and it is your most coveted feast?"

Innamorata ~ 415

Offal-Eater's gaze darted in a panicky way. A tremor ran through him. He cleared his throat and said, "No, no . . . there is always the most forbidden delicacy. I have tasted a morsel of it but once. I fear I shall never taste it again, though it is the only thing that sustains me, that fills my belly, that grafts fat to these horrible bones . . ."

Offal-Eater carried on, but Truss's mind was turning in another direction, like a carriage wheel loosed from its axle. He was thinking of another game that would enliven his dull and slow-passing hours. And he was thinking of how he would cajole Mordaunt into playing it with him.

His eyes flitted to the other leech, who was staring at Offal-Eater in undisguised revulsion. He was difficult to look at for long intervals, Truss had to admit, and he had quite a bad smell. But he was all the more entrancing for it. What a creature! And what a world, which still had such alluring creatures in it!

"I will show you to the kitchens," Truss said. "There you will have all the pluck and tripe you could wish to eat. Indeed, you will have more than any man could consume without bursting."

"There is nothing that will overfill me," Offal-Eater said. His voice was hoarse with excitement.

"Oh?" Truss arched a brow. He glanced over again at Mordaunt, who, this time, met his gaze and set his jaw. He understood. And Truss was overjoyed for it. "Well, let us see if that is true."

The kitchen was not Mordaunt's favorite place in the castle; it was, in fact, his least favorite place. It stank of oil and grease and the dramatic amount of sweat that poured from the armpits of the chef, Gower. It was ill lit and hot even in the coldest months of winter. And now, with summer at its apex, the chamber was almost unbearably warm, the air suffocatingly heavy and cracked through with the sounds of slamming pots and jangling cookware. Mordaunt tried to hold his breath.

Their new companion, this Offal-Eater, only heightened the squalid, repellent aura of the kitchen. He scuttled behind them like a hermit crab, occasionally dropping onto all fours and then rising again, panting with exertion and arousal.

The kitchen was more crowded than Mordaunt had ever known it to be, preparations already under way for the wedding. The din was deafening, spoons tapping against soup pots, knives thumping against cutting boards, and of course the incessant sizzling of butter and fat. Gower was shouting over it all, nearly bawling out his instructions, as the lesser cooks chittered in panic and scurried about, chastened mice in stained aprons. Truss, Mordaunt, and Offal-Eater passed through unnoticed.

Truss was leading the way, his footsteps jolly. He even hummed a wordless tune under his breath. Mordaunt had recognized at once the look in the other leech's eye, the gleam of hideous excitement that meant he had found a new, crass way to amuse himself. But Mordaunt had come along. What did it say about him that he had been unable to refuse the bright canary's call of such novelty, such degenerate thrills?

A shiver went down his spine as they passed the larder, exuding its dank coldness, and then through the dim, narrow corridor to the outermost chamber of the kitchen. Here was Truss's destination. The rubbish heap.

The stench was almost unbearable, even for Mordaunt who, in performing his leech's duties, regularly attended to the vilest mechanisms and excretions of the human body. But the corpses he worked upon were—by order of the Septinsular Covenant—always fresh, often still stiff with the rictus of death, not yet near to rot. This, here, was a decidedly posthumous scent. The scent of things left to putrefy, quicker and more odiously in the summer's heat.

Here was a feast fit only for flies and maggots, yet, upon entering, Offal-Eater clapped his hands together in uninhibited joy. He squealed, a repugnant, piggish sound.

And then he fell upon the pile as a lover into crimson sheets. He writhed; he clawed; he opened his mouth and tore at whatever he could with stained yellow teeth. There were hunks of offal that he swallowed whole and others that he chewed, his cheeks expanding to grotesque proportions. The paunch of his stomach stretched like a taut wineskin. All the while he was groaning, moaning, taking part in a crazed but solitary ritual, a bacchanal for one.

Mordaunt looked on in silence. He really was a most deviant creature, this Offal-Eater. The revulsion that Mordaunt felt as he watched him took on a joyous feel, almost erotic, as though his disgust was the smoke in a prophet's pipe. He was aroused by it, the sensation of himself as superior to this wretched thing, this thing that could not even be called a man.

He glanced over at his fellow leech. Truss was watching with rapt attention, one hand fisted in the front of his robe, twisting and twisting the fabric. Mordaunt recognized the same arousal within Truss, the burning eyes, the slightly parted lips. They were both so distracted by their own impassioned disgust that, for a moment, their original purpose there was forgotten.

But Truss was the first to break from this trance. He tore his gaze away from Offal-Eater and said, "I will bet you he can eat half the pile."

Feeling rather gutsy, Mordaunt replied, "I will bet you he can eat the whole pile."

Truss gaped at him; he was used to Mordaunt's conservative bets. "No," he protested. "It cannot be. His stomach would sooner burst."

"I think the rubbish will be gone before his appetite is."

And indeed, as the moments wore on, that seemed to be precisely the case. Offal-Eater gnawed and nibbled; he chewed and swallowed, and yet each bite seemed not to sate his hunger but to augment it. Mordaunt grew almost weary from watching it. Even such a freakish spectacle could not hold his interest indefinitely. But Truss—more imaginative in these matters—was speaking again.

"Offal-Eater," he yelled, over the sound of this frenzied feasting, "would you eat a kitchen cat?"

Offal-Eater paused, a string of intestines hanging from his mouth. "Yes, yes," he said, "and again, yes."

This revived Mordaunt's curiosity as well. "What about a lizard? A snake? A fetal puppy?"

"Yes," he replied, "yes, and yes, and yes."

So it went on like that, almost interminably. Truss wrangled a kitchen cat and Offal-Eater ripped its abdomen open with his teeth. He drank its blood and ate it, bones and all, before proceeding to vomit up its fur and skin. A fetal puppy could not be procured so easily, but Mordaunt swore he would marshal one up before the day was through.

Having consumed every scrap and morsel of rubbish in the room, Offal-Eater then grew unerringly still. He lay flat on his back, arms and legs splayed out to his sides, in the position of a man strapped to a rack. His chest rose and fell faintly with his previous exertions, and he still exuded a smell that was fetid past all conception, but otherwise, he made no impression upon the world.

A hushed silence fell over Truss and Mordaunt as well.

After several moments passed, Offal-Eater lifted his head. In a hoarse, weary voice, he said, "Thank you, Rosencrantz. Thank you, Guildenstern."

"That is not my name," Mordaunt said.

"Nor mine." Truss frowned.

But Offal-Eater said no more. He lay his head back down again on the dirt floor. His eyes closed, and he sank immediately into what seemed, to Mordaunt, a perversely restful slumber. That left only him and Truss to watch in stunned amazement, saying no more to each other, either, for what they had witnessed was beyond words.

In that silence, which was not even broken by the hum of blackflies—they had all fled with the vanishment of the rubbish—Mordaunt began to think. He was remembering that Offal-Eater had spoken, earlier, of a *forbidden delicacy*.

I have tasted a morsel of it but once. I fear I shall never taste it again, though it is the only thing that sustains me, that fills my belly, that grafts fat to these horrible bones.

And now, having seen Offal-Eater consume near everything that Mordaunt could possibly imagine, and understanding that there was nothing so vile that he would *not* consume, Mordaunt thought he knew what that *forbidden delicacy* was.

Innamorata ~ 419

VIII
PARTS ARE CHOSEN

Agnes's dreams did not fully leave her, even upon waking. She found her limbs tangled in the sheets, which were cold and damp, and then could not make herself rise; flat on her back, lying awake as if in the throes of a fever, she felt a strange and perverse urge to stay there. If this was indeed guilt, then perhaps she could sweat it out. It would take only time, grueling and miserable moment by moment—but the moments would pass anyway.

Only she could not stay, because she had business in the castle. She would finish the writing of the masque today, and then she would marshal up the actors from among the inhabitants of the Outer Wall. Escorted by members of the Dolorous Guard for her safety, Agnes would select the most beauteous, the most refined in their manner, as refined as a peasant could be. She would take them up with her into Castle Crudele and dress them in costume and teach them their lines; she hoped she might find some who could read. And it would be a glorious spectacle, one of whimsy and passion and intrigue, every second a vivid, colored thing, expelling all vulgar thoughts from the audience of nobles, making them fall over themselves with newfound devotion to the Crown.

Or so Agnes hoped. She loved Liuprand and she believed she could make others love him, too. She dressed and sat down at her writing desk, picking up the quill in her right hand. The purpose of this masque was to reflect only the grand spectacle of life, none of its banal drudgeries. If there was hate, it would be matched in its ferocity by desire. If there was grief, it would be matched in its potency by joy. Her quill raced across the page. She was not that gray, wilting creature. She was—as each proud, bragging beat of her heart reminded her—alive.

And that realization, at last, chased away the thoughts of Marozia. For the rest of the morning, Agnes worked dutifully and without distraction at her task.

In the afternoon, Agnes was able to select her actors, two dozen of them, the most graceful of the inhabitants of the Outer Wall. It was a rather artless charm that most of them had, but it could be shaped and molded, made into something sophisticated. With gilded masks and passionate red paint on their lips, it might be forgotten, momentarily, that these were creatures that knew *only* life's banal drudgeries and none of its grand dramas.

She arranged the actors in their places; she taught them their lines. She chose the silks and velvets that would be cut for their garb, all of them richly colored, with a sheen that would sparkle in the candlelight. Masks for every and every one, hiding the faces that were mundanely marked by pox scars, by pimples, by wrinkles and sunburns and the chapping of harsh winds. The actors rotely followed her instructions, never moving unless directed, standing still until their knees quaked beneath them. Agnes was quite pleased.

As the hours of the day wound on, Agnes's pleasure turned to anticipation. With every moment that passed, as the sun lowered its belly like a large yellow beast, her excitement only grew. Indeed, when the first striations of dusky blue appeared on the horizon, her composure slipped, and she startled her actors by clapping her hands together very suddenly to dismiss them. They lumbered out of the hall, a herd of bewildered cattle. And Agnes slipped away.

Through the winding corridors, up the long and forgotten staircase, dust-cloaked, abandoned by all but two. It had been three days since their last meeting here, and Agnes's heart ached with longing.

When she arrived at the landing and pushed open the heavy, iron-gridded door, she was shocked and more shocked to see that it was not Liuprand alone who stood within.

There was another man there, or perhaps it was better that he should be called a *creature*. His shadow on the wall was a man's shadow, but what cast it lacked the basic elements of humanity that would put a mind at ease. He had bones, and stretched, taut yellow flesh, but with no fat to gird and brace them. What few teeth he had were broken and would make a poor inheritance for her house. Thrasamund, Master of Eyes, would be similarly bereft with what could be found within this creature's skull: two dull, bleary orbs, which seemed to look both everywhere and nowhere at once. His colorless hair was in patches; when he breathed, it was with a strained, labored wheezing sound, air rattling through the corroded bellows of his lungs.

Agnes was left without words. He captivated her, horribly, and commanded the attention of all her senses. She did not even notice Liuprand approaching her until he spoke.

"My love," he said. "How I've missed you. How it has pained me, to spend these last evenings alone."

"What is that?" she whispered. "There in the dark?"

"Nothing to concern yourself with." Liuprand drew his arm around her. "Look away from him—and see what I have done."

It was difficult, but Agnes managed to divert her gaze and take in the entirety of the room around her. The changes took her breath away. No longer was the altar massed with melted wax; it had all been scrubbed off, scraped clean, leaving shockingly fine and polished marble below. What now gave the room light was a number of torches placed along the wall, tongues of flame flicking in their braziers. But what was most impressive, most shocking, was that beside the green velvet chaise, a large tub had been constructed from brick and stone, and filled to its brim with water. Flower petals floated on its surface, lilac and protea, white orchid and hyacinth.

Agnes looked up at Liuprand. His blue eyes were shining like sunlight on the evening sea. "Do you like it?"

Agnes, who still could not speak, merely nodded. The greatest gift of all was so simple, in truth: It was to love and be loved in return.

Liuprand inclined his head toward the creature in the corner. "Go now," he said. "I have no more need of you."

The manlike thing raised a hand and gave an awkward, crooked wave. In his bullfrog's moan of a voice, he said, "Farewell, Stella, hyacinth girl. Farewell, Lord Marchino." And then he turned and scurried from the room.

Agnes frowned, unspoken question in her mouth.

"Ignore him," Liuprand said. "He is a wretch that I found among the inhabitants of the Outer Wall. I had Pliny bring him here to perform these labors, as no one within Castle Crudele could be trusted with such a secret. This creature—this Offal-Eater, as he is called—is mad; even if he persuades anyone to listen to his ramblings, he will not be believed. It is impossible for him to reveal us."

Slowly, Agnes nodded. And then, as Liuprand's hand slid along her bodice, she was possessed by a fevered frenzy of passion, the strange creature all but forgotten. She tugged at the buttons of Liuprand's shirt while he snapped the laces of her corset in a single deft tug. Her gown fell away from her. The rest of his clothes were shed soon after.

With a sudden swiftness, Liuprand lifted her up into his arms. She uttered a small noise of shock. He carried her, in the style of a bride, toward the tub and stepped within it, lowering them both in increments into the water. It had been heated, and Agnes's bare flesh burned pleasantly as she was submerged.

The petals of a white orchid drifted past. Her black hair spilled out around her, made even sleeker in its wetness, as shiny as a mermaid's tail. Liuprand released her to perch gently upon his lap; one hand cupped her head and the other the small of her back. She felt him growing stiff against her thigh.

Agnes was recalling—as she knew Liuprand was, too—that night in the House of Blood, where they had committed their first act of lustful treason. When she had finally laid down her grief and given up her fear, and opened herself up to him like a night-blooming flower, shy in the sun but glorious under the moon. That reminded her of what she wished to tell him, but before she could, Liuprand kissed her on the mouth, and all her reason and wisdom was forgotten.

She shifted her lips and seated herself upon him, moaning as he slid inside her, inch by inch. He was steel sheathed in silk, hard and soft both at once. He thrust up into her, tangling his fingers in her hair, jerking her head back to expose the column of her throat, which he then lavished with his mouth and tongue.

Her release built within her, a banking of coals in her lower belly, from which a heavenly fire rose and laced through her veins. He came with a lion's roar, muffled against her shoulder, but there was nothing to deafen the cry of ecstasy that broke from Agnes's lips. The sound lifted from her like an ivory-winged bird, soaring to the ceiling and fluttering there among the rafters. And then, in its absence, virtually no sound at all. Only the labored gasping of two lovers in the dark.

When Agnes recovered herself, she slipped off his lap and sat beside him, leaning her head back against the edge of the tub. Liuprand's throat bobbed and his lashes fluttered wearily. Her own tiredness settled upon her like a velvet mantle, but she shoved it away, unwilling to surrender to sleep and to dreams. The real world demanded her attention. Turning to Liuprand, she said, "I have an idea to propose to you."

He opened his eyes and looked upon her earnestly. "What is it, my love?"

"I have been writing my masque. I have the actors now, and the script, and I think it is going rather well." The liplike petal of an iris bobbed through the water and caught itself in her hair. "But there are two parts I could not fill with the actors from the Outer Wall. They are . . . wanting of beauty and charm."

Liuprand's gaze was steady; he hung upon her every word.

"And you are the most graceful and glorious creature to ever touch

Drepane's shores." Agnes lifted a hand to his face, brushing her thumb across his cheekbone.

"I am no such thing," Liuprand said, "but go on."

"Will you do it?" Agnes asked. She leaned closer, close enough that he could feel the whisper of her breath. "Will you take the main role yourself?"

Liuprand shifted slightly so that their eyes were perfectly level. He lay his hand over hers and gently prised it from his cheek, kissing her scarred palm and each of her fingers.

"I told you once that I am your disciple," he said. "I follow every command you give me, and endeavor to grant every wish that so much as flits through your mind." He smiled against her hand. "Yes, Agnes, of course I will do it. There is nothing you could ask of me that I would not debase myself to execute."

IX

THE PROCESSION

The arrival of the guests began at the earliest hour of dawn, and was announced by the tolling of the great brass bells in the tower of the Outer Wall. Phylus, the bell-ringer, took the ropes in his callused hands and yanked with all the force that his aged body could muster. And as the reverberation shuddered through his bones, there was a desperate scrabbling at the base of the tower, beggars and paupers and scullions scattering in all directions, striving to be the first to share the news with the inhabitants, and hopefully earn a coin or a head of cabbage for their trouble.

First to arrive was the delegation from the House of Bones; their master, Amycus, was precise and proper in all things. Their banners were black and white, their sigil a pale raven perched on a skull, with a bleak field of ebon behind. There were no windows on Amycus's carriage, no angle from which he could be glimpsed, leaving the inhabitants of the Outer Wall bereft. He was a curiosity, this boy-man who spoke with a bird's voice. And yet his procession vanished through the barbican without offering even a peek of the diminutive lord.

Next came the delegation of the House of Lungs, and a more divergent spectacle there could not have been. Lord Hartwig's carriages were emblazoned in garish colors, showing, in progression, a painting of a great hunt: naked youths with spears against a backdrop of gold and green, an ivory stag with an enormous coronet of antlers, gored, its wounds weeping dramatically. Rubies, not red paint, made up the blood, and the stag's eyes were chips of sapphire. As the carriages trundled past, a few were bold enough to reach out and swipe at the gems, as if they could rattle them loose. But the jewels stuck fast, and the peasants were bereft once again. So distracted they were by the finery of the carriages that they missed the Master of Lungs himself, though he sat proudly upon a pure-white mount, in a glorious brocade cape of velvet.

The more worldly of the inhabitants were surprised to see the delegation of the House of Flesh appear next. They had the longest journey, from the remotest part of the island, an arid and sun-scraped territory separated from the rest of Drepane by forbidding black peaks. Perhaps the length and the many possible treacheries of the passage had caused the Master of Flesh to come with a sparse retinue: a single carriage, lacking any ornamentation save for the gossamer drapes that revealed only the silhouette of the lord behind them. He appeared as no more than a shadow on a wall, and the assembled peasants let out a long, disheartened sigh as he passed.

Was it so much to ask that these great lords came in the most sumptuous trappings of wealth and supremacy? The days of the peasant-folk were so dreary, so colorless, that they yearned for a vivid spectacle to tint, however briefly, the drab canvas of their existence.

Their hopes were modestly lifted by the arrival of the House of Hearts. Their colors were the tender pink of an infant's earlobe and the muted red of the inner petals of a still-ripening rose; however, when taken together, these pastel shades made a lovely sight indeed. They suggested the soft beauty of a sunrise, and most of the peasants were not so lacking in sophistication that they could not appreciate a subtler form of glamour and of art. The Master of Hearts sat with his lady wife within one of these dawn-hued carriages, their hands joined in a faithful knot. The peasants sighed again upon seeing them, only this time it was a low, besotted sigh, as if the love of the lord and the lady had imbued them, in passing, with a similar satisfied fondness. They were, however briefly, at peace.

And so it was rather startling to see next the House of Eyes, though their retinue was certainly not lacking in opulence or spectacle. Lord Thrasamund's carriages, colored sunset orange and vivid green, were heavy, sturdy things, and they beat the earth with their wheels as they passed, stirring harsh clouds of dust into the air. The peasants gasped and choked, but when the dust cleared and they had Lord Thrasamund within their sights, they felt suddenly galvanized, shot through with gall and with purpose.

He was a craggy giant of a man, his shiny bald head compensated by the most exuberant ginger beard. His eyes were set low over his hooked nose, and his gaze was as fierce as an eagle seeking quarry. The peasants absorbed this ferocity, this drive, and their spines stiffened. Each one suddenly recalled a moment when he had been wronged, with no recourse, or an occasion during which she had been cheated and left with naught but her futile fury. A murmuring of jilted anger came from the crowd. Lord Thrasamund's simmering ire had infected them.

But when his carriage passed through the barbican, his anger vanished with him. The peasants blinked, as if newly roused from slumber, and wondered what had happened. The once-powerful sentiment was now no more than a half-remembered dream.

And then at last, at very long last, came the House of Blood. Their carriages were crimson, and so were their banners. A dozen carriages there were, twice as many as the next-largest retinue, and they were oddly silent as they passed through the crowd of peasant-folk. A hush fell over the assembly, and it made the gonging of the bells feel obscene, an affront not only to etiquette but to nature itself. The retinue had turned the world into a grim place—not gray or drab, but black with dread and wretchedness. Even the wind ceased its gusting. The air was still and suddenly thick with the tang of copper.

Maleagant stood at a distance from the tight knot of the crowd. She saw, over the tops of the peasants' heads, the carriages in procession, in their fleeting rainbow of colors. And she felt, as the other inhabitants of the Outer Wall did, the noxious disease of emotions that the nobles inflicted. She felt love and outrage and loathing and even the cold prickle of nearing death.

The wise woman shuddered. Yet here, in the horrible mass, the feelings imposed upon the peasants were not so appalling as what she could glimpse beyond grotesque and miserable reality. In her mind's eye, the future unfurled like a tapestry: threaded here with gold, and there with silver, veins of blue and cross-stitches of purple. But most of all, it was stained gruesomely and appallingly with red, for blood.

X

THE SANCTION OF THE SLUGGARD

Agnes was not viewing the procession, nor could she be found in the entrance hall, greeting and making pleasantries with the noble guests. Instead, she was in one of the back rooms, checking the fit of a cloud-sprite's costume. The actor who wore it had gorged himself these past few weeks, taking full advantage of his new position within the castle, and now the pale fabric strained about the paunch of his stomach. Agnes frowned, yanking the silk tighter, fingers quavering about the buttons. This was the fiddly sort of task that her damaged hand still protested, and she wished she'd had the foresight to enlist one of the castle seamstresses to aid her in these final moments.

"Stand *still*," Agnes ordered through gritted teeth. "And let me not see you sneaking sweet rolls off the feast table."

"Apologies, lady," the cloud murmured.

At last she managed to fasten the buttons. She let out a breath and stepped back, raising a hand to wipe her forehead. The organization of this masque had required more labor than she had imagined, and in truth, she would be glad to see it done. But she would be even gladder to see how it impacted the guests, how it roused their spirits, how it filled their hearts with love for Liuprand and the Crown. Agnes no longer had any doubts. She had written with the full force of her own passion, and she knew her efforts would succeed.

All around her, the actors were in their garb, their masks fixed to hide their plain peasant faces. They stood stiff and at the ready, and if any of them expressed dolor or apprehension, it would not be noticed.

Their exteriors had been transformed, like an old, weather-worn statue painted over again in bright colors.

Agnes smiled. In only a few short hours, the wedding would be finished, and the true spectacle of the evening would begin.

More than half a decade had passed since Castle Crudele had sustained such an assembly of illustrious guests, and the great hall had been transformed to more than adequately suit this momentous occasion. Every single candle within the castle, it seemed, had been marshaled to line the walls, to fill the arms of the candelabras, and to light the eight chandeliers that hung from the ceiling. The whole chamber gleamed with their languid brightness.

A great many flowers had also been plucked and arranged about the dais. White flowers, from Agnes's private garden, though she doubted that any of their guests would understand their significance, save for perhaps some old retainers from the House of Blood. Within each bouquet was a long stalk of delphinium, its purple vertebrae climbing almost defiantly upward, straining toward the false sunlight.

The tapestry that hung behind the dais had been commissioned for the ceremony. Majestic and enormous, it covered the whole of the wall from the floor to the ceiling, and showed an abstract scene: In the center, the winged lion of Seraph stood in profile, one paw extended decorously.

The creature to which this paw was offered was not one that could be found in the pages of Pliny's encyclopedia. It had the hind legs of a deer with the curling horns of a bull; however, it also had the sleek black feathers of a raven and a mouth full of very sharp canid teeth. Its snout, long and wolflike, ended in a heart-shaped nose. Its face had half a dozen eyes, and the shaggy fur on the rest of its body was a deep crimson red.

This exceptional and freakishly fashioned beast served a great purpose. Agnes could pinpoint the way that each feature represented one of the seven noble houses of Drepane, and she smiled to herself at Liuprand's cleverness. Already she noticed many of the guests gesturing toward the tapestry. There was a surprised yet pleased tenor to their whispers. They understood what Liuprand intended them to understand. So far all was well.

And each house had made a plentiful, enthusiastic showing. The plots on either side of the aisle were full nearly to bursting, every seat in the pews occupied. The Houses of Hearts and Bones and Lungs were on the right side, and the Houses of Eyes and Blood and Flesh were on the left. The plot for the House of Teeth was filled by inhabitants of Castle Crudele: Waltrude and Pliny and several other of the more cherished servants, and of course Drepane's golden prince. Sitting between Liuprand and Pliny, Agnes held a wriggling Tisander on her lap.

Indeed, the only empty seat in the great hall was the throne. But it would not remain so for long. Of all the tasks left to Liuprand before the wedding, this had been the most odious and the most onerous—yet he had, after many months, succeeded in it. The door to the left of the dais opened, and the rasping, gurgling respirations of the king could be heard.

He was carried into the room on an opulent litter, which was hefted by twelve of the Dolorous Guard, six on either side. Their armor clanked; their knees wobbled under the strain. Agnes felt her chest tighten as she watched this precarious undertaking—if even one of the men faltered, the litter would slip, and the king would roll to the ground like a boulder in an avalanche.

She could not recall the last time Nicephorus had left his chambers, and for good reason. In these past six years, he had grown huge beyond all conception. So large, in fact, that he was bound to his bed; he could not rise without assistance, and he could do little more than while away his days with food and drink and sleep. Occasionally, he had whores brought to his chamber and ordered his servants to couple with them while he strained and strained to work himself over, but it was said that this only made him weep for his own deficiencies.

The worst had come two years ago, when his feet had begun to swell in size and turn black and gangrenous. The Most Esteemed Surgeon had visited his bedside and proclaimed that they would need to be amputated, lest the infection spread to the king's vital organs. And so now he sat, footless upon his litter, his ankles ending in bandaged stubs. He wore no special regalia for the occasion; he could not be moved sufficiently for the seamstress to take his measurements. His naked form was instead draped with a large blanket, which slipped off his shoulders occasionally to reveal the endless, dimpled rolls of fat.

A heavy silence fell over the great hall. The mists of the revulsion in the air could almost be felt, could almost be tasted, like sour wine.

Slowly, tremulously, the Dolorous Guard mounted the dais. They had been instructed, on pain of death, not to utter so much as a groan of strain or exertion, and so they were silent save for the grinding of pauldrons against breastplates, of gauntlets against the litter's wooden frame. Squeaking, grating noises that made Agnes flinch and want to cover her ears, but even that, she feared, would further shame the king, and would disgrace this entire enterprise with the filth of Nicephorus's depravity.

The Sluggard, indeed. He could not fit the throne so, as instructed, the Dolorous Guard set the litter down on the dais, right in front of the chair, and he leaned back against it, head on the seat, arms flopping out to his sides like the useless tentacles of a beached squid. Berengar's golden crown sat crooked upon his brow, too small to be properly worn.

The king inhaled deeply. Mucus rattled in his throat, making the sound more of a groan than a breath. The chamber was, otherwise, as still and silent as death.

"Now," came the deteriorated, rasping voice of Nicephorus the Sluggard, "we may begin."

XI

GAMELYN

He mounted the dais so agilely that it seemed an insult to the king, though surely it was not meant as such. It would have been impossible for a man, in the flower of his youth, to degrade himself sufficiently so as not to shame the hideous lump that sat before the throne. But there was a low murmuring of relief as the bridegroom took his place before the crowd; the assembled guests were glad to have their attentions diverted from the Sluggard in all his grotesqueness.

And a more diverting sight there could not have been than that of the Master of Blood, Gamelyn. He was a tall youth with long, well-formed limbs—more lean than muscular, though he was not lacking in vigor; Agnes could see the rippling robustness of his body through the crimson garb that he wore. The precise shade of his hair had evolved with age. Where it had once been bronze, it was now a darker, deeper red, like wine from a goblet. His face had also lost some of the softness of childhood, his cheekbones high and prominent, his jaw sharp and strong.

These were the glimpses of his grandfather in him, the late Lord Fredegar's virile graces. Agnes could find nothing of Unruoching in his son's features—the weak chin and the weaselly, shifting gaze. No, it was his mother who had gifted him the rest of his fine looks. He had the surpassingly green eyes of Ygraine, and by extension of Thrasamund, for he was the product of not one but two ancient and noble bloodlines.

The intensity of those eyes could not be unrecognized, though perhaps it was only Agnes who felt chilled to the bone beneath their stare.

The eyes thrust her backward in time. She was not looking at the creature before her, at the man grown, but rather at the boy in the dungeon, the boy who had watched his father's torment and seen clear through to its cause. The boy whose anger had been cold and silent, but still naked as day. The boy who had been taught, at only twelve, how to rage and how to hate.

To calm herself, Agnes began to stroke one of Tisander's golden curls between her fingers. She was being overly suspicious, overly fearful; Gamelyn was not even looking at her. His unfeeling gaze was instead cast blankly out over the crowd, lingering on nothing in particular. His handsome face betrayed no sentiment. There was only a brief and very subtle twitch of his full-lipped mouth.

"They say he is the greatest swordsman since Berengar," Pliny murmured, and Agnes startled to hear his voice. When the meaning of his words sank in, she was perturbed even further. He could only know such a thing if he had spoken to some of the retainers from the House of Blood. She had not thought he would dare approach any of his former compatriots.

Liuprand scoffed quietly. "A skill sharpened against squires and wooden targets," he said. "He has never known the field of battle. He is no warrior, no Berengar come again."

"I only relate what I have been told, my prince."

Yet Agnes found she could picture it easily, those sinuous arms swinging a sword so deftly that it looked like no more than a whirl of silver in the air. Silver and crimson were his house's colors, which appeared discordant against the House of Berengar's navy and gold.

She could not help but compare these two men: the bridegroom who stood on the dais, the Master of Blood, and the prince who sat beside her, Liuprand the Just. That Gamelyn was an able swordsman she did not doubt. And he was an exceptionally fine example of his species, with all the features and proportions of beauty and nobility. But he was not Seraphine. If he were to stand beside Liuprand rather than beside the slumped body of the diminished king, his own deficiencies would have been made apparent. Liuprand would tower over him by a head. His limbs were long and lean and he looked nimble in his movements, but Liuprand was certainly stronger by brute force, broader, built thickly of muscle. Agnes had seen how he could splinter wood into dust in the palm of his hand.

Even the most well-bred and well-trained native of Drepane could not match the pure power exuded by those with the blood of Seraph. Liuprand's golden aura pulsed from around him now; Agnes could feel its warmth and instinctively sidled closer.

But she did not have long to bask in this glow before the doors to the great hall opened. Every guest in the pews rose, and so did Agnes, hefting Tisander up onto her hip.

Being within the plot closest to the dais, Agnes had to crane her neck to see over the crowd and down the aisle. The door closed and, for a moment, there was no answering sound. And then she heard, very faintly, the measured padding of slippered feet on the floor. Two sets of footsteps, each with a rhythm of their own.

It took another moment before Marozia came into view. It had been so long since Agnes had laid eyes upon her cousin that her appearance was a shock, not least for what she wore. It was a gown of black wool, stiff in its construction, unlike the sumptuous garb of silk and velvet that Agnes had known her to prefer. The neck of the dress reached her chin, covering the entire column of her throat. She had on black gloves; not a single jewel adorned her fingers, not even her wedding ring. Her earrings were but small golden studs, and her long dark curls were contained within a mesh hairnet.

Agnes had never seen her cousin wear black. In the ancient days of Drepane, before Berengar, before God had been vanquished and his prophets put to the sword, black had been the color of mourning, worn to honor the dead. It was the color that Adele-Blanche had dressed herself in every day that Agnes had known her, that spiteful and perverse shade that communicated her disdain for the Septinsular Covenant and the royal line that enforced it.

Marozia was clever enough to know this. She would not have forgotten their grandmother's garb or her reasons for wearing it. And

Agnes could swear she saw the same glimmer of perverse pleasure in her cousin's eyes as whispers rose from the crowd, whispers questioning this uncouth choice of attire. Only the oldest among the guests would recognize the color for the significance that it once held; yet the others still knew it was an insult, a protest against what was to come. Marozia had made herself into such a sight of disquiet that one almost did not notice the child in her arms.

The bride clung to the front of her mother's gown with one tiny clenched fist. Her other hand was in her mouth, and her thumb-sucking was vigorous enough that it could be heard from quite a distance. Spittle shone on her chin, and so did the tracks of tears on her cheeks. The blood of Seraph had gifted her golden hair, which fell in loose, rumpled coils to her waist, and deep-blue eyes that were wide with bewilderment. Her white gown was taffeta and lace—the gown of a grown woman, only shrunken in its proportions, trying to highlight a bustline that did not exist and nip in at a waist that was not there. The absurdity of it was so poignant that the whispering quickly ceased, and a glacial silence returned to the air.

A long, diaphanous veil fluttered out from the crown of her head. It was long enough to brush the floor, and it would have, if not for the second figure trailing behind the princess and the bride. Ninian, the handmaiden with her mismatched eyes, walked stiffly after Marozia, holding up the gossamer fabric so that it stretched like a web of spider-silk. She herself wore a gown of ashen gray, her hair braided into a tight crown that made Agnes's scalp prickle to see it. She had no jewels, no adornments, not even a heel on her slippers, and her gaze was cast coldly to the ground.

The procession was slow. Marozia must have wished it to be, to drag out these moments of discomfiture and unease. It was not the king she sought to embarrass—for he was incapable of such a sentiment—but the prince, her husband, and even the guests themselves. She wanted them to turn their heads away in shame. Agnes had been lost to her for a very long time, but still she recognized the look on her cousin's face. For all her many talents and virtues, she had never been skilled at disguising her emotions. Beautiful, capricious Marozia, with both the serpent's hypnotizing stare and its deadly teeth.

The princess reached the end of the aisle and ascended the dais. While she had tarried in her grave walk, two new figures had taken their places on the dais as well. One was the Most Esteemed Surgeon, who was arranging himself in quite an awkward position before the king, trying to avoid tripping over the splayed-out stumps of his legs. The other was the lady Ygraine, who stood thin and shivering behind her son.

Agnes could perceive the bruises of a sleepless night beneath her eyes—just how many sleepless nights had she passed, in these six, nearly seven, years? Had her dreams been haunted by the sounds of her husband's gurgling screams as he choked on the precious blood from Lord Fredegar's casks? Did she walk the halls of her castle and remember how her beloved had perished of thirst and hunger behind an impenetrable wall of stone?

It was not the first time Agnes had been given to wonder these things; she had imagined, in her mind's eye, Ygraine pressing her face to the newly built wall and whispering empty comforts to her husband on the other side. She had imagined how Ygraine's tears would work their way into the masonry, causing the mortar to dampen and separate back into grains of sand. She had imagined all this and more, even after she had made the vow to strike guilt from her heart. Agnes shifted her gaze away in shame.

Marozia turned so that Meriope, the little bride, faced her bridegroom before the crowd. She wriggled in her mother's arms, still sucking at her thumb, but otherwise made no sound. With her face only in profile, and partly obscured by the veil, Agnes could not discern her expression. She could not tell if Meriope understood her fate, even as it played out in front of her, like a mummer's farce.

"This noble lord, Gamelyn, Master of Blood, and the princess Meriope, of the House of Berengar, have gathered here today to be wed." The voice of Most Esteemed Surgeon arched out awkwardly over the crowd, as a bird uncertain in flight. "By my own endlessly scrupulous hands, I anoint their union. If anyone in attendance has cause to protest it, let them speak now or hereafter hold their tongue."

No voice, no whisper rose from the audience. Tisander had gone stiff in her lap. He was a child wise far beyond his years, but even he seemed consternated by the scene before him, his little brow creased and his mouth turned downward in a grimace. He saw only the aberrant nature of the moment, and not its necessity. He could not know all the labors that had been performed and all the blood that had been shed to bring it forth. He did not know how the gyre of fate had twisted and warped to construct this scene. Even Agnes, who had witnessed it all, who possessed an adult's wisdom and reason, could not quite comprehend it. Injustice upon injustice. Betrayal upon betrayal. Abuse upon abuse. But there was no other recourse. To restore the world's order, all debts must come due.

"Then I endlessly seal these two in lawful union. This binding is absolute, and can be broken only by the cruel artifice of death."

Gamelyn, in a swift, practiced motion, reached into his pocket and produced a ring. It was so small that Agnes could not make out any of its features, not even which stone had been picked to adorn it. Marozia had to gently prise her daughter's hand from her mouth and extend her fingers by force. That, finally, drew a low whimper from Meriope. It was a childish keen of confusion, and it went through the air like shears through silk. The crowd flinched.

But Gamelyn did not fumble. He only paused, to wait out the whimpering, and then slid the ring onto his bride's spittle-slicked finger. His face was angled away from the crowd, and shadowed. Agnes perceived no emotion from it.

A few more words from the Most Esteemed Surgeon and then it was done. The wheel was set once again in its groove. The world had been put back to its proper course. And now the gyre turned on.

Liuprand rose from his seat and climbed the dais in one long, able stride. Towering over his lady wife, and indeed even over the Master of Blood, he clapped his hands once to capture the attention of the audience.

"I must thank you all heartily for your attendance and your graceful observance of this ceremony," he said. "To further demonstrate my gratitude, I have arranged a performance for your pleasure. Please follow me into the feasting hall, and enjoy the fruits of the skillful and clever Lady Agnes's labors."

XII

THE FRUITS

Agnes was filled with a wondrous exhilaration as the guests began to file into the feasting hall. She passed Tisander into Waltrude's arms and then slipped forward through the crowd, darting among the guests so that she could come out ahead of them, and to the back room where her actors were waiting. They were all in their costumes, all arranged precisely to her pleasure. Her blood pulsed delightedly in her veins and rose in a hot flush to her cheeks.

From the next room she heard the shuffling footsteps of the guests, the scraping of chair legs against the stone floor as seats were taken, the clinking of glasses as wine was poured. *Any moment now*, she told herself. One of the lion cubs coughed, covering his mouth with his paw. Her jittery excitement expressed itself in a long, tremulous exhale.

The door opened, and Liuprand appeared in the threshold. His cheeks, too, were flushed pink, eyes shining with that boyish earnestness that made Agnes fall more in love with him by the moment. "Are you ready, Lady Agnes?" he asked.

"Well, not quite," she replied. "There is one performer who has not yet donned his mask."

Liuprand smiled. "I had trouble putting it on myself. I'm afraid I must beseech your help."

"Oh," said Agnes, and she had to bite her lip to keep from smiling broadly back, "then I shall happily grant it."

He came to her—as close as they dared when in the company of the actors, even though their gazes were dull and not prying. Without a word, Liuprand knelt and bowed his head.

Agnes fixed the mask on him, fingers trembling at the illicit touch—against the nape of his neck, along the line of his jaw—which was as much as they would ever be allowed in front of strangers' eyes. Their love was for the darkness, blooming only in the secret cover of night. Six years and it still struck her with an old jolt of pain to think of it.

She withdrew her hand, and Liuprand rose. Now from the feasting hall came only the low hum of wordless whispers. Agnes beckoned her actors to their places. And then she slid on her own mask.

The masque began with death, as this was the history of their island. The harps played an eerie, almost discordant tune as her reaper walked the length of the stage, trailing his gray robes. Agnes had chosen a very tall man for this part and ordered him to fast for two weeks, in order that he should have the emaciated look of a revenant. And indeed, his hollow cheeks and spindly limbs, along with the sheen of hopeless hunger in his eyes, gave very much the effect she had desired.

He did not entertain so much as he did haunt the audience, in his sallow, flesh-colored mask and the coarse white horsehair she had fashioned into a wig. The crowd murmured their unease; what sort of masque was this, they wondered, that began in so grim and treasonous a manner? But this was all according to Agnes's design. Death's shade made slow, lumbering circles about the stage, the ghastliness of the moment accentuated by his isolation. He was utterly alone as he circled.

At last, when the discomfort of the audience had reached its peak, just before it would be diminished by degrees into boredom, a passel of actors rushed the stage. They were dressed finely, if innocuously, in garb that befit a lesser noble house. Agnes—wisely, she thought—

would not want to offend any of the houses in attendance, for the fate of these actors was calamitous.

They hovered at first around the edges of the stage, miming conversation, drinking from empty goblets. But one by one, death approached them. His walk was almost solicitous, and the nobles paused in their feigned ministrations, tilting their heads in exaggerated curiosity, as their expressions could not be seen behind the masks. The harp strings quivered to silence.

Death reached out. He had a dagger hidden in his sleeve and now it slid forth, gashing the air and the front of the nearest noble's frock. The fabric fell away and there were gasps from the audience, but there were no red ribbons to stand in for blood, no hands clutching at a falsely slit throat. Instead only the noble's clothes were pared away, revealing the shock of his naked body beneath.

And still it was terrible. The audience did not quite comprehend why the ordinary features and faculties of the human form suddenly took on a grotesqueness in the candlelight. Agnes had selected the most unremarkable of actors for these roles; they were neither fat nor thin, old nor young, fit nor ill. She had applied no cosmetics to them. What the audience saw before them were the same sights they saw when they looked in the mirror each night, yet somehow it made them all flinch and avert their eyes.

The lady Agnes was clever, and she knew the secret that most did not. The secret was that humanity is wretched in its essence, and we loathe to be reminded of our own rote repulsiveness. We hate to remember that we have bones that creak and grind at their points of juncture, blood that pulses wetly and turbidly through our veins, and muscles that distend and undulate when called upon to move. A man hates most of all his own heart, his own lungs, his own eyes and flesh and teeth, and he is grateful when he can displace this hatred onto another, when one is so openly, so garishly odious that it appears exceptional. The most blessed sights in the world are the most vulgar, and the most frightful are the most mundane.

Death does not transform; death merely reveals. And so death paced across the stage and disrobed each of the nobles, showing them all in their vile, banal humanity. There were sickened groans from the audience. Agnes could have done little more to excite them to sentiment.

The slain nobles rose and followed the reaper in his circling, like naked ducks in a row. Their footsteps dragged; their shoulders slumped; they seemed to have no will of their own, only what had been imparted to them by death. The audience shuddered and wept, more desperate with each passing moment for relief. They wished for something that would dress the world in the bright garments of romance once again.

And so then he came, robed in the finest fabrics of gold, in the shiniest of jewels, and lending his own pulsing aura of light to the presentation. If there were any in Drepane who doubted the grace and fairness of their prince, such qualms were now put to permanent silence.

He did no more than ascend the stage, the glimmering blue of his eyes showing through the holes in the mask, and the audience fell about with sighs and weeping. At last there was proof that the world held beauty. Here was such a glorious example of humanity that all could forget how hideous it was in its normalcy. What great heights humanity could reach! The prince was evidence of it. The crowd cried out in relief.

Liuprand was playing Berengar, and so with nothing but the wave of his hand, he vanquished death. The nobles reassumed their clothes. They fitted their plain faces again with masks. And then came the next group of actors, the cloud-sprites and the sunbeams and the seabirds and the lion cubs, showing what wondrous creatures the world contained when it was bathed in the House of Berengar's golden light.

But what occurred next was a surprise, to the audience and even to the prince who had been well prepared for his part. Lady Agnes emerged quietly from the back room, and, while attentions were focused on the gamboling cubs and the fluttering seabirds, she tipped back the lid to a large wooden trunk. From within there was a great whirring sound, and then a mass of moths lifted into the air, their wings palpating like the beat of a thousand tiny, bravely stirring hearts.

The audience saw a lovely feast for their eyes, these brilliantly colored and variably sized moths forming a vivid tapestry over their heads. But the prince saw more. He saw that the features of the moths had been carefully chosen, and because he knew the language of rustling wings, he knew that the lady was sending him a coded message. A message of love. Black wings, white wings, iridescence gilding their membranes and their antennae. Love and resolve. The scattered flight of these moths was a vow, as true as words spoken, in a tongue that no other on the island had the privilege to know.

I will love you forever, said Agnes to the prince, voicelessly.

The mask could not hide the prince's smile, nor could he be persuaded to keep his joy a secret as Agnes herself mounted the stage. She wore a gown of silver, with a low neckline that bared her shoulders and her collarbones and the cleft of her breasts. Woven through the silk were pearls and diamonds, and every inch was embroidered in glimmering thread, baroque swirls and patterns of flowers and reaching ivy. Her black hair was pulled half back, in a crown of braids laced with silver ribbons, and the rest hung loose and sleek to her waist. Her jewelry was modest so as not to distract from the glamour of the dress, or from the costume's true spectacle: a pair of large, gossamer wings unfolding from her back.

As she strode toward the prince, moths perched on her bare shoulders or in her hair and then, at intervals, took flight again, giving her the appearance of constant movement, of a living, vacillating canvas. Liuprand reached out his arm. Lady Agnes reached back. Amid the swirl of moths and under the gleam of candlelight, their fingertips brushed.

What a beautiful sight it was for the audience, a rich and lively painting, rendered in the most exquisite strokes. It was as though the moon extended one of its silvery beams to meet the matching, outstretched shaft of the sun. They thought of it as such: theater, performance, art. They did not guess at the truth that undergirded the pageant. They were far too happy to be free of the hideous sight that was common humanity. Clever Agnes had foreseen this. She had arranged it all, putting in place every piece so that she *could* dance with her beloved, just once, in the light.

The moths, trained and as intelligent as the raven perched on Lord Amycus's shoulder, eventually retreated to the trunk where they had been concealed. The actors stood in a line and bowed deeply. Applause rained through the hall, with all the brash clamor of a summer storm, and Agnes and Liuprand, their hands joined, bowed as well.

But there was a single face that remained unmoved, a single gaze that had, despite the efforts of the lady Agnes, seen the truth that lay under the showy scene. Beauty could not disguise it. Not to the one who could perceive the world in such a manner that she easily ascertained the desires of others. It was a skill that she had not had the chance to exercise in quite a long time, removed as she had been from humanity in her lonesome tower.

Princess Marozia saw that dreadful and wonderful thing that was love. She saw it in every facet of her cousin's form and every subtle movement undertaken. She saw it reflected back in her husband, the prince, even behind his mask. Years unspooled before her. A waking dream, in which she witnessed each secret meeting, each stolen kiss, each frenzied, passionate coupling, all of which had occurred within these cold halls while she had driven herself half to madness, alone.

She was watching Agnes and Liuprand so intently that she hardly even noticed that she had begun to pick at the skin around her fingernail, unwinding that white band of flesh in the *prick-prick-prick*ing rhythm of pain. From her eyes fell a single tear. And from her hands, a drop of precious blood.

XIII

HAPPY AND DAUNTLESS, AND SAGACIOUS

The feasting hall was aroused with noise, all the pleasing, joyous sounds of celebration. Agnes sat at the head table to Liuprand's left, and from this vantage point she could survey the scene before her completely. It was a happy one. Her masque had left so much exuberance and pleasure in its wake.

Beside her, Liuprand had slipped off his mask and was indulging heartily in food and drink. He sipped from his bright goblet and smiled as, in turn, each noble house came to greet him and pay the appropriate honors. The king had already retired for the night, to his own private, gluttonous feast, which would have been too embarrassing and grotesque to witness. And so it was Liuprand alone who represented the Crown, the House of Berengar, and he did so with all the grace that a golden prince should.

First came Hartwig, Master of Lungs. A man of pride and vanity, it seemed he had strived not to be outdone by any of the other guests or even by the spectacle of the celebration itself. He wore the most magnificent doublet, silk and velvet and stitched in every shade of thread that could be dyed, from every root and plant on Drepane. His face was beauteous enough, at a distance, though when he approached the table Agnes saw the efforts that had made it so: wax applied to the corners of his eyes and his brow to draw back the flesh and smooth the wrinkles that came with age.

Hartwig had no wife and was yet to legitimize an heir, but he was attended by two of his favorites, both pale, lissome youths, with hair as long as a woman's. They looked closer to boys than to men, and they stood at a slight distance behind Hartwig, as if fearful to approach the prince, their mouths drawn into sullen pouts.

"Lord Hartwig," Liuprand said.

"My prince." Hartwig bowed deeply. "I offer my most heartfelt congratulations on the wedding of your daughter. And thank you for the gift of the masque. It was an exquisite performance to witness."

"That is all thanks to the labors of the lady Agnes," Liuprand replied. "I played only the smallest part."

Hartwig turned to her and placed a hand over his chest, giving a rather theatrical sigh of his own. "The spectacle moved me greatly, lady. You have a talent for provoking sentiment."

"Thank you, my lord." Agnes felt her stomach flutter at the praise. "I am glad to hear that it touched you."

"Is all well in your lands?" Liuprand asked. "How fare the House of Lungs and its vassals?"

"Our lands prosper, and the Painted Hall is happy. It would be a great honor to host you and the princess, should you wish to visit the south."

With the mention of the princess, Agnes's skin prickled and she turned away from Hartwig. She had not wished for her gaze to fall to the other end of the table, but it did nonetheless. There, holding the tiny bride on her lap, was Marozia. Her plate was empty and her goblet full, not a single sip drunken. Meriope laid her head on her mother's chest and blinked sleepily; the hour had grown late, and Waltrude had already taken Tisander to bed. Agnes imagined it would be a trial to keep the little girl awake for the remainder of the festivities.

Initially the bridegroom had been seated appropriately at his wife's side, but the order had become rearranged, and now Ygraine sat between Marozia and Gamelyn. She was very thin, and her gown, the color of a bruised peach, seemed to drag about her, like the shedding husk of an insect. A saffron-yellow shawl covered her shoulders and part of the braided mass of hair at her nape. Agnes once again had the impression of diminishment and immense sadness. She was a beautiful woman, but her obvious grief reduced her.

Yet she was not silent, not brooding. She was speaking, rather intently, to Marozia, both of their mouths moving in rapid whispers. A part of Agnes was gladdened to see it, gladdened to see that both the lady Ygraine and her cousin were not so lost to their anguish that they could not establish a rapport. It was to both of their benefits, after all, for the Crown and the House of Blood to remain familiar to each other.

Occasionally, when there came a pause in the conversation, Ygraine would turn to the other side and whisper to Gamelyn. She loved her son—Agnes could tell from the way her green gaze grew soft when she looked upon him—and her son loved her in return. He leaned into her touch and even allowed his mother to pat his cheek or stroke his hair, as if he were a boy and not a man grown and wed. Watching them in this manner, Agnes grieved, briefly but deeply, for what she could never have.

In the time she had spent observing the bride and bridegroom and their mothers, Hartwig had taken his leave, and Lord Amycus was approaching the dais. Accompanied by his wife, Pharsalia, who looked near to twice his height, and of course his raven, he gave a steep bow.

"Lord Amycus," said Liuprand, "and Lady Pharsalia. A pleasure."

The Master of Bones whispered something to his raven. The raven squawked out, *"The honor is mine, Your Highness."*

Agnes did her best to remain unperturbed by the queer lord and his even queerer animal. She glanced at the lady Pharsalia. Her dark hair was streaked with silver, and her face was weary and lined; she had given her husband seven children, but only four had lived past their childhood years, all of them girls. She was too old now to give her husband a son, and so it was said that Lord Amycus bedded a new woman every night, while his wife looked on, to shame her.

When Agnes turned back, the raven was croaking again.

"The abyss is watched, Your Highness," it said. *"Should you ever wish to inspect its soundness yourself, the House of Bones will host you gratefully."*

"Thank you," said Liuprand, "for your ever-dauntless vigil."

Amycus—or rather, the raven—offered his honors once more, and then he departed, leading away his wife like a child's horse-on-a-string. Agnes was momentarily preoccupied by the sight of Pharsalia's retreating back, and so she did not at first notice the next solicitor: Lord Vauquelin, Master of Flesh.

He was a tall man, and broad, with lank black hair to his shoulders. Agnes was rather surprised by how pale he appeared; she had thought that the sun would have tanned him, in his warm and dusty lands. But his face was a shock of white, and only when he grew closer to the dais did she realize that this was accentuated by the application of powder, giving him, overall, the appearance of a risen corpse.

"Lord Vauquelin," said Liuprand as the Master of Flesh bowed, "thank you for your attendance. I know the passage is not easy from Pelekys."

"No," Vauquelin agreed, "though it has been well worth the trials. The ceremony was lovely, as was the masque that followed. Lady Agnes is a great mind."

"Thank you, my lord," Agnes said, feeling the same twinge of pleasure at his flattery. "Your praise honors me."

"And where is the lady Volumnia?" Liuprand asked. "I hope she is not absent for unfortunate cause."

"No, my prince," Vauquelin replied, "my wife is well. But such long journeys do not agree with her. She sends her most happy regards."

It was whispered that the lady Volumnia had, in her age, grown half as fat as the king, and an ordinary carriage could no longer accommodate her. Secretly, Agnes could not imagine how this was so—no woman, even one of prestige and nobility, would be permitted to feast endlessly. Depthless hunger was a privilege reserved for men alone.

But Agnes suspected this talk was not true at all, merely the uncharitable opinion of vociferous rumormongers, an aspersion cast upon Vauquelin and his house. If the House of Teeth had been famed for its cold asceticism, the House of Flesh was famed for its lustful indulgence. Yet there were few who knew, in truth, what occurred in that arid and distant territory, what strange practices they followed, what debaucheries were encouraged by Vauquelin's hand.

And perhaps it would never be known, at least not by Agnes, for, unlike the other solicitors, Vauquelin did not invite Liuprand to his keep, Pelekys. He only gave his honors again and then departed to the table where he sat with two retainers, the sole men who had joined him on his jeopardous quest. They wore light, loose-fitting tunics, and their sole adornments were heavy, hammered disks of bronze hanging around their throats and their wrists. They had the same white paint as their master on their faces, which made them look both freakish and austere. Their appearance intrigued Agnes, who had never directly spoken to anyone from the House of Flesh before, but she did not have long to ponder it—two figures were approaching the dais.

They walked, as they seemed always to do, hand in hand. Lord Rabanus and his beloved wife, Perpetua, of the House of Hearts. Their garb was velvet, soft pinks and tenderest reds, the same colors that bedecked their banners. Perpetua wore a rather impressive divided hennin, her airy veil fluttering with her movements. The Master of Hearts bowed, and his lady wife curtsied, and Liuprand looked upon them with more fondness than she had seen him regard any previous solicitors. It was the fondness of familiarity. Agnes sat up straighter in her seat.

"My dear prince," Lord Rabanus said, "we have been absent from each other for too long."

"Far too long," Liuprand agreed. "I hope it has not been trouble that has kept you away."

"No, my prince, all is well," Rabanus replied. "We have merely been arranging the betrothal of our own eldest daughter, and we hoped that tonight you might offer your blessing."

Rabanus gestured toward one of the tables, where his retinue sat. Among them was a doe-eyed maiden of no more than twenty, wearing a hennin that matched her mother's, its veil a gauzy, gossamer shade of rose.

"Rosalynde," Liuprand said, smiling brightly. "It seems like yesterday she was only a child, clinging to her mother's skirts."

"She was only fearful in your father's presence, my prince," Perpetua said, her brow arching. "Otherwise she was a bold and clever girl, and remains endowed of these traits as a woman."

"I would expect nothing less, from a daughter of your house. And I expect, as is your custom, that her betrothal is one born of love, not duty."

"Of course," said Rabanus. "We wish for all of our children to be as joyous in their matrimony as we are."

A marriage for love was as aberrant on Drepane as the customs of the House of Teeth under her grandmother's regime. Agnes could have grieved, again, for what she would never have, but curiously she did not feel her own deprivation in that moment. She only felt the happiness that Lord Rabanus and Lady Perpetua seemed to impart upon her. It pulsed from them, like the aura of golden light that radiated always from Liuprand. Agnes reveled in its glow, basking like a lizard on sun-warmed stones. She was—at least for the moment—content with the order of the world.

As though he could sense this stirring of sentiment in her, Liuprand placed a gentle hand on her shoulder. Agnes could not remember the last time he had touched her with another's eyes upon them. To Rabanus and Perpetua, he said, "I do not believe you have yet had the privilege to meet the lady Agnes, Mistress of Teeth."

"It is an honor," Agnes said, with a dip of her head.

"Likewise," said Lady Perpetua. "And your masque was a great privilege to witness." She paused, gaze flickering briefly to Liuprand and back again, and then went on, "I am deeply heartened to know that the prince enjoys the companionship of such a gifted and virtuous lady."

Alarm bolted through Agnes, but Liuprand answered swiftly and calmly, "Yes, we have become good friends over the years."

And there seemed to be no subterfuge on the faces of Rabanus and Perpetua, at least none that Agnes could discern. They both smiled back uninhibitedly, their eyes made bright by the lambent glow of the candles, the rings on their joined hands gleaming.

"Perpetua was my mother's childhood companion," Liuprand said, turning to Agnes. "She was a lady-in-wait here at Castle Crudele. She could only be persuaded to part from my mother's side when she became enamored of Lord Rabanus, and he with her."

"It was no easy choice to leave," Perpetua said. Her fingers, still dovetailed with her husband's, clenched ever so slightly, knuckles whitening. "I did not relish being absent from my oldest and dearest friend. I had always thought we would raise our children together, that we would grow old . . ." A shadow passed over her face. "But fate does not always arrange itself to our wishes."

"*Fate*," murmured Lord Rabanus. He gave a brisk shake of his head. "It was not fate that stole away these dreams, my love. It was a far baser and more mundane depravity. The barbaric malice of a man who yet draws breath in these halls."

Agnes felt the words go through her with a chill. The king had long since departed, but to utter such calumnies against him, in his own castle—throats had been slit in this very chamber for less.

Perpetua squeezed her husband's hand, a gesture of both comfort and warning. "Please know, my dear prince, that the loyalty of our house is to you, always to you."

Liuprand dipped his head. "The Crown is most grateful for such unbending devotion."

"No, my prince, you misunderstand," Perpetua said. Her voice was soft and low but not without conviction. "It is not the Crown to which we offer our honors tonight, nor our pledge of loyalty. It is to *you*. Liuprand the Just, prince of Drepane, son of the brave and unjustly slain Queen Philomel. You have our hearts and our steel. It is to the benefit of all that our king is a sagacious ruler, fair and gracious and valiant. You will be such a king. And the House of Hearts will do all that is in our power to make it so."

XIV

WITH BARBARIC LUSTER

Liuprand ordered chairs to be brought up so that Rabanus and Perpetua could join them at the high table for drinks and for merriment. In their circle of four, there was much laughter, loud and uninhibited, and wine imbibed to coax it out. Agnes had not ever seen Liuprand carouse in this manner, and it gladdened her that for once he could shed the prince's stiff restraint and revel like an ordinary man.

They spoke of times that had passed, and the wine seemed to embellish even the moments of grief, making them into a fable of sorts, safely confining them to the realm of stories half remembered and ancient, distant dreams. Agnes even recalled tales of Adele-Blanche and managed to imbue them with humor, making her grandmother into a whimsical figure, stripping her of all her cruelties and her legendary coldness. She found that she could indeed smile at the memories that had once caused her so much anguish. They were now so distant from her, in this moment of flushed elation and artless passion, that they seemed almost as if they had happened to another girl, another woman, not Lady Agnes, Mistress of Teeth and secret consort of the soon-to-be king.

So many of her idle fears slipped away in the haze of drink. When Liuprand laid a hand on her arm, she did not stiffen with the panic that they would be found out, that someone clever and perceptive would see what lay beneath the seemingly innocent touch. There was only the lady Perpetua, and the lord Rabanus, kind, gentle souls of humor and sympathy.

It was duty that stole away this moment of unbridled happiness.

Two figures were approaching the dais, one familiar to Agnes, and the other not.

"Lord Thrasamund," said Liuprand, lifting his gaze. "Good evening."

"Good evening, my prince," Thrasamund replied, though his bow was brief and shallow. "I have been waiting some time to greet you and pay my honors."

"Yes, and I thank you for your patience. Lord Rabanus and Lady Perpetua are old friends, and we found plenty to discuss." Liuprand's face was delicately but unmistakably flushed. "Your attendance at this ceremony is very much appreciated."

Thrasamund's face, by contrast, was pale and gelid. "Well understood, my prince; however, if my house could beg a moment's word—"

"Of course," Liuprand cut in. To Rabanus and Perpetua, he said, "I should give my full attention to Lord Thrasamund and his son, but I will call for you again when I am finished."

They both nodded in assent and departed, the pale-pink veil from Perpetua's hennin floating out behind her. While Rabanus continued ahead, Perpetua gave one brief glance over her shoulder, a glance that met Agnes's eyes. Her expression was odd, almost fearful, the happiness drained from her so suddenly, like clipping the stem of a rose.

When Agnes returned her attention to these new solicitors, Liuprand was saying, "You are most welcome, Lord Thrasamund, and I am happy now that our two houses are joined—though perhaps in an abstruse manner—through the bloodline of your grandson."

"Yes," Thrasamund agreed, "it is most fortuitous. The profit of this betrothal is many-sided."

His tone was leery, lacking the gaiety that was appropriate for the circumstances. Yet if Liuprand noticed, he pressed on as if there were no discrepancy between the quality of Thrasamund's voice and his words.

"It is my aim to cultivate familiarity and goodwill among all the noble houses of Drepane and the Crown," he said. "I hope you can see my efforts already—or rather, the efforts of the lady Agnes, whose brilliant mind constructed the masque."

Thrasamund's gaze shifted to Agnes, and he dipped his head. "Lady," he said. "I believe it has been many years since we have last looked upon each other."

"Many years indeed," Agnes replied. She had not laid eyes on the Master of Eyes since the desecration of Adele-Blanche, and his appearance had not much changed in that time. His bald head still shone like a polished bead, and his beard was just as boldly red. What did seem different now was his manner. She had not once heard his hearty laughter in the feasting hall. He had given none of the jocular and effusive speeches he was known for. His spirit seemed to have retreated into itself, like a fox hunkering down sullenly into its den.

"And," said Thrasamund, in that same dispassionate tone, "I am given to understand that you have never met my son and heir, Childeric."

With one hand, he beckoned the other man forward. In stark contrast with his father, Childeric of the House of Eyes bowed deeply to the waist, and did not stand up straight again until Liuprand said, "My lord, you may rise."

"Thank you, my prince," he said. His voice was heartfelt, dripping with the honeyed sweetness of sincerity, which, to Agnes, came as a great relief. "And thank you for this splendid affair."

"You are most welcome, my lord. Your attendance is appreciated by the Crown."

"A propitious evening it has been for us all," Lord Childeric said. "Though I must confess that my favorite moment of the night was the masque. Lady Agnes, it is an honor to make the acquaintance of a woman so clever and so artistically inclined."

The other guests had laid similar flatteries upon her, but Agnes felt an even greater earnestness from Childeric—perhaps it was not so much his words but the way in which his chest swelled as he spoke, as though he were anxious to impress her with his plaudits. It was innocent, in a way, boyish, though he was of an age to her and Liuprand and looked it. It occurred to her then as strange to be a man of such high status, near to thirty—and not yet wed. She could well imagine how many ladies would be falling over themselves to marry into the most noble and most venerable House of Eyes. Yet . . .

It could not be his appearance that had prevented his finding of a wife. Childeric was a handsome man, though perhaps in a rather nondescript way—he looked in some respects a copy of his father, only duller. His red hair was not quite so bright, his eyes not quite so canny. But his openness was appealing. He had a distinctly congenial manner that was not common among nobles and lords.

Agnes realized she had gone for too long without speaking, and hurriedly replied, "Thank you, Lord Childeric."

In a rather natural way, Thrasamund and Childeric came to occupy the chairs that Rabanus and Perpetua had abandoned. It became apparent that, indeed, Thrasamund also had much to discuss with the prince. The House of Eyes and its lands were not so prosperous as of late. A drought, a wildfire, a small uprising by a lesser noble house. His wife, Quirine, absent from this affair, was suffering from great fearfulness over these troubles, causing her to remain hidden in her stronghold.

Thrasamund would ask the Crown for gold and for arms, though he was not as beseeching as he ought to have been. All throughout he retained his icy manner. But—and perhaps there was the wine to thank for this—Liuprand did not appear to take offense. He continued his discourse with Thrasamund.

Meanwhile, Agnes faced Childeric. He wore a brocade of emerald green, a bit too deep and rich for his coloring. They looked at each other for a moment in silence, and then Childeric leaned forward, across the table.

"I must confess," he said in a low voice, "that I have been an admirer of yours long before this moment."

"Oh?" Agnes arched a brow. "And how did that come to be so, when I have not left Castle Crudele in all the years since my husband's passing?"

"Words travel like falcons on the wind," Childeric replied. "Your story is well known across the island."

"A woeful tale," Agnes said. "I cannot imagine why it would inspire admiration."

"I do not find it woeful," said Childeric. "I find it poignant. It is a tale of courage, of resilience. Another lady might have broken into pieces after such a tragedy. But you have conducted yourself with such elegance and such dignity. You have brought a renewed honor to the House of Teeth and to the line of Adele-Blanche."

"I see." Agnes felt a flush rise to her cheeks. She had not known at all that this had become her reputation. She knew only what occurred within the castle's cold halls. "And do you find, upon our first meeting, that I am deserving of such high regard? That these tales are true?"

"Not quite, my lady," said Childeric. "I find that the stories do not do you justice enough. In particular, they are lacking in praise for your beauty."

Such facile flattery should not have charmed her, and yet it did. Agnes found herself flushing more fiercely. *The wine,* she thought, *it is the wine and not the words.* But it was a pleasant feeling to be praised, even in so unsophisticated a manner, and she reached for the carafe and poured herself and Childeric each another goblet.

"You are forthright, my lord," she said, "even brazen. We have met but once."

"Perhaps I would have been more temperate in my youth," Childeric said. "But why should I stifle my passions now? I have the great gift to be seated before a beautiful woman. I intend to enjoy this favorable position for as long as I am given to hold it."

"Very well," said Agnes, biting her tongue to subdue her smile, "but I am not some serving girl who will ruck up her skirts in a shadowed corner of the scullery."

"No, of course not. You are a noble lady, most exquisitely bred." Childeric's gaze skimmed down her throat, past the necklace of teeth, and to the swell of her bustline, straining against the silver silk. "I do not propose a hasty, hidden coupling."

Agnes, mid-sip of her wine, set her goblet down. "I had not realized this was a *proposal*."

"Then forgive me," Childeric said, "for I have misjudged my position—and perhaps yours as well. In the tales that are told across the island, you are lonely, shackled by your widowhood, confined to this castle for the pleasure of the princess. I thought that you would welcome a betrothal to another lord of fine pedigree."

"I am not a trodden creature to be pitied." Agnes's heart pounded fiercely. "Nor am I a helpless maiden to be rescued."

"No," Childeric agreed, "you are not a maiden. Perhaps you were when you wed Lord Fredegar, but years have passed since then. Years in which—forgive me, lady—your fruits have begun to wither. I had assumed that as Mistress of Teeth you would desire an heir, and as a woman, you would desire a child. Motherhood is not yet out of reach—"

"Enough," Agnes said. "Speak no more of this."

Slowly, and somewhat unsteadily, she rose from her seat. She had not appreciated until that moment how wine-addled she had become, for her vision doubled and her head felt suddenly full of cotton. Agnes drew a breath to compose herself.

Childeric rose, too, though with far greater poise and alacrity. "My deepest apologies, lady. I did not mean any offense."

The flush on her cheeks was anger now, not joy, not drunkenness. "Leave me be."

"Wait." Childeric's hand shot out and gripped her about the wrist. "Lady, please. I have been too forward—too hasty—and I am sorry."

Agnes tried to wrench herself free but found that the wine had made her weak and sluggish. She made a low, pleading sound, halfway between a whimper and a gasp—and it seemed that noise, against all odds, cleaved through all the clamor of the feasting hall, all the far louder voices, because Liuprand's head snapped up.

"What are you doing, Lord Childeric?" he demanded. "Unhand her."

Instantly Childeric released her. "Apologies, my prince. I only wished to express my admiration for Lady Agnes, my appreciation for her beauty and her many graces. Perhaps I was . . . overenthused."

"False flattery," Agnes bit out, clutching her arm to her chest, as if it had been injured.

"Not false," Childeric protested. "No, never."

"You thought to ply me into accepting your marriage proposal," Agnes said, "so that I might produce you an heir."

"So *you* could produce an heir." Childeric's pitch rose, and as the rest of the hall fell silent, his words seemed to slash at the air. "Was I so wrong to think that a woman of your age and stature would wish for it? Surely—"

He cut himself off. Liuprand had risen.

"You proposed marriage?" Liuprand asked. "In this manner—under this circumstance—while at a royal wedding feast?"

"I see now that this was unwise," Childeric said hastily. "Please, my prince, it was not meant as a slight. I believed the lady would welcome a suitor, as a balm to her unhappy widowhood. Surely—surely you would want more for her than to languish here during her remaining fertile years. I could give her the gift of motherhood, such as all women desire."

Heat rushed through Agnes's veins. Fury, shame, anguish—she felt each one like the piercing of an arrow. Tears sprang up and gathered on her lashes, though only Liuprand was near enough to see.

And indeed he saw them. Their gazes met, and he recognized her misery in that moment, her outrage, but mostly her despair. He recognized all within the fraction of a second, as quick as the pulse of blood behind a bruise, and a glaze came across his exquisitely blue eyes. It was a barbaric luster such that Agnes had witnessed only once before, in the dungeon of Lord Fredegar.

One more beat passed. And then Liuprand had his hands about Lord Childeric's throat.

He had lunged across the table, and it overturned, causing all the bright goblets and the golden plates to crash to the floor and shatter. Wine streaked the stone. Agnes cried out.

Within moments Liuprand had Childeric pinned to the ground. His huge body loomed, his golden cape spread from his shoulders.

Childeric was gasping, clawing helplessly at Liuprand's hand, trying to pry his fingers loose. Shouts came from the mouths of the women in attendance, and even some of the men. Their tables overturned. Their food and wine spilled.

"Release him!" roared Lord Thrasamund over the din. "That is my son—"

Liuprand's hold slackened on Childeric's throat, but only so that he could pull back his arm and strike him brutally across the face. There was the crunch of bone as his nose broke, and blood spurted from the site of the wound. Blood—*blood*—

Agnes screamed, or at least she thought she did. Her mouth was open and her throat was raw, but that terrible, animal howl was not coming from her. Through the haze of her drunkenness, Agnes searched the room.

It was the lady Ygraine who screamed. She wailed and shrieked and tore at her clothes. Gamelyn reached for her, pinning her arms to her sides so she could no longer thrash, but she fought him, and they both sank to the ground. Huddling against her son's chest, she sobbed.

And then there was Marozia, too shocked to move, holding on to her daughter and watching in utter stillness and silence. Meriope hid her face in her mother's skirts, not weeping, perhaps too young to understand the horror, too bewildered to produce tears.

Agnes could do little but look on, panic rising as her drunkenness ebbed. It knifed through the haze. Liuprand pummeled Childeric and there was nothing just about it, nothing princely. It was barbarism, as sloppy as a tavern brawl.

Only Thrasamund was roused to action. He grasped at Liuprand's cape and attempted to wrest him away, but Liuprand merely shrugged him off, with a mindless, oxlike twitch, and the great lord fell back against the toppled table as though he had been dealt a blow.

"Get . . . away . . ." Thrasamund growled as his retainers rushed to his side to right him. "Stop this madness—stop—"

At first Childeric had struggled, but now he lay still. Yet Liuprand pounded on; he was beyond reason now, excited only by his wine-stirred rage. The stench of blood hung in the air, almost sweet as it mingled with the splattered remains of the feast. The only sounds were Ygraine's muffled sobs and the wet, vulgar slap of skin on bloodied skin.

Finally, Agnes was able to summon up some half-numb courage. She stumbled forward and placed a shaking hand on Liuprand's shoulder, gently, so as not to startle him. Then—slave as he was to her touch—Liuprand stopped. His shoulders slumped. His fists slackened. His labored, uneven breathing filled the hall.

When he looked up at Agnes, his eyes were glazed. Childeric's blood soiled the sleeves of his doublet, red to each elbow.

"Agnes," he whispered.

But before another word could fall from his lips, Thrasamund and his retainers descended. They slid Childeric's unmoving body out from under Liuprand, leaving a lugubrious trail of blood in their wake.

Liuprand rose unsteadily to his feet, as if hobbled by the hugeness of his own form; even now, half bent, he towered over the next tallest man in the room. Agnes saw for the first time a perversity to his size, how it made him something beyond human. It was as if a bitter god had descended from the heavens to punish, with his own hands, the minor crime of a mortal man. And such a minor crime it was, Agnes thought in despair: words, as insubstantial as air.

"Come now!" Thrasamund shouted, beckoning his retainers. "The House of Eyes recants all its honors and renounces all its vows! Your savage cruelty will not be forgotten, Liuprand of the line of Berengar! You have lost our loyalty to your cause!"

His retainers flocked to him. Four men together hefted Childeric's body onto their shoulders, and Agnes was shocked to see that—very faintly—he did now stir. His eyes were too swollen to blink, but his mouth moved voicelessly.

"And the House of Blood will follow," Thrasamund snarled. "Come, Gamelyn. Take your lady mother. And take the child, too. She is your possession now."

Gamelyn had his arms still braced about his mother and did not move. His expression was one of cold shock. When he continued to stare on in stillness, Thrasamund barked an order to one of his retainers, and the man approached Marozia.

Brusquely, and without a sound, he grasped Meriope and lifted her off the ground. She had been holding fast to Marozia's gown, and the fabric tore in her tiny fists.

"Mama!" Meriope cried. "Mama, no!"

These were the first words Agnes had ever heard her speak.

Marozia reached for her, but Meriope, writhing and wailing, was transferred into Gamelyn's stiffly raised arms. At last his icy façade cracked, and his lips curled upward, subtly, in disgust. Then the circle of men closed around them, herding the guests of both houses to the door.

Their heavy, hurried footsteps, and Meriope's continued wailing, created a terrible din. Marozia gave chase, hiking up her skirts and breaking into a run, arm outstretched and fingers straining, straining, straining toward her daughter. But the hosts of the House of Eyes and the House of Blood were too far ahead. They beat open the great doors and vanished through them. Marozia to fell to her knees, empty hand still held aloft, and let out one single, broken sob.

 # XV

THE PRINCESS AND THE MISTRESS

Agnes was a connoisseur of silence, but even she had never heard quite such a silence before.

It was unique not only for its totality but for its brittleness, too. The air in the chamber had a fragile quality, like glass. Even so much as a sharply drawn breath could shatter it.

All around were the ruins of the feast, the broken goblets, the toppled tables, the wine and food spilled and splattered, and of course the blood. It was in garish smears across the floor. It soaked the hem of Liuprand's golden cloak. And the whole room reeked of it, that salty tang, like rusted metal, like water from a stinking, stagnant pool.

The guests from the remaining houses did not speak or even move. The women did not attempt to wipe the stains from their skirts, and the men did not call out to their retainers for aid. Agnes's gaze cast about the room and she saw only blankly horrified faces, wide eyes. Perpetua's chin was quivering, and she gripped tightly her husband's arm. Beside her, Lord Rabanus stood as still as a corpse.

It was Marozia alone who shifted. Her arm fell, while her shoulders, cloaked in that stiff black cloth, drew up around her ears. She stared unblinkingly down at the floor, her chest heaving.

Something fell silently from her face—a tear?

And Agnes found she could not bear it, any of it. The pressure of the silence was like the pounding of mallets against a thin, taut drumskin. It echoed through her bones; it gave a hot pulse to the blood in her veins. She thought she had conquered silence, that indeed, she had even conquered pain, but now, in the ebbing haze of her drunkenness, she knew she had done no such thing. How arrogant she had been, how witless. Her pain had only learned new shapes and new currents.

The silence was shattered at last by Agnes's shallow, stuttering gasp. She was appalled at herself, at her lack of restraint; surely it was the wine that had slicked the path for her to make such a sound.

But before any heads could turn, before she could be burned with those dozens of eyes, Agnes fled from the feasting hall.

She hurried down the corridors, arms wrapped around herself as she shivered, not even quite sure where she was going. Her body was leading her and her mind was merely jerked along after it, like a horse choked by its bridle. Her vision blurred and multiplied.

Agnes only made it halfway down the corridor before she heard footsteps and realized that someone was following.

Bewildered, panicked, she turned. She could not have predicted what she saw when she did: Marozia, holding up the black skirts of her gown and striding briskly after her.

Agnes let out a startled noise of shock. She paused briefly and blinked, as though her cousin were a mirage, a vision that she could vanish. But Marozia's pace only quickened, her slippered feet striking the stone floor.

And Agnes, her forehead pricking with a cold sweat, her heart careening in her chest, broke into a run.

She hastened through the corridors, making indiscriminate turns, clambering up spirals of stairs. She was still clumsy with drink and tripped once, twice, thrice over her skirts.

Somehow Agnes's frantic flight led her to the parapet. As she emerged, she felt the hot gusts of summer night air blast her cheeks, blowing back her hair. The darkness was misty and muddled, smoke-colored clouds blotting out the stars and moon.

"Don't you dare run from me!"

Marozia's voice shot out like an arrow, and Agnes felt struck by it, pinned in place. She stopped, bracing herself on the balustrade, panting with exertion. Her whole body trembled.

In a single beat, Marozia was upon her. One of her hands clamped down on Agnes's shoulder, and the other grasped the front of her gown. She slammed her back against the balustrade, hard enough that Agnes's teeth rattled in her mouth.

"Traitorous whore!" she screeched.

Agnes raised her own hand to Marozia's shoulder, trying to shove her away, but her cousin had the advantage of a clear head, and her movements were not hampered by the clumsy sluggishness of wine. Agnes could not push her off.

"You may have fooled those dull cattle in the feasting hall, but I see how you swan your treason right before their eyes!"

The sky rumbled with thunder, drowning out the end of Marozia's words. It was a dry summer storm, such that would make wildfires bloom wherever lightning struck the parched and depleted land.

Agnes swiped helplessly at her cousin's face, yet that served only to further enrage her. With a quavering howl of fury, her grip slackened for a moment—but then her hands came around Agnes's throat.

The sudden pressure, the shrinking of her breath, made Agnes seize with terror. Lightning cracked the sky, and it blanched Marozia's face, clarifying every feature: her lips, pulled back into a snarl, her white teeth bared, her eyes glossy with the sheen of wrath.

"Marozia!"

Liuprand. He emerged from the staircase and approached them, each stride long and powerful, his previous quivery drunkenness now shed. The lightning washed him, and Agnes saw the blood still drying on his gold doublet and gold cloak, turning the silk a muddied, reeking red.

Marozia's attention was diverted for no more than a second, eyes flickering to Liuprand and then back to Agnes again, and never losing their rageful gleam.

"Martyr, you think yourself," she bit out, "so meek and so innocent. But you have always coveted what is mine. My title, my beauty, my children . . . and now you have taken my husband, too, out of a barren spinster's sourness and spite."

Her grip on Agnes's throat tightened. Agnes could only wheeze, and a red haze fell across her vision.

"Release her," Liuprand ordered, encroaching another step. *"Now."*

Marozia turned her head—slowly, and as she did her hands began to shake, so fiercely that Agnes could feel their trembling through her skin, to the very marrow of her bones. The corners of Marozia's mouth dragged down into a grimace that Agnes recognized, one that presaged tears, only there was no weeping now. Just the faint gathering of water on her dark lashes.

"She's your *daughter*," Marozia whimpered. "Your own blood."

"Let her go, Marozia," Liuprand said. "You've gone too far."

Her cousin's nails dug into the flesh of Agnes's throat. And then there was a terrible, groaning, creaking sound, coming from below. Through the mist of her darkening vision, Agnes saw, with horror, that the stone of the parapet was beginning to break apart beneath them. That was why, she realized dimly, Liuprand remained at a distance. If he moved so much as a pace more toward them, the ground would give way completely.

"I have done my duty." Marozia's voice thickened. "Followed every law to the letter, every posthumous order. All while you have snuck about, shirking yours for stolen kisses and fleeting pleasures, shaming our family—our house."

Agnes scrabbled at the hands around her throat but could win herself no reprieve. Her chest burned with the very last embers of breath, and the stone beneath them continued to groan and crack.

Her vision had ebbed to near-total darkness. She could only see the blurry canvas of her cousin's face, her mouth a passionate smear of red, her eyes two black gashes. Tears wavered on her lash line, but still they did not fall. Her eyes only burned and raged and hated.

And then, all of a sudden, she was released. Marozia let her go so brusquely, so unceremoniously, that Agnes dropped to her knees on the fractured ground. She saw the vanishing swish of her cousin's skirts as she knelt there, sucking in desperate, rasping breaths. Marozia brushed past Liuprand on the parapet, dark gown fluttering after her, while Agnes was too stunned and pained to move, listening to the creaking and groaning of the stone.

This will be my end, she thought, *either way.*

But in half a heartbeat Liuprand had his arm around her waist and was hauling her to her feet. He pulled her to safety just as the ground at last crumbled away, into the sea below. Where each bit of rock broke the water's surface there was a harsh, violent sound, like the crunch of bone.

Then the ocean swallowed the sounds and the tide rolled on again, returned to its ceaseless, restless rhythm. Liuprand clutched Agnes to his chest as she wheezed and gulped. Another bolt of lightning scattered the clouds. And Marozia was gone.

XVI

DISTANT EMBRACES

"It would be best if you did not try to speak."

By the large, open window of her bedchamber, Agnes sat, slightly hunched, in a chair that had no back. This was so Pliny could move about her more easily, dabbing on a salve that smelled so bitter as to sting her nose. Her hair was pinned up on her head in a pearl-enameled clasp. Pliny pressed his fingers to her sternum and, very gently, adjusted her posture. Agnes rolled back her shoulders and tried to straighten her neck, but a dull ache pulsed from her throat as she did. She winced.

"Apologies, lady," Pliny murmured.

Agnes swallowed, and even that—especially that—provoked another bolt of pain. The salve was warming her skin, though the rest of its promised healing properties were yet to emerge. *Soon,* she thought vaguely, with a hope that was not very hopeful.

"It will take time," the leech said, as if he had read these thoughts. "Not even a day has passed."

Agnes heard the words, but could not grasp their meaning. What had been mere hours felt the length of lifetimes, and yet, in some manner, it seemed as though not a moment had passed at all. If ever she allowed her mind to wander she was there again, on the lightning-blanched parapet, Marozia's hands at her throat. Panic swam up. Her lungs seemed to seize and then wilt like cut flowers. She crumpled forward in her seat.

"Lady?" Pliny's hand hovered, hesitant, above her shoulder. "Do not mourn. You will be well again."

Slowly, Agnes sat up. She had not wept but the tip of her nose prickled with heat, as though she might, at the slightest provocation, dissolve into tears. Yet what good would it do, to weep?

Agnes's gaze slid to the mirror.

The face that stared back at her was one of ghastliness and of horror. A throbbing necklace of bruises ringed her throat, deep purples mottled with sickly greens and garish blacks. Each was the shape of a finger, ruthlessly pressed. Small gauges showed where teeth had been driven into her skin, Marozia's hands clenched around the regal bauble of their house. It gave the impression that Agnes had been both choked and bitten.

Her cheeks were pale and wan with lack of sleep, with the food and wine she had vomited through the burning chasm of her throat. And her eyes—the whites were now flooded with red. The look of it repulsed her. Agnes turned away.

Pliny was mixing a poultice of chamomile and honey when there was a knock upon the door. The leech glanced at Agnes for permission. She nodded, and he called out, "Come in."

It was Liuprand. He seemed to have passed a similarly sleepless night, for there were deep, dark circles under his eyes and his golden aura flickered and waned, like a candle flame blown about by the wind. He had shed his bloodied garb and came instead in vestments of navy, with a heavy, woolen cape that dragged over the ground.

"Pliny." He inclined his chin to the leech. Then, as he turned to Agnes, his voice lowered and his gaze grew soft and he said, "My love."

Agnes swallowed, to yet another scrape of pain, and opened her mouth. She was halfway to forming words when she remembered Pliny's directives. Her lips fell shut again.

"I have instructed her not to speak, my prince," the leech said. "It will irritate her wounds and prolong the healing process."

"I see." Liuprand's expression was suddenly awash with grief. "Then furnish her with a quill and parchment, Your Scrupulousness."

"Yes, my prince."

As Pliny went to fetch them, Liuprand approached her. Slowly, unsteadily, Agnes rose from her chair. It had been a long time, a very long time, since Liuprand had come to her chambers, for fear that such a visit would arouse suspicion. Agnes felt a cold vise of panic grip her, more instinct than reason. Because what was the use of discretion now?

Liuprand paused a pace away, eyes wavering.

"Look what has been done to you," he whispered. "All because of my arrogance and folly. I wish that I could suffer your pain instead."

Pliny laid out the parchment and quill on her desk. Agnes took it and scratched out a message, then handed the paper to Liuprand.

The fault lies with me. I should not have been so wounded by simple words.

"No," Liuprand said. "Lord Childeric's conduct was a grave insult. Punishment was warranted . . . but I should not have allowed my temper to rule me. Perhaps, without the influence of the wine . . ." He shook his head. "It is an ignoble man who cannot prevail over his worst impulses. I had never thought I would be such a man. Uncivilized and indulgent, vulgar and weak."

You are not that man, Agnes wrote, pressing her quill tip firmly to the page. *One such lapse in thirty years does not make you a brute. And you acted to defend my honor, not out of arrogance or vanity.*

Still, Liuprand grimaced. "Would that I had waited and reproved Lord Childeric in a more suitable manner. Then we would not have lost the confidence of both the House of Eyes and the House of Blood. All your efforts, gone to waste for my impulsive sin. I have kept the truth from my father yet, but when he learns what has transpired . . ."

Insulate the king from this knowledge now. Intercept all missives until we have come to a solution. It is fortunate that he is all but confined to his bed. Agnes chewed her chapped and bitten lip. *There will be some way to repair it. To atone with Lord Thrasamund.*

"Perhaps. But it will require cleverness and, on my part, abasement. I already filled Lord Thrasamund's coffers and paid a dowry to the House of Blood. There must be more, some other manner in which I can offer recompense." He sighed. "To rob a lord of his heir, a man of his birthright, and a parent of their child—it is a beastly thing I have done. At least when I offer my regrets, the message will be heartfelt."

Faintly Agnes nodded. Fear, as chill as a mountain wind, was prickling her skin. She was not thinking of Lord Thrasamund, or Lord Childeric, or even of the blood and the shattered goblets. She was thinking of a young girl with golden hair, and her mother. She was remembering the sound of their broken sobs.

"I know," Liuprand said softly—for he could always read her face. "That is another matter that must be addressed. And it is far more vital than the first. Lord Thrasamund is not the only one with whom we have lost confidence."

What Agnes thought then she did not say, or rather, did not write. In her mind, the words churned queasily, like gray laundry being wrung. *That confidence was lost long ago. This was only the truth laid out baldly, at last.*

Liuprand took a step forward and closed the space between them. Pliny was busying himself with his herbs and poultices, but Agnes knew that the old leech had sharp ears, and Liuprand knew it, too. He lowered himself so that their faces were level.

"I understand," he murmured, "that you and the princess have not been allies as of late. That loathing has blossomed where once there was love. Yet I do not believe that so much time has passed, so much distance grown, that you cannot still sense your cousin's mind. Her heart." He laid a gentle hand on Agnes's chest, where her own heart pulsed and fluttered. "Has she gone completely to madness?"

Agnes's fingers clenched around the quill. She leaned over, stiffly, and began to write.

I do not think so. Fury, yes. And for fair cause. But even now I do not believe . . .

She paused, her quill tip halting on the page. A sharp and sudden pain lodged itself between her ribs, causing her breath to catch.

I do not believe that she will act out of malice. She is capricious, but she is not cruel.

Liuprand inclined his chin, rising again to his full height. "Indeed. She has already had her fit of pique." Delicately, and without touching her, he gestured to Agnes's bruised throat. "And to expose our secret would shame her, as well. She is proud enough that she would not wish for the world to know how her husband and her cousin carried on under her nose."

Yes, Agnes wrote. *If there is one thing that Marozia has yet to shed, it is her pride.*

"I dearly wish it had not come to this," Liuprand said. He let out a soft exhale. "If it were no more than a gash upon my honor, then I could have borne it—but you have been harmed, and that is what I cannot bear."

With utmost tenderness, he took Agnes's face into his hands. Indeed, his touch was so gentle that she could almost not feel it at all, and, unexpectedly, it drew from her a great swell of grief. Here he was before her and yet she was apart from him. This was what their folly had done.

"I swear, Agnes," he whispered, "that I will never let such harm come to you again. I would fall upon a sword before I would let you be pricked by a needle. I am your servant and I am your shield. My soul has been fashioned for the purpose of loving you, and I would sooner welcome death than be stripped of this duty, this design. I would endure the blackest torments, such that my mind cannot even conjure—the most appalling agonies. Do you believe me?"

Her throat burned too much for words, her neck even for so little as a nod. Agnes merely stared up at him, into the eyes of her lover, her protector, the guardian of her honor, the champion of her heart. What had she done to deserve such a being? And what would she do to keep him?

Liuprand could not remain long in her chambers; their secret was still a secret, even if there was now one more mind that knew it. Agnes dismissed Pliny, as well.

Her empty stomach scraped as it churned, but she was in too much pain to consider eating or even drinking. Her hand darted out for the jug of water that Pliny had left out for her, and then recoiled, as if she had been burned. Her hair remained pinned up in its pearl clasp. The thought of letting it down, of feeling it brush against her bruised throat, made Agnes flinch.

She wore only a nightgown, which fell about her limply, a shapeless garment of white linen. Her feet were bare against the floor's cold stone. As she cast her gaze about the room, it landed once more on the mirror, on her own reflection. The wan, haunted face with its red eyes stared back at her. It was not a woman's face. It was a ghost's, a girl's.

Agnes's feet took her out of the chamber and down the corridor. She was not even certain of where she was going until she arrived. Hesitantly, her fingers flexing and twitching, Agnes pushed open the door.

Marozia's old chamber was empty, as it had been for more than half a decade. The canopy had been removed from the bed, the mattress stripped bare. A dense coat of dust lay over everything, and the air was thick and stale. No candles were lit, and the hearth was long since cold, but the window was open, so the darkness was incomplete, striped with irregular slants of pale light.

Agnes walked forward, though the floor seemed to swallow the sound of her steps. The silence, unlike the darkness, was complete and unyielding. It engulfed Agnes in a familiar, almost relieved fashion, as the embrace of a long-lost friend. She felt the heavy air shift, folding her into this voluptuous grasp.

Slowly, though without faltering, Agnes approached the bed and sat. Like the air, like the silence, the mattress remembered her shape and drew her down. Ignoring the pain of such movements, Agnes lowered herself onto the bed and curled up on her side.

Her mind was flooded then, not with thoughts, not with words, only with images, the bright surging of memories. They blinked and flashed, one after another. She saw her hands moving briskly over scarlet cloth as she dressed Marozia. Scarlet, then bridal white, that long lace train. She saw her cousin's collarbone and the shadow of dark curls across it as she fell into Agnes's arms, weeping. She saw her fingers, coaxing bread into Marozia's mouth.

She saw Marozia's head, pillowed in her lap, sweat plastering her hair to her reddened face, her throat pulsing with each scream of her labor. She saw the flash of white teeth as her lips parted to form these wails. She saw the glaze of wordless agony in her eyes.

What Agnes felt as she lay there, the ghost of Marozia beside her, was beyond articulation. She let her lashes flutter closed, relenting to the dream. She let tears wash her cheeks. Agnes let her thumb slide into her mouth, and she sucked it greedily, until she was lulled to sleep.

XVII

RIMMED IN RED

Waltrude had mixed the wine and water herself, but still the leech did not drink. The carafe between them remained untouched. He sat across from her at the table in the little princeling's chambers, close enough that her hand could reach out to touch him, ghosting through his beige robes. Yet she did not dare. He was not a creature to desire comfort, or to offer it. So Waltrude merely looked on as Pliny's stare, which was unblinking, grew glazed with a grief that seemed quite unlike him. He was also not a creature to linger on what had been lost.

"You have seen her, have you not?" At last, the leech's eyes slid to Waltrude.

"Seen, no," Waltrude replied, "but heard—yes, heard. A great many things I have heard. I have thought to ask you which are true."

"All and none," Pliny said. "Words are only representations of things, flitting shadows on the walls of our minds. I can tell you what I was given to witness, but it will still not be exactly the truth."

Waltrude did not like this version of Pliny, morose and submersed in enigmatic philosophies. With a stifled sigh of irritation, Waltrude said, "Then speak."

The leech was silent a moment, his gaze watchful. As lost in obscurities as he seemed, he was still canny and missed nothing, not even Waltrude's quiet, ornery exhale. *I have known him too long,* she thought. Seven years was hardly a notch on the long white branch of her life, and yet—*We have become as accustomed to each other's flaws as our virtues.*

"You departed after the masque," said Pliny, jolting her from these thoughts, "with the young prince Tisander. You took him straight to bed, and remained in his chambers for the night—yes?"

Waltrude nodded. "Yes."

"And did he sleep in peace?"

"Yes," said Waltrude, "as a dormouse in its winter nest."

"Then he heard nothing from the feasting hall, or from the corridors, or the parapet?"

"No." Waltrude frowned. "Nor did I."

"That is for the best," said Pliny. "He will not be haunted by such horrors as we witnessed, and he will still regard his father as a just and noble man."

This greatly alarmed Waltrude. Her heart beat faster, and the skin of her neck prickled with cold. "I grow no younger, Pliny the leech. Tell me—what transpired that night while I sat ignorant in the dark?"

Pliny drew up his narrow shoulders around his ears, giving him the look of a bald, dour vulture on its perch. When he spoke, his voice was low and bitter. "The success of the lady's masque did not presage what was to come," he said. "At the outset, all was joyous, at least at the prince's table. The guests came one by one to give their honors. The prince and the lady amused themselves especially well with the Master of Hearts and his lady wife—I am told she was once handmaiden to the queen." He paused, his lips thinning into a grimace. "Much wine was drunk by all."

"By all?" Waltrude shook her head. "No, it cannot be. The prince does not indulge himself in such mortal pleasures. He has always been ascetic by nature, heedful and restrained."

"Yet is he so restrained? For years he has carried on with his mistress while his legal wife languishes in a locked tower. We who know him well can see this as love—as heed of another duty. He has sworn a vow with his heart that even the laws of man cannot trespass." Pliny's voice grew yet lower. "But others will not think the same."

Waltrude's chest had become almost unbearably tight. "Go on."

There was a beat of silence, and the leech again averted his gaze as he spoke. "The last house to come pay honors was the great House of

Eyes. Lord Thrasamund approached with his son and heir, Childeric—a man of good, if facile, humor, and graciousness to compensate for his lack of wit. Yet Thrasamund had none of his usual jocular disposition. He was remote and cold, even while asking for gold and arms from the Crown. And perhaps . . . perhaps if the prince had not been too deep in his goblet, he would have recognized this for the ill portent that it was. Had he only quarreled in words with Lord Thrasamund instead."

"What was Lord Thrasamund's grievance?" Waltrude recalled him very dimly as a pleasant, boisterous man, not given to sulking.

"He did not say," Pliny replied, "though it is plain enough for those with half a mind to see. His daughter was in attendance. The dowager lady of the House of Blood, Ygraine."

Ygraine. Waltrude remembered her from Agnes's calamitous wedding to Lord Fredegar: a rather nondescript slip of a woman, pretty enough though no great beauty, but well mannered as befit a lady of her stature. And she had already performed the foremost duty of her station: She had given her husband a son, and the House of Blood an heir.

Her late husband, Waltrude amended. Indeed she remembered as well the horrors of the scene in the dungeon. Ygraine on her knees, a dreadful sight, and even more dreadful as the moments ticked on. As the blood poured and Lord Unruoching choked. She had swooned then, and fainted, and her retainers had carried her out. Waltrude had not imagined she would ever hear of the woman again. She knew well what happened to ladies whose minds were lost to grief.

"She has remained all these years a ghost of herself," Pliny said, "mired in her sadness. Time has not strengthened her spirit. She has only withered. I saw so myself at the feast."

Waltrude looked down at her hands. They were ancient hands, more bone than flesh, hands that had served two kings, reared two princes, and attended two queens. The kings had both gone uncaringly to their vices. The princes were gentle boys who had become men she struggled now to recognize. And the queens had died.

"What of her son?" Waltrude asked. "The Master of Blood. Gamelyn."

"I have not known him since he was a boy. He was sweet then, his only flaw being the ordinary impatience and impertinence of youth. But I cannot say how he has grown. Manhood can as easily corrupt virtues as it can engender them."

"Yes," Waltrude said. "That I understand well myself. I ask only for the sake of the little girl . . . Meriope. Her husband's character will shape the rest of her life. If she is to be happy, it will be all to his credit. And if she is to suffer—"

"It is not Lord Gamelyn alone who steers her fate," Pliny cut in. A rare thing for him—he was nothing if not always courteous, rigidly observant of etiquette. "He did not wish for this. That much I could read on his face. What man wants a bride who was not so long ago weaned from her mother's breast? She is closer to an infant than to a woman. His disgust showed itself openly."

Waltrude drew a breath.

"Will he be cruel to her for that? Perhaps. I am no longer given to know what occurs within the halls of the House of Blood. His father, the late Lord Unruoching, was a coarse and barbarous man, all the more cruel for his stupidity. Yet his grandfather, the late Lord Fredegar, was just and kind, possessing every virtue that a man in his position ought. Has Gamelyn drunk the poison of his father? Or sipped the nectar of his grandfather? I confess I cannot say."

"You said that Gamelyn alone does not steer the girl's fate," Waltrude reminded him. She had to suppress a shiver. "How do you mean?"

The leech shifted, leaning forward over the table and resting his chin in his folded hands. His soberness could almost be felt, like an emanation of chill air.

"I mean," he said lowly, "that this matter was settled at the Crown's discretion. The House of Berengar is still preeminent in all things. The king may be gone to madness and gluttony, but the prince knows the truth of this arrangement: not a marriage, but a treaty. Not a bride, but a hostage. The girl is a pawn in her father's game for peace. So if there is sympathy between the House of Blood and the Crown, Meriope will be treated accordingly. And if relations sour, she will pay the price for it."

All along Waltrude had known this. How could she not? She had seen the tortures inflicted upon women for the crimes of men. Even queens were not exempt. And the princess in the tower knew this, too. For all her grief, her mind was sharp, her teeth sharper still.

"The prince, then," she said thickly. "Pliny . . . what has he done?"

"He has sacrificed his daughter for his love. He has wrecked his honor for his heart. And he has lost the sympathy of two great houses. A crime committed in the haze of drunkenness, in the fever of passion. I did not think him capable of such an act. I must see it only as a lapse. A mistake that will not be repeated, not a true reflection of his character. Else I would . . ."

Pliny's voice faded into silence.

"You are wise to arrest yourself before treason, Your Scrupulousness," Waltrude bit out. "No man is without fault, even such a one as our prince. What is this terrible act, which you cannot bear to even put to words? If you are even half as old as I am, surely you have seen worse. What transpired in your old master's halls—"

"The blackest and bitterest tragedy, yes," Pliny cut in. "The anguish of Lord Fredegar's death has not worn thin. Yet that crime was already repaid twice over, with Unruoching's blood, and now with the young girl's maidenhead. The prince has taken more than was his right."

"To the minds of some men," Waltrude murmured, "everything that a prince takes is his right."

"And those men will continue to swear for the House of Berengar. Rabanus, Master of Hearts, and Amycus, Master of Bones—their loyalty is unshakable. I have seen it affirmed myself. Vauquelin's lands are too distant for anyone to know his mind, but his influence is as paltry as the crop yield at Pelekys. Hartwig is vain enough that flattery will sway him to a new cause each moment. But the House of Eyes and the House of Blood? Their faith has been lost. It has been trampled upon. Its throat has been savagely cut."

All this and still Pliny would not speak plainly of Liuprand's crime. Perhaps he meant for her mind to conjure its own monsters. But in the silence, behind her eyes, Waltrude saw only Philomel's broken body in the sheets. She blinked and saw the princess, her daughter, clutching her skirts. She blinked once more and saw—

Lady Agnes. She pushed open the door and led Tisander by his hand into the chamber.

The boy ran first to her, throwing his arms around her waist, and then to Pliny, clambering into the old leech's lap. Impressively, Pliny seemed to shed his gloom at once, and he smiled at Tisander without inhibition.

"Lady," he said, rising to his feet, the child propped on his hip. "I was to meet you in the library."

"No," Agnes said, "it is best that Tisander have his lessons here today."

Waltrude's head snapped up in shock. Her voice—a low, rattling wheeze, like the wind through a hollow reed. She was further shocked to see that the lady wore a high-necked gown of gray, its lace collar buttoned primly to her chin, her hair held high on her head with a pearl clasp. An old gown, it must have been, for the healthy swell of her breasts and hips made the fabric strain at its seams. Waltrude had not seen her dress in this manner for years. She had not seen the lady's hair bound in at least as much time.

"I did tell you, lady," Pliny said softly, "that you should try not to speak."

"It cannot be helped," Agnes rasped. "There is much to communicate, and writing will not suffice."

Waltrude, who had forgotten a moment her courtesy, rose to her feet and greeted the lady with an unacknowledged nod. Her face was the color of cold porridge, and her eyes were rimmed in red. It was a ghoulish sight that made Waltrude's stomach queasy.

"Very well," said Pliny. "I will give the princeling his lesson in his chambers. And—should you like it—I have another poultice for your throat."

Agnes fell to silence for a moment. Her lashes fluttered over her bloodshot eyes, and she looked very weary.

"Not yet," she croaked. "I must have words with you first. I am in need of your counsel."

At last, her gaze slid to Waltrude. Other than tiredness, the wet nurse could discern no emotion from her visage. The lady swallowed, winced, and then said, "Occupy Tisander for the moment. Pliny and I will speak in my chambers."

"Yes, my lady," Waltrude replied. Turning to Tisander, she held out her arms. "Come here, my sweet dove."

Pliny transferred the child to her, but Tisander whined and squirmed, and in another moment won his release. His legs carried him unsteadily across the room to where Agnes stood, and he fell against her, burying his face lovingly in her skirts. His tiny fists gripped the gray silk.

"No," he whined, "I don't want you to go."

Agnes knelt down and brushed a golden curl from his forehead. "I will return soon, my dearest love, and I am not going far. Perhaps you can practice your numbers in the meantime. Count as high as you can, and I will be back before you reach the limits of your knowledge. Yes?"

Tisander's lip stuck out and trembled. He looked into Agnes's eyes, even raised a hand to touch each of her cheeks. Then at last, he mumbled, "I can count *very* high."

"Of course you can. You are the cleverest boy. Now go to Waltrude."

Reluctantly, Tisander turned and went to Waltrude's side. He leaned into her, and Waltrude patted the crown of his head. "We will be fine here, lady," she said. "Go to your business."

Agnes nodded, wincing once more. Waltrude could not tell precisely what was causing this pain in her; perhaps it was nothing that could be perceived by the naked eye. Perhaps a knife had been turned inside her. Perhaps the blade had been stuck so deep between her ribs that it had vanished.

Without another word, she turned, gray skirts swishing over the floor. Pliny, however, cast one last glance back at Waltrude. There was a weariness, too, on his face, making the wrinkles seem more apparent than ever. Whatever he had seen had aged him.

As Waltrude led Tisander over to the table, she found that she did not feel weary herself. There was a tension in her old muscles, a stiffening in her ancient bones, and a cold rush in her veins. She was no prophet, no wise woman such as lived in the Outer Wall; she could only look backward, sifting through the sand of nearly a century of memories.

She had seen such things before. Injustice, dishonor, secrets kept at greatest cost. And so she knew—even without a seer's power—that the order of the world could not be resettled without sacrifice.

XVIII

AN IMMODEST PROPOSAL

Corks. Stones. Twelve eggs, twelve apples. A lamprey, swallowed without chewing, the bones crunched between his teeth. Bull's lungs and bull's liver, the latter filched from the chef's chopping table, for there were some others who hungered for these innards, someone else in the castle who had a formidable appetite. Though none like him. There were no others like him.

He had been turned out of his house before he could grow the first hair on his chin, his mother beating him black and blue with her frying pan, for he had once again eaten all six of the pork pies meant for dinner, and the turnips, and the bread. For years—how many, he did not know—he had roamed the Outer Wall, begging for coin on street corners. His only honest work had been when he discovered that many would pay to watch him devour oddities and refuse. He could consume a yowling alley cat in a matter of moments, ripping open its throat with his teeth. He was especially fond of snake meat. It had a most sublime flavor.

He was forced to cease this act abruptly when a child went missing, but he did not like to think of that.

Now he sat slumped against the rubbish heap, a fish bone digging into the small of his back. Unlike other creatures, he was not made weary by his hunger; instead it imbued him with an impossible strength. It was a sort of transcendent power, one that allowed him to brawl with the stray dogs and make them cower and turn belly-up; one that allowed him to go many days without sleeping, kept awake by the keenness of his senses, gaze sharp as a kestrel's, ears pricked like a bloodhound's. The scraping pain of his empty stomach seemed to him a gift bestowed by an unearthly force, akin to the future-sight of Madame Sosostris.

He had liked the wise woman, and now he missed her. Weeks he had spent shut up in the castle's cold dark halls without so much as a glimpse of the sun. He even longed for the company of the street dogs. Lying with them in a greasy, flea-bitten pile, he could keep warm at night.

Listlessly, he plucked up the fish bone and ate it. Then the rotten pit of a summer peach. He licked the sour juice from his fingers. He scratched at one of his scabs, the one in the crook of his elbow, which scabbed and bled and scabbed again by the day, for he could never suppress the niggling urge to pick it. He was opening up the cut again when two figures appeared in the threshold.

"Oh," he said. "It is you."

The short one, Rosencrantz, stepped forward, out of the shadows and into the pool of oily torchlight. His familiar, Guildenstern, remained back a pace, nose wrinkling under the hood of his robe. *Symbiotes, they are,* he thought, *not two leeches but a leech and its host.* Who was the host? And who the bloodsucking stooge?

"I see you continue to enjoy the profits of your labor," said Rosencrantz. "A worthy reward for your services, yes?"

"Yes, oh yes." He dug his nail into the scab. "There is never an end to the feasting here. Always morsels left behind. Always fed. Never deprived. No longer too hot or too cold. Starved only of sunlight, but what do I need of that? I can smell as well as I can see."

"Indeed," said Guildenstern dispassionately. "You must be quite grateful, then, to whoever plucked you from the Outer Wall."

He nodded in an eager, fervent manner. "Grateful forever and ever. I do not forget a thing. Neither a compliment nor a slight. Neither a boon nor a burden."

"That is good to hear," Rosencrantz said. "It will make our task far easier."

Guildenstern gave him a pointed look. "How many times did I tell you—a soft touch is to be employed here. You are too hasty always."

"He will not understand a soft touch. He is half mad, listen. We must be forceful."

"Too forceful and our cause will be miscarried. We were ordered to work in whispers."

"Whispers need not be subtle. Only quiet." Rosencrantz dovetailed his fingers and began to twist them restlessly, as if kneading dough. "I should not like to linger overlong here."

"Very well," said Guildenstern, with a revolted breath. He turned away from his companion and cast his gaze over the rubbish heap. "You are a loyal creature, that much I can see. One who does not easily forsake his oaths, too. That is why we do not come to you beseeching or threatening, with pleas or with demands. We come to you with promises."

He had begun to grow impatient with this intercourse. His hunger was reasserting itself. He fished for a morsel in the pile and retrieved the soggy pink shell of a crustacean. It was rubbery on his tongue, and he savored the rotten tang as he chewed and then swallowed.

"I have been promised many things before," he said, briefly serene as his hunger was, for a moment, sated. "Since I was but a mewling child. Their vows always wear thin when it is discovered that my appetite never does."

"I can assure you that this is a vow that has never been sworn before."

Just as quickly as the bite settled in his belly, he was hungry again. Hungry for food and for plainer speech. "What is it then, Guildenstern?"

"That is not my name, but perhaps it is best that you only know me under this false epithet." He stepped forward into the light and stood shoulder-to-shoulder with Rosencrantz. "You spoke before of a forbidden delicacy. The only sustenance that truly sustains you. You despaired that you would never taste of it again. But put away this despair, creature. Do not mourn your belly's emptiness any longer. I swear to you here, in the dark and filth, that you will taste this delicacy again. It will fill you as you have never been filled before. You will be sated—

that I can promise beyond all remission. Loosen your tongue for me now, and you will be glutted, surfeited at last. This I swear to you, by the hands of the Most Esteemed Surgeon himself."

The words poured over him, as sweet as water from a mountain spring. Drool began to gather at the corners of his mouth. He parted his wanting, sucking, slavering lips, and then his own words fell from his tongue, like flesh from a rotted limb—wretched and yet so very, very easy. In truth he had never been a loyal creature, at least not to the oaths and laws of men. He was always and only loyal to his own hunger.

XIX

ONE SPECKLED, ONE WHITE

The moth never thought she would be called to such a task. She, like all the others of her kind, had grown complacent, safe in the blooming garden, the greatest labor of her days flitting from one flower or willow frond to another.

She knew that her ancestors had been message-bearers and heralds, but she did not imagine herself an heir to this legacy. The heroic winged envoys of Berengar were long dead; their stories were recalled with misty affection. This disrupted none of the garden's serenity, for not a creature there had been alive to witness the plague and the pillaging, and it was inconceivable to think that war might ever come to the island again.

The moth was chosen not for her particular bravery or intrepidness, but for her coloring, though she did not know that. She only knew that a gray-clad lady had entered the garden and reached out an arm, beckoning. Her fingers were tipped with nectar, and the moth flitted down from her perch. Gratified, she sipped the nectar, and her antennae twitched and hummed as she listened to the lady's rasping voice.

"You are a good and clever creature," she murmured, stroking, very gently, the tip of the moth's wing. "Will you serve me, as your kind once did the conqueror-king of Drepane?"

The moth was moved by curiosity, or perhaps stirred by an ancient, hereditary urge, passed down from those undaunted ancestors. As if sensing her acquiescence, the lady then fixed a small scroll of parchment to her leg. She whispered her instructions and promised another taste of sweet nectar upon her return.

And so the moth took flight, leaving behind the garden for the first time in her life.

The winds were propitious, the hot summer breeze gusting her toward her destination. The moth was slightly unsteady, buffeted about in the air like a bee drunk on pollen. She passed over bone-white beaches and scorched plains, dead trees forking up at odd angles. She passed over a dry riverbed, a furrow in the land, and knew, with some unconscious certainty, that this was her path.

She followed it over an open field that bore the scars of a recent skirmish, tattered tents flapping and dented breastplates littering the parched brown grass. Rather than cowing her, these sights enlivened her; she became ever more conscious of the importance of her duty. This was precisely what her ancestors had done, steered by the war-wise hand of Berengar.

At last this gash in the earth led her to a place occupied by the living. She did not know, as she first glimpsed those shining gray towers, like pieces of shale pointing upright, that she was descending upon Ironmanse, the ancestral keep of the House of Eyes. She circled once the tallest tower, which at its peak was as narrow as an embroidery needle, and then fluttered down to a nearby window.

She perched there for only a moment, glimpsing the firelight and the other goings-on of a castle within, before a man appeared to block her sight. He was a craggy, rather loutish-looking man, cloaked almost unbecomingly in all the jewels and finery of a noble lord. His head was as bald and shiny as a shucked pearl, but his beard reached his waist and was a thick, lustrous, impassioned red. Yet for all this, his face was set and cold.

He stared down a moment at the moth, lips pressed into a thin line, devoid of color, and then clipped the parchment from her leg. He unfurled it, and his jutting brow descended like a storm cloud over his eyes as he read.

The moth waited, her antennae quivering.

His gaze scanned the page once, twice. The parchment crinkled in his hand. With a barked command, he summoned another man to his side, a figure too concealed in darkness for the moth to see.

"The miscreant wretch of a prince wishes to treat with me," the red-bearded lord rumbled. "His words are beseeching; it is almost piteous. He writes like a supplicant. For all his brutish strength and pretending virtues, he knows what it is to kneel. I hear he has taken his father's cock since he was a child."

The moth was too much an animal to understand his words, and too much an animal to know that she was bearing a second, silent message, one that perhaps even the red-bearded lord did not comprehend. She did not know that the soft-voiced lady had carefully chosen her among all the moths in the garden for the color of her wings: one speckled, one white. This was a dead language, resurrected only in odd elements, and known by two alone.

Still she waited, and more words passed between the men, and at last there came another scroll of parchment fastened to her leg. She flicked off her weariness and flapped her wings, rising again into the blustery summer air. It had grown dark, and the sky was riotous with stars.

As the white monument of Castle Crudele appeared in the distance, the moth was glad to see her journey's end. She lilted gently back down into the garden, where the lady was waiting. Her skin was pale and luminous in the dark, but her eyes were the faded gray of rain-drenched stone.

She took the note and fed the moth yet another helping of nectar in thanks. Then the moth flitted off, to ensconce herself in the petaled embrace of a white flower, heedless to the gravity of what she had done. She drifted to sleep and dreamed only a moth's idle dreams.

XX

THE MASTER OF EYES

Agnes marked the passage of days by the fading of the bruises on her throat, by the slow and painful reclamation of her voice. The burst blood vessels in her eyes repaired themselves—whether by Pliny's tonics and poultices or by the simple progression of time, she did not know. But when she rose each morning, she felt a more puissant creature, more whole.

She went to her usual haunts, fulfilled her usual duties, yet all the while there was a prickling along her spine, an uneasy churning in her stomach. When she was with Tisander, she would often fall to distraction, trailing off in the midst of a sentence she was reading aloud. Frowning, he would turn in her lap and lay a hand gently on her cheek. He spoke no words, but the question was evident in his too-wise, too-knowing eyes.

"Apologies, my sweet dove," she would say then, blinking away the film that had fallen over her eyes. "I am well. Let me begin again."

Agnes came to understand that it was not her body that needed healing but her heart. And it was no shriveled thing, wrung like a sponge—it was strident and bragged more fiercely than ever. This was the perplexity of mortal life. The more alive she had become, the more she learned to ache. When she had been that small, shrinking, gray-clad maiden, she had put away her pain, along with her voice, along with her need, and in that she had hidden herself from love, too. The lack of it was not even near as agonizing as the surfeit.

She wondered what her arms had even done, before they had held the child. What had her mouth done before it could whisper Liuprand's name? She had been so stubbornly proud not to feel her heart. She had lived in the dismal safety of dreams. To wake was to grieve.

And grieve she did, for what she had lost, for the world that had broken apart under her feet. But when she at last surfaced from the dark waters of lamentation, she had known there remained something which she could repair. It would require a quill and parchment and a willing messenger. Those she had found easily enough. She knew too that it would require forfeit. Yet more grief before all was well again. The yielding of her own heart's blood.

She was with Waltrude in her chamber when the bells of the Outer Wall rang. The wet nurse jolted, and Agnes turned her head toward the window. It was the earliest hour of dawn, when the sky was more white than colored, like a pale cheek yet to fill with a flush. Waltrude dropped the laces of her corset and then fumbled to grasp them again, but Agnes stilled her.

"Not this gown," she said, and stepped toward her wardrobe. "Another, finer one, with its bustline low."

Waltrude nodded and proceeded to dress her in silence. Agnes selected a gown of deep violet, which bared her shoulders and her bust, and especially drew attention to her throat, where the ancestral necklace of the House of Teeth hung. Her hair was left loose. She wore no other jewelry save the pearl ring, which she never divested herself of, not even while sleeping or bathing.

All the while Agnes shivered, nervousness causing her teeth to chatter. If Waltrude asked, she would blame it on the castle's coldness. Not even the most oppressive summer heat could penetrate the stone. The days of drought that ravaged the rest of Drepane, that starved the Outer Wall and its environs, had no effect on the inhabitants of Castle Crudele.

When the last lace of her corset had been done, Agnes turned to the door. Before she could push through it, Waltrude's voice at last rose.

"Shall I come with you, lady?"

Agnes swallowed, and there was the subtlest twinge of pain in her throat. "No," she said. "Keep watch of Tisander. Remain at his side through all his lessons today. And . . ." She paused a moment. ". . . stay within sight of Pliny the leech."

If Waltrude was perturbed by these unusual instructions, her face did not show it. But the wet nurse had always been too clever for her station. The years had only sharpened her senses and whetted her wisdom. Agnes suspected that now, as always, she understood more than her expression allowed.

Waltrude dipped her head. "Yes, my lady. I will go now."

Agnes was determined to be quick, so that she would arrive in the great hall before any others could enter. But she was not quick enough. By the time she reached the chamber, her pulse pounding from her exertions, Liuprand was already there. Around him were two dozen men of the Dolorous Guard, stiff in their gray armor, swords drawn.

"Agnes!" He strode toward her, breaking the ring of soldiers. "What are you doing? Return to your chambers now; I will have the Dolorous Guard escort you. It is not safe here. A contingent from the House of Eyes has come. They are at the barbican now."

"I know." Agnes found it difficult to speak around the knot in her throat. "I have summoned them."

Liuprand's eyes widened—first in disbelief, and then in shock and horror. "Why?" he asked, his voice so plaintive that, for a moment, Agnes regretted all. "Why would you do such a thing, and how?"

Agnes drew a breath. She had dreaded this exchange perhaps more than anything else when she had first drawn up her plan. "I sent a missive to Lord Thrasamund, pleading to treat with him. I—I may have signed it with your name. But I used only words that you have already spoken on this matter. It was a heartfelt plea. I wrote exactly as you would have, yourself."

Liuprand's mouth opened, then closed again, beyond speech. He closed his eyes and gave the faintest shake of his head.

"Oh, Agnes," he whispered. "You should not have done this—you have put yourself in grave danger. If Thrasamund is to discern any trickery, he will grow more embittered, more rageful. He will think he has been wronged once again." Liuprand exhaled, a thin sound, almost defeated. "I fear what you have begun."

Agnes wished they were not in sight of the Dolorous Guard so that she might lay a hand on Liuprand's cheek. That she might comfort him with her touch as well as her words.

"Do not be afraid," she said. "I have not been reckless in this, I swear. I have passed many days and nights in reflection and preparation. Please allow me to speak to Lord Thrasamund when he arrives. I believe I can soothe his wounds. I believe that I can set all right again."

Liuprand just stared down at her, brow furrowed as if he were trying to hide the pain of a wound, mouth drawn into a grimace.

"Don't you trust me?"

"I do, Agnes. Always I do. It is Thrasamund I do not trust. He may have acquiesced to this meeting, but you cannot know his true intentions. I have wronged him gravely. Already I have furnished him generously with gold and arms—what else will he demand, to restore faith and sympathy?"

"Please," Agnes said. "Keep faith with *me*. Believe in my art, as you did with the masque. I am not a mere pawn upon the board. I am a player in my own right."

With these words, Agnes proved her point—she knew precisely how to cut to Liuprand's heart. He sighed again, more deeply and more gravely this time, and then he said, "Very well. I will allow you to speak with Thrasamund. But you must remain at my side, and behind the Dolorous Guard."

Relief made Agnes's knees quiver. "Thank you. Thank you. I will not fail, I swear it."

It was at that moment that the doors to the great hall groaned open, and the retinue from the House of Eyes poured forth. It was not a small retinue; Agnes had expected as much. Thrasamund, despite his concession to the meeting, would come with all the instruments of defense.

His armored men formed a bastion, closing a tight circle around their lord. Over their helmets, however, Agnes glimpsed the shining crown of Thrasamund's bald head and the hard, fierce set of his brows. Her task was not close to finished. Persuading him to this summit had only been the smallest part of it.

"My Lord Thrasamund," Liuprand said. He had to raise his voice nearly to a shout, so that it would arc out past the steel wall made by the Dolorous Guard. "I am most grateful that you have come. You are welcomed eagerly and with all the warmth Castle Crudele can offer."

"Not very much warmth then."

Liuprand flinched, though only Agnes was near enough to see it. "It is not the most hospitable structure, I grant. But the House of Berengar is glad of your visit."

"Let us not lose more time to pleasantries. This is no convivial appointment, and I do not wish to remain overlong." Thrasamund's words rolled like boulders down a mountain. "You pleaded your apology by ink and paper. I should like to hear it from your mouth as well."

Liuprand exchanged one last look with Agnes—his gaze was soft, as it always was when he laid it upon her, though now there was the wavering of guilt within it, regret dancing like moonlight on the water. His chest swelled; he drew himself up to his full height. And then, clearing his throat, he said to his men, "Part."

With the clanking of armor, they did, forming but the smallest gap for Liuprand to step through. He had not been anticipating Thrasamund's visit and wore his rather quotidian doublet of navy with braids of gold, though it was better this way, Agnes thought; she would not want Thrasamund to believe that Liuprand was swanning his house's superiority or the wealth of the Crown. Yet still he was the most majestic creature, closer to a hero in a storybook than to a mortal man. His beauty was almost beyond description. The warm aura of light that pulsed from him made one feel blessed merely to be in his presence. And now, as he bowed his great head, it seemed an aberrance of nature, like a lion cringing before a sheep. Surely his remorse could not be doubted.

"Lord Thrasamund," he said, "I offer my most sincere and heavy-hearted condolences. I acted rashly and brutishly; there is no excuse to be made. I have long strived to promote goodwill between the great houses of Drepane and the royal line of Berengar. To think that I have brought all my work to ruin with a single act of impulse and barbarity brings me untold shame—yet I know it is still a mere shade of the anguish you must feel, to have lost a son. It is a grief I cannot begin to fathom. I pray you can forgive this lapse of mine, and I pray still more that you can find some manner of peace, even as you mourn Lord Childeric."

At the conclusion of Liuprand's speech, silence fell upon the great hall, a very heavy silence. Agnes began to pick at the white skin around her fingernail before she could stop herself. Her mind formed no thoughts other than a single word, repeated over and over in a steady, grueling rhythm: *Please. Please, please, please.*

And then, extraordinarily, from behind the row of his men, there came Thrasamund's low and throaty laugh.

"You are as eloquent as your father is fat, Prince of Drepane," he said. "I dearly hope that you do not take offense to that and rob me of yet another child. I do not have any more to spare."

Agnes saw Liuprand's fists clench at his sides. "No, my lord. Not again. Never again."

Thrasamund chuckled blackly. "Well, you speak with resolve; that much I cannot doubt. But mine is a more twisted grief, a perverse mourning for the living. Should you like to see the fruits of your effort, my prince?"

Liuprand glanced at Agnes, brow furrowing. Her heart winced, to see his bewilderment—she had kept this hidden from him, too, else he would never have consented to such a meeting. Agnes did not know if she would ever forgive herself for her deception.

When there came no reply, Thrasamund laughed again, the same brusque, humorless sound.

"Part," he said to his men.

Greaves and gauntlets clattered as they stepped to the side, arranging themselves into a half circle that revealed, at last, the Master of Eyes in his entirety. A distinguished lord in all respects, of towering height, even if he was still a head and a half shorter than Liuprand, and robed in a doublet of deep green.

But Agnes did not waste more than a moment's attention on Thrasamund. She was looking at the figure to his left. She had been told, in letters and in vagaries, of his condition, yet even now she struggled to recognize him—so diminished he was in his form. He sat, not stood, in a large and cumbersome wheelchair, a blanket draped across his lap. One arm hung down limply, fingertips nearly brushing the floor, while the other was thrown over his chest in an awkward, strained angle that made Agnes's skin rise with horror. And his face—his jaw was slack, spittle forming in the corners of his mouth. A woman, small and hunched, at least half as old as Waltrude, leaned over and dabbed at it with a handkerchief before it could drip.

Yet for all this Lord Childeric's eyes were gleaming and sharp. They cast about the chamber, nothing muddled in his stare, nothing unfixed or unaware. He saw all and understood. His gaze landed on Agnes, and then on Liuprand, and he remembered.

She would have preferred there to be malice in this stare. It would have been well earned. But instead there was only the flashing of fear.

 # XXI
PROGENY

Silence reigned again in the great hall of Castle Crudele. Ordinarily Agnes had an exceptional tolerance for it; she could endure lengths of unimpeded silence that others cringed and stammered to fill. Yet now she found herself struck mute and dumb, and each moment dragged out endlessly, agonizingly. Her mind produced only wordless sounds—a rushing, a churning, as if she had been thrust underwater during a sea squall.

"So you see," Thrasamund said, "my son lives, as I have reported in my correspondence—if one can call such a wretched state *life*. He cannot speak or move his muscles of his own accord, but his wits are intact. I suppose I should thank you, for at least leaving him with that." His gaze cut to Liuprand. "The Just, indeed."

"I am most deeply sorry," Liuprand said, though his voice was weak. "If I can offer anything that might ease this burden, my lord, please tell me and it will be yours."

Thrasamund smiled thinly. "Were there anything that could change his circumstance now, I certainly would ask it of you—yet the Most Esteemed Surgeon himself cannot heal such wounds."

Liuprand swallowed. His throat pulsed; Agnes read his anguish plainly. "Let me send more gold, at least. And I can furnish you with the most adept and experienced leeches; they will ensure he is always kept comfortable, within the limits of his condition."

"I have leeches of my own, and you have sent gold enough already."

Agnes had waited all this time; now was her chance to speak. She took one uncertain step forward, and then another, until she stood right beside Liuprand. She cleared her throat. With a tremulous breath, she said, "My lord, I have another remedy to propose."

Thrasamund's brow arched. "Lady, you have done enough. Your honor has been defended; my son has more than paid the price for his folly. What could you offer me now?"

"I offer just what your son asked for." Agnes inclined her chin. "I will wed Lord Childeric. I will be his wife."

There was no opportunity for silence to follow, no deadened air, for Liuprand let out a stammering noise of shock. Agnes kept her gaze straight ahead; she knew that if she glanced at him, she would lose all nerve and fall to weeping. She met Thrasamund's eyes steadily.

He regarded her in turn with suspicion. "Forgive me if I am reticent to believe you make this offer in good faith and candor. You refused my son's proposal once. Why would you accept now, when he is but a shell of himself?"

"Marriage need not be a match of love," Agnes said, swallowing. "But it is an arrangement that may benefit both sides. The Master of Blood was wed to Meriope for similar purpose. To restore concord, to make amends. Your son will have a wife of most noble pedigree, and through that, a line to the Crown. My spurning of Childeric set this woeful turn in motion. Allow me now to make it right."

Thrasamund continued to stare at her intently for a moment, before looking to Liuprand. Something unreadable glimmered in his stare. "And what do you, my prince, think of the lady's terms?"

Liuprand's blue eyes were limpid yet impassive. Yet another moment passed before he said, "The lady is wise and sincere in all things. I can assure you that this offer has been made in good faith."

"Hmm." Thrasamund steepled his hands. "If this has the prince's sanction . . . but, Lady Agnes, you understand that this marriage will come with the same requirements as any other, despite the extraordinary circumstances. I have no other son. Childeric remains my heir; even in this state, he will someday wear the title Master of Eyes. And so it is necessary that he himself produce a male child that will continue our line."

Agnes dug a fingernail into her palm. "Yes, my lord," she said softly. "I understand."

"Well then," Thrasamund said. He rolled his shoulders back and puffed out his chest, as a soldier to be fitted with his armor. "This is a most unexpected offer, but I will consider your terms, lady. I cannot agree to such an arrangement hastily and without deliberation. I should ask the prince if he will allow my retinue to stay at Castle Crudele for several days, while I ponder this offer."

Liuprand looked surprised at being addressed, blinking as if he had just been roused from slumber.

"Of course, my lord," he said, in a stiff tone. "You will have lodging here for as long as it takes you to decide."

Thrasamund turned to his men, mouth opening as he prepared to direct them; Childeric's nurse dabbed again at the spittle dripping down his chin and stroked back the hair that had fallen over his forehead. The tenderness of her touch made Agnes's eyes sting, and reminded her that she had not yet fulfilled her purpose here. Clearing her throat, she said, "Lord Thrasamund, there is one more thing . . ."

He froze at once, gaze narrowing. "Ah, I should have known that there would be further demands made of me. Your cleverness cannot be doubted, and neither can your artful wiles."

"No," Agnes said. "This is no attempt at trickery. It is only . . . a question." She paused and allowed a moment for her chin to quiver, so that when she spoke her voice did not shake. "I mean to inquire about the well-being of the lady Meriope."

Something in Thrasamund's gaze now shifted—an emotion that Agnes could not discern; it was gone again quickly, like a silver fish briefly surfacing from the water before darting back down again. His lips flattened into a cold sort of smile, and he said, "My grandson is no brute."

"I did not mean to imply such," Agnes said hurriedly. "But for the sake of my cousin, her mother—I know she wishes to hear news of her daughter."

Thrasamund's smile gained a keener edge. There was another

quicksilver flash in his eyes, only now Agnes recognized a bit of private amusement in it, one that made the hairs stiffen on her neck.

"The Lord Gamelyn would not be so cruel as to leave a parent in despair over the welfare of their child," he said. "The princess is not ignorant of her daughter's fate, I can assure you."

Slowly, Agnes nodded. Yet still she felt a chill, and gooseflesh prickling the length of her arms. "Thank you, my lord," she said. "That is all I wanted to know."

"Then I should like to take my leave now." He glanced pointedly at Liuprand. "I will reflect on today's turns and give my answer soon."

"Yes," said Liuprand. His voice was vague now, his gaze unfixed. To the Dolorous Guard, he said, "Go, all of you. Show Lord Thrasamund and his retainers to their chambers. Ensure they are comfortable; tell the kitchens to prepare food, should they want for it. Then close the barbican, and return with haste to your posts."

XXII

THE CHAINS OF DESIRE

Gone was Lord Thrasamund and his contingent; gone were the men of the Dolorous Guard. The great hall of Castle Crudele was empty save for its prince and his mistress. Agnes was trembling, and now she could not lie and say it was only from the cold. Her cheeks were too flushed with the heat of blood.

Yet Liuprand would not look at her. He stared only at the threshold where Thrasamund and his retinue had vanished, his bright gaze driving into the darkness of the corridor. Agnes felt, for perhaps the first time since she had come to be his lover, a pricking of fear as she regarded him. But she did not fear for her own well-being—she feared what Liuprand might do to himself, what tortures he might inflict upon his person, maddened by grief.

"Please understand," she began, laying a gentle hand on his arm. "Please—you can see why I have done this."

Agnes felt his muscles stiffen under her touch, and, at long last, he turned. His face was shockingly pale, all of his puissant golden aura gone white. His eyes were rimmed with tears, unfallen.

"I cannot see, Agnes," he said lowly. "Just as I cannot see any future that is empty of you. That is no life, for me. It is a form of posthumous existence at most. If you are gone—" He choked. "—then so is all my reason for being."

She could not look at him without tears leaping to her eyes, as well. "Please," she managed again. "Do not speak such, I cannot bear it. Your pain is the only thing that might sway me from my course."

"Then let it sway you!" Liuprand's voice rose suddenly to a shout, and he grasped her tightly by the shoulders. It was not rough enough to hurt; he could never hurt her, even in the blackest of rages, but it was unexpected enough that Agnes gasped. "Let it drive you from this wretched and hopeless turn! You would doom us both to unending misery."

"No," she tried, weakly, "it is only that . . . I can see no other way to make this right again. Thrasamund has rejected every other entreaty. And worse, your name has been sullied, your legacy tainted—all in defense of my honor."

"I care *nothing* for my legacy," he bit out. "I care nothing for the decrees of men. It is no more than the mindless grumbling of sheep and swine. Let them brand me with any epithet they wish, for good or for ill; I do not care. Let Liuprand of the House of Berengar die, and let me rise again, reborn for the sole purpose of your veneration. That is the only worth of my life."

Agnes shook her head fiercely. "It cannot be so. All your life you have labored selflessly for the betterment of the island, for the well-being of all who live upon Drepane. I will not have this be for naught."

Liuprand opened his mouth to reply, then snapped it shut again. A glazed look came over his face. He released Agnes and stepped back, drawing himself up to his full height, casting his eyes about the great hall. He fixed his gaze for a moment on the throne, empty for years, ever since King Nicephorus had grown too fat to fill it. He let out a long, tremulous breath.

"And why should I prize their well-being so?" he murmured, almost to himself, in a voice strangled with bitterness. "Why should I toil endlessly for their advancement, for their happiness, at the expense of my own? They are capricious and dull, crude and witless. I killed one man and they called me just. I near to killed another and they called me cruel. Yet they will say that my greatest crime is loving you."

Agnes could scarcely bring herself to look at him. A single tear ran a path down her cheek, and spilled to stain the velvet of her gown.

"You have undermined yourself again and again in my defense," she whispered. "Can I not repay such devotion with a sacrifice of my own? Would you take this choice from me?"

Liuprand's head dropped. He squeezed his eyes shut, then raised a hand to press hard against his temples, obscuring for a moment his visage. His shoulders rose and fell mightily, and his breathing grew rapid and short. Agnes was terrified that she might, for the first time, see him weep.

"No," he said, the word muffled by the cover of his hand. "I cannot accept it. Any other torment I could endure, but not this."

A sob rose in Agnes's throat, but it did not spill past her lips. Silence reigned again in the great hall. Nothing could impinge upon it; even the distant, rote noises of the castle's daily drudgeries seemed to have gone quiet. It was as though there were no servants, no scullions, no guards, as though Castle Crudele were empty of all but two. And in this silence, in this emptiness, the cord stretching between them swelled and thickened. Its straining seemed to make it only stronger. Under threat of snapping, it fortified itself.

Agnes sensed this, and finally, the sob tumbled from her mouth.

"So you cannot bear it," she choked out, through her tears. "I was a fool to think that I could, either. But what can we do? I have made the offer to Lord Thrasamund; it would be perfidy to rescind it now."

Liuprand let his hand fall from his face, and he looked up at Agnes again. He did not weep, but the anguish was plain in his eyes.

"I do not know," he said quietly. "We must hope that Thrasamund rejects the offer himself. Perhaps—perhaps we can, in a subtle manner, sway his mind, yet make him believe the decision was his own. I must think on it."

Still tearful, Agnes nodded. "I will think on it as well. And I am sorry—I am sorry that I have tried to protect you yet only caused you more grief."

Liuprand drew in a breath, and his great chest swelled. He moved toward Agnes and grasped her by the shoulders again, this time with utmost gentleness. He lowered his head until their faces were close, their noses near enough to brush.

"My grief is a condition of my love," he said softly. "It is the abject law of humanity, that one cannot exist without the other." He leaned yet closer, touching his forehead to hers. "Do you love me, Agnes?"

"Yes," she whispered back. Her heart bragged with the inexorable truth of it. "With every fragment of my being, forever."

"Then," he said, and kissed her briefly but tenderly on her brow, "all will be well."

XXIII

A WET NURSE'S SORROWS

Waltrude paced the length of the princeling's chambers, wringing her bony hands. Hers were not the hurried, frantic footsteps of someone a quarter or even half of her age; her gait was slow and burdensome, but nonetheless it betrayed an unsettled mind. Indeed she could not recall the last time she had been so ill at ease. And it had begun even before the arrival of the contingent from Ironmanse.

It was her mistress's disquiet she had sensed, and it had seeped into her, like mud into a peasant's cloth slippers. She could always tell when the lady Agnes's nerves were bad, because she retreated into silence, that old trick, long since abandoned but resurrected occasionally as it was needed. These past days she had been so quiet, her gray eyes so distant and dim. The matter had not been helped by the temporary loss of her voice.

Waltrude had learned, at long last, its cause. Pliny had not been forthcoming but she was not such a one to easily relinquish her curiosities. And thus finally the leech had recounted all he had witnessed at the wedding feast, and all that Agnes had endured after, relayed to him by the lady herself. These recollections grieved him; Waltrude could tell from the quality of his speech—far from stiff and formal, as was his ordinary manner, but instead thick with emotion. Bitterness and ill portent. It had sent shivers along Waltrude's spine.

So many more questions she had as she looked out the princeling's window to the courtyard, where a further group of men waited before the closed barbican. They wore the colors and banners of the House of Eyes, and though all were armed, their weapons remained sheathed and they had scarcely moved at all for hours. They only shifted and murmured among themselves—complaining, Waltrude imagined, of the heat, of the stench from the Outer Wall, of their master's tarrying. Since his arrival at dawn, Lord Thrasamund remained yet within Castle Crudele.

It is a good omen, Waltrude thought, fingers dancing along the windowsill. *He is considering the prince's entreaties, whatever they may be. He has not stormed out in righteous fury.*

She wished to share these thoughts aloud, to pick the leech's mind, but she could not, for Tisander sat just beside Pliny at the table, having his lessons. Such a clever boy he was, wise far beyond his years. This was occasionally unnerving to Waltrude. There was a steadiness to his gaze that no child of his age should possess. Where his knowledge was lacking, his perception made up for it. He seemed almost frightfully adept at reading the hidden thoughts and secret desires that did not show plain on a person's face.

Now—as though he could indeed read Waltrude's thoughts, precisely—the boy looked away from his book and up at her. "I'm weary of this," he said, just the hint of a whine in his voice. "I want a story, Waltrude, *please.*"

Waltrude exchanged a glance with Pliny, whose expression was clouded and unreadable. After a moment, he gave a single, brittle nod.

"Come here, then," Waltrude said—and the boy leapt from his seat and ran to her arms. She lifted him and settled him on her hip. "What sort of story would you like to hear?"

He was quiet a moment, toying with the collar of her frock, his brow puckering in deliberation. Then he looked up at her and said, "Tell me about my papa when he was a child."

"Ah, so you want a true story," Waltrude said. She crossed the room and sat down in Tisander's abandoned seat, balancing the child on her knees. "But first, can you guess? Do you think your papa a cuckoo bird fallen from its nest?"

"No," Tisander said, giggling.

"A squirming baby seal, washed to shore?"

"No!"

"And what about a wolf cub, tumbling out of its mountain den?"

"No, no, no," said Tisander, clapping Waltrude delightedly on each cheek. "You are being silly."

"Yes, a bit silly," she agreed. "Your father was only a little boy once, just like you. Gold of hair, blue of eye. His favorite place was the library. He could read before he could walk. He loved his mama dearly, and kept always to her side. He did not much care for the rough play-fighting of the other boys. His soul was a gentle one; he had no constitution for violence, even when it was pretend. He had two kittens and called them Feather-Tail and Bright-Paw."

Tisander was listening raptly, that sober gaze of his unwavering. But the boy was not the only one. With a quick sideways glance, Waltrude saw that Pliny was watching her intently, as well. His lips were pressed into a thin line, almost white with the reduction of blood—and his eyes were fixed and unblinking.

"It is all true," Waltrude insisted, shifting her gaze back to Tisander. Discomfort prickled her skin. "And now he is a man grown, but his heart remains as it was: fair and humane, more inclined to be injured by the cruelties of the world than to inflict them himself." She swallowed, and then with greater conviction went on, "He is a good man, and will be a good king, and you will follow in his footsteps, sweet one. You have the blood of Berengar, but just as important, you have the blood of your father. His kindly nature. His noble intentions. Under his rule, Drepane will flourish."

Waltrude now glanced pointedly at Pliny, but the leech had averted his gaze.

Satisfied, Tisander laid his head on Waltrude's breast, his lashes flickering. "I wish to see him," he said, with a soft sigh. "My papa . . . will he come tuck me into bed tonight?"

"I imagine so," said Waltrude. "And Agnes, as well—neither wishes to ever be too long parted from you."

With yet one more contented sigh, Tisander closed his eyes. Waltrude indulged herself to stroke his golden curls, finding as much of her own comfort in the gesture as she wished to impart upon the boy. Yet this moment of peace was not long-lived. When she looked up, she found that Pliny was staring at her again.

She felt like snapping at him—it was unjust, this dour sulking of his, when Waltrude could not so much as glare back. For weeks he had persisted in this glum and bitter behavior, his disquiet rising from his flesh like barbs, and only further irritated with time, not soothed. Waltrude felt it, even if Liuprand himself was still ignorant to how he was beginning to lose his leech's faith.

Over Tisander's head she frowned, sure to keep her displeasure invisible to the little boy's eye.

Pliny continued to glower at her, wordlessly, and Waltrude's chest began to smolder with something greater than mere annoyance. Had he not helped to raise that cruel, stupid man, Unruoching? Who had come to slay his own father and aggrieve the lady Agnes so? He had no right, she thought with anger, to pass such judgments upon her and the boy she had reared. He had been at Castle Crudele for seven years; she had been here for seventy. He could only know a small part of what had caused the prince's lapse. For all he had endured, at his father's hand alone, he could by now have become a tyrant.

Yet you reared the king, as well, a voice in her head whispered. *He was a sweet boy, as gentle as his son, and look what has become of him.*

Waltrude closed her eyes a moment—she could not entertain such musings; they would lead her to ruin and madness. When she opened them again, Pliny was staring still, and she could bear it no longer. She stroked once more the princeling's hair and said, "Perhaps I shall look for your father, sweet one, and bring him here. Would you like that?"

Lifting his head, Tisander nodded. There was a slackened, sleepy expression on his face, and Waltrude realized that the hours of the day had passed and dusk was settling now, the dark, deep purple of an infected wound. Thrasamund's contingent remained outside the barbican. They were no longer jostling and muttering; they had gone silent and still. A hot, heavy wind swept over the courtyard and then came through the window, carrying with it the vile human scents of the

Outer Wall. In the distance the moldering bell tower made a faint impression on the clotted purple clouds.

"Very well, then," Waltrude said, and lifted Tisander gently from her lap. "Stay here with Pliny, and I shall fetch him."

The boy went obediently to Pliny and raised his arms to be picked up. The leech did, settling the princeling on his knee. Tisander was weary of his lessons but not so tired that he was yet ready to sleep, and would eagerly accept a story read aloud to him. He rested his chin on Pliny's shoulder, and his small mouth cracked with a yawn.

Waltrude locked stares with the leech one final time. No words passed between them, only this charged look. His eyes were lidded and cloudy with secret thoughts, treacherous thoughts, though so far contained only within the lockbox of his mind. She almost wished he would speak them aloud, so she might make a rejoinder, defend the honor of the prince to which he had sworn his now-faltering allegiance. Yet even Waltrude's uncommonly sharp gaze could not penetrate Pliny.

She turned and went into the corridor, the leech's name still a whisper on her tongue.

In the hallway, Waltrude's steps became hurried. In a pace as urgent as she could manage, she wound her way through the corridors and up the spiral of stairs. All the while her mind raced, each thought like the bolting of a spooked horse.

The world has sullied him, as it sullied his father.

No—it is your rearing that has tainted him, as black rot consumes a ripe fruit.

Were you only wiser—were you only younger, or older—were you a softer touch, or a sterner hand—

Ah, she would not survive such anguished musing for much longer! She had to speak with the prince. He was the only one who could dissuade her from this self-torture. Perhaps he need not say a word; perhaps merely seeing him as he was, beautiful and noble and just, would reassure Waltrude that he was not some brutish creature, that he had not been transfigured as though by the work of magic.

By the work of love, she thought. Only his affection for the lady Agnes could drive him to such lengths. A ruinous thing, then, love. He had gorged himself on it, just like his father had gulped down every succulent morsel on his plate. A glut of love was more dangerous than a dearth of it. Liuprand had drunk from the ever-flowing fountain of romance, and look what it had done to him.

The hour was late and Waltrude knew, with a sense of unfolding dread, where she would find the prince. Not once in these seven years had she disturbed his meetings with the lady. Even now she was fearful of it. What occurred behind the closed doors of the chapel was not her right to witness.

Yet as she approached, her resolve only grew. *I must hear the justifications from his mouth. I must see the gentleness of his gaze myself.* She was halfway there now. The last stretch would be most arduous—climbing all those steep, crumbling stairs to the most airless and disused section of the castle, visited only by two. She was astonished by her own desperation, which seemed to imbue her with an impossible strength and an even greater endurance.

So fixed was her course, so intent was her mind, that it did not even occur to her that she might encounter any obstacles on her way. Thus, when she rounded a corner and nearly collided with two figures in sepia robes, Waltrude was startled to a gasp.

"Good evening, Your Scrupulousnesses," she said when she had recovered herself. "What brings you here at this twilight hour?"

The taller and thinner of the leeches—she vaguely recalled his face, but not his name—gave a faint, ghostly smile. "Does illness or injury cease to occur in the dark?"

Waltrude lifted her chin indignantly. "Do you often answer a question with another question?"

"Only when the question is inane," the thin leech said. The stout one merely leered at her. "We have our duties to the inhabitants of the castle, as you have yours."

Her mouth twitched in irritation. "And who requires your services tonight, Your Scrupulousness?"

"Ah, we are sworn to discretion in this matter—our oaths to the order require that we keep our patients' secrets. Should I ask who, tonight, is suckling your teats?"

"That is no secret to anyone," Waltrude bit out. "There is but one child in the castle, and he is grown well past that need. Unless perhaps you should find yourself wanting for a bit of comfort at my breast? I have not yet nursed one as gray as you, but some men never outgrow their infantile appetites."

At this the stout leech scowled, and looked as if he might make a reply, but the taller one waved a hand to silence him before he could speak. The thin leech—his name was still lost to her—merely smiled on with indulgent contempt.

"Your back may be hunched, but your wit is sharp," he said. "I shall not forget it. But I do suggest we end this intercourse now."

Waltrude narrowed her eyes. "And why should we? Is your task truly so urgent?"

"Yes," said the stout leech, and his voice was not what Waltrude had expected. He spoke with too much earnestness, the word coming out in a rush. His companion was clearly the one who possessed the wiles for them both. "Most urgent."

The thin leech's lip curled. "That's enough," he said. "Our duties are not within the purview of a milk cow. You should concern yourself only with what little milk remains in your breasts, and what few years remain of your life."

"Better a milk cow than a worm," said Waltrude. "You ought to wriggle back beneath your rock."

"No, I do not think I will." The thin leech drew himself up to his full height, which was not so impressive—even Pliny was taller, and looked more robust besides. "It is you who should return to your pen. You will come to thank me for this counsel."

"I did not ask to be counseled." Yet a strange coldness was pricking at her. It seemed not to emanate from the stone walls or the marble floors, but rather from the leeches themselves, as if they had brought with them all the chill dankness of the dungeon. "Your purpose here—whatever it is—is of no greater importance than mine."

"Take the advice, woman," the stout leech rasped out. "If you do not heed us now, you will wish that you had."

Waltrude shivered, but she held her chin aloft. "I have lived many years and made many errors in that time; regret is nothing too foreign or too appalling to me."

"You do not know *appalling*. I promise that you do not."

It was the thin leech who spoke, and his voice was like a draft of the larder's air. He was no clever animal. Few of his kind were, save Pliny, who, even when he vexed her, retained always his poise and wisdom. Waltrude wished that she had not abandoned him, that she had allowed him to chafe her so. She wanted now for his grace, for his considered words, for his reluctance to anger or spite. He was more temperate than she. He would have been able to reason with these men, where she was only moved to a choking rage.

"Remove yourself from my path," she said lowly. "I will not ask with such courtesy again."

"Waltrude," said the thin leech, and she was both shocked and disturbed that he knew her name, "I am doing you a kindness. You do not comprehend it yet, but you will."

"How about a game of chance?" the stout leech piped up. From the folds of his robe he removed a coin, a Seraphine silver, scratched and worn with the face of the Dogaressa on one side and the winged lion on the other. He rolled it through his fingers with surprising deftness. "I shall play you for the opportunity to pass."

"Enough, you lout," spat the thin leech. "Do you think of nothing else but your own mirth? And your luck is abysmal; it always has been."

"A man's fortune can change, as the stars rearrange themselves every night."

"The stars do no such thing," said Waltrude. "Let me through."

The stout leech held out the coin on the palm of his hand. There was a scratch, which appeared to be intentional, erasing the Dogaressa's eyes. Now she was a blind woman, trapped in this metal cast.

A feeling of misery began to form in the base of Waltrude's belly. It thickened and hardened, like a pearl in the clutch of an oyster. Then it rose and rose, through the cavern of her stomach, and to the hollow of her throat. It rolled on her tongue. It rattled the rotten yellow gate of her teeth. It was a sob, she realized, one of furious protest and darkest despair, such that she had never felt before. Even as she laid eyes on Philomel's broken body, she had not wept. And perhaps now this was the profit of her silence: All the years had not withered her pain; they had augmented it. A great pearl it was now, one that would fetch a hefty price.

"Move," she whispered, yet her voice cracked the word, broke it apart in two pieces. "Make me ask again, and you will regret it. I am here on the prince's errand."

The two leeches exchanged glances. For such dull and simple creatures, the look that passed between them was unreadable. Waltrude could only feel the shaking of her own knees beneath her, and the strenuous beating of her aged and burdened heart.

"You do not understand what you ask," said the thin leech. She thought she could detect the faintest hint of pity in his voice. "Your wit may be sharp, but your knowledge is lacking. Return from whence you came, Waltrude. I swear this plea of mine is a beneficent one. You will wish you had heeded it."

"Then let me wish. Wishes come to nothing in the end."

The stout leech flicked his coin. It turned so many times in its ascent that it seemed no more than a flash of silver, winking in the corridor's crude darkness. As it rose and then began to fall again, the leech said, "Call face. Call lion. Do it now, *do it.*"

Waltrude was too bewildered to speak.

The coin landed back down on his open palm. The three of them peered over at it. And the thin leech smiled.

XXIV

FLOWERS AT BLOOM, CUT TOO SOON

One by one, Agnes lit the torches on the wall and basked a moment in their burning warmth. She could scarcely believe now that she and Liuprand had for years accepted the cold and the dank of the abandoned chapel when all along they could have improved it, and so easily, too. The torches suffused the chamber with a heady and golden light. The altar was a lovely thing underneath the wax and grime, shining white like the brightest and most intact shell on the beach. The tub had been emptied and filled again, the water refreshed and scented with new flowers and oils.

A hyacinth drifted across its surface, as lazy as a lily pad in a pond. Purple were its petals, and lush despite the passing of its blooming season, which was early spring. It was summer now, and a hyacinth should not be so vividly colored. Agnes still knew the whims and the temperaments of all these flowers, knowledge that had been imparted to her since she was old enough to follow her grandmother through the gardens of Castle Peake.

Frowning, she approached the tub and knelt at its edge. Her fingers skimmed the water's surface until she was able to coax the hyacinth into her palm. She lifted it and held it to the light. Dampness made its petals an even darker violet, and it glistened with droplets like morning dew. Beautiful, fragile, and contrary to reason. Agnes would have expected to see phlox or coneflowers, a daylily or a dianthus, all summer blooms.

She was stunned, momentarily, by its impossible loveliness, which was against nature's laws. If anyone were to learn the trick of inducing flowers to bloom out of season, of keeping their petals florid and open all year, it would have been Adele-Blanche. But as with the secrets of raising the dead from their graves, the determination to uncover it had died with her grandmother. No other creature would be so resolved to defy the fundaments of nature.

Agnes sniffed the hyacinth. It had an even sweeter scent than she remembered, perhaps made all the more potent to her by its perversity. A hyacinth needed the fullest exposure to the sun; she recalled her grandmother carefully adjusting the placement of the stalks, peeling open the petals in the direction of the daylight. It was the only time that Adele-Blanche would ever be seen on her knees.

She cupped the delicate bloom in both her hands and stared intently, as if she might persuade it to give up its secrets. It would be wrong to say that the sight and the scent of the flower engendered a fondness in Agnes, a longing for times that were now forever gone. When last she had held such a flower, she had been a silent and gray, shrinking creature, less alive than the plants in her grandmother's garden. If anything, Agnes's fondness was for the fact that this *was* the past, that she could recognize it as such, that those times would never be here again. The flower reminded her that she had swelled and flourished and bloomed.

Hyacinth girl, said a voice from the low part of her consciousness, though it was not her voice. It felt as if someone else had snuck the thought into her mind.

Agnes let the flower fall from her hand and drift back into the water.

She had passed the rest of the day deep in thought, contemplating her now-injurious position. She had made the offer to Lord Thrasamund, and it could not be rescinded. So desperate she was to restore Liuprand's reputation and honor that she had cornered them both like treed foxes.

Her only hope now was that Thrasamund would find some reason of his own to refuse her. Agnes had run through every option in her mind, from the subtle to the flagrant, from the clever to the whimsical, that might make Thrasamund spurn her. She envisioned herself feigning madness, perhaps falling into a mimed fit at the dinner table. But the idea left the taste of bile in her mouth. She could not think of it without thinking of Ygraine, wailing and weeping and tearing at her clothes. Thrasamund would not wish to see such a scene played out again before his eyes. And Agnes could not bear to make a mockery of the woman's real pain.

Perhaps the marriage might be annulled after some time, when it failed to produce a child. But she expected such a thing would be blamed on the impairments of Childeric's condition, not hers. His defect could be seen.

Yet even that plan would take years to see its profit. Her stomach began to churn and her skin began to rise with gooseflesh, and Agnes laid a hand on the altar to steady herself. She would have to believe that Liuprand had come to a solution of his own. She had utmost faith in him; it was as imperturbable and irrevocable as her love. He was wise and noble and good. He was driven single-mindedly to please her. The strength of his devotion would prove itself in this; he would not allow harm to come to her, and he would not allow her to be absent from him. That she knew above all else.

He would be here any moment now.

Agnes paced about the altar, waiting. Her heart was humming and her blood was running hot in her veins. Soon, soon she would feel his arms around her, his lips on her lips, his hands on her breasts, and his hardness nudging her entrance. She started to tug at the laces on her bodice, loosening them so that she would be ready, at once, for him to take her.

The gown slid further down her shoulders, baring more of her skin to the torchlight. Her thighs were wetted now with her own slickness, her own anticipation. Agnes considered a moment letting her fingers slip beneath her skirts, bringing herself to the edge of pleasure as she waited. She bit her lip in contemplation.

But before she could make up her mind, the chapel door scraped open.

Agnes lifted her head, searching for Liuprand in the gloaming half-light. Yet there came only the flash of steel, and the sound of clinking armor.

Terror seized her. She stood fixed in place, clutching her loose gown to her breast, the other hand gripping the edge of the altar. She did not utter even the smallest sound as the precious, sacred air of her chapel was cleaved apart with the bodies of strange men.

No, not strange—not all of them. At the head of the troupe was Lord Thrasamund, Master of Eyes, his red beard made redder by the amber glow of the torches. His gaze, under that powerful brow, was set and fierce.

Agnes could not speak. The men, some wearing his house's colors and others the crimson garb of the House of Blood, spread out and arrayed themselves around the altar, closing her in.

"He left you alone here." Thrasamund's voice was rough and low. "Ah, or he has tarried too long."

Even her mind could not form words, much less her tongue. Her very breath seemed to die within her throat.

One of the men turned and said, "Should we stay to our course, my lord?"

Thrasamund himself was silent a moment, as the torchlight danced with the shadows upon his craggy face.

"Let us act now," he said, "and let him see the profit of his dallying. He will not witness it, but he will be racked brutally with the knowledge that he was too late to save her."

The men converged and set themselves upon her. More than a dozen there were, yet it took only one man to grasp Agnes's left arm, and another her right. They hauled her forward, around the altar, and pressed her to her knees at Lord Thrasamund's feet.

The Master of Eyes regarded her with such intensity as befit his house's name. Her hands were now twisted and pinned behind her back and Agnes's gown slipped further, exposing her breasts. Her hair, long and loose, tumbled over her shoulders as her head was forced down. She had to crane her neck painfully to see the lord's face.

"Beautiful, but not nearly so beautiful as your cousin," he said. "Love is the most mysterious of all humanity's afflictions. The more I probe it, the less it seems to be governed by wisdom or reason. I can glimpse nothing in you that should cause a man to forfeit his crown."

Agnes's breath came now in thin, labored gasps that made her chest heave. A plea formed on her lips, but her bewildered fear kept her muzzled and stifled. Still she could not speak a word aloud.

"Yet," Lord Thrasamund went on, in a softer tone, "I find myself moved by the very same inscrutable sentiment. How much love for one can inspire hate for another."

From his belt he seized a dagger, its blade glinting keenly. The men jerked Agnes back so that her throat was bared, a long and supple column of white.

As the blade neared her, at last, at *last,* Agnes managed to produce a sound.

"Liuprand!" she cried. "Liuprand! Liuprand—"

"This is for my son," said Thrasamund, his voice still soft below her screaming, "and for my daughter."

He drew the blade swiftly across her throat, the flesh opening like the petals of a flower. Red blossomed from its fount and poured forth over her breast. And, with this torrid rush of blood, the lady Agnes was forever silenced.

XXV

WOUNDED LION AND TRODDEN SERPENT

Two men of the House of Eyes dragged Agnes's body and set it upon the altar. The pouring of blood slowed to a trickle and then ceased altogether, though it had painted Agnes's chest in darkest, deepest crimson. They arranged her limbs at her sides, spreading her hair out across the white stone, and as they performed this unholy ritual, the men spoke to one another in whispers.

"Surgeon's hands, she's a pretty thing. I've never slain a lady before."

"You did not slay her. Our lord did. And his cause was just. The prince's pain is the only fair price for his crimes."

"Her crimes, too. Little better than a common slattern she was, carrying on with her own cousin's husband. Blood is a fair price for such debauchery as well."

"Too right. No wounded lion or trodden serpent is more dangerous than a woman scorned."

"Nay, not a woman scorned—worse. A mother grieved."

"The princess has very well had her vengeance now."

The door to the chapel was propped open so that yet more bodies could filter in. Another troupe of men, in the colors of the House of Eyes. Their expressions were both fixed and blank with the purpose that their lord had instilled in them, all of their previous humanity shed. They touched the swords at their belts, reassuring themselves of their resolve and their potency. Their armor and mail shielded them from the dangerous compulsions of compassion or regret.

Along with the men scampered another creature: thin and diminished in form, yet not remotely in spirit. He galloped like a dog, bare feet scrabbling the floor. His face was so wan, so hollow, that he would have resembled more a corpse than a living thing, if not for the lustful sheen of his gaze, aroused and animated by hunger.

He threw himself on the altar and latched his yellow-toothed mouth around the lady Agnes's wrist, masticating furiously and letting out a moan of pleasure.

"No!" barked Lord Thrasamund. With a sweep of his arm, he knocked the creature off the altar; it fell, back flat, on the chapel floor. "You dull wretch! We're saving her for the prince."

"But they said," the creature whimpered. "Rosencrantz and Guildenstern, they said that I would have the forbidden delicacy. If I told."

Thrasamund scowled in anger. He snapped his head up and cast his gaze about the room. "You, girl," he growled. "You said you could keep this vulgar being's appetite in check. He will have more than enough to feast upon later, when our first task here is done. The bloodshed now is paltry compared with what will come."

With tremulous steps, the handmaiden slipped from the throng of men. Her mismatched eyes remained on the ground as she mumbled, "Yes, my lord."

Still whimpering, Offal-Eater righted himself and slunk away. He hid within one of the chapel's unlit corners, where the darkness was oily and otherwise unpenetrated. Hunched over like a gargoyle, he rubbed his hands briskly up and down his bony arms, as if to banish a chill.

"The rest of my men," Thrasamund said, "they will arrive soon, yes?"

"Yes," Ninian whispered back. "My mistress ordered the barbican open herself."

"Good," said the Master of Eyes. "Then we wait only for the prince, now."

Of all Lord Thrasamund's flaws, it could not be said that he was hasty or slipshod in his plans. He set his men about the chapel in a strict order, four at the door, six around the altar, and at least two in each far-flung area of the room, so that there would be no successful flight, no skirmish from which his side would not emerge the victor. Ninian shrank back, keeping near to Offal-Eater in his corner. There settled then a great silence, the air thickening as the odor of blood wafted from Agnes's corpse and impugned the chapel with the scent of salt and death.

And in the silence and death-choked air, Liuprand arrived at last.

He came surging through the door, his gait uneven, encumbered by fright and urgency. He very well may have tripped of his own accord, but Thrasamund did not leave even that up to chance—the moment Liuprand stepped through the threshold, the men guarding the door each plunged their swords into the backs of his thighs.

With a mighty cry, he fell. The floor itself seemed to crack as his knees struck the stone. Blood spread beneath the fabric of his breeches, like a dark shape moving under ice. A stammering noise of pain he uttered, yet not a single word.

Gasping, he tried to get to his feet, but he seemed to struggle overmuch—not with his fresh and weeping wounds but rather with the enormity of his own body. The hugeness of his form labored against the efforts of his spirit. When he did rise, it was clumsily; he swayed like a drunkard as he staggered to the altar.

Finally he laid eyes on Agnes's body. At first there appeared to be no recognition on his face. He regarded her with the dull stupor of a very young child, to whom even the mundane sights of the world are beyond conception. His mouth opened, wordless still in its uncomprehending horror.

But all those in attendance should have desired his unending silence. For when Prince Liuprand screamed, it was the most terrible sound.

It was an animal howl, and it lit the chapel with the fire of his anguish. Some of the men let their swords clatter to the ground as they hurried to clap their hands over their ears. From her corner, Ninian began to weep piteous tears. Offal-Eater scratched furiously at his skin, gnashing his teeth, letting spittle foam and trickle from his mouth.

Liuprand screamed and screamed. It turned into a bitter and broken wail. He clawed his way onto the altar and took Agnes's lifeless body into his arms. Cradling her corpse to his chest, his great, powerful frame was racked with sobs.

"She died calling out your name." Thrasamund stepped up to the altar, a cold smile on his face. "Would that you had arrived only a moment sooner. Can you hear it, my prince? Her helpless, terror-stricken screams? Can you imagine the agony of her final moments, believing that you had abandoned her?" His eyes were emerald but infinitely dark. "I shall never let your mind be empty of it. Her cries will haunt you, even in your dreams."

His savage howling had now ceased; there was only the sound of his rasping, heaving sobs. The blood on Agnes's body soaked through his doublet, while the wounds on his legs leaked still, staining the white stone of the altar red.

"Was all this anguish and torment for love?" Thrasamund's voice grew low. "Or was it lust only, the basest mechanisms of your body? You could have had your pleasure with any common whore or even forced your own wife, if she were unwilling. Yet you bedded the princess but once. Forsaking her night after night, to lie with her cousin instead—a lady of less beauty, less esteem, less charm. I wonder if it was merely the perverse desire of a man who, so glutted on every privilege and virtue of life, found excitement in the pursuit of the only thing forbidden to him."

"No," Liuprand moaned, softly. "No, it was love, it has always been . . ."

A small glimmer of amusement danced in Thrasamund's gaze. "Is that so? You were not driven at all by the desires of the flesh?"

Words were lost to Liuprand again. He choked on yet another sob, rocking Agnes's body in his arms.

"Prove it, then," Thrasamund said. His smile was colder and colder still. "I will believe you are such a creature who loves purely and chastely if you can resist your carnal urges now. Even in death, your lover is beautiful, is she not?"

There was no comprehension on Liuprand's face, no thoughts in his mind and no feelings in his heart but that wretched and searing anguish. Thrasamund gestured to his men, and two of them came to join him at the altar.

Even as the men descended upon Liuprand, the prince still could not understand. He struggled in only a perfunctory manner, and vainly—he was too confounded by his agony, too grief-addled, to protest much. He held tight to Agnes's body, his sobs scraping and strangled with fresh panic, as the men pressed him down onto his belly and began to strip off his bloody breeches.

Thrasamund looked on and did not speak, but the satisfaction in his eyes burned like sparks from a greenwood fire.

When the men had completed their task and the prince was naked to the waist, one of them looked up at their master with a furrowed brow. "He is not hard yet, my lord."

"Then help him to surface his prurient passions. They are within him, I am sure, and they must be drawn out."

Obedient to his lord, the man reached beneath Liuprand's feebly writhing body. He found his manhood there, limp, and began to stroke him roughly to hardness. The other man grasped at Agnes's gown, tugging to free her of it, and when he could not, he took his knife and slashed apart the velvet and silk. The fabric fell from her and left her corpse naked to the chapel air.

Naked, and pressed beneath her still-living lover. Had she not been dead, she would have felt Liuprand stiff against her thigh. For her earlier efforts she was still slick there, and the mingling of their blood wetted her further.

It was far easier than either of the men had imagined, to maneuver the prince's form to its course. It was like fitting a wheel into a well-worn groove. Aided by the slipperiness of the blood, to be sure, but also by the familiarity of the act to both of them. Even in death, Agnes's body seemed to yearn for him; it recognized his shape and readied itself to be filled.

And Liuprand, who lived, and whose mind was still, for some part, intact? Could he have protested more adamantly this violation? The deep heart of the matter may never be known. But what can be said is that he was once a creature who prided itself on its lack of greed, its renunciation of all such low impulses and embodied cravings. Yet now, in his love, he was ruined. His asceticism had been flayed from him; he was an animal skinned, his abject humanness laid bare. He desired her body even when her soul was gone from it. Thrasamund had spoken truly: Her corpse was as beautiful and sensual as her living form had been, and when Liuprand thrust into her, he groaned with relief and with need.

Beneath him, Agnes's body was jostled up and down the altar, her head rolling limply with each forceful ingress. Thrasamund's men had long since removed their hands, and he worked over her of his own accord, panting and heaving with exertion. His thrusts were long and vigorous and deep, almost violent in their desperation—perhaps this was the moment in which Liuprand's mind fully escaped him. Or perhaps he knew he would never see his lady Agnes again and in some hideous way believed that this was the final expression of his great and irrevocable love.

With a strangled moan, he released himself inside her. He collapsed, shoulders rising and falling in hopeless heaviness. Blood drenched the place where their bodies were joined. Still cached in the corner with Offal-Eater, Ninian became ill; she doubled over and vomited all down her frock and onto the floor. Most of the men, by now, had turned their faces away. The ones that looked on did so with the blackest, most vulgar arousal in their eyes.

Only Thrasamund watched with little perceptible emotion. His satisfaction seemed incomplete, insufficient, as if even this gruesome scene had not been as vile a torment as he had hoped. But he did not allow this discontent to prevent him from action. He drew his dagger once more and cut the doublet from the prince's back himself. Liuprand was as naked now as his slain lover.

"So now it has been proven," said Thrasamund, his voice low. "You are no more noble a creature than all the rest, even for your crown and for your precious Seraphine blood. You are base and crude, vile and depraved. What right have you to rule us as if you are a god and we a lowly, lesser race of men? If you had not taken her yourself, I would have given her body to be forced and defiled by my dogs. But you have let your true nature be known. You, Liuprand the Just, golden prince of Drepane, heir to the throne of Berengar, are no better than a beast."

Liuprand was panting, his eyes flung wide and wheeling with a wild, animal panic; every moment seemed to prove more the truth of Thrasamund's words. His face was flush against the curve of Agnes's throat, near enough that her death wound was dripping its sluggish black dregs upon his tongue. As if by instinct, he licked his lips, and then—realizing the horror of what he had done—he choked, and another sob wrung from deep in his chest.

"There, have your fill of her," Thrasamund murmured. He laid a hand on Liuprand's naked back, almost a comforting gesture, had he not then squeezed it and raked his nails along it, provoking from the prince a pitiable moan. "Indulge your every appetite now, for this is the last feast you will ever have. From here on your body will know nothing but ache and longing. Your manhood, too, has spilled its final drop." A faint, rumbling laugh. "Would that your father had not needed an heir, else he could have gelded you sooner, kept you like one of Hartwig's eunuch boy-slaves."

Liuprand did not beg—what would he have begged for? If there is no reason or wisdom to be found in love, there is even less to be found in pain. His mind had no more capacity for thought than a fish has for flight. His heart beat, but only to force his anguish gruelingly through his veins. He grasped at Agnes's face, turning it toward his, as if he could make her eyes look upon him, her eyes that saw nothing anymore. He tried to wake her with a kiss, but both their mouths were slippery with blood, and his lips could not find purchase upon hers.

Here was what remained of his once-grand and encompassing love. It had been a bright thing, lustrous as the sun itself, and it had painted the world all in gold. Had any saneness remained in him—had he even still the ability to speak—Liuprand might have begged Lord

Thrasamund to robe the world once more in its colored vestments, to apply the varnish of passion and romance that made all things charming and luminous again.

For without passion's tints and romance's pigments, the world was too repugnant and painful to bear. Even Thrasamund's men, who had previously shed all such sentiments, began to feel the chamber's lack of love and started trembling. Their faces went pale; sweat dewed their brows. Those who had looked on with avarice and lust now had the air of illness about them, and they averted their gazes at last. They stared with too-great intent at the torches smoking on the walls, at the flowers drifting across the surface of the water, and at other inhuman things, which were not so alive—or so dead—as to repulse them.

This seemed, finally, to please Thrasamund. His smile was broad and almost artless; for a moment, he was a shade of the jovial man he had once been. He gave the flesh of Liuprand's back another cruel squeeze and let his fingers sink in deep enough to draw blood.

"Have you the strength for another bout?" he asked, chuckling with unreserved glee. "I can wet her thighs with more blood, if you wish."

Liuprand only moaned, wordless.

"Very well."

Thrasamund raised his head and cast his gaze about the chamber. He beckoned two more of his men, who came to crowd the altar. At their lord's direction, they seized Liuprand about the arms and tried to lift him, but his body was huge and iron-heavy, and the prince had gone utterly still. It took yet another pair of men to heave him successfully from the altar. His legs, with their garish and oozing wounds, dragged limply behind him. A trail of blood smeared the floor in his wake.

"You." Thrasamund jerked his chin toward Ninian, cached in her corner with Offal-Eater. "Come now. And you may as well bring the wretched creature with you. My men have set upon Castle Crudele with every sword that the House of Eyes can muster, and they are eager to take their vengeance. This thing will have what he was promised, too. Let him tell me if Seraphine blood tastes of honey and wine."

Silently, Ninian stepped out from the darkness and beckoned Offal-

Eater to follow. He bounded after her, yet she cast one brief, solitary glance back. It was a look that made her mismatched eyes turbulent, dozens of emotions passing through them like flotsam on the foaming tide, but none among them could be counted as regret. She loved her mistress with every beat of her heart's blood, and she had hated her abusers in equal measure, and here was its profit. She would not be shamed for it. It was too long that she had craved revenge, and the time for any misgivings had passed. She was a cold creature now, as the princess had trained her, and she had executed her mistress's orders to their ends. She slipped through the chapel door and was gone.

The men who had arranged Agnes's body remained stood at the altar. There was a hollowness to their gazes, and when the one spoke, his voice was hoarse. "What should we do with her, my lord?"

Thrasamund tilted his head. He put a finger under his chin, feigning contemplativeness. This was the bloody theater of his old self, shining once more through the gauze of bitterness and malice.

"What did our ancestors do," he said, "before the conquerors slit their throats and killed our customs?"

The men exchanged stupid glances.

"Fool of me to expect an answer from you dullards." Thrasamund let out a revolted breath. "Did you not have a grandmother, a wet nurse, who whispered to you such stories at their breasts? The old ways may have died, but they were not sufficiently desecrated as to be beyond resurrection. Let this lady be the first in a century to be dedicated in accordance with Drepane's ancient traditions. It is the line of Berengar, and his laws, that will be snuffed out now."

Thrasamund's retainers knew no more of Drepane's bygone customs than a flea knows of the laws of men. But they were obedient to their lord and they listened. They nodded as he spelled out his orders and gave not even a whisper of protest. They had no sense of a world before Berengar's conquest, but their fathers and grandfathers had served the House of Eyes for generations; their loyalty was, too, a groove well worn.

And so they reached for the lady Agnes, whose corpse was beginning to grow cold. The blood had dried, and it nearly stuck her to the stone. But they managed, nonetheless, to drag her from the altar and heft her into their arms, one man holding her wrists and the other her ankles, her body swinging between them like a pendulum. Her long black hair brushed the floor.

They carried her through the open door, out of the chapel that now held only the stench of death within, the remains of love corrupted and gone foul. Thrasamund closed the door soundly behind him, with the quiet rasping of iron against stone. And then all three men, along with Agnes's corpse, began their winding descent.

XXVI
PROGENITRIX

Despite being built by the hands of the conqueror—or, more rightly, by his Seraphine masons—Castle Crudele was not fitted to serve all the needs of mainland nobles, much less kings. That is to say, there were not many appropriate facilities for the purpose Thrasamund sought. All of Drepane had been, for a century, governed by the laws of the Septinsular Covenant, and the line of Berengar was not exempt. Not until this moment had any man seriously questioned the supremacy of the Covenant. Even Adele-Blanche, the great witch woman, the sharp-toothed striga herself, had only dared to prod gingerly at these laws, testing their firmness by conducting her secret rites, playing her traitorous music upon the instrument that was her granddaughter Agnes. And yet even her best-laid plans and posthumous orders had not been enough to persuade Castle Crudele to give up its secrets.

It had been years now since Agnes herself had given these orders even a passing thought, and no other living creature within the castle had reason to dream of, much less to scheme about, what lay beyond the veil of death. Life was itself trial enough. The more thoughtful creatures, those with the most reasoned minds, such as Pliny the leech, pondered its many questions and probed its many elements, but strove no further. Their philosophies skimmed the waters of existence yet never plumbed its sepulchral depths.

Lord Thrasamund was not such a one as to even entertain these abstruse questions about life, and so of course he did not contemplate its inverse, either. His thoughts lay—as most men's do—with only what his eyes could see or what his hands could touch. The matter before him was one of means. How could he arrange the world so it suited his desires? Though he and his men had taken Castle Crudele, he had no intention of seeking out its mysteries. It was no more than an object to him. That its foundation had been watered with blood and that its walls had contained every depraved horror had no relevance to his aims. He felt their unnatural coldness, but still—its stones were merely stones. He had no sense of their hideous power.

The Master of Eyes led his men down into the castle dungeons, and they stumbled after him, carrying the body of the lady Agnes among them in their trembling arms. She was still a slight woman, even with the healthy accumulation of weight in recent years, but the absence of a soul seemed to make her physical form more burdensome. Her corpse dangled limply, just inches above the ground.

In the deepest depths of the dungeon, where the floor is little more than packed dirt and the ceiling sparkles with the dampness of the heaving earth, there is, at the end of a narrow corridor, a door. The door is made of dense and cumbrous gray stone. Rather than a knob, as an ordinary door would have, there is only a lock: a bolt of iron that is far too heavy for a single man to lift alone.

It was so cold in this corridor that the breath of Lord Thrasamund and his retainers plumed out in clouds of white. They laid Agnes's body for a moment in the dirt while they raised the enormous latch. There was the hushing of iron against stone.

The chamber within was as black as the inky innards of a squid. The Master of Eyes thrust his torch into every corner, briefly scattering the shadows there, and finding only dank and squalid air. Not even so low a creature as a worm inhabited this place. The only life was that which Thrasamund and his men had brought with them, their own weakly sputtering spirits, like a lamp burning the last of its vivifying oils, so feeble against death's colossal darkness. Some animal part of their minds seemed to recognize this, and all three shivered.

This chamber had once been a vault that had contained the riches of the Crown, gold carried on ships from Seraph to furnish Drepane's new rulers. Yet now it lay empty—every coin spent without return. For seven brief years it had stored the gold of the House of Teeth, siphoned in a slow drip from Castle Peake, but now the spigot had been turned and this watercourse dried to a parched ditch. Princess Marozia had ceased all deliveries of goods and coin from the House of Teeth to Castle Crudele weeks ago. Had the prince not been so preoccupied with his mistress, perhaps he would have noticed.

Now Thrasamund's men carried Agnes's body to the vault and lay her within. The blood was drying black on her naked limbs. This chamber would be her resting place, serving a function that no chamber had served on Drepane for a century. A tomb, as there were on the mainland, where there was no Covenant, no leeches, no desecrations.

It was not that Thrasamund cared especially about preserving Agnes's corpse—this was an act of defiance against the Crown and the House of Berengar. Drepane's great houses would no longer observe the rites forced upon them by the conqueror's line. The Septinsular Covenant would be torn up and burned, itself desecrated. The time of Seraphine supremacy was ended.

And so her body was not arranged in any particular manner; it was left slumped on the floor, hair tangled to obscure her face, limbs folded at awkward angles that would have, in life, been painful. But—for all death's horrors—she would never feel pain again.

"Let us go now," Thrasamund said, beckoning the men with a wave of his torch. "I should not like to miss the slaughter." The sounds of clashing steel and rending flesh could be heard from upstairs.

The men followed their lord immediately. They, too, were anxious not to miss the grand massacre above and were equally impatient to leave this place that was so cold and hostile to the living. They departed the chamber, closing the great stone door behind them and letting the latch fall back into place with grim finality.

And so Agnes lay alone in the dark, left for death to feast upon slowly. Within days her body would begin to soften with rot. Within weeks her flesh would putrefy and ooze like an open wound. Within months only bones would remain.

Or rather, *should*. Death should have picked over Agnes's body like a crow upon a carcass. But as it was, death merely flew past, casting her briefly in its black-winged shadow and then vanishing again. Time itself seemed to turn gelid around her.

Agnes was expired, extinct, forever gone, and her soul had departed from her stiffly preserved body. That much, without a doubt, was known.

Yet all was not still within the tomb. In the years that came, some would say that here, finally, was the profit of all Adele-Blanche's plots and schemes and cruel abuses. That she had, incidentally, come upon some truth, that her strategy had, by mere chance, hit its mark, but that she herself had perished before she had ever seen the flourishing of her design. Perhaps her herbs and tonics, the scars she had drawn upon her granddaughter's body, the human flesh she had forced her to consume—perhaps some latent magic lay in these devices, after all.

Still others would say that it was the appalling legacy of Castle Crudele that had worked its alchemy upon her. That the cold stones themselves contained vile powers of sorcery and enchantment, the blackest arts, thought to be extinguished long ago beneath the blade of Berengar. That perhaps the violence of his conquest had not snuffed out these dark magics but rather driven them into hiding; or even, perversely, had strengthened them, but made them lie cleverly in wait.

There were but few who would say that this was the work of love. That the prince's passions—some beauteous, and others grotesque—were so powerful that they could trespass death itself. That the Seraphine were a superior race of men. Their virtues more consummate, their faculties more potent. Their seed, perhaps, more vital.

All of this might be true, or none of it. It could as easily be the greatest secret of the world or an outpouring of peasant superstition. The only inexorable fact was this: that, in the darkness of her makeshift tomb, while her body was held in the otherwise imperturbable rictus of death, something stirred, at last, in the lady Agnes's once-barren womb.

APPENDIX
THE GREAT HOUSES OF DREPANE AND THEIR RETAINERS

THE HOUSE OF BERENGAR AT CASTLE CRUDELE

NICEPHORUS THE SLUGGARD, the king of Drepane

LIUPRAND, the prince of Drepane

WALTRUDE, a wet nurse

THE EXARCH, the patriarch-in-exile of the church of Seraph

THE MOST ESTEEMED SURGEON, the head of the Leeches' Order

TRUSS AND MORDAUNT, leeches

THE OUTER WALL

MALEAGANT, a wise woman

NINIAN, a girl

OFFAL-EATER, a vagrant

THE HOUSE OF TEETH AT CASTLE PEAKE

ADELE-BLANCHE, the Mistress of Teeth

MAROZIA, the granddaughter of Adele-Blanche

AGNES, the granddaughter of Adele-Blanche

SWALLOW, a leech

WRESTBONE, a leech

THE HOUSE OF EYES
AT IRONMANSE

THRASAMUND, the Master of Eyes

QUIRINE, the wife of Thrasamund

CHILDERIC, the son of Thrasamund and Quirine

THE HOUSE OF BONES
AT ABYSSWATCH

AMYCUS, the Master of Bones

PHARSALIA, the wife of Amycus

THE HOUSE OF BLOOD
AT BITTERNEST

FREDEGAR, the Master of Blood

UNRUOCHING, the son of Fredegar

YGRAINE, the wife of Unruoching

GAMELYN, the son of Unruoching and Ygraine

PLINY, a leech

CENDRILLON, the dungeon-keeper

THE HOUSE OF HEARTS
AT THE LOVELORN TOWER

RABANUS, the Master of Hearts

PERPETUA, the wife of Rabanus

THE HOUSE OF LUNGS
AT THE PAINTED HALL
HARTWIG, the Master of Lungs

THE HOUSE OF FLESH
AT PELEKYS
VAUQUELIN, the Master of Flesh
VOLUMNIA, the wife of Vauquelin

ACKNOWLEDGMENTS

Thank you to my agent, Sarah Landis, for your unfaltering support, and for always meeting me at my most peculiar and unhinged. Thank you to my editors: Tricia Narwani, the fairy goth-mother this book needed, and Sam Bradbury, who, after half a decade of working together, did not balk when I presented this inscrutable tome. Thank you to the teams at Del Rey and Del Rey UK for both embracing and making more scrutable this book's strangeness. Thank you to Mervyn Peake for imbuing me with a love for your world, and for helping me to create mine. There will never be another like you.

Finally, this book owes a great debt to the work of Dr. Natalie Cleaver, whose paper "Humanism's Other Inheritance: The Brutal Intertextuality of Boiardo's Rocca Crudele" enhanced my understanding of the *Orlando innamorato*'s Rocca Crudele interlude and inspired many of the metafictional elements of *Innamorata*.

THE HOUSE OF TEETH DUOLOGY

WILL CONCLUDE IN

BOOK TWO.

ABOUT THE AUTHOR

Ava Reid is the *Sunday Times* bestselling author of *A Study in Drowning*, *Lady Macbeth* and other novels. Her books have been published in more than fourteen territories. She lives in the New York area.

avasreid.tumblr.com
Instagram: @avasreid

ABOUT THE TYPE

This book was set in Dante, a typeface designed by Giovanni Mardersteig (1892–1977). Conceived as a private type for the Officina Bodoni in Verona, Italy, Dante was originally cut only for hand composition by Charles Malin, the famous Parisian punch cutter, between 1946 and 1952. Its first use was in an edition of Boccaccio's *Trattatello in laude di Dante* that appeared in 1954. The Monotype Corporation's version of Dante followed in 1957. Though modelled on the Aldine type used for Pietro Cardinal Bembo's treatise *De Aetna* in 1495, Dante is a thoroughly modern interpretation of that venerable face.